the
witch's
heart

The Witch's Heart

GENEVIEVE GORNICHEC

ACE
New York

ACE
Published by Berkley
An imprint of Penguin Random House LLC
penguinrandomhouse.com

Copyright © 2021 by Genevieve Gornichec
Penguin Random House supports copyright. Copyright fuels creativity,
encourages diverse voices, promotes free speech, and creates a vibrant
culture. Thank you for buying an authorized edition of this book and for
complying with copyright laws by not reproducing, scanning, or
distributing any part of it in any form without permission. You are
supporting writers and allowing Penguin Random House to continue to
publish books for every reader.

ACE is a registered trademark and the A colophon is a trademark of
Penguin Random House LLC.

Library of Congress Cataloging-in-Publication Data

Names: Gornichec, Genevieve, author.
Title: The witch's heart / Genevieve Gornichec.
Description: New York : Ace, [2021]
Identifiers: LCCN 2020022385 (print) | LCCN 2020022386 (ebook) |
ISBN 9780593099940 (hardcover) | ISBN 9780593099957 (ebook)
Subjects: LCSH: Mythology, Norse--Fiction. | Loki (Norse deity)--Fiction. |
GSAFD: Love stories. | Occult fiction.
Classification: LCC PS3607.O5979 W58 2021 (print) |
LCC PS3607.O5979 (ebook) | DDC 813/.6--dc23
LC record available at https://lccn.loc.gov/2020022385
LC ebook record available at https://lccn.loc.gov/2020022386

Export Edition ISBN: 9780593335925

Printed in the United States of America
1   3   5   7   9   10   8   6   4   2

Jacket design and illustration by Adam Auerbach
Book design by Tiffany Estreicher

For Poppy

THE
WITCH'S
HEART

PART I

LONG AGO, WHEN THE GODS WERE YOUNG AND Asgard was new, there came a witch from the edge of the worlds. She knew many ancient spells, but she was especially skilled with *seid*, a magic that allowed one to travel out of body and divine the future. This greatly appealed to Odin, the highest of the Aesir; when he learned of her abilities, he offered to impart upon the witch his knowledge of the runes in exchange for teaching him *seid*.

She was uncertain at first. She'd heard enough about Odin to make her hesitate. But she knew he did not share his secrets lightly, which meant her knowledge of *seid* must be of great value to him indeed. So she swallowed her suspicions about this grim one-eyed god and accepted his offer.

As they practiced *seid* together, the witch found herself drawn farther down than she'd ever traveled before, where she brushed against a place darker than the beginning of time itself. This place frightened her, and the secrets contained there were great and terrible, so she did not dare go deeper—much to Odin's displeasure, for the knowledge he sought above all else was hidden there, and it seemed to him that only she could reach it.

The witch was also teaching her magic to the Aesir's rivals, the Vanir, a sister race of gods whose home she had passed through on her way to Asgard. The Vanir could think of naught but gold with which to reward the witch for her services, though she cared little enough for it.

But when Odin realized she was traveling between Asgard and Vanaheim, he saw an opportunity. He turned the Aesir against the witch and called her Gullveig, "gold-lust." They drove spears through her and burned her three times, and three times she was reborn—for she was very old, very hard to kill, and far more than she appeared. Each time she burned, Odin tried to force her down to the dark place to learn what he wanted to know, and each time she resisted. And when the Vanir heard of the Aesir's treatment of her, they became furious, and thus was the first war in the cosmos declared.

The third time she was reborn, Gullveig fled, though she left something behind: her speared heart, still smoking on the pyre.

That was where *he* found it.

Some time later, he tracked her to the deepest, darkest forest at the farthest edge of Jotunheim: the land of the giants, the Aesir's bitter enemies. This forest was called Ironwood, where the gnarled gray trees were so thick that there was no real path through them, and so tall that they blocked out the sun.

He did not have to venture into those woods, though, for by the bank of the river that divided Ironwood from the rest of Jotunheim he found the witch, staring across the water at the dense forest and mountains beyond. She sat upon a rough woolen blanket with a thick cloak about her shoulders and a hood pulled over her head. The sun was shining, but she sat in the shade, hands folded in her lap, leaning against a tree trunk.

He watched her for a time, shifting from foot to foot, scratching his nose, listening to the quaint gurgling of the river and the whistling of songbirds. Then he sauntered up to her, his hands clasped behind his back. He could see only the bottom half of her face, but her skin looked pink—tender, healing, *new*. When he got closer, he noticed the skin of her hands was the same. She seemed to be resting peacefully. Part of him didn't want to disturb her.

Then again, he'd always found the idea of *peace* to be quite boring.

"How long are you going to stand there?" she rasped. She sounded like she hadn't had anything to drink in an age and a half. He figured that breathing in the smoke from one's own pyre three times would have that effect on a person.

"You're a difficult woman to find," he replied. Truth be told, he wasn't sure how to proceed. He'd come to return what she'd left in Odin's hall—and for something more, though he didn't know exactly what.

Something had drawn him to Ironwood that day with her heart tucked into his haversack. And he had a feeling that whatever was pulling him down this path was important, was special, was *interesting*, for he was so very easily bored.

And now here he was, enticed by the possibility of some excitement and hoping the witch would not disappoint.

SHE didn't reply at first, opting instead to study the strange man who'd approached her. The sun was shining behind him, so she couldn't quite make out his features—just a deep green traveling cloak and hood, brown pants, brown leather shoes, and the silhouette of wild hair.

"I really admire your work," he said conversationally. "You know—sowing chaos wherever you go. Making mighty beings fight over your talents. It's impressive, really."

A moment passed before she said, "That was not my intention."

"What was it, then?"

She did not reply.

"Well, if you're planning on doing it again," he said, "I would *love* to watch and possibly participate, so long as I don't get caught. But I'll let you know up front that I shall not, under any circumstances, make you a promise I can't talk my way out of. I'm not usually this straightforward about it, so consider yourself lucky. I'm letting you know as a friend."

"A friend?" The word was foreign to her.

"Yes. I've decided it just now." He cocked his head. "Am I your first friend? What an achievement for you."

She ignored the question. "Seems a rather one-sided decision on your part."

"Well, I see you're not exactly surrounded by admirers." He studied her. "You seem to me to be nothing more than a harmless witch from the backwoods—I haven't heard anyone talk like you for a very long time. I'm surprised the Aesir could even understand your accent. Who are you? Where do you come from?"

"I don't know," she said after a moment. She inclined her head such that she could see him, but he couldn't quite see her. "I could ask you the same question about yourself, and you probably wouldn't know the answer, either."

"Oh yes?" He settled down on his haunches and peered at her.

She could see now that he had a pale, angular face, a sharp, slightly upturned nose that gave him an impish look, and shoulder-length dark blond hair that fell somewhere between wavy and curly. His eyes were grass green; his smile was mischievous.

The witch nodded once in reply.

His smile faltered a bit. "And how could you possibly know that?"

"I know things," she said. "You may have heard."

"I *may* have heard that your knowing of things was what got you stabbed and lit on fire, multiple times. Perhaps from now on you should just play dumb."

"Well, that's no fun," she said, only half joking, her hand moving instinctively to the vertical slash between her breasts—the place where they'd stabbed out her heart.

"That's the spirit!" He laughed as he rummaged around in his bag. After a moment he pulled out a wad of cloth and held it out to her.

She took it—and started when she felt the bundle pulsing rhythmically in her hands.

"Your heart," he explained. "I was going to eat it, for some reason, but I decided that maybe you should have it back."

"*Eat* it?" she asked, making a face. "Why?"

He shrugged. "I don't know. To see what would happen."

"You would've eaten the heart of a witch, and that cannot be good for your well-being," she said dryly; she frowned as she unwrapped it. "It seems to have healed quite a bit from the fire. But . . ."

"But there's still a hole in it," he finished for her. "You got stabbed. Perhaps it shall heal completely if you put it back where it belongs. Do it now—I won't look."

"It can wait." She replaced the cloth and looked at him. "Thank you."

"You're welcome." He sat down now, stretched one leg out, and propped his elbow up on the other knee. "So, I take it you're not going by Gullveig anymore. What do they call you now?"

"I'm not sure." She looked at him sideways as he plucked a long piece of grass out of the ground, put it in his mouth, and let it dangle lazily there, and she noticed the splash of freckles across his nose and cheeks, and how the sun behind him turned the outline of his curls a violent orange.

She was still not sure what to make of this man. It was difficult to decide how much she should tell him.

"You don't know your own name?" he asked, raising his eyebrows.

She shrugged. "I thought I would like to travel, in which case they would call me something depending on the nature of my wanderings." She cast a glance across the river at the gray thickets of Ironwood. "Though I may yet decide to rest here for a time."

"And what will you call *yourself*, then, if you stay?"

She considered this for a moment or two before she said, "Angrboda."

His wrinkled his nose, and the blade of grass drooped. "What? 'Proclaimer of sorrows'? That's an odd name. Why would I want to be your friend if that's all you're going to do?"

"*You're* the one who decided we were friends," she said. "And besides, it's not you to whom I'll bring sorrow."

"Are all witches as cryptic as you are?"

"I don't know if I've *met* any other witches, though I think some used to live in these woods, too, long ago." She looked to the other side of the river again and lowered her voice almost reverently.

"They say there was one witch here who bore the wolves that chase the sun and moon, and raised many others still."

"Right. I heard stories about them, growing up. The Old One and her wolf-children."

"You heard those stories in Asgard?"

"Well, I'm not *from* Asgard. Anyway, everyone knows the stories out here."

"You're a giant," she said. It was a guess on her part, but she did not make it sound like a question. "Giant" was a misnomer: a name, not a descriptor, for giants were often no larger than the average person. And while her visitor was certainly dressed like one of the Aesir, sometimes there was no physical way to tell a god from a giant.

But this man, traveling alone and undisguised . . . There was something wild about him, something about his eyes that spoke of deep forests and midsummer nights. Something untamed, unharnessed.

He cannot be a god, can he?

He shrugged a shoulder at her deduction. "Sort of. Anyway, it seems rather empty around here now. No wolves . . . no witchmother . . ."

"Indeed." She looked across the river again, feeling a pang in her empty chest. "But maybe it was me. Maybe I was their mother."

"You don't remember, though?"

She shook her head. "I don't."

Silence fell between them, and he shifted. She got the feeling he hated when conversations lulled; he had the air of one who enjoyed hearing his own voice.

"Well," he said at last, "I'll have you know that I'm going to make it my personal mission to ignore all your depressing prophecies and do whatever I feel like doing."

"You can't just *ignore* prophecies."

"You can if you try hard enough."

"I'm not quite sure that's how it works."

"Hmm." He put his arms behind his head, leaned against the tree, and said haughtily, "Well, maybe you're just not as clever as I am."

She gave him a sidelong look, amused. "What do they call *you*, then, Sly One?"

"I'll tell you if you show me your face."

"I'll show you my face if you promise not to recoil in horror."

"I said I'd tell you my name. I can't promise anything more. But trust me, I have a strong stomach—I was going to eat your heart, after all."

"My heart is not so full of vile things, I promise you." Nevertheless, she lifted the hood, revealing heavy-lidded blue-green eyes and the brown stubble of her burned hair. These had not been Gullveig's colors, but Angrboda figured that she should leave *that* particular name and all its associations behind her and never mention it again.

This was a new phase in her existence. She was going to keep the witchery to herself from now on, thank you very much. No more *seid*, no more prophecies, no more getting into trouble. She'd already had enough of that for several lifetimes.

"And here I thought you were going to be some hideous ogress hiding under there." He raised his hands and curled them into claws. "Angrboda Troll-woman, so ugly that men flinch away in terror to look upon her face."

She rolled her eyes. "And what's *your* name? Or do you intend to break your promise?"

"I intend no such thing. I am a man of my word, Angrboda. I'm

the blood brother of Odin himself," he said loftily, and put a hand
to his chest.

Ah, there it is, she thought. She did not remember Odin taking
a giant for a blood brother when she was in Asgard. But then again,
that could have been centuries ago, for all she knew—she remembered very little of her time in Asgard and next to nothing from
the time before that. Perhaps her strange visitor just hadn't been
present in the hall where she'd been burned.

Or maybe he was and was watching it, rapt. Like all the rest.

"And I can't *believe*," he went on, "that you would besmirch my
good name by implying that I'm an oath-breaker—"

"I would have to know your name in order to besmirch it,
would I not?"

"You're besmirching the *idea* of my good name."

"The idea of your name itself, or the idea that it's a good name?"

He blinked at her and mouthed the word *Oh.*

"I shall make up a name for you if you don't tell me what it is,"
she said.

"Ooh, very interesting." He wrapped his arms around his knees
like an excited child. "What did you have in mind?"

"You won't like it, that's for sure. I'm going to call you the worst
name I can think of, and use my witchy magic to make everyone
else call you that, too."

"'Witchy magic'? Oh, I'm *so* frightened."

"Don't *make* me make you eat this," Angrboda said warningly,
holding up her cloth-wrapped heart.

"Hmm, maybe that's what I should've done in the first place."
He sat up straighter and gave her a mock-predatory leer. "Maybe
I'll gain your power. Here, give it back."

She held it away from him when he reached for it and said, in her most ominous voice, "Or maybe something much, much worse will happen."

"How do you know?"

"I don't. I'm only saying."

"Well then, I suppose I can't blame you for wanting to hang on to it after what happened."

"I won't be parting with it anytime soon—that's for certain." She put her heart back in her lap and looked down at it. *Not ever again.*

A few moments passed. When she looked up at him again, he was giving her a crooked smile. She returned it hesitantly—she didn't know what her smile looked like now, if it was grotesque or unbecoming or just frightening.

But his smile only widened, betraying none or all of his thoughts.

"My name," he said, "is Loki Laufeyjarson."

"You use your mother's name instead of your father's?" she asked, for Laufey was a woman's name.

"I do. And I honestly can't believe you don't know of me, for all the time you spent in Asgard. The gods are *so* very serious, and it gets quite boring sometimes, so I'm prone to amusing myself to keep things lively—mostly at the expense of others, but that's neither here nor there. They can't help that I'm rather the wittiest person around, after all."

"And the most humble, too, no doubt," Angrboda observed, with straight-faced sincerity.

Loki studied her for a moment as if trying to decide whether she was joking. When her expression didn't change, his wry smile widened into an appreciative grin.

"You know, Angrboda," he said, "I *do* think we're going to be the best of friends."

◆　◆　◆

ANGRBODA made her home on the far eastern side of Ironwood, where the trees clung precariously to the steep mountains bordering Jotunheim. She stumbled upon a clearing near the base of one such mountain, where she found an outcropping of rocks that led into a cave quite large enough for her to stand in. Upon entering, she realized there was a hole carved into the rock above her, under which sat the remains of a hearth.

It was all eerily familiar. Like it had been waiting for her.

She rebuilt the hearth into a long fire with stones she gathered from the woods. The cave itself was as large as any modest hall in Jotunheim: spacious enough for furniture and with plenty of room for storage near the back, where the ceiling was lower. By day, the inside of the cave was illuminated by the sun coming in through its mouth; by night, she kept her hearth fire lit against the total darkness of her new home.

"A cave?" Loki said, blinking, the first time she showed him inside. "Why not build a hall?"

"I'm *hiding*. A hall would be too obvious."

Loki just shrugged at that. She noted that he didn't comment on whom she was hiding from—even though he was one of them. She knew she should've been worried as soon as he'd revealed his association with Odin, but something told her that he wasn't what he seemed, and that instinct was what kept her from fleeing to find another cave every time he departed hers.

Angrboda saw him now and again after that first day, whenever he would come by Ironwood. He was a natural shape-changer, as she soon discovered, and he could make rather good time from Asgard to Ironwood when he took the form of a bird, and he didn't just drop by for nice banter. Sometimes he stayed a night or two, comically snoring facedown on her floor using his balled-up cloak as a pillow.

She rarely slept.

She didn't know how much time had passed since they'd met by the river, but her light ash brown hair had grown long and straight and fine; she often put it in a thin braid draped over her shoulder or pinned it back in a loose bun at the nape of her neck. Her cave-dweller-pale skin had healed quickly after her burning, giving her the look of a much younger woman, but the dark circles under her eyes were ever present.

She'd put her heart back where it belonged, too, by leaving her body enough to numb the pain but staying connected enough to move her hands. She'd opened the wound where they'd speared her, and so there remained a vertical raised scar between her breasts.

But it still felt like something was missing from her. Like that hole in her heart had not yet fully healed.

She got along fine regardless. There was a stream that branched off the river beside which she'd first met Loki, and it meandered near enough to her cave that it wasn't a hassle to go back and forth to fetch water and wash what few articles of clothing she had. She'd accumulated a meager pile of furs on which to sleep, too, but not enough food to eat. Animals were scarce in Ironwood.

One day she was out checking the snares she'd placed among the trees, and when she saw that they'd yielded nothing, she wandered over to the stream to catch some fish. For hours she sat by the bank, bored out of her skull and with no bites on her line. She had nearly dozed off against a tree when suddenly an arrow whizzed past her head and planted itself in the bark three inches from her face.

After a shocked pause, Angrboda looked around, wide-eyed, for the source.

Another giant emerged from the trees across the stream: a woman, broad-shouldered and dressed in a short woolen tunic and pants, with a bow in her hands, a pack on her shoulder, an empty quiver at her hip, and a bunch of fat rabbits hanging from her belt.

"You're not a rabbit," said the woman. She seemed a little too disappointed.

"You nearly killed me," Angrboda replied, blinking furiously.

"What are you *doing* here, anyway? Don't you know this place is dead?" Although she appeared no older than Angrboda, the woman looked down on her as though the ancient witch were nothing more than a naughty child.

Angrboda did not appreciate this and stared right back at her in silence.

The woman appraised her for another moment before saying, "Why don't you grab my arrow out of that tree and come share a meal with me? It's the least I can do after almost shooting you."

"Worse has been done to me," Angrboda said, throwing her makeshift fishing rod aside. The stream was shallower than usual this season, and she needed only hop across a few rocks to get to the other side.

While Angrboda started the fire, the other giantess deftly skinned two of the rabbits and introduced herself as Skadi, daughter of Thjazi, and added with pride that she was known in Jotunheim as the Huntress for her skills with archery and trapping. She was pretty in her way, with thick pale hair in two braids under her fur-trimmed cap, and strong, skilled hands. Her eyes were a glacial blue.

Skadi just nodded when Angrboda introduced herself, only the slightest hint of confusion in her expression at the name.

"So, do you live near here?" Angrboda asked as Skadi started boiling the rabbit meat in a small iron pot she'd drawn from her pack.

Skadi shook her head. "I live in the mountains, but farther north and farther inland. Where are you from? I can barely understand your accent."

"I'm very old," Angrboda said truthfully. "Older than I look. If you're from the mountains, where are your skis?"

"It's not snowing here yet. I had to leave my skis along the way."

"What brings you here, then? There's naught but small game in these woods, and it's scarce enough. Surely the mountains are better hunting grounds for you."

Skadi used her knife to stir the contents of the pot and grinned across the fire at Angrboda. "It's because of a story we tell here in Jotunheim. They say the witch who birthed the race of wolves is still here somewhere. She's one of the ancient giantesses of the forest—supposedly they all lived here in Ironwood a long, long time ago. I come by sometimes when I'm out hunting, but I've never found anyone. Then I saw smoke rising from the foothills earlier today and couldn't resist coming to take a look. I suppose it was just you, though. Right?"

"Aye, it was." Angrboda paused to choose her next words carefully. "I *am* a witch, but surely not the one you seek."

"A witch," Skadi echoed. "What sort of witch?"

Angrboda shrugged.

"What can you do?"

"Nothing impressive, I suppose," Angrboda mused. "My home isn't even furnished." She didn't have so much as a pot to cook stew in. A witch she might be, but Angrboda was no craftswoman when it came to the tools and furniture she needed to be more comfortable in this new life of hers.

Skadi paused and stared at her—partly with suspicion and partly with the are-you-*stupid* look that Loki had given her when he'd first seen her new residence. Angrboda kept looking right back at her and pulled her cloak tighter around her shoulders. Night was falling.

"Huh," Skadi said at last and resumed stirring the food with a look on her face that implied she wasn't thinking about stirring the food. "You must be able to do *something* if you call yourself a witch. Some of the witches I've heard of can do *seid*. Like Freyja. Can you do that?"

"You know of Freyja?" Angrboda asked cautiously.

"I've heard talk. You hear things when you're a trader. You know of the war?" Skadi prompted, mistaking Angrboda's distant expression for confusion. "Between the Aesir and the Vanir?"

Angrboda nodded. During one of his visits, Loki had told her of what had transpired after she'd fled Asgard.

"I know of it," she said, "but I hardly know the details. In fact, I've heard there was no war at all, just the declaration and then the truce. But how did the truce come to be?"

"An exchange of hostages," said Skadi. "Njord of the Vanir and his son and daughter, Frey and Freyja, in exchange for two men from among the Aesir. One of whom was Mimir."

Angrboda's eyebrows shot up—another familiar name. "Mimir? Odin's most valuable adviser? These Vanir hostages must be important indeed for him to suffer such a loss."

"Oh, don't worry," Skadi said darkly. "The Aesir hardly play fair. Odin got him back in the end—his head, at least . . ."

Angrboda shuddered. "Still, even to make such a trade in the first place . . . what of these Vanir? What's special about them?"

"Njord is a sea god of some sort, but his daughter, Freyja, is said to be the most beautiful of women, and they say she taught *seid* to Odin himself."

"Is that so?" *Good. Let them say that,* Angrboda thought. *Soon no one will remember a thing about the witch they burned thrice, and I'll be left in peace.*

"Yes," Skadi continued, "and Freyja lives among the Aesir now. I've heard she has her own hall and everything."

Angrboda shifted and pulled her cloak yet closer around her. Freyja—a young woman before the war—had been the first one in Vanaheim to beg Gullveig to teach her *seid,* and she remembered as much only because the girl had been both stunningly beautiful and astonishingly persuasive. Her face and Odin's were the only two Angrboda remembered clearly from her time as Gullveig.

"So, can you do what Freyja can, then?" Skadi asked her.

"Yes and no," Angrboda said slowly, hoping to steer the conversation away from *seid.* "But I do possess some other useful skills."

Skadi seemed contemplative. She poured the stew into a small wooden bowl she had with her and handed it to Angrboda, as she herself ate right from the pot.

"I'm trying to think of how to help you," said Skadi. "For I intend to do so. But I'm a trader. This is a business venture, and the nature of the business is that you have to produce something in exchange for something else. So what can you do?"

Angrboda paused and considered this. Besides *seid,* what *could* she do? She didn't remember much from the time before . . . except for her magic. That was as much a part of her as her very soul and as clear in her mind as her breakfast this morning.

"I can make potions," she said. "Though I don't have access to the ingredients at the moment." She gestured to the thick, barren trees surrounding them. "There's not much to work with out here."

Skadi grinned. "One of my kinswomen has a great garden. I could trade my game for whatever plants you desire. Then I could give the plants to you in exchange for the potions, which I can then turn and trade for whatever else you need . . . for a percentage, of course."

"Of course," Angrboda echoed, grateful that Skadi was amicable to the idea in the first place. "You'd be doing most of the work, after all. You may take what you wish from your trades—my needs are few." She paused. "Though I have to wonder what you'd be getting out of all this. I'm very far removed from any trading paths. Or any paths at all, for that matter."

Skadi shrugged. "You're not wrong about that. But it all depends on whether or not your potions are any good. If they are, I can make better trades, so the trips will be worth my while. What sorts of things can you make, then?"

"Healing salves, for one, and charms to cure illness," Angrboda said, and took a sip of her stew—it was delicious, especially since she'd been living off scrawny rabbits charred on sticks over her hearth fire for quite a long while. "And potions to stave off hunger—especially useful in the winter."

Skadi was impressed. "Those will fetch a high price. Provided that they work."

"Trust me," Angrboda said with a hint of a smile. "They work."

As it turned out, Angrboda was correct: Skadi bartered her potions around Jotunheim and received so much in exchange for them that she would often show up at Angrboda's cave with household items—knives, spoons, linens, woolens, a cooking pot, an ax for woodcutting—and game, which she had either caught herself or traded for. Their arrangement was such that Skadi brought her large wooden boxes filled with small lidded clay pots, padded on all sides with unspun wool so they would not break in transit.

Angrboda filled the pots with her potions and passed them back to Skadi, who gave her a new box of empty pots in return.

Some of the items Skadi brought back gave the witch cause to believe her potions were making their way beyond Jotunheim. Skadi said she did have a few contacts who traded with dwarfs in Nidavellir and dark elves in Svartalfheim, and even with humans in Midgard. The items from Midgard included such things as fine textiles Angrboda had never even heard of.

"This one is called silk," Skadi had informed her when she'd arrived with a particularly beautiful, shiny length of fabric. "The humans traverse vast oceans in their longships for the sake of trading. This cloth has come quite a long way."

"I have little use for such finery as this," Angrboda said, awed as she ran her fingers over the smooth surface of the silk. She ended up trading it back to Skadi for something far more precious: a small pot of the finest honey Angrboda had ever tasted, and which she hoarded like a dragon.

In addition to teaching Angrboda how to set a *proper* snare to catch fresh game, Skadi eventually started towing logs down from the higher mountains on her sledge and leaving them outside Angrboda's cave. When Skadi had a nice large pile of logs, she declared that they were going to build some furniture.

"I don't know how to build furniture," Angrboda said lamely. *I'm certain I could figure out how to magic something together, though it wouldn't be pretty.*

"I'll show you. I have the tools," said Skadi, and produced them from her pack. "Trust me, we mountain women know how to do *everything*."

And so Skadi built her a table and two benches, and a bed frame, which was then tucked against the wall and laden with blankets and furs atop the two swaths of linen Angrboda had sewn together and stuffed with straw for a mattress. Skadi made her a smaller table and cabinet for her potions soon after, but the Huntress's best creation was her last: a sturdy chair to place near the fire. Angrboda carved it with patterns and swirls and placed furs on the seat to make it more comfortable.

Skadi also brought her ample candles to light her dark cave— and especially her worktable, as it was against the cave wall such that she had her back to the center fire as she mixed potions. The candles had come just in time, for the long dark of winter was on its way. Angrboda usually spent this time huddled in the back of her cave, surviving on one of her hunger potions, which she cobbled together with what small plants she could find in Ironwood. Those potions had worked well enough, but their taste had left much to be desired—the ingredients had never been quite right.

But now she had Skadi to provide the plants to make her concoctions palatable, and anyway, she didn't need to take her own hunger potions any longer; thanks to Skadi, she also had a store of dried meat and some goats for milk. The goats arrived well-fed, for which Angrboda was grateful, as there was little greenery for them to graze on in the mountains and the forests at the edge of the world.

Maybe things will be different this year, Angrboda hoped. *Every spring Ironwood seems a bit greener. But perhaps it's just my imagination.*

LOKI still came to bother her at his leisure. She was fine with that, as she enjoyed his company, though she did find him to be a little much at times. Peace and quiet were the only companions she could rely on; Loki was interested in neither peace *nor* quiet, but then again, he didn't seem to be all that reliable himself, and one of his favorite pastimes was complaining about how uninteresting she'd become since leaving her Gullveig roots behind.

He was, however, slightly taken aback when he barged into her cave one day to find it completely furnished, and she relished the look of surprise on his face as he took it all in.

"You're just in time for dinner," she said as she stirred the stew pot over the hearth.

"You even have a table now? You're really moving up in the world, aren't you?" he exclaimed. "Where did you get all these things, anyway? You even have a door! I thought you'd *never* get one."

Angrboda shrugged. She hadn't wanted anything too noticeable to mark the entrance of her cave—which looked more or less like a pile of moss-covered rocks jutting out of the mountain base, with smoke rising from the unseen chimney hole—but she'd decided she rather did need a door of some kind, so Skadi had nailed some wood together into a panel to cover the cave's mouth.

Angrboda tried not to let it unsettle her that they'd found a set of ancient iron hinges already secured in the entryway when they'd measured it for the door. Skadi had seemed perturbed herself at the find, but had said nothing except to deem the hinges functional before securing the new panel to them.

"I've been trading," Angrboda said presently. "Potions for possessions. It's quite lucrative."

"Trading with whom?" Loki asked, arching an eyebrow. "Don't tell me you have other friends now, too? I'm impressed."

"As you should be."

"How are things here?" Loki poked a rabbit hanging from the ceiling. "Boring? Menial?"

"More or less."

"I see you have a garden now," he said, smirking.

"I do at that," she replied with a smile and ignored his condescension. Earlier that year, Skadi had brought her some seeds, gardening tools, and even a simple straw hat with a wide brim, and Angrboda had gotten to work. She was quite proud of the garden, too; she grew just enough to feed herself with fresh root vegetables, cabbage, and herbs for seasoning.

"How wonderfully domestic," Loki said dryly. "What are you cooking?"

"Rabbit stew."

"Do you ever eat anything other than rabbit?"

"If you don't want my rabbit stew, you can leave."

"And to think, you were once a powerful witch who did interesting things."

"I still *am* a powerful witch, and you would do well not to forget it." She spooned the stew into bowls and passed one to him, and they sat down on opposite benches at her new table. "How are things with the gods?"

He prattled on, pausing only to eat. And as Angrboda listened, she tried not to wonder at the bitterness creeping into his voice as he told his tales of Asgard.

ONE rainy night a short time later, Angrboda was sitting in her chair by the fire when Loki appeared at the mouth of her cave, drenched and stumbling. He closed the door behind him, facing away from her, his shoulders hunched and shaking. His hood was up. She could not see his face.

"Loki?" she asked hesitantly, standing. "What brings you here so late?"

He shuffled over and sat on the bench, put his head down on the table. His breath came in ragged, wet gasps, and his fists were clenched so hard that his knuckles were white.

Alarmed, Angrboda went over and sat on the bench beside him, carefully placing a hand on his shoulder. He twitched away and lifted his head a bit to reveal a small puddle of blood on the table. Angrboda paled and made to rip his hood back, but he put his head down on his arms and would not move.

"What did you do?" she asked him.

"Nothing," he said, his voice muffled and odd. "Why do you assume that I did something?"

"Because 'things' are generally what you do. It seems to me in the time we've known each other that you can't keep your mouth shut to save your life." Her scowl deepened as she took note of the blood now seeping onto his forearms. "What happened?"

"*Nothing.*"

She put her hand on his shoulder again. "Let me see your face."

"No." Loki sat up, his features still hidden by the hood, and at this point Angrboda could see the blood soaking the front of his tunic. "Leave me be."

"You wouldn't have come all the way here in the first place if you wanted me to do *that.*"

"I had nowhere else to go," he said, very quietly.

Angrboda threw the hood off his head and he turned his face away. She could feel his shoulder shaking feverishly under her hand, and she moved closer to him and said, "I cannot help unless you show me."

At last, he turned to her so she could see the source of the blood: His mouth was a mangled mess, crudely stitched shut with a thick cord and without much care for evenness. He'd clawed about half the stitches out, and the bloody cord was dangling free on one side.

The breath left her as she stared first at the wounds and then at his green eyes, which were bloodshot and glassy as he looked back at her helplessly.

Angrboda didn't say anything more. She drew her knife—a recent gift from Skadi, a fine blade with an antler handle and a thick leather sheath that hung from her belt—and cut the dangling cord as close to his face as she could, and her nimble fingers began to gently pull the stitches out. Loki winced at her touch, his eyes watering, but he said nothing. When she was done, she had him hold a dry rag to his mouth to stanch the bleeding and told him she would be right back. He stared past her with glazed eyes and nodded.

The rain had let up a bit. She fetched two pails of water from the stream and poured one into her pot above the fire, and when it was hot, she wetted a clean linen scrap and dabbed silently at his mouth. This time, Loki did not so much as flinch.

"Shall I ask what they did to you," she said at length, "or what *you* did to *them* to deserve it?"

"I made some mischief and fixed it, as I'm wont to do. But in the meantime, I simply could *not* stop myself from shooting my mouth off." He rolled his eyes. "As you would say."

She gave him a wan smile as she continued to dab his lips. "Shocking. What sort of mischief was this that you pulled?"

"You know of Thor's wife, Sif? Well, while he was off drinking with the rest of the gods, I snuck into their chambers while she slept and cut her hair off. She didn't so much as stir as I did it, but in the morning, you could hear her screaming all over Asgard. And then they heard *me* screaming as Thor chased me down and threatened to break every bone in my body if I didn't fix it."

Angrboda blinked and gestured for him to hold the rag to his mouth. "And why, exactly, would you do such a thing to her?"

"It was more a prank on Thor than a prank on her. He loved her hair." Loki gave a shrug, but his voice sounded oddly pained as he added, "I thought it would be funny."

"I question your sense of humor," Angrboda said dryly. She crossed the room to her potions cabinet, where she got to work making a fresh healing salve. "Among other things. What happened next?"

"I lost a bet. I went to the dwarfs seeking new hair for Sif and got two more items out of the deal. Then I went to another pair of dwarfs and bet them they couldn't make items as fine as the first set, but the gods liked the second set better. If it weren't for my own boundless cleverness, I wouldn't have a head right now."

"How so?"

"I bet my *head*. They couldn't have my neck, you see. So they settled on sewing my mouth shut with an awl."

Angrboda said a quick chant over her salve in its tiny clay pot, then turned and gave him a sideways glance. "That's a stupid deal, and the outcome was stupider yet."

"Not completely. Now the Aesir have nice things, thanks to me."

"What sort of nice things?"

"Well, Thor now has a hammer with a short handle—make of *that* what you will—and *actual* golden hair for Sif. Odin has a spear that won't miss and a magical ring, and Frey has a golden boar and a ship that you can fold up and take with you, and which always has a fair wind."

"Those seem like great gifts. You can put the rag down now."

"Yes, well, it didn't stop Thor and Frey from holding me down as the dwarfs sewed my mouth shut." He watched Angrboda with the wariness of a child being presented with something new for dinner as she came back over to him and stuck her finger into the clay pot. When she smeared some of its pasty green contents across his mouth, he made a face at her. "Is this the stuff you sell to your friend Skadi? People trade her actual *goods* for this?"

"This will heal the wounds faster than they would heal on their own. But you'll have scars. They'll be worse on the side where you clawed your face like an animal. And this is fresh and more potent because I made it for *your* wounds, so it will work faster than the pots of *stuff* I trade to Skadi to distribute to just anyone."

"That makes me feel *loads* better."

"As well it should. You're in good hands, if I do say so myself."

"You mustn't be so humble."

She rolled her eyes. "I try. Very occasionally, I succeed."

"I knew that knowing a witch would come in handy one day. When can I wipe this off my face?"

"When you stop bleeding." Angrboda smeared the last of the pot's contents on his mouth with more force than she intended, causing him to wince. "A little gratitude would be nice."

"Gratitude? I can't imagine where you'd get *that* from. Maybe you should trade some more of this smelly stuff to your friend Skadi and see if she can find you some."

"Stop moving your mouth or you'll undo all I've done." She sighed, put the clay pot down on the table, and folded her arms. "I feel as though this won't be the first time I'll have to get you out of trouble."

"You're not getting me out of trouble. You're fixing me. I got *myself* out of trouble."

"And which is the more difficult task, I wonder?" Angrboda picked up a new rag and dabbed the beads of fresh blood that had formed on his lips and seeped through the layer of salve. "See? You've started bleeding again from talking so much. You should probably just keep your mouth shut for a while and let the damage heal."

Loki reached up, took her wrist, and gave her a crooked smile. "Not likely."

That smile, bloody and twisted though it was, gave her pause. Her hand stilled, the rag pressed against the corner of his mouth.

"Thank you," he said, his eyes half-lidded and his expression uncharacteristically soft.

She shook herself and pulled away from him, and started collecting all her bloody or otherwise soiled rags into one of the buckets. "You are a wholly irritating man, Loki Laufeyjarson."

He made a rather offended noise at that. "Wait, what?"

Angrboda picked up her bucket. "I'm going down to the river to wash these. There's more water in the other bucket for you to clean yourself up."

"I *could* just go stand out in the rain for a bit and save myself the trouble." He tugged off his muddy leather shoes and soggy woolen socks and threw them in a heap at the cave's entrance.

"I'd rather you didn't," she said, pursing her lips as she thought of all the dried mud she'd be sweeping out of her home tomorrow morning.

Loki got to work unwinding the long strips of cloth that wrapped each of his calves: a common garment for men. "I really am irritating you, aren't I?"

Angrboda ignored his question, carried the bucket over to the door to her cave, and peered outside with a frown. The rain was coming down harder than before. "Perhaps I won't bother with this until morning." When she turned around, she immediately looked away, as Loki had just cast off his bloody tunic and had it between his thumb and forefinger as he dunked it in the other bucket.

"That's not how you launder clothing." She sighed and set her bucket down, then bustled over to him to snatch the tunic, sneaking a brief glance at him as she did. The small bit of muscle on his body was visible only because he was thin. She told herself not to look too closely, and directed her attention to the tunic; she spread it out on the table and started working at the bloodstains with a rag.

"My pants are dirty, too," Loki said innocently as he reached for the drawstring on said garment.

Angrboda put a hand up to stop him. "You needn't take them off just yet."

"So you want my dirt in your bed?"

"When did my bed become a factor in this?"

"I could always wear one of your dresses to sleep in. I quite like dresses. Unless you only have the one. And it seems rather dirty to me. Do you sleep in that?"

Angrboda decided not to ask about the dress comments. "Why is it any concern of yours what I sleep in? And I don't suppose you're under the impression that you're sleeping in my bed tonight, it being *my* bed and all."

"Then I suppose we'll have to share." Loki shrugged a shoulder. Much to her relief, his pants were still on. "I'm *wounded* and I've crossed *worlds* today to get here. The least you can do is give me a decent place to sleep, Angrboda Iron-witch."

Angrboda gave a small smile, for the name had a ring to it. "I suppose you're calling me after my home, then?"

"No, I'm calling you after your steely disposition."

"How kind of you." She finished and hung his sopping tunic off the back of her chair to dry. "Your pants aren't dirty enough to need washing, but I'll try to get the spots out, and the pants needn't come off your body for me to manage that."

"Fine." He flopped down on the bed. "I'm hungry."

"Then get up and get your own food. Am I your mother?"

"No, and I'm grateful for that." He sprawled out and put his hands behind his head, bent his knee, and propped the other ankle up on it. "If you were my mother, I'd have a rustic accent like yours. No, my mother was a piece of work."

"It must run in the family," said Angrboda as she sat beside him to scrub at a patch of blood on his pants. "Why do you use her name in Asgard, then? Why not call yourself after your father?"

"Well, she was more like the Aesir than my father was. Or at least I think she was." He scowled. "I don't know. Maybe she was one of them. He was a giant for sure, though. That much I remember."

Angrboda paused. "You don't know?"

Loki looked over at her, oddly serious. Her salve was doing its work; she could see the scabs starting to form beneath the green paste. "I don't remember much before Asgard. Don't tell me *you* remember much before you were Gullveig."

"No, and it has long troubled me," she said, finishing up the last spot on his pants. They weren't pretty, but the stains were less noticeable than before. She handed him her last clean rag. "Here— you can wipe your mouth off now."

"Maybe it's not important, then," he said. He obeyed and then tossed the green-smeared cloth into her now-overflowing bucket. "It doesn't really matter where we came from, does it? We're here now. We're ourselves. What more can we be?"

Angrboda stood and deposited her own rag with the laundry, feeling suddenly drained. She put more wood on the fire, then grabbed her bone comb from the table, undid her braid, sat down in her chair, and started untangling her hair. As she did so, she heard Loki shifting on the bed, but neither of them said anything more.

"Do you ever stay still?" she asked when she was nearly done. When he didn't reply, she turned around and saw him sprawled out on his stomach under a pile of furs, snoring unconvincingly.

Angrboda got up and went over to the bed, meaning to take one of the furs from him so that she might make herself comfortable on her chair for the night, for she still did not sleep much. But when she got closer, she saw he was shivering and was reluctant to take anything from him.

After hovering there for a moment, she removed her belt, the cloth square she'd tied about her waist as an apron, and her woolen overdress, leaving only a linen underdress she'd been meaning to wash. Had she been alone that night, she would not have changed it—but after a sideways look at the "sleeping" Loki, she pulled another linen gown out of a chest Skadi had made for her and discreetly changed into it.

A short time ago, she'd come to Ironwood with only the clothes on her back. She considered herself fortunate to have the time and the means to make herself some spare garments, and out of such quality fabric as the warm wools and thick linens Skadi had procured for her. It seemed Skadi's suppliers of plants also grew flax and owned many sheep, and apparently had a lot of time on their hands to prepare, spin, and weave.

That was just fine with Angrboda, who found such activities frustrating and tedious where many women found them productive and cathartic. *The more power to them,* she often thought. *I'll gladly trade my wares for theirs.*

"I thought you weren't inclined to share," Loki murmured as she slunk into the bed beside him. He stuck out his upper lip. "Is it because I'm cold and wounded?"

She sighed internally and was grateful that she'd changed clothes with some modesty, having suspected him of being awake. In her experience, when he was *really* asleep—usually facedown at her table—his snoring was far more obnoxious.

"Perhaps it's because you're pathetic and I have an overwhelming urge to care for pathetic people," Angrboda said under her breath. "Almost like your urge to keep talking when you should probably stop and think instead."

By way of a response, he proceeded to move over such that there was the smallest possible space between them without their bodies actually touching. And within minutes he was asleep, leaving her awake to listen to his snoring. Leaving her to feel an odd fluttering in her chest, an unwelcome stirring inside her, like something was awakening that would be better off asleep, better off in the farthest recesses of her mind, where it couldn't bother her.

But Loki was nothing if not bothersome.

A loud clamor awoke her, followed by Loki's muttered curses.

Angrboda sat up and rubbed the sleep from her eyes, but she felt considerably more awake when she saw the mess Loki had made of her cooking utensils.

"I was trying to make breakfast," he whined when he noticed her looking. Thankfully, his tunic had dried during the night and he had put it back on.

"Out of what?" she asked, climbing out of bed.

"Uh," he said. "Dried animal meat and some eggs, I suppose. That's all you have in your stores. And I'm *hungry*. You're a bad hostess."

Angrboda ignored that, considering she had not only healed him but also washed his clothes and allowed him to share her bed last night. "How are your wounds?"

"Well, I'm talking, aren't I?"

"That tells me exactly nothing of import." She approached him and examined his mouth. His gaze softened again, as it had last night. Something in her chest fluttered—her heart, she realized—and she cursed it.

"See?" he said quietly, gesturing to the scars. "All healed."

Angrboda shook herself and stepped away from him, suddenly

claustrophobic. He was taking up too much space—both in her cave and in her head.

"Have a drink. I'll go gather some berries to go with breakfast." She could see the sun shining through the cracks in her door and figured it for a warm morning, so she decided to forgo her woolen overdress, but still put on her belt and tied her apron atop it. Then she poured a cup of ale and slid it across the table to him.

Loki took a sip and said, "This is a lot better than usual. Did you make this batch differently?"

Angrboda reddened a bit as she grabbed her basket. She didn't need to be told that Skadi was a better brewer than she was, so much so that the witch had stopped making her own ale in favor of her friend's. "No. I've been trading for it. Drink as much as you want."

"You don't have to tell me twice," Loki called after her as she left and closed the door behind her.

The rain had ceased sometime in the night. She took a huge breath of the crisp autumn air and immediately felt better.

Since she had first come to Ironwood after her burning, the woods had grown greener and greener each spring, and she could not help but notice that the green seemed to be spreading from the area in which she had made her home. Perhaps Ironwood was showing its gratitude at having just one inhabitant again.

As she got farther from her cave, the thickets of trees became denser, the forest darker. There was nothing in Jotunheim east of Angrboda's cave, for it bordered the mountains at the very edge of that world. But Skadi came from the north, and Angrboda was now heading south along the mountains' edge, trying to find plants whose berries she or the animals hadn't yet touched. Soon enough she passed into unfamiliar territory; even Skadi couldn't find traces of animal activity in this area, so it was pointless to set snares here. But as the rest of her usual haunts had been picked clean, she figured she'd at least have a look around.

The trees seemed to close in on her. Several times she thought she heard footsteps over her shoulder—but when she turned around, no one was there.

She kept walking but couldn't shake the feeling she was being followed. She almost thought she heard someone whispering behind her, repeating something she couldn't make out—and then a cacophony of voices laughing and singing, carried on the wind—

Mother Witch.

Startled, Angrboda stumbled on a rock and lurched sideways, and her basket went flying. When she had picked the dead leaves and sticks out of her loose hair, she fumbled for her basket, and that's when she noticed she had fallen into a clearing. Looking down to see what had caused her to trip, she saw a small rock and then noticed there was more than one, forming a circle with a small gap, all half-buried in the underbrush.

A foundation, Angrboda thought. *As if for a home.*

Looking past this, she saw that a circle of foundations lay around the outside of the clearing, more visible than the one over which she'd tripped. In the very center was another ring of rocks not so closely packed together, which Angrboda assumed had once enclosed a fire.

The wind picked up and she thought she heard voices again—women whispering, children laughing, the howl of a wolf. They were as distant as a faded memory, but she could have sworn—

"I thought you went to get berries," said Loki from behind her, and Angrboda jumped and put a hand to her chest in surprise. He gave her a crooked smile when he noticed how startled she was. "Am I interrupting something?"

I was just imagining it. Angrboda willed her heartbeat to get back under control. "What are you doing here?"

"I came to see what was taking you so long."

"Ah." She had not even heard him following her. She went down on her haunches and looked out over the foundations again, frowning.

Loki crouched beside her and looked in the direction she was looking. He stuck out his upper lip and said, "I mean, I *supposed* that all you did all day was stare at rocks, but—"

"Someone used to live here," she said quietly.

Confused, Loki stood and then crouched again. "Oh. I see. Maybe your witchy magic scared them away. Or maybe it was your face, Angrboda Troll-woman."

She elbowed him in the ribs, and he made a show of flopping over and clutching at his chest.

"What if these were troll-women as well?" she asked mildly, gesturing to the clearing.

Loki arched his eyebrows and sat up. "The Jarnvidjur?"

For some reason, the word sent a chill through her. "Those are . . . the women who lived here with the wolves? From the stories?"

"Well, yes."

Angrboda stood, casting a last glance at the clearing before turning around and walking off. She heard Loki get up and follow her, oblivious to her uneasiness at the discovery of these ruins as he complained all the way back to the cave.

"But what about *breakfast*?"

HE was gone for a time after that, leaving her to dwell on her thoughts.

She didn't go back to the clearing. She was afraid that if she did, she would just sit there, listening to those whispered voices on the wind, waiting for something to happen, waiting for the memories to awaken within her and explain why she felt such an attachment to that ancient place.

But still she stayed away. Without Loki there to startle her from her reverie again, she feared that she would turn to stone in that clearing, staring at rocks just as he'd said, until she became one of them herself.

One night sometime later, Loki came in and sat down beside her, looking troubled. She took part of the woolen blanket off her shoulders and draped it over his. His closeness made her heart skip a beat, and she cursed it. There it was, that dizzying, claustrophobic feeling—but this time, she couldn't flee.

Loki didn't notice. His gaze was fixed on the fire, but hers was on his mouth. His wounds had healed fully by now, but as she'd predicted, the scarring was worse on one side than on the other.

"Doesn't it scare you?" he asked.

"What?"

"The fire. Aren't you frightened? After what happened?"

Angrboda shook her head. "No."

"Didn't it hurt?"

"Can I tell you a secret?"

"Depends. Do I have to promise to keep it?"

Angrboda leaned in, ignoring the tightening sensation in her chest as she moved closer to him, and lowered her voice. "The healing was worse than the burning. Because when I was burning, I could leave my body. I didn't feel a thing. That's how I put my heart back, too."

"Really? I'd heard that was part of the nature of *seid*. But haven't you sworn off such things, after what happened to you as Gullveig?"

Angrboda shrugged a shoulder. "Yes, but I didn't go far." *If I did, I'd risk alerting Odin of my whereabouts.* That was one of many reasons she'd vowed to avoid using *seid*. If she went too far, she'd risk brushing up against Yggdrasil: the tree connecting the Nine Worlds, the axis of the universe. It was now Odin's own means of transport, and she dared not go anywhere near it.

When Loki didn't say anything, Angrboda turned to him and changed the subject. "So, what's going on? You only come here when you're bored or troubled, and you seem more of the latter today."

"That's not true." Loki pressed his lips together as if trying to keep himself from speaking, but the words started tumbling out anyway. "But, well . . . recently, there was this builder who came to Asgard with his horse. Offered to build a wall, in exchange for Freyja—and the sun and moon, too, but we all know Freyja is the real prize."

"Indeed," Angrboda murmured. "Surely the Aesir didn't agree to this."

"Mmm, yes, except they did," said Loki, shifting uncomfortably. "With some slight alterations. Courtesy of yours truly."

"And what were these alterations?"

"Well, it was suggested that the builder do the work in less time, and he agreed, so long as he could use his horse to help him. The Aesir considered this and asked me for my opinion. I told them to go for it—what do I care? We needed a wall, and this stranger was willing to build it. I didn't see the problem."

"Then what *is* the problem?"

"The *problem* is that the builder's stallion is supernaturally strong, and the wall is nearly finished. The Aesir are about to lose what they'd wagered, and they say it's my fault and now I have to fix it. Or at least that's what Odin told me, when he had his foot on my throat and was threatening my head. So now I have to do something, and I know what. It's just . . . not going to end well. I have a feeling. But it's better than getting killed."

"Perhaps the only solution is to keep your mouth shut next time, before someone shuts it *for* you," Angrboda said lightly. "Again."

Loki grinned at her, the light from the fire dancing in his eyes. "I would very much like to see them try."

A short time after he left, while she was out collecting firewood, a horse came up beside her and nudged her arm. She was so startled at the touch that it nearly caused her to drop the kindling she was cradling like an infant.

"Oh, hello," she said absently. Then it occurred to her to wonder what a horse was doing wandering around in her woods and how it had approached her without a sound, so she paused and stared at it.

It stared back at her with abject misery.

"Huh," said Angrboda. "What brings you here in such a form, Loki?"

I'm in trouble, said the mare in her head.

"What sort of trouble?"

You'll see in a few months.

Angrboda considered this.

"Loki," she said, "please don't tell me you shape-shifted into a mare and lured the builder's supernatural stallion away so he couldn't finish Asgard's wall in time to win his prizes."

A beat of silence passed.

The mare flicked its tail, irritated. *And here I thought you didn't do your prophecy magic anymore.*

"I didn't need magic to put two and two together. Come along, then," she replied, patting its muzzle in what she hoped was a comforting manner before leading it back to her home.

Angrboda did not end up spending that winter alone. Instead, she had Skadi barter for hay above anything else, and she cared for the horse.

Now that it was snowing outside, Skadi was faster than ever in her trips from Ironwood to Jotunheim proper. The woman was in her glory on a pair of skis—even with her reindeer and a sledge in tow.

One time, when Angrboda invited her inside for dinner before she took off to the mountains again, Skadi was surprised at the pregnant mare hunkered down in the corner, wretchedly munching on hay as if it were the last thing it wanted to be doing.

"So *that's* why you've needed so much hay lately," said Skadi. "Where did you get a horse?"

Angrboda shrugged and stroked the mare's mane. "This one wandered up to me in the woods one day and needed help. Who was I to refuse?"

"So you're going to be curled up here with a horse all winter, feeding and cleaning up after it?"

The mare whinnied, and it almost sounded like an extremely Loki-like snicker.

"That's the idea," said Angrboda, unfazed.

Skadi sighed. "You are an odd woman, Angrboda, even for a witch. Do you have those potions for me?"

Angrboda handed her a large box of clay pots, their woolen padding packed securely around their neat little rows. "There you are."

"Once the passes fill with snow, I won't be able to see you," Skadi said. She eyed the mare and then looked back to Angrboda. "Are you *sure* you have enough provisions to last the winter?"

"Indeed. You've outdone yourself, Skadi, I assure you. We'll be fine."

Skadi embraced her suddenly, then pulled away and put her hands on the other woman's shoulders. "Take care of yourself."

"You, too," Angrboda replied, then shut and secured the door behind her.

So that's Skadi, said Loki.

"That's Skadi." Angrboda stroked his forehead. "So . . . you, me, and the goats." The goats had their own shelter outside—which Skadi had constructed along with the latrine, some ways away—but Angrboda figured she'd have to bring them into the cave when it got too cold. "It's going to be a long winter."

I'm stuck like this for longer than that, Loki said sullenly. *Can't you just . . . whip up a potion and a chant to get me out of this faster?*

Angrboda smiled. "I'll see what I can do."

AND so Loki and Angrboda passed the winter in the cave, and Angrboda's potions once again worked their magic: Instead of taking nearly a year, the mare gave birth in the spring to a gray colt. Skadi came as soon as the mountain passes cleared, with new furs and big game and early springtime plants for Angrboda to use in her concoctions so that they might start up their trading arrangement again.

Skadi wondered at the colt, for it had eight legs and she'd never seen anything like it before. Loki and Angrboda were amused at her amazement; they were used to the colt by now.

Angrboda was surprised to see that more of the gray trees in Ironwood now had leaves in the spring and that there was grass in the clearing outside the entrance to her cave—enough for a mare to munch on while the colt galloped playfully about. Angrboda often ground her plants and mixed her potions outside to watch them.

It was early autumn when Loki told her he was taking the colt he'd borne back to Asgard as a gift to Odin. Its name was Sleipnir, and it would come to be known as the best horse among gods and men.

Angrboda argued. She wanted to keep the colt; she found she had a certain fondness for Sleipnir despite his peculiarity. But Loki refused. He would not tell her why, besides citing the fact that Odin was the All-father and deserved a horse such as this, and she could do little to change his mind.

On the morning he decided to leave, Angrboda was sewing in her chair when a sudden *whoosh* made her look up to see air swirling around the mare like a tornado. When it dissipated, Loki was standing there, hunched and haggard and very much naked.

"A little warning would have been nice," Angrboda said, pointedly looking the other way.

"Yes, I suppose it would have been." His voice was hoarse from disuse, but he sounded more than a little relieved. "You wouldn't happen to have any spare clothes, would you?"

Later on, as they stood in the clearing at midday, Angrboda once again tried to change his mind about parting with Sleipnir.

"You never go anywhere anyway. What would *you* do with a horse?" he said, now fully clothed. Angrboda had hastily shortened one of her dresses into a tunic and happened to have on hand a pair of pants she'd been mending for him. He'd have to go barefoot for now.

"I'm not saying *I* would keep him," she said. "I'm saying *we* would. He's charming."

As if on cue, Sleipnir trotted up to Angrboda and nuzzled her hand, and she smiled and stroked his mane.

Loki just looked at her, then shook his head and led the colt away, chin held high. Angrboda watched him go until he disappeared. The hole in her heart seemed to always be present now—after months of Loki's company and then the addition of a baby animal, her cave seemed colder and darker in their absence.

BUT Loki had apparently decided not to linger long in Asgard; to her surprise, he returned before nightfall.

Angrboda was cleaning up from supper when he entered. Newly man-shaped, he looked tired and drawn from the months and months he'd spent as a horse, more so than he had when he'd left that morning. When he'd been trying to put on a show.

For his sake, she hoped it had lasted all the way to Asgard.

"Did Odin like his gift?" she asked, turning to him.

"Yes," he replied. He'd swapped the clothes he'd departed in for his usual Asgardian garb; she tried not to be offended by that.

She sat down on her bed pallet and regarded him. He leaned against the table, arms folded, seeming determined not to look at her. In the firelight, the bags under his eyes were even more prominent.

"Come here," she said, holding up the corner of the large woolen blanket she'd draped across her shoulders and beckoning for him to sit beside her on the bed. He approached her reluctantly and sat down. She put the blanket over his shoulders so it covered them both, and he shivered and pulled it closer around him, staring at the fire.

The silence between them could have lasted a thousand years.

"They think I don't know what they're saying about me," Loki said at last. "I bring them a great gift and I'm rewarded with . . ." He waved his hand and gave up trying to describe it.

"And you *care* what they say?" Angrboda asked. "Why?"

Loki shook his head. "You live in a cave. You don't know what it's like to live with a bunch of—"

"Aye, I know what it's like." She reached out and placed her hand on his. "To be an outsider."

"And how did that work out for you?" Loki said bitterly, and pulled his hand away. "Oh, that's right. You were stabbed and lit on fire, multiple times. And now you're hiding out here on the edge of the world all by yourself. I would rather be considered disgusting and shameful among the rest than be alone like you."

"Is that what they called you? Disgusting and shameful?" Angrboda asked, ignoring his jab at her. Although her memories as Gullveig were vague enough, she recalled feeling like she didn't belong—and the moment they'd turned on her, *burned* her, she'd felt a lot of things. But the emotion she could recall most distinctly was not fear or anger, but the feeling of being used.

She imagined Loki must be feeling the same thing. And she did not wish that on her worst enemy—let alone the man before her, who made her thrice-burned heart flutter so annoyingly. The thought of him in such pain made her chest burn with fury.

"More or less," said Loki, and he shrugged. "But I just decided that I don't care."

"So you won't be going back?"

"Oh, I will. I'm just going to get *better* at not caring."

"You're a fool," said Angrboda, clenching her fists in her lap. "It'll be the same if you go back. I don't know how I can be of any further help to you if you insist on remaining in Asgard. It's not going to end well." She gave him a pleading look. "This will keep happening, Loki. I say this only because I—I care for you."

She wished she could take back the words—Loki had always seemed to her to be the type to flee at the first mention of feelings, and she wasn't particularly keen on discussing such matters, either—but her words were true enough, so she let them linger in the air between them.

Loki suddenly regarded her with suspicion. "Wait. You . . . don't find me repulsive? You don't think—what I did, what I *can* do, it's not something—?"

Angrboda rolled her eyes. "If that were the case, do you think I would've spent the entire winter literally and figuratively cleaning up after you?"

"I—well, I mean—"

"You seem to have lost your way with words, Sly One."

He glowered at her. "Everyone else—"

She placed a finger over his lips. "From now on, once you cross this threshold, you must either stop caring—as you said you would—or bring your bothersome feelings elsewhere. Do I make myself clear?"

"Are you saying that it's bothersome that I *have* feelings, or that I should single out specific feelings that are bothersome and leave *those* at the door?"

Angrboda thought for a moment. "The second one."

"And who gets to determine that?"

"I suppose you do."

Loki stuck his tongue out and made to lick her finger, but she pulled it away and glared at him. He just grinned at her.

"Did you hear a word I just said?" she demanded.

"Yes."

"Then what did I say?"

"Feelings at the door. I shall do so on one condition: that I can bring inside the *most* bothersome ones."

"That's no condition at all," said Angrboda, cross and not a little offended. "You really weren't listening to me, were you?"

"Of course I was," Loki said lightly, brushing an invisible speck of dirt off his pants. He paused and considered his next words, which was not something she recalled seeing him do before. "I just figured you might want to make an exception for these particular feelings, bothersome though they may be . . . because they're about you."

Angrboda stared at him. He stared back at her, and for once he seemed to be absolutely serious.

"What? I care for you as well," he said. "As much as I hate to admit it. Caring about things makes life more complicated, doesn't it? Best not to care about anything at all, in my opinion. And then you came along. I find it quite bothersome indeed."

Angrboda was taken aback by his response, which she had assumed would be an attempt to change the subject. Suddenly *she* was the one who wasn't ready to have this conversation, and yet here they were, and she had started it.

"Do you, now?" she said, trying to keep her voice even. "Is this a game to you, Loki? You found me, you've shown up time and time again to bother me and insult my hospitality, you mock me for being uninteresting—"

Loki started to say something, but she cut him off.

"And yet somehow I believe you," she finished. "You may be made of jests and cleverness, Loki Laufeyjarson, but there are some things even you cannot hide."

Like the way I've seen you look at me.

"Some *feelings*, you mean," he said, sighing. "I suppose I *must* get better at hiding those. But for now . . ."

Angrboda found she couldn't sit still under his gaze, and she got up. Put some more kindling on the fire. Sat back down under the blanket with him. He moved closer to her, and she turned and looked at him again.

"If I'm such a bore, why are you still here?" she asked slowly.

"You're not a bore. I'm all jests, remember?"

"Still. The fact that you've kept returning means something." She moved her hand up to place it on his shoulder. She couldn't look him in the eyes, afraid her words would fail her.

"What more would you have of me?" she asked. *So much for locking all my bothersome feelings away at the bottom of my cursed heart.*

"I would have all of you," he said quietly, brushing her nose with his. "I would have everything."

Said cursed heart seemed to have jumped up and settled itself in the general vicinity of her throat, and Angrboda glowered at him and twisted away.

"You're going to break my heart with this business with the gods," she said thickly.

"Break your heart? I would never," said Loki, affronted. "I was the one who gave it back to you, remember?"

"So you did," Angrboda replied, "but—"

He cut her off with a kiss, which she returned without even thinking—like it was something for which she'd been waiting a million years—and she *knew* he felt it, too, because as soon as their lips made contact, it was as though some floodgate inside of her broke, and emotion overcame her like a wave and she couldn't stop it no matter how hard she tried. Which was, admittedly, not very hard.

She didn't know what sort of emotion had been loosed, but despite the repressed longing that had been building in her chest, it seemed as though her excitement was laced with trepidation.

What am I doing?

Somehow she couldn't make herself care. Her eyes squeezed shut as she wrapped her arms around his neck, as she felt his hands on her hips, pulling her closer, then pushing her—gently, but insistently—down onto her back. It was as though her hands were moving on their own, sliding off his green tunic and tossing it aside. One of his hands was moving up her thigh, bunching her dress, pulling it up to her waist as he kissed her so powerfully that she couldn't move to sit up.

And the manner of that action struck a chord, somehow—perhaps it was a fear of being *used* again, but suddenly she felt the tiniest mote of regret for letting things get to this point.

Angrboda pulled away.

Loki reared back from her, confused. "What's wrong?"

She propped herself up on her elbows and, rather than trying to work out her anxieties in this particular moment, said the first thing that came to mind: "I meant what I said, you know. You're going to break my heart."

"Of course I'm not," he said petulantly, rocking back on the bed to balance on his knees, now wearing only his pants. "If your prophecy magic is telling you that, it's a poor judge of my character."

Angrboda shrugged and didn't look at him.

He leaned forward again and kissed her, less forcefully this time, and ran a long finger along the line of her jaw as he pulled back again. Then he gave her that half-lidded look that had sent her heart fluttering a few times before and said huskily, "How could I repay your kindness in such a way?"

"I don't know," she murmured. But the answer didn't matter. Not really. Not anymore.

She wanted this as much as he needed it.

And on the off chance he was telling the truth about such feelings for her, they would cross that metaphorical bridge when they came to it.

She sat up, reached over, and untied the drawstring on his pants as deliberately as she had pulled the bits of cord from his lips those months ago—only this time she moved slowly, not out of regard for him, but to make him squirm. He was still on his knees, and his breathing quickened as she worked. When she looked up at him, her own mouth twisted in a way to which she was unaccustomed.

"You're smiling," he pointed out, surprised.

Angrboda's expression went blank again, and she demurred. "Was I?"

"Yes."

"Hmm."

"I'd like to make you do it again."

"I'd like to see you try." Angrboda pulled her dress over her head and cast it aside so she was left with nothing to cover her except the long hair that fell over her breasts, obscuring them.

Loki stared and continued to stare as he settled over her and brushed her hair aside. He didn't ask about the scar on her chest— maybe he realized what it was from, or maybe he was too distracted to comment on it. Or to comment at all, for that matter.

"You seem to have lost your way with words again, Sly One," she said for the second time that night, but this time the words caught in her throat and sent a shiver of excitement through her.

He seemed to snap out of it then, but his eyes didn't leave her as he got his pants the rest of the way off and kicked them aside. He looked her in the eyes and grinned.

"I don't think I need them anymore," he said, and kissed her again.

I will give you whatever you need, Angrboda decided then.

After all, you gave me back my heart.

ANGRBODA was more tired than she remembered ever being, but still she did not sleep. Every time she began to doze, she was kept awake either by her heart fluttering madly in her chest or by Loki's lips somewhere on her body. By the time dawn came he was sprawled half on top of her, snoring into her hair.

The fire had nearly died and there was sunlight streaming through the chimney hole. Angrboda had almost drifted off again when there was a loud knock on the door, followed by Skadi shouting, "Angrboda! Are you awake? The sun's been up for hours!"

"Wake up," Angrboda whispered to Loki, shaking him. He lifted his head groggily and blinked at her. At her insistence, he rolled off her and stumbled to his feet, muttering to himself.

Angrboda shoved him toward her storage area in the back of the cave and gestured for him to crouch in the shadows behind a chest and some baskets. "Just until she leaves. Please—I know it will be a challenge for you, but try to keep your mouth shut."

Loki made an indignant noise but did as he was told.

Skadi knocked again. "Hello?"

"Give me a moment!" Angrboda called, throwing some kindling on the dying embers of the fire to make it look like she'd been awake for longer than she had.

"I have to piss," Loki complained in a low whisper from behind the chest.

"You'll have to hold it until she leaves," Angrboda hissed back as she wrapped one of the blankets around herself and kicked their discarded clothing under the bed.

When she opened the door, she was greeted not just by Skadi, but by another giantess as well, who was carrying a basket of plants. Angrboda pulled the blanket tighter around her body and raised her chin. She could only imagine how she appeared—having Skadi see her so indecent was one thing, but a stranger, too?

Skadi was dressed, as always, in a man's tunic and pants. Since the autumn weather was unseasonably warm, she had abandoned her usual kaftan for thinner wools and forgone her furs altogether, though she still wore a cap and her leather hunting boots with their pointed toes.

"Good morning," said Angrboda.

Skadi looked her up and down and raised an eyebrow. "Rough night?"

"You could say that," said Angrboda, brushing her sex-tousled hair behind her ear in what she hoped was a casual way. "Can I help you?"

"We brought you some of the ingredients you need," said the other woman, who was regarding Angrboda with something not unlike disapproval. She was young and very pretty, but her disposition did not seem to match.

"Angrboda, this is my cousin Gerd," said Skadi. "She lives near the mountains, and has a great garden and grows many plants. Her mother is a fine weaver and her father has hundreds of sheep. Most of the plants and fabrics I trade to you are from her—she was interested in finally getting to meet you."

"Though I mistook the long hike for a short walk," Gerd grumbled, wiping the sweat from her brow and smoothing back her loose, mousy hair. She was a little shorter than Skadi, but rounder, paler, softer, and dressed in much finer garments. If not for the slight traces of dirt under her fingernails, Angrboda would have guessed the girl had never done a day of work in her life.

Skadi just smirked. "Gerd, this is Angrboda, the witch of whom I've spoken."

"It's a pleasure," said Angrboda.

"Charmed," said Gerd, who seemed more interested in trying to see over Angrboda's shoulder. "Is there a man here?"

"Perhaps. Then again, maybe it's a woman," Angrboda replied, looking her dead in the eyes. "Is that a problem?"

"Is he your husband?" Gerd asked, staring right back at her.

"How do you know they're a 'he'?" Angrboda said placidly.

Skadi's face twitched just the slightest bit, but she said nothing.

Gerd looked confused. "If you're going to lie with a man, you should be married to him. But I take it you're not married, witch, else you wouldn't be living in a cave."

Angrboda looked to Skadi. "You keep the most charming company."

"She's family," Skadi said with a shrug. "But you know I'll trade with anyone."

"Even loose sorceresses, it appears," said Gerd.

"Just give her the plants, Gerd." Skadi sighed, rubbing her temples, and Gerd obeyed her with a huff.

Angrboda took the basket primly and held it to her chest to keep the blanket from falling off and revealing her nakedness. "Thank you."

Then Skadi's brow furrowed as she stared at something just above the basket—and Angrboda realized with a start that it was the scar on her chest that had drawn her friend's attention, and she moved the basket up to cover it. Gerd was too busy staring around the clearing with distaste to notice.

Skadi gave her a questioning look. Angrboda returned it with one that clearly said, *Another time.*

Angrboda then invited them inside for a meal, but both women declined and departed. As soon as she shut the door, she heard a huge sigh of relief from behind her, followed by the sound of urine hitting an empty ceramic jug.

"Will you live?" she called idly to the back of the cave as she set the plants down on the table and took off the blanket, tossing it back on the bed.

"Fortunately for you," Loki said when he was done, and wandered over to her. "Rest assured that the entire time those two were at your door, I was cursing your name."

Angrboda snorted and took to sorting the plants. "Perhaps you shouldn't have had so much ale last night."

"It was my first day as a man after *months* as a horse," said Loki. Still naked, he stretched in the lazy, self-assured way of a cat before putting his arms around her waist from behind. "Do you always walk around naked? I should visit more often."

"On the contrary, I'm generally fully clothed, despite living alone."

"That's a shame."

"Perhaps I would be more disposed toward nakedness if you *did* visit me more often."

"Then perhaps I can take you up on that." He breathed the words into her temple. "It was a good night."

"It was," she said, and turned to face him.

They kissed, but Loki pulled away after a moment or two and said, "Perhaps Skadi's cousin was right. Perhaps I *should* marry you."

"*Pfft.* And what makes you think I would have you?" she asked, but her heart leapt.

"Well, you've already had me. Every which way, I might add, but I'm sure we could find some more."

Angrboda considered this as she put her arms about his shoulders, and found that her previous fear of being used had dissipated enough that she could joke about it in tones of fake seriousness: "But you've taken advantage of me already of your own accord. Now it would be your *duty* to take advantage of me, as my husband."

"And usually I'm not one for such responsibilities, but I think I may be able to handle this particular obligation," he replied, just as seriously.

"Don't the Aesir have responsibilities? As gods to the humans and such?"

"Eh," said Loki. "I only became Odin's blood brother for lack of anything better to do. I figured that gods did interesting things. It was for boredom, mostly."

Angrboda brought her hands up and pushed his wild hair behind his ears. "Or for loneliness?"

"Maybe," Loki said shiftily. "Boredom and loneliness often coincide."

"I understand."

He pressed his lips together and ran his finger down the scar in the middle of her chest, and she tensed eagerly at the memory of his rough lips on it last night.

"But it's a small price to pay for freedom," he said, seeming lost in thought, "which I no longer have as I used to. At least, that's what it feels like lately, being among the gods."

Angrboda nodded.

"I tire of control," he went on. He put his other hand on the small of her back, pulled her to him. She kept her arms around his shoulders. "But I don't want to be alone."

"I see."

"And you've never tried to control me."

"I haven't."

"And you care for me."

"Perhaps against my better judgment, but yes."

"You don't care what I do, as long as I come back eventually."

"I wouldn't say that, exactly . . ."

Loki put his forehead to hers. "So will you be my wife?"

Angrboda pulled him closer. So much had happened, and so quickly—but she couldn't deny what she had felt for him even before this, though part of her was still convinced that he was going to suddenly back away and tell her it was all a joke.

But when he only continued to look at her, she realized that she could get used to seeing this strange expression of utmost sincerity on his face, and she knew her answer.

"I would be honored," she said at last.

AFTER yet more long days and short nights with her, Loki left again. Angrboda was more than used to this; after all, he'd been visiting sporadically for years and years. But part of her had hoped it would be different now, although that part soon resigned itself to the fact that Loki was Loki and did what he wanted, and she stopped focusing so much energy on waiting for him, instead channeling it into organizing her stocks for the winter.

There was also a certain thing that she had to tell him, which served only to make the wait that much harder.

Angrboda had grown restless during the autumn while he was away. Winter was close at hand in Ironwood by the time Skadi dropped by for one last visit before the mountain passes snowed her in.

"So, you'll be spending the winter by yourself?" she asked as she plopped a great bag of dried meat down near the table.

I hope not, Angrboda thought, handing her a cup of ale. "It seems that way. Me and the goats."

"And the baby, too," said Skadi. "Or am I wrong?"

Angrboda instinctively put a hand to her stomach, which was barely bulging. "How did you know?"

Skadi took a swig from her cup. "I'm observant. Though I've never *observed* any men around here—who is the baby's father?" She smiled, but only barely. "Not a wolf, I hope."

Not in a manner of speaking. "No. It's my husband."

Skadi gave her a long unfathomable look. "You have a husband?"

"Yes."

"And where is he?"

"Away."

"I see," said Skadi doubtfully. She seemed a little offended. "Will he be back before winter?"

Angrboda shrugged.

Skadi sighed. "You can't stay here."

"I'll be fine; I assure you. Besides, I have enough food here for myself."

"Indeed?" said Skadi, eyeing her belly again. "But enough for two, if your husband returns?"

Angrboda had nothing to say to that, for she'd been fearing the same thing. Her appetite had increased somewhat, but should Loki come back and spend the winter with her, there was a chance her stores wouldn't be enough to feed them both.

Skadi looked satisfied. "That settles it—you're coming to the mountains with me. My father will welcome you. He has a particular interest in magic. You'll just have to ignore his occasional foolishness—he sort of grows on you after a while, I promise. Lately he's taken to going on fool's errands, so you may not even have to meet him right away."

Angrboda regarded her friend calmly, suppressing her growing alarm. What if she wasn't here when Loki deigned to make an appearance? Would she not see him until the passes thawed in the spring?

"How will we get there?" she asked. "I've no skis or snowshoes, and I'll be slow."

"You can ride on my sledge."

"There'll be no room for me on the sledge if we take all the supplies back up the mountain."

"We'll take as much as we can fit on the sledge with you. This cave of yours is cold and dry enough that the food will keep until you return."

"What about the goats?"

"They'll be fine until spring. They're animals. Think about this," said Skadi. "Is waiting here all winter really what you want to do, at the risk of your baby's health?"

Angrboda sat down heavily on the bench. "You're right. Of course you're right. I was being foolish. I'm just not . . ." She drummed her fingers on her thighs, then motioned to her abdomen. "I'm not used to this quite yet. I wish I had someone to share it with."

"Isn't that the point of being married?" Skadi scoffed. "Some husband you have."

Angrboda shifted and looked down at her hands, because she couldn't deny she was thinking the same thing.

"Well, you have me," Skadi said.

"It's not the same. You're not my husband."

Skadi gave her a scathing glare. "Of course. I'm only your friend. What do I matter?"

"That's not what I meant—"

"Of course." Skadi's eye twitched. "Wait. He doesn't know, does he?"

Angrboda shook her head. "I've not yet seen him."

Skadi slammed her cup down on the table and stood. "Pray I never meet him, or he'll come out the worse for it. Come, grab as much as you can carry and let's get moving." She paused. "But don't grab too much. You're with child. Pick light things. Here, I'll get the sack I just brought in and take it back to the sledge—that's the heaviest."

"Soon I'll have you securing my boots for me as well," Angrboda mused.

"Just you wait, my friend," said Skadi. "Before long, *someone* will have to."

Angrboda stowed her heaviest woolen dresses in her traveling basket and donned her cloak and hood, then followed Skadi outside and closed the door to her cave, and stacked rocks and twigs and dead grass in front of it so it would be hidden when the snow fell.

As Angrboda was finishing up, a falcon perched itself on a tree branch near her head and peered at her. She looked at Skadi—who was busy rearranging the supplies on the sledge and muttering to herself—and then back at the bird and whispered, "It's about time."

Sor-ry, said Loki. *There was this business with a giant and some golden apples. Business in which I may or may not have been involved . . .*

"I'm leaving for the winter," Angrboda said. She was not in the mood for his stories of mischief-making, although she knew he was itching to tell the tale. If he'd have shown up but half an hour ago, she would be spending all winter curled up in his arms. Now it was too late, and if he revealed himself, Skadi would probably spear him with one of her skis.

Loki seemed to sense the brooding air emanating from the Huntress, for he retained his falcon form. *I can see that. Where are you going, anyway?*

"The mountains."

Ugh. Why would you want *to go there?*

"I was invited. And Skadi has sworn violence on my absent husband for leaving me to winter alone. I'd stay a bird if I were you."

I'm sorry, he said, fluttering down to perch on her shoulder. *I'll come visit you, then.*

Angrboda shook her head. "The weather will be too bad. Do yourself a favor and stay in Asgard this winter." Her news of the baby was on the tip of her tongue, but she held it back; this wasn't how she'd pictured telling him. He might be quite expressive while in animal form, but something in her wanted to see his face when he heard, so she could gauge more accurately how he felt about the whole thing.

Because after her conversation with Skadi, part of her was desperate to know whether she'd made a mistake in agreeing to be his wife. His reaction to her pregnancy would be very telling.

"I'll be back here as soon as the passes clear," she added.

The falcon bobbed its head, then gave her an affectionate peck on the cheek before flying away. By this time, Skadi was ready to go; she gestured for Angrboda to come sit on the sledge and made sure she was bundled up in furs.

The trip would take two days, and each mile took her farther from her home. And Angrboda realized then that the last winter with Loki—even as a mare—had been too short, and the ones before them barely memorable. This was going to be the longest winter of her very long life.

THEY stayed the night in the giant Gymir's abundant hall, and Angrboda once again had the pleasure of finding herself in the company of Gerd, who was the daughter of Gymir and his wife, Aurboda; although Skadi had referred to Gerd as her cousin, their fathers were distant kin.

Gerd didn't seem to notice Angrboda's pregnancy and Skadi didn't mention it, and they were off again the next morning after they had exchanged some of their supplies for the hospitality. At least now their sledge would be lighter.

The next day, they found Skadi's father Thjazi's hall, Thrymheim, empty—save for a few reindeer grazing near the storehouses, tame enough to roam freely. Unlike in Gerd's parents' hall, there were no servants, not even guard dogs barking at the gate.

"We don't need much, my father and I," Skadi said when Angrboda observed this. "Those who live close enough to disturb us—well, they know better."

Skadi did not seem particularly surprised that her father was absent. As she unloaded the contents of the sledge into one of his storehouses, she muttered darkly to herself about wild-goose chases and golden apples and quests for immortality.

Angrboda caught the bit about the golden apples but decided to keep what Loki had told her to herself.

She did not have long to wait, though, to find out what such apples had to do with Skadi's father—for within a fortnight of Angrboda's arrival, Gerd was at their door, freezing and irritated. Once they had invited her inside and poured her a cup of ale to warm her, she told them what she'd heard from her parents, who had heard it from others: that Skadi's father, Thjazi, had been killed by the Aesir after abducting the goddess Idun and her golden apples of eternal youth.

"What happened?" Angrboda asked, for Skadi was too stunned to speak.

"Thjazi captured a man called Loki first and threatened him until he agreed to find a way to get him Idun, and he did," Gerd began.

Angrboda was almost glad that her husband had hinted at his involvement in this matter; otherwise she might've visibly started and given herself away at the mention of his name.

"And then to get her back," Gerd went on, "Loki flew into this very room and turned Idun into a nut, they say, and flew back to Asgard."

I wasn't aware he could project his shape-shifting powers onto others, she thought, wondering if this part of the tale was true.

"But Thjazi followed in eagle form, and the Aesir lit him on fire when he arrived, and killed him." Gerd stared down into her cup. "I'm sorry, cousin."

Skadi did not shed a tear. She just balled her fists in her lap and stared down at them. Angrboda put a hand on her shoulder, and no one spoke for a while.

"Who is this *Loki* person?" Skadi said quietly.

"Odin's blood brother, who's reckoned among the Aesir," said Gerd. "He's a giant as we three are, and they say he gets the gods into trouble constantly and then gets them out again, as he did this time."

"Which makes him a traitor," Skadi spat. "The gods hate us. They look down on us. Why would *anyone* do such a thing as join them?"

"The benefits, I suspect," said Gerd. "There must be something to marrying one of them or otherwise becoming their kin, as he did."

"This Loki is going on my list of men whose throats I'll slit if I ever come across them," said Skadi. She turned to Angrboda and added, "Along with your useless husband."

Angrboda resolved not to mention they were one and the same.

"Oh, you're married now, then?" Gerd said to Angrboda. "Why don't you cover your hair, as married women do?"

"It's a recent development," Angrboda admitted, although the truth was she'd forgotten about this custom. "I've not had a chance to make myself a head covering."

Gerd seemed offended by this. "My mother has plenty of spares. I'll have one for you when next we meet."

It was nearly nightfall and at this point Skadi had invited Gerd to stay the night and she'd accepted. Soon after, Gerd fell asleep on a pile of furs in the corner, and Angrboda and Skadi were left to talk by the fire in the middle of the hall.

"Are you all right?" Angrboda asked her after a time.

Skadi shook her head.

Angrboda moved over and sat next to her on the bench, took her hand. "I'm so, so sorry for your loss, my friend." *And I wish I could tell you that I'm sorry for the hand my husband had in your father's death as well.*

"I will avenge him," Skadi said, shaking. Tears were coming to her eyes now, to Angrboda's immense relief—she'd been more worried at the fact that Skadi was *not* weeping. "When the passes thaw, I will go to Asgard with sword and shield and all the armor I have, and *I will avenge him.*"

"Perhaps they will compensate you instead."

"And perhaps I will spear them all through before they can so much as speak a word." The tears now dripped down Skadi's face, and she turned to Angrboda and said, "Where did you get that scar? That was them, wasn't it? They did that to you?"

"Yes," Angrboda said quietly. "But that was in another time. Another life."

"There's no such thing. And time doesn't matter unless you're keeping track of it." Skadi sighed. "I will go alone, after I take you back to Ironwood. And there's nothing you can do to stop me. This is something I *must* do."

"I understand," Angrboda said, but it was only a half-truth: She understood that the loss of Skadi's father did merit some sort of compensation, which Angrboda was sure the gods would provide. But the concept of *vengeance* was something she could not quite grasp.

Not fully, anyway.

Not yet.

❖ ❖ ❖

So she spent the winter curled up with Skadi near the fire and listened to the other woman's stories, for she herself had few to tell. Skadi had traveled much on her skis and knew almost everyone who lived within a week's journey of Thrymheim, and she knew mostly everything *about* them, too. Yet in her sleep Angrboda would hear her mutter or cry about her father. And if there was anything to do during the winter, it was sleep, so she heard more emotion from Skadi during those times than when her friend was awake.

To her surprise and relief, the matter of the scar on Angrboda's chest did not come up again, so occupied was Skadi with her mourning. It would have caused her more grief to see her friend in such pain had Angrboda not been so consumed with excitement about the child growing inside her—an excitement that Skadi would occasionally share, but more often not.

When spring arrived and the passes cleared, Skadi did as she had promised and took Angrboda back to Ironwood. Once they dug up the entrance to her cave and checked that the food supplies had kept, Skadi unloaded the sledge.

Angrboda was more than happy to be home. It felt as though she had been away a long, long time. She put a hand on her stomach and felt her baby kick, and smiled a rare smile.

"How can I repay you for this?" she asked Skadi. It had been a harsh season, and Angrboda truly *did* doubt that she would have come through it as healthily as she had if she'd stayed in Ironwood.

But for all its severity, the winter had been blessedly short. She was only six months along in her pregnancy when she arrived back at her cave, and not showing very much at all. *A late autumn, a short winter, an early spring. The best any of us could hope for.*

Skadi just shook her head in response to the offer. "It was

enough that you were there for me. I would have lost my mind and let grief consume me had you not been at my side. Consider us even."

Angrboda shifted. "So you still intend to avenge your father, then?"

Skadi's gaze hardened. "I do."

"Then, good luck. And if you need to be healed, you know where to find me."

Skadi nodded and left, and Angrboda wondered if this was the last time she would ever see her friend.

IT was not long at all before Loki was at her door, but by then she was already preoccupied with cleaning and gave him only a peck on the lips when he entered the cave instead of the passionate, lingering embrace she'd been envisioning all winter. He looked surprised, like he was expecting a warmer welcome than *that*, and blinked at her from his place in the doorway.

"You've gotten fat," he commented as he watched her bustle about.

She whirled on him, lip curling.

"Not that I mind," he added hastily, palms up in surrender. "It's a good look for you."

"Well, thank heavens for that," Angrboda snapped. "And for your information, I have *not* gotten fat."

"Well, from what I can see—"

"Think about it, Loki. Think very, *very* hard."

After a few moments, Loki's mouth formed an O shape. Angrboda folded her arms.

"So . . . who's the father?" he asked, half-jokingly, but she could see a bead of sweat on his brow.

Angrboda gave him a deadpan look. "Oh, I don't know . . . my husband?"

"Then I suppose this is a bad time to mention that the Aesir made me take a wife among them." His gaze was fixed on her belly. "When did this happen?"

"I suspect the night you got back from delivering your eight-legged horse-child to the All-father," Angrboda said. Then her brain took a few steps backward and she bristled. "A wife?"

Loki walked up to her and put his hands on her hips, staring down at the bulge. "Shouldn't you be bigger by now?"

"Why did they make you take a wife?" Angrboda felt like she needed to sit down, for her heart was pounding so angrily that she feared her head would explode.

"Sigyn is *much* bigger than this and she got pregnant at *least* an entire moon after. Maybe more." Then he caught the way she was staring at him and said, "Sorry, what was the question?"

"The matter of your wife in Asgard," Angrboda said through gritted teeth as she sat down heavily on the bench.

"Oh," said Loki. He plopped down next to her and leaned backward against the edge of the table, his thigh and shoulder pressed against hers, crossing his legs at the ankles. He addressed his next words to the cave wall. "Right. They made me marry her—I suppose they're trying to keep me in line. I told them I already had a wife in Jotunheim, but they disregarded it. And as such, they don't recognize *you* as my wife, and made me take another."

"They *made* you marry her," Angrboda echoed in disbelief. "It seems to me that you cannot be *made* to do anything you don't want to do."

He turned to look at her now: an intense, steady look meant to gauge her reaction. "It's not my intention to keep things from you."

Angrboda balled her fists on her knees. "Do you love her?" And then, after a long and terrible silence, the inevitable next question: "Do you love *me*?"

"I . . ." He sighed, stood up, and knelt down before her, put his hands over hers. "Can I tell you something?"

Angrboda stared blankly down at their hands and said nothing. He had never *asked* to speak before. Loki asking if he could talk was much like a fish asking if it could swim while in the act of doing so.

But Loki seemed to be gathering his thoughts, which Angrboda had rarely seen him do, as words seemed to continuously spill out of him. She was perturbed enough by this turn of events to finally make eye contact with him, despite blinking back tears of frustration.

"I think you were the reason I figured I might be able to love someone," he said. "Why would I give you back your heart only to break it? I suppose that must mean something, right?"

"You *suppose*?" she mumbled, swiping at her eyes.

He reached up and wiped away a tear she'd missed, and his words were quiet and hoarse with those feelings he'd been so determined to hide at first. "And I do so hate to see you cry, and I hate even more that I was the cause of it."

"Before *you* came along I wasn't sure if I could love, either," she said, and tried not to sound as resentful as she felt. Then she softened those words by adding, "I had always been fine alone. And I still am. But I'm better when you're here."

"Well, it relieves me to hear that you're not always lovesick and pining for me." Something about his tone made her feel like he was more than ready to get off the subject of love and feelings. She was happy to oblige him in this regard.

Angrboda rolled her eyes. "Who would pine for the likes of you?"

"Who wouldn't?" Loki asked loftily.

"*I* wouldn't, apparently."

"Sigyn would. She's probably doing so right now, at this very moment."

"I'm not Sigyn," said Angrboda, and it seemed as though something dark and awful blossomed in the pit of her chest as the other woman's name rolled off her lips.

"Of course you're not," said Loki. "You live in a cave."

"What?" Angrboda looked around her, feigning shock.

Loki patted her hand in a manner that positively dripped condescension. Angrboda had to admire his ability to keep a straight face as he said, in a sympathetic tone, "I thought you knew."

Angrboda put a hand to her chest. "I would be lost without you."

"Yes, I know. Everyone would be. Anyway, *you* live in a cave. Also, she *obviously* thinks more highly of me than you do." He peered at her with mock suspicion and tapped his temple. "Your earlier sarcasm has been noted."

"She's *obviously* gotten confused somewhere. But I suppose you *do* have some redeeming qualities."

"I'd be most interested to hear them."

"Well, for one, you gave me back my heart." She squeezed his hands and moved them up to place them on her stomach. "And more yet."

"It kicked me," he said, blinking.

"I suppose that means she likes you. Also, she hiccups."

"How do you know it's a she?"

"I don't. Call it wishful thinking on my part."

"I don't care either way, as long as I don't have to clean up after it."

"Oh really?"

"Yes. I guess I'll . . . hold it, or something, or maybe try to make it laugh. But as soon as it starts dripping with excrement, I'm handing it back over to you."

"You're absolutely useless."

"Babies just cry and make a mess and you can't put them down anywhere because they just roll off whatever you set them on."

Angrboda snorted. "Maybe I won't let you hold the baby at all, if you're going to be haphazardly placing her on tables and benches."

"And their heads are big. Really big." Loki held his hands up, half a foot apart from each other. "*This* big. So big that even you, with the size of your hips, will have no lack of trouble pushing it out of you."

"Excuse me—the size of my *what?*"

Loki blinked, opened his mouth, closed it again.

Angrboda stared at him with raised eyebrows, waiting for him to repeat his last statement.

"And if you try to sit them up," he went on after a beat, "their heads simply loll over because they're *so big*. Babies are very inconvenient."

"*You're* inconvenient."

"I know. I have to work at it sometimes, though. Babies don't even have to."

Angrboda shook her head at him.

Loki grinned as he leaned up and kissed her—and it was a better kiss than the one she'd given him when he walked in, to be sure. A proper kiss. "Can we now move on to the matter of my not having seen you all winter long?"

"I was beginning to think you'd never ask," she replied.

❖ ❖ ❖

THEY ended up in the clearing outside the cave entrance, curled up atop a blanket. The spring night was seasonably warm, but Angrboda couldn't remember the last time she'd slept outside. She was always surprised to remember how many stars there were. For some reason she'd thought there would be only emptiness beyond the mountains that bordered Ironwood—perhaps that was part of why she rarely ventured out after dark, for fear of that void, for fear of realizing just how far on the periphery she really was.

And yet the sky told a different story.

"Are there so many stars in Asgard?" she asked Loki. They were facing each other, resting on their sides, his stomach pressed against hers, limbs entwined.

"Just about," he replied. "They're only stars. They look the same from everywhere, I promise you." He pointed to two stars in particular, burning brighter than the rest. "Those are brand-new, though."

"How do you know?"

"Well, you know your friend Skadi?"

"Of course I know my friend Skadi." Angrboda sat up laboriously. She'd feared the worst, not having heard from Skadi since she'd left to avenge her father. She was surprised to hear Skadi's name pass his lips—but then she remembered he'd seen her on various occasions, such as when she'd brought hay to the cave when he was a horse, and stopped by that spring and marveled at his son, Sleipnir, and of course last autumn when he'd come to see Angrboda as she was leaving for the winter. "Do you have news of her?"

"Calm down. She's quite well," said Loki, and she lay back down beside him. "She came to Asgard demanding blood, but . . .

she came to a compromise with the Aesir. She took a husband from among them and demanded to be made to laugh, which I alone succeeded in doing, at my own peril." He pointed at the stars. "And Odin took her father's eyes and made them into stars. They're just there, you see?"

But Angrboda wasn't looking at the stars. She was remembering the story that Gerd had told them, about what fate had befallen Skadi's father, and she recalled her friend's grief and rage and lust for revenge. As a result, she had a hard time believing what she was hearing.

"She took a *husband*? *That* was her recompense? That's ridiculous!"

"Yes. His name is Njord, and he's of the Vanir. A sea god. One of the hostages that got traded in the war. He's Frey and Freyja's father. And why is it ridiculous? A husband is more than fair compensation."

"She did not want a husband," Angrboda ground out. For some reason the news of Skadi's marriage made her angrier than she would like to admit. A new feeling twisted in her chest—something like envy, not unlike what she felt when she'd first spoken Sigyn's name. "How did they talk her into such a thing? That's preposterous."

"Well, that's what happened."

She set her jaw, the unknown feeling in her chest writhing furiously. "And he treats her kindly, this husband? This Njord?"

"The Vanir treat everyone kindly, for the most part. But the last I heard, it wasn't working out between them—he hates the mountains; she hates the sea. Surely it won't be long until the marriage dissolves."

"That's unfortunate," said Angrboda, not meaning it at all.

"Is it? They seem incompatible."

"I'm just glad she's alive." Angrboda sighed and settled down a

bit. Skadi had barely concealed her fury when Angrboda had pro-
fessed to have a husband, and now Angrboda was cross with her
for the same reason. It was better to let it go, she decided.

"She was made to choose her husband by his feet alone. She was
hoping for Baldur, Odin's own son, the youngest and fairest of the
gods. He's not even grown his beard and everyone is lusting after
him, goddesses and giantesses alike." Loki rolled his eyes and
smirked at her, pushing her hair back behind her ear. "What if
Skadi had chosen me?"

Angrboda snorted. "She would have sooner kicked you where
it hurts than marry you, had she found out that you were my
husband—she's muttered about the things she would do to that
man, should she come across him."

"Well, Skadi's payment for her father's death was twofold: a
husband and a bellyful of laughter, and I was personally responsible for the 'laughter' end of the bargain," Loki said. "My testicles
have suffered enough on her behalf, thank you *very* much. I tied
them to a goat to make her laugh. She has a rather sick sense of
humor, don't you think?"

Angrboda blinked at him. "Why . . . would you tie your testicles
to a goat?"

"I was telling a story," Loki said defensively.

"I would like a reenactment, please."

"No. That would mean tying my testicles to *your* goats, and *your*
goats are unsociable and mean."

"They are not."

"They are, too."

Angrboda pressed her lips together, unable to fully hide her
amusement. "Was it a true story you told?"

"Perhaps."

"Which means you've tied your testicles to a goat on more than one occasion."

"It's not something I'm proud of," said Loki with gravity.

Then Angrboda noticed some smallish scars on his arm . . . then on his shoulder . . . then on his chest. "Where are these from?" she asked, prodding at one.

"Oh," he replied. "Those are from when Skadi's father turned into an eagle and dragged me all over creation until I agreed to bring Idun and her apples to him."

"And you did."

"I didn't exactly have a choice. And then the gods all got old without the apples, and I laughed at them, and then they threatened to kill me unless I got them back, which I did. Problem solved. I'm sure they're starting to mistrust me, though. You should see the way they look at me sometimes."

"Does it bother you?" Angrboda ventured. "That they don't trust you?"

"Not particularly," he said with a shrug.

"Not yet. You live among them. Living among those who mistrust you will take its toll eventually." She paused. "You are always welcome here. You know that, right?"

"I know. And I thank you for not asking me why I won't stay."

"I know that you don't know. That's why I don't ask."

Loki sighed. "So, why does Skadi want to injure your husband bodily, again?"

Angrboda shifted. "For not being here."

"Ah," he said.

They were silent as they watched the stars for a while.

"I was thinking of creating a charm," said Angrboda sometime later.

"What sort of charm?"

"Well, first of all, it's said that Odin can see all the Nine Worlds from that chair of his. Is that correct?"

"It's correct," Loki said slowly. "It's not just said. He *can*, if he chooses."

"I want to hide this place. So that only those who have been here will be able to find it." She looked at him. "To be safe."

Loki arched an eyebrow. "What interest would anyone have in finding you?"

Angrboda shifted. "I've always been afraid the Aesir would come after me. But now I'm connected with you, and soon we'll have a child to worry about, too. That calls for more substantial measures."

"But they don't know you're *you*. Just that I have a wife in Jotunheim."

"But if you keep making mischief and then disappearing, they will start wondering where you've gone. It's only a matter of time before someone follows you here."

"You're being paranoid. What would they even do to you if they found you, anyway?"

"You forget your own words—they stabbed me and lit me on fire, multiple times." *And there's still the matter of what Odin wishes me to reveal to him, and the place I'd have to go to get it.* The thought made her shiver. *He burned me thrice and he'd do it again. And I have so much to live for now.*

She steeled herself. It wouldn't come to that, because he'd never find her once her protection spell went up.

Loki seemed skeptical. "So you think you can perform a spell that could hide you from even the All-father, who sees *everything*?"

"You forget again, my love." Angrboda half smiled and lowered her voice, ran her finger along his cheek. "Whatever they've told you, they burned me for a reason."

"Huh." Loki leaned up and over her, grinning. "Perhaps one day it will pay off for me to have a witch for a wife."

"I'm not getting you out of any sort of trouble you have in mind."

He kissed her. "I didn't have any in *mind*, but I'm sure I'll come up with something soon enough. It never takes me long."

"Then, as I said, you won't have my help."

"Are you sure about that?" he asked, kissing her neck, trailing kisses down the scar between her breasts.

"Absolutely," she replied with finality, "and any attempts to change my decision would be futile."

The kisses continued ever lower. "I'll keep that in mind."

As the night quickly passed—as their nights together so often had, rushing past in a haze of passion—she found that she wasn't even startled by the awareness that he could probably make her do whatever he wanted. Just a kiss, just a caress, just a *word* and she was his entirely. And while his way with words was not mere bragging on his part, his way with touch required no boasting whatsoever: Such actions spoke for themselves.

She was more surprised that she *wasn't* surprised, perturbed, or troubled by the fact that she cared for him so deeply, as she once might have been.

Later they continued to lie there, the breeze cool on their damp skin. Angrboda stayed awake, for the child inside her was kicking excitedly, while Loki fell asleep in her arms. She took to running her fingers through his sweaty curls. He looked deceptively peaceful in sleep.

She would do anything for him, she realized then, with a sudden fierceness that made her heart race. Anything for him—anything for the child inside her, pressed between them and evidently incensed by her mother's quickened pulse. Anything for them. *Anything.* And for some reason, this scared her, as if the thought itself were a promise she knew that she couldn't hope to keep.

HE stayed with her as the days grew longer and the nights shorter. But before long he was off again, speaking of Sigyn and the Aesir, and his absence bothered her where it had not before.

Angrboda took this time to work on her spell. She sewed three small sacks out of some leather scraps and filled them with little stones she'd carved with runes, over which she'd chanted for nine days and nine nights. After that, she placed the sacks in a wide triangle around her cave and the clearing. The first two she placed in the hollows of trees, marking the trees with more runes to disguise them.

The last sack she put higher up behind the cave to give the triangle even sides. She had to clamber up onto the rocks to place it, which was a challenge for her in her current state though the incline wasn't steep. But she succeeded in hiding the sack in a hole in the rock face and disguised it as she had with the trees.

Once the charms were all in place, she immediately felt more at ease. She would just have to hope that such a blind spot would go unnoticed by Odin—along with the fact that, should he be seeking Loki's location, her husband would sometimes be beyond his sight.

For whatever reason, the baby seemed to like to sleep during the day, only to wake and flail about at night, to Angrboda's growing discomfort. The witch took naps whenever she could and worked by firelight, weaving and mixing potions and sewing.

Lately she'd needed to adjust her clothes to better fit her present shape, including cutting a slit down the front of her dresses that could be secured with a brooch—it would come in handy for feeding the child after it was born.

Then there came a night when she awoke from a brief and restless sleep to a pain contracting in her belly. It was so strong that for a moment she could not move.

When she finally raised herself to a sitting position, she felt something wet and frowned, reached down to touch the bed, her dress, the insides of her thighs.

Her hand came away wet with blood. In the same moment she realized the baby wasn't moving. She tried to remember the last time it *had* moved, but as it usually did not do so during the day, she could not recall.

A sudden panic gripped her. She was far enough along in her pregnancy that her child might survive outside the womb, but some instinct told her that what was happening was *wrong*, that the connection she had to the life growing inside her was slowly being severed.

The baby was dying, and by the time she gave birth, it might be too late to save it.

Her mind raced. Did she have any potions to help? Any at all? Any spells? She could feel her bedclothes soaking further now, and a strangled whimper escaped her lips as she grappled at the furs and blankets, dragged herself back against the cave's wall, curled up around herself on the bed. And she thought and thought, and came up with nothing.

Her heartbeat had quickened, and that made her only option all the more obvious as she let the rhythm lull her into a trance, steady as the beating of a drum.

Ba-dum, ba-dum, ba-dum . . .

She descended without even thinking, shedding her body like a snake sheds its skin, her lips forming words she didn't know how she knew.

Sacred words. A chant. Calling back the baby, her daughter. Angrboda could almost feel Yggdrasil as she reached out, could almost skim her fingertips over the fabric binding the universe together—luckily the child had not gone that far, but Angrboda certainly would've risked using the World Tree if it had come down to it.

Angrboda felt her daughter's presence and latched onto it in her mind, bidding the child return to her body. And as the witch repeated the words over and over, her own pain started to subside. Then, at long last, she felt the child kick.

Angrboda would have cried with relief were she not so terrified.

In the morning she found herself still curled up on the bed in her soiled shift, the furs and blankets around her mussed and stained. She felt numb with shock, but at least the child seemed fine.

It took until late that day for her to gather the will to get out of bed, get some water to clean herself up, and eat. That was around the time she realized that she was still too distraught to cry.

THE dreams began that very night.

Having spent most of the day awake but abed, Angrboda put a few more logs on her hearth fire after supper, lit some candles for extra light, and settled down in her chair to repair the cuff on one of her older dresses. She soon found herself distracted, and before she knew it, she had nodded off.

Later, she wouldn't be able to tell if she had been awake or asleep when she felt the presence. Felt someone circling her. *Calling* to her, in a manner similar to the one she used to call to her daughter. Speaking words she knew but didn't. Beckoning her closer. Drawing her out, and pushing her down.

Someone noticed what I did.

And this someone wanted something from her.

She sank deeper and deeper and felt herself brush against the edge of the dark place—the person's voice seemed to be pushing her toward it, pushing her to look over the edge, to plunge headlong into the depths of that fathomless void.

No. She knew what was down there, knew it from her time as Gullveig, from her days of *seid*—if she went down there, she would come back with things she didn't want to know.

Things she *shouldn't* know. Things *no one* should know.

She'd told Odin as much when she'd refused to go down there for him, and she'd burned for it. Thrice. *It can't be him again,* she thought, for she could not make out who this person was; they had concealed themselves from her, and so lacked Odin's distinct presence in her mind. Had his mastery of *seid* grown so powerful that he could mask himself completely?

No, she thought again. *Leave me alone.* She resisted, tugged herself away, and felt the chanter rear back. Felt their surprise.

And then their fury.

She jolted awake when she felt the heavy woolen dress slide off her lap and land in a heap at her feet. Her chest heaved and her hands shook as she slid off the chair and arduously bent down to pick up her sewing. When she had managed to haul herself back into her seat, she found she was too tired to continue sewing, but not too tired to realize the risk of falling asleep again, so she was at a loss for what to do.

For one of the first times since she decided to make her home in Ironwood, Angrboda desperately wished she wasn't so alone.

ONE summer morning Angrboda went down to the stream, which was a challenge at this late stage in her pregnancy. She sat there for a long while, enjoying the quiet and the soothing running water, until she heard the rustle of leaves, and Gerd emerged from the trees on the other side of the stream carrying a pack basket. When Angrboda nervously sat up and greeted her, the first words out of Gerd's mouth were, "Have you heard Skadi's gotten married?"

"Indeed. Some time ago. Care to join me? I had planned on bathing but I can't seem to muster up the energy."

The offer had been made out of politeness, not friendship, but nevertheless, Gerd hopped the few rocks to the other side and sat down on the bank beside her. "I have something for you, as promised."

And she dug around in her basket and extracted a piece of undyed linen, finely woven.

"It's a head covering," said Gerd as she offered it to the witch. "I came to realize my mother's are far too fine for your tastes. Hers are all silk, or dyed, or brocaded with gold thread and tablet-woven bands. You're a much simpler woman than she—no offense meant."

Angrboda had to concede this. "Thank you, Gerd. This is a fine piece, and I'll wear it happily."

"And if you wish to make it a bit fancier and help it stay in place," Gerd added, "I've also tried my hand at tablet weaving." From her bag she pulled a long band of yarn, woven into swirls and whorls of blue and green, accented with yellow. "But you can also wear it as a belt. Or cut it up and use it as trim for a dress."

"Your work is exquisite," Angrboda said, awed, as she took the band and ran her fingers over the tightly woven pattern. "Thank you for this. I shall treasure it."

Gerd beamed. "You're quite welcome. And there's more yet." She then extracted from the basket some more swaths of linen, these ones soft yet heavy. "They're swaddling clothes for your child. My mother made them as a gift for you—your potions healed my father's sickness last autumn, and she's eternally grateful. When Skadi told us you were with child, she insisted on making you something special."

"Please thank her for me," Angrboda said, and meant it. "These are generous gifts."

"It's the least I can do," Gerd said, shifting, not looking at her. "For being so impolite to you before. I apologize."

"I was not so polite myself. I'm sorry as well. But I find I have to ask . . . did Skadi put you up to this?"

"Of course she did. And you're welcome." Gerd put the cloths back into her basket. "I'll carry these back to your . . . er . . . *cave*, when you're ready. Also, Skadi wants you to know that she's well and will soon be by to see you but is staying in Asgard for the time be— Are you all right?"

For Angrboda's fists had clenched and her face was white. Her first contraction had just hit.

"Isn't it a little early for this?" Gerd asked, panicking as she helped Angrboda back to her home. "So is it—is it happening right *now*, or—should I go get—?"

Not as early as before. This is better. The contractions were small and far apart, and Angrboda found that she was not comfortable in any position, so she just walked back and forth in the clearing. "There's no time to go anywhere."

"If there's time for you to pace like that, there's time for me to go get someone," Gerd said shrilly, adding that she had watched her mother attend births but had never supervised one. Angrboda shook her head. Gerd sat down by the cave entrance and took to petting the goats as a way to distract herself as Angrboda continued to pace.

Gerd stayed with her, and late in the evening the contractions became so painful that Angrboda could no longer stand. It took her a while to find a position in which she found it natural to deliver; after much frantic reorganizing on Gerd's part and tired instruction on Angrboda's, Gerd ended up layering blankets over a pile of furs, and Angrboda half leaned, half squatted against it.

Far later in the night, a shaking Gerd knelt before her, ready at any moment with a blanket over her hands to catch the baby. She let Angrboda hold on to her shoulders to steady herself, not saying a word about the woman's fingernails digging half-moon welts into her skin, or anything but what words of comfort a young, inexperienced maiden could provide. For the girl's own sake, Angrboda bit back as many of her screams as she could. But just the look of pain on her face seemed to frighten Gerd.

As the labor wore on, though, Gerd seemed to become more comfortable in her sudden role as midwife. And when the baby was finally born in the very early morning, Gerd caught it and patted its back to clear its lungs, and cut the umbilical cord. When Angrboda heard the first wail escape her child's mouth, she sagged back against the blankets in relief.

"A girl," Gerd said as she wiped the wrinkly pink baby off and placed her in her mother's arms. She wadded up the blankets that had collected some of the birth mess and sat back and stared at both of them. "She's beautiful."

"She is. Just look at her." Angrboda felt her eyes fill with tears as she cradled the baby, who had stopped crying—which caused Angrboda to panic for a split second, until she noticed that her daughter was staring at her in wonder, and not with the baby blue eyes of a newborn.

She has her father's eyes, she thought, staring back at the infant with equal amazement. *And she's looking at me like she's surprised that she's here.*

Is it right that a little baby like her should look so wise?

"Does your husband have dark hair?" Gerd asked, because the baby had been born with a full head of downy black hair, and Angrboda's hair was a far lighter brown. Loki's was fair as well, but Gerd did not know this.

Angrboda shook her head. "I'm not sure where the color came from."

"Do you have a name for her?"

"Her name is Hel." It was a name she'd been pondering for a while—it had come to her the night she'd called her daughter's soul back from beyond, and it had stuck with her, almost as if Hel had named herself.

She put the baby up to her chest to nurse, but Hel seemed content to just continue staring at her in fascination.

"She's . . . not a *normal* baby, is she?" Gerd asked. "She's not crying."

"She looks very concerned about her new living situation," Angrboda agreed. *There's something curious about her, I suppose, but it's not a bad sort of curious.*

She's absolutely perfect.

Gerd was the first to notice the problem, so engrossed was Angrboda with her baby's pensive little face. "There's something wrong with her legs . . ."

She was right. Hel was moving her legs, but they were the

wrong color—pale white, not pink like the rest of her, and the skin was stiff and cold. And they seemed to be turning *blue* as the seconds passed.

Suddenly Hel started crying again, but this time it was a shrill cry of pain, and everything about the night Angrboda had almost lost her rushed back into her mind all at once. In her happiness, she had all but forgotten about it.

Angrboda said to Gerd, "Go to my cabinet. Go *now*, and get the pink vial in front—quickly!"

Gerd was on her feet in a second, scrambling, and grabbed the vial and handed it to Angrboda, who opened it and poured its contents down her daughter's throat, frantically muttering chants under her breath. Hel coughed but swallowed and started to calm down. The color did not return to her legs, but they did not continue to stiffen, either. Soon enough Hel was staring at her mother again and actually seemed content to nurse.

Angrboda looked up at Gerd then, who was looking back at her with unconcealed alarm. "What just *happened*? What did you give her?"

"I don't know. I don't know," Angrboda whispered back. Her daughter's legs were still cold, yet still moving. "It was a healing potion. It didn't heal her all the way—I don't know what it was, but I stopped it. For now."

"She seems all right now," Gerd said shakily. "I mean . . . her legs looked like that when she came out. I didn't want to say anything because she seemed fine, but if she was like that the whole time, why did she panic? Why did it get worse all of a sudden?"

"Maybe it was because she realized it. She was warm when she was inside me, and she can move them. Maybe she just hadn't noticed." Angrboda hugged Hel closer to her. "And maybe it will happen again. It looked like the flesh was dying, being eaten away somehow—I'll make a better potion. To preserve it. To *stop* it."

It's my fault it happened. It has to be. If she was dead, I made her come back. It was something about how I saved her that night, something about my chants.

Or perhaps something about me.

Gerd swallowed and picked up the soiled blankets, put them outside the door. "I'll wash these tomorrow. I won't be able to find my way to the stream in the dark."

She then took the cloth from her bag and handed it to Angrboda, who swaddled Hel when she was done eating, keeping the wrapping loose so she could easily check her daughter's legs. Then Gerd assisted her in cleaning herself up and helped her into bed.

Gerd ended up falling asleep at the table afterward, and Hel fell asleep in Angrboda's arms sometime later. But the witch herself, for all her fatigue, could not sleep.

This is my fault, she thought. *I keep coming back. I cannot be killed, not by fire or a spear through my heart. Is it not backward that a mother who is reborn time and time again should bear a daughter who is half-dead?*

Did I keep all the life for myself, instead of passing it on as I should have? Or did I not have enough to give?

But Hel seemed content to sleep, safe and loved. And, still unable to look away from her daughter's perfect face, Angrboda realized then that maybe her heart was healed after all.

GERD insisted on staying a few days to cook and clean. Angrboda thought the girl must have chores to do at home, but she was too tired to argue. And when Gerd finally left, it was only to come back a week later with Skadi in tow. Angrboda almost cried then—not only at the sight of her dearest friend, but also at the several jugs of ale Skadi had brought along to replenish the witch's stores.

She invited them both inside for dinner and Gerd once again insisted on cooking. Angrboda was exhausted from lack of sleep—due to both her newborn and her fear of the mysterious chanter from her dreams—and let her have her way.

"So I'll be looking for a man with black hair to castrate," Skadi said in place of a compliment, as soon as she saw Hel. "Where *is* this husband of yours?"

"Don't concern yourself with it," Angrboda said as she cradled her sleeping daughter. "Tell me of Asgard."

Skadi shrugged and took a sip of ale. "I take it Gerd has told you what happened?"

"I didn't have to," said Gerd. "She knew. How *did* you know, Angrboda?"

"So, how are things with your husband?" Angrboda asked hastily to change the subject.

Skadi and Gerd exchanged a suspicious glance, and then Skadi said, "We've separated. It only took me one night to realize I couldn't live by the sea—the gulls and the waves are too loud. Yet I stayed nine nights, and Njord stayed nine in my hall, but he could not sleep for the howling of wolves. We parted on good terms, and I shall still see him sometimes. He's a good man, and still my husband. And I will always be welcome in Asgard." She took another swig of ale. "I am reckoned among the gods now. There are humans in Midgard who pray to me on hunts."

"That must be wonderful," Gerd said wistfully. "To be worshipped."

"It's nothing special," Skadi said, but in a tone that implied it certainly was.

Skadi and Gerd stayed the night, seeming unbothered by Hel's waking up every few hours to nurse, though the baby didn't cry very much. When her friends left, Angrboda took to sitting outside, feeding the goats with Hel in a sling on her chest, and keeping a lookout for her troublesome husband, never getting her hopes up.

She found it strange that his absence bothered her less and less in the wake of Hel's birth. Worrying about him, wondering about all the reasons he hadn't come to visit—it would take up time and energy that she was unable and unwilling to expend. As far as she was concerned, Loki could do whatever he wanted—she had a daughter to take care of now.

TWO full moons passed before she saw Loki again.

The nights were starting to get colder. He entered when Angrboda was asleep, curled up around Hel, who was set in a depression in a pile of furs so she could not roll off the bed platform, and so Angrboda could not roll over and accidentally smother her.

Not that Angrboda moved much in her sleep. Not that Angrboda *slept* much even before Hel was born, but she was certainly asleep when Loki came in; she was roused by the sound of the door opening and shutting.

Loki took off his shoes and put some more wood on the fire, then crossed the room and looked at the bed in silence—as if, for once, he wasn't quite sure what to do.

Angrboda turned her head to look at him. "It's about time."

"I couldn't get away," he said, actually sounding apologetic. He carefully climbed over her and positioned himself on the other side of Hel, so the baby was settled between the two of them. "Sigyn had her child last week. If I left, I wouldn't hear the end of it."

"From whom?"

"From all of Asgard."

"How is she? And the child?"

"Both healthy. The baby is a boy."

"Ours is a girl."

Loki observed the still-sleeping baby with uncertainty. "What did you name her?"

"Hel."

"Hel? What kind of a name is that?" Loki laughed, and Hel stirred at the sound. She screwed up her face to cry, but when she opened her eyes and saw him, her features went slack and she looked him dead in the eye and held his gaze.

"She does that," said Angrboda. "She really enjoys staring at people. Sometimes I think she can see into my soul."

But Loki was staring back at the baby, and his entire expression had changed. He was as much in awe of her as Angrboda had been on the day she was born, and Hel in turn seemed enamored of her father—so much so that, all of a sudden, she smiled widely at him with her little pink tongue lolling out.

"She's been sort of smiling sometimes, for no reason," Angrboda said, surprised, "but this is her first *real* smile. And it's for you."

Loki was not paying the least bit of attention to her. He was suddenly smiling at Hel like Angrboda had never seen him smile before, and he reached out his finger so the baby could grip it in her tiny hand.

In that moment, Angrboda realized she was witnessing love at first sight.

Hel, attempting to stick his finger in her mouth, kicked happily and the blanket fell off her feet. Loki's eyes widened. "Why are her legs . . . ?"

"She can feel them. Look." Angrboda squeezed one of her

daughter's tiny toes, and Hel squirmed. Angrboda then found the words spilling out of her faster than she could stop them as she told him about the night Hel had nearly been lost.

"You can do that?" he said when she was done. There was an eagerness in his voice that Angrboda did not like. "Bring back the dead?"

"I'm not sure she was dead," Angrboda said, but she was still uncertain. "But aye, I saved her."

"And you think this has something to do with her legs?"

"I don't know, but they're dead. Dead flesh, but growing with her. I've tried potions and salves—none are harmful to her, I would never do that, the worst they do is *not* work—but nothing seems to reverse it. If I just keep trying, maybe I can revive them, but for now the most I can hope for is to stop her legs from rotting further—"

Loki leaned over and silenced her with a kiss. "We're odd. She's odd. She fits right in, does she not?"

"That's . . . abnormally sweet of you."

"I have my moments."

Hel seemed determined not to close her eyes until she was sure her father wasn't going anywhere. But eventually she fell back asleep, nestled between her parents without a single care in the world. Like a proper baby, Angrboda thought.

"How long will you stay?" Angrboda whispered, right before she fell asleep.

"As long as I can," he whispered back and kissed her again. And it seemed to her then that all would be well, if only for a time.

IN the days that followed, Loki spent most of his time with the baby, sitting on the bench with his elbows on his legs and Hel set between them, with his arms held out on either side of her to keep her from falling, his hands cupping her head. This was an optimal position to stare at her and have her stare back at him in return. He was willing to part with her only when she needed to eat—and, as promised, when she soiled her swaddling clothes.

At least Angrboda had been able to coerce him into going down to the stream and washing the baby's dirty linens; that was more than she had expected from him. She even suspected that, during the times she took short naps or went out to do her own washing or gardening, he might have changed Hel once or twice himself. As a result, she found herself wondering if her husband would ever cease to surprise her. She rather doubted it.

"You're not bored with her yet?" Angrboda asked as she swept the inside of the cave. The head scarf Gerd had made her turned out to be quite useful in keeping the hair out of her face, and Angrboda had quickly gotten used to donning it every morning. She found she liked Gerd's tablet-woven band better as a belt and wore it over her plain leather one, from which hung her antler-handled knife for decoration.

"She can fit her *whole fist* in her *mouth*. I wish I could do that. Such talent! I wonder if we can teach her some tricks."

"She's not an animal, Loki."

"She tried to put her foot in her mouth, but she didn't like the taste. She made a face. Probably because of all that green stuff you keep putting on her." Loki very much enjoyed giving Angrboda constant narration of everything she already knew Hel did. She supposed it was better than his not caring at all.

"They're salves to *stop her flesh from rotting off*," Angrboda said for the millionth time. "Not just *green stuff*."

Loki ignored her. "Though I suppose the 'dead flesh' bit might be why her feet taste bad. Isn't that right, Hel?"

Angrboda continued sweeping. "Whatever you say."

"She burbled. That means yes."

"Then what means no?"

"Cooing."

"Once again: whatever you say." Angrboda set the broom aside and sat down beside him on the bench, holding her arms out. "Now, if you're quite finished hogging my daughter—"

"*Our* daughter, thank you. Hel, do you want your stinky old witch mama to hold you now? Feel free to coo and stay with me forever."

Hel burbled.

A beat passed.

"Fine," said Loki, and passed Hel over to Angrboda. "She must be hungry. Surely that's the only explanation. Or she's about to have explosive diarrhea and wants to spare me, bless her little heart."

"Or perhaps she's just fonder of me." Angrboda smirked. She unpinned the front of her dress to nurse Hel—she'd extended the keyhole slit in her neckline downward, to provide easier access for her fussing child—and in doing so realized that she and Loki had actually been fully clothed more or less since he'd arrived.

"I highly doubt it," said Loki, scoffing. "Sorry, Boda, but *I'm* her favorite."

"Why does she have to have a favorite?"

"Because I said so, and I'm her parent."

"I'm her parent, too, don't forget."

"Yes, I suppose, but—"

"You *suppose*?"

"She looks more like me than you. That means I'm her favorite."

"As if she can control what she looks like."

"I'm a shape-changer; she could be, too! What if she saw me and decided that she wants to look more like me than like you because I'm her favorite?"

"She looked like you *before* you graced us with your presence."

"Yet more evidence supporting my argument."

"I don't even know how to argue with you."

"I'm the best at arguing, so it's a futile endeavor on your part."

Later on, when they had successfully put Hel down for the night—or rather, when Angrboda had, as Loki was always more of a nuisance than anything when it came to calming their daughter down enough that she would fall asleep—they sat outside the cave mouth, covered in a blanket. The summer was nearly over, and with its end came the first crisp fall breezes.

Not wanting to scare him away with any sort of serious matters when he was so taken with the baby, Angrboda had kept her own anxieties close to her chest when it came to the presence of the chanter in her dreams, whom she could still feel every time she fell into a deep enough sleep. But this fear was beginning to weigh on her.

"I've been having dreams," she told him as she sat there with her head on his shoulder and his arm around her waist.

"Congratulations," Loki said dryly.

Angrboda pulled away and looked at him. "Dreams in which I leave my body."

Loki frowned. "On purpose?"

"No. It's . . . it's as though I'm being drawn out, as if someone is seeking me. Someone wants something from me, and I don't know what."

"Well, why don't you let them take you and see what they want?" Loki suggested.

"Because I don't know what will happen if I do."

Loki mulled this over. He seemed too untroubled by this, and too dismissive. But of course he saw no reason to panic—he didn't know the gravity of what she was implying.

She was going to have to tell him the truth about *seid*. She'd rarely spoken of it to him—or even to Skadi or Gerd, for that matter—for fear he'd become too interested, as Odin had. For fear that, on the off chance any word of Loki's witch-wife and her abilities made it back to Asgard, Odin could turn his blood brother against her.

It wasn't that she didn't trust Loki in this regard; it was that she knew personally just how persuasive Odin could be, and the lengths to which he'd go to get what he wanted.

"Loki . . . when I leave my body, I'm connected to everything. I'm part of all the worlds, and part of Yggdrasil, the World Tree. I can see everything, and if I really wanted, I could learn things I shouldn't know." She paused for effect. "Things that haven't happened yet. Do you know what I'm saying?"

Loki sat up straighter. "Indeed?"

Angrboda nodded. "Such is the nature of *seid*. Please don't ask me to tell you more."

"Why not?" He gave her a puzzled look. "Is it so complicated?"

"No, it's just . . . knowledge of the future is dangerous, and it's— it's gotten me in trouble before." She gave him a meaningful look.

Loki put his hands up. "That's where Odin and I completely part ways. Knowing the future would be too much of a burden. It's just another form of control. No, thank you."

Angrboda sighed with relief.

"So you truly think it's Odin who's after you again?" he asked.

"It doesn't *feel* like him. It doesn't feel like anyone I know." Angrboda shook her head. "But if it *is* him, then I know exactly what he wants. Where he wants me to go. I don't know how to explain it. There's this . . . *dark* place at the very bottom of everything, a place I've never been, a place that has knowledge I've never tapped into before. Knowledge that terrifies me. Whatever this person wants to know, it's nothing they *should* know. Nothing *anyone* should know."

Loki shrugged. "Maybe they're *just dreams*—did you consider that? Maybe you're capable of having dreams that don't mean anything, just like the rest of us."

"It's more. I know it. I can *feel* myself being pulled while I sleep. There's a voice, chanting in my head. Ever since . . . ever since I called Hel back."

Loki looked skeptical at that but said, "Perhaps it really *is* Odin, then. It sounds like something he would do." He shifted. "He practices *seid* even though it's women's magic, and nobody says anything. But I give birth to *one* eight-legged horse and never hear the end of it."

"They're *still* on about that?"

"It's a good story," Loki admitted.

"Aye, and one told at your expense. They continue to mistrust you?"

Loki shrugged. "I can't say that I blame them."

"No good can come of your remaining there. You know this."

"I'm Odin's blood brother. I can't just *leave*. And besides, the only way I *can* keep myself entertained there involves mischief. That's why they have no love for me."

"Well, you are loved here. Is that not good enough?"

He gave her an unfathomable look then, and kissed her on the temple and held her close. "How long do you really think we can continue this?"

"Continue what?"

"This arrangement we have."

Angrboda jerked away and stared at him. "You mean our marriage?"

"I *mean* that I'm starting to think you were right before. About Hel's safety. And your own."

"I completed the spell to hide this place," Angrboda said. "We're perfectly safe. You needn't use that as an excuse. What's gotten into you?"

"I have to go back sometime," Loki said, but it sounded as if leaving was the last thing he wanted to do. He looked over his shoulder at the cave mouth. Angrboda followed his gaze, searching for the pile of furs atop which their daughter slept soundly.

"Then go," said Angrboda. "I care little. Hel will surely miss you, though. I fear she'll become bored, only having me to stare at all day again."

"I don't think so. You have a very interesting face."

"You can go *now*, if you choose. Unless you'd rather sit here and continue to insult me."

"I don't consider 'interesting' an insult."

"I know. But your tone suggested otherwise." Angrboda pulled away from him, pulled her legs up, and folded her arms on her knees. "Is she beautiful, this other wife of yours?"

"Yes," Loki admitted. He reached over and cupped her cheek, ran his thumb along the darkened hollow of her eye. "But so are you. Even though you look like you haven't slept for at least these nine ages past."

"I just told you about the dreams. Coupled with a newborn daughter and a husband like you, you should hardly be surprised."

"You didn't sleep before that, unless I tired you out."

She rolled her eyes and flinched away from his hand.

"Did you watch me sleep?" he asked.

"Only when I was bored enough."

He ran a hand through his hair and gave her a come-hither look. "It's because I'm so handsome, isn't it?"

"Oh yes," she said. "You're positively dashing. I can hardly keep my eyes off you."

"I have that effect on people," he said loftily. "It's a curse."

"I do believe you've changed the subject."

Loki sighed. "Sigyn is a good woman, and loyal. But you have more . . . gravitas."

Angrboda raised her eyebrows. "You think I possess such a quality as 'gravitas'?"

"Absolutely. That was one of the first things about you that intrigued me, Angrboda Iron-witch." He gave her an odd look when she made a face at the nickname. "You've . . . never really thought about yourself, have you?"

"No. Should I?"

"Perhaps." Loki sat as she did now, wrapping his arms around his legs. "I often think about myself. But that's because I don't understand me. Not one bit."

"None do."

"*You* do."

"Hardly."

"That's a point I would argue, but maybe another time." Loki looked skyward. "When my son was born, I thought something in me would change. I thought something would *happen* to me. But it didn't. The weeks passed and I just—I didn't feel any connection with the baby. I know Sigyn is disappointed with me, and I can hardly bear it. So I left."

Angrboda listened silently.

"And all that time," he went on, still not meeting her eyes, "I started to think that maybe there was something more wrong with me than even I thought—that maybe I was even more different than they all say I am."

"You became a father," Angrboda said. True, he had borne Sleipnir, but she doubted that he had any nurturing feelings for his first child. "It's a transition—you need time to adjust. The connection will come, and all will be well. You were scared. Maybe that fear was keeping you from bonding with your son."

He scoffed at the word "fear," but then he looked thoughtful. "Maybe it was. I know I was apprehensive about coming back here to meet our child. I was afraid I would just look at her and feel . . . nothing. I didn't want *you* to be disappointed with me, too. I don't want things between us to change."

He looked at Angrboda then, and she back at him, and she said, "That's because I love you, and you love me. And even as I speak these words now, they terrify me, but I know them to be true. More than anything else, I know this. And so do you."

Loki took a deep breath and let it out slowly. "You're not wrong. But I don't think the gods consider me to be capable of such a feeling as love. It's as you said: They mistrust me. Maybe it's because I never talk to any of them as I talk to you now, as I've *always* talked to you. My existence feels like an act. It *is* an act."

"You can't believe that," said Angrboda, but truthfully she wasn't sure.

"I only ever show them one face, and that's all they know, and that's all they use to judge me. That, and my deeds. Of which they . . . disapprove. To say the least."

"Have I not seen all these faces of yours?"

He pursed his lips in a grim smile. "I'm afraid you haven't."

"Fine, then. All the more reason not to listen to a word they say," Angrboda said hotly. "Have I not told you this?"

Loki sighed. *"Anyway.* The moment I first looked upon Hel's face, I realized that no matter what anyone says, maybe some good truly *can* come of me. She's the living proof."

Angrboda didn't respond for a long while. But when she did, she whispered, "I felt exactly the same."

HE left again soon after that but did not stay away long.

Angrboda had a feeling that Loki was deliberately missing Skadi's appearances. Her friend was showing up more than usual, as winter was nearly upon them and Angrboda needed to build up her stores. She assured Skadi that her husband *would* be around this winter—she was certain of this now that Hel was in the picture. Loki had not stayed away for more than a week or two since the moment he'd met his daughter. And since Angrboda wasn't in the high mountains with Skadi this year, he could come and go as he pleased even in the dead of winter, being a shape-changer.

He did just that.

Loki came back one time with a small wolf figurine he'd carved for Hel. He was not so crafty with his hands as he was with his words, but Hel immediately stuck the figure in her mouth and sucked on it. And when her first teeth began to appear, she chewed on it, looking irritable all the while.

"Do you ever get the feeling she's like a little adult in her head?" Loki asked Angrboda one night at the beginning of winter as they watched their daughter sleep.

"How so?" Angrboda asked.

"She seems frustrated all the time. Like she already wants to be independent and is mad that she's too little."

"Perhaps that's normal for babies. Even for one like ours."

"She also stopped biting you since that time she made you bleed when she was nursing. And she cried because she was sorry she hurt you. Now she only chews on that wolf I made her. It's like she *knew. And* she stays still when you put that green stuff on her legs— what sort of baby *stays still?*"

By midwinter, Hel was sitting up by herself, as her parents discovered one night when they finished making love in front of the fire and turned to find her sitting up in her pile of furs. Hel was staring at them like they had both lost their minds, dangling her drool-saturated wolf figurine from her mouth in confusion. Loki and Angrboda looked at each other, then back at Hel, who gave a pointed burble.

By the end of winter, Hel was crawling, and they spent half their days chasing her around the cave. They took to keeping her in the sling when they ventured outside so she wouldn't crawl away and get lost in the thick, gnarled foliage—which, to Angrboda's pleasure, was once again greener this spring than it had been the year before.

It was near the end of spring that Angrboda discovered she was again with child, and this time, she didn't have to wait until six months into her pregnancy to share the news with Loki. It received a lukewarm reception from him, but she was too preoccupied with Hel to think much about it.

"*When,*" said Skadi, when she came by at the beginning of summer and once again noticed Angrboda's condition regardless of its subtlety, "do I get to cut off your husband's balls and feed them to your goats?"

"I should like to have a few more children by him yet," Angrboda replied primly as she arranged her clay pots of potions in a box for Skadi. "Then he's all yours."

Skadi hoisted Hel, now a year old, onto her lap. "Honestly, are you sure you're not just conceiving these children yourself?"

"He was here during the winter."

"Prove it," said Skadi, ever suspicious.

"Her first word was 'Dada,'" Angrboda said, nodding at her daughter. Hel had perked up at "Dada" and looked toward the door, then seemed disappointed when Loki didn't enter.

"Huh," said Skadi. She looked angry all of a sudden and held Hel closer, for she'd grown quite fond of the child during her visits. "This poor little girl. Maybe I should stick around until he gets here and then cut his balls off. Shouldn't I, little one?"

"I'd rather you didn't." Angrboda passed the box over to her. "I know how he is, that's all. We're fine without him."

"I wish you *had* conceived this child yourself," Skadi muttered, reluctantly trading Hel for the box of potions. "It's one thing to be without a father entirely and to not know what one is missing—which, in your situation, wouldn't be much—but to have one who only shows up at his own pleasure? And with Hel so attached to him!"

"Hel knows this is the way things are. We're *fine*."

Skadi got up and started toward the door, then stopped and turned. "Will you promise me something?"

"That depends."

"Promise me," said Skadi, carefully, "that you're not just letting him come around to use you and then leave."

Angrboda frowned and her heart rate jumped a bit at her friend's words; it seemed old anxieties died hard. "Do you really think I would do that?"

"It seems to me you would, because you already do."

"That is not the case," Angrboda said, her tone icy. "I promise."

Skadi shook her head, glowering. "It's not something I wanted to touch upon—I knew it would make you angry. But perhaps you should consider directing your anger at this husband of yours and not at me."

"He wasn't the one who suggested what Gerd did on the day she and I met each other, and what you suggested just now."

"He's the one who's doing this to you, if it's as you say," Skadi snapped. "Is he truly your husband, or are you just his plaything?"

"You have officially worn out your welcome for today, my friend," Angrboda said coldly and shifted Hel in her arms. "You don't know how it is between us. Those are matters for a husband and wife to know, and no one else's business."

"Those matters *become* my business when they compromise your well-being," Skadi shot back, and then added acidly, *"my friend."*

"My well-being is not being compromised. As such, it is not your business."

"I apologize for my concern, then. Obviously I had nothing to worry about." Skadi straightened, and her voice took on a business-like quality. "Thank you for your hospitality. I shall be back soon with the goods you requested. Have more of the potions ready by then."

Then Skadi left and slammed the door behind her. Hel glanced up and gave her mother a deadpan look, such that Angrboda was reminded utterly of herself.

"Mah," Hel said. It was a sound she had learned from the goats, but she somehow managed to make it sound disapproving.

"What?" Angrboda said, defensive.

"Mah, mah, *mah.*"

"She was out of line!"

Hel stuck the wolf figurine back in her mouth and said no more on the subject. Angrboda got the feeling that she'd just lost an argument to an infant, and oddly enough she wasn't even surprised about it.

This child was Loki's, too, after all.

IT was not until midautumn that Angrboda exchanged more than just civil pleasantries with Skadi, when the latter started coming by more frequently with winter supplies. Skadi looked more troubled every time they met, until Angrboda finally had to ask why, exactly, this was.

"You conceived in the spring, did you not?" Skadi said.

"Late spring, yes. And?"

"And are you sure the child is alive in there? You don't look much bigger than you did a few months ago."

"I can feel his heart beating. He's alive."

"So you know it's a boy, then?"

Angrboda just shrugged.

Loki showed up again at the beginning of winter, right before the first heavy snowfall, and expressed the same sort of confusion Skadi had. He was soon distracted by Hel, though, and said no more to Angrboda about it.

At this point, Angrboda was completely convinced that Hel understood every single word uttered to her. And when Hel spoke these days, it was not in random syllables but in complete sentences—the first of which was, of course, an inquiry as to her father's whereabouts. This led Angrboda to give her a simplified explanation about Asgard and the Aesir, to which Hel responded by sticking her wolf figurine back in her mouth and, quite literally, chewing it over.

Angrboda had a feeling that Hel had asked simply for the sake of asking—she always talked absently to her daughter, mostly for lack of anyone else to talk to, so Hel must have known all about where Loki was. But after the child had asked her directly, Angrboda started speaking to Hel more and more, and Hel, for her part, just gave her an unblinking stare. There was a certain satisfaction to this silence, though, as if Hel were pleased that her mother was speaking to her as she would a grown-up.

This changed whenever her father came around, at which point Hel instantly reverted back into a toddler, clinging and wailing at Loki's heels. Such behavior drove Angrboda mad, and it tried her patience further that they were all cooped up together for the winter.

For the first time, she wished he would just *leave*.

"She's getting too big for that sling," Angrboda told Loki one day when he was carrying Hel around in it for absolutely no reason other than because he wanted to. "She hasn't let me carry her in it since she started walking."

"That's because she *likes me better*. Right, Hel?"

Hel nodded enthusiastically.

"There you have it."

Angrboda gave her daughter a *look*. Hel blinked innocently and chewed on her wolf figurine. It now seemed the only time Angrboda even got to touch the baby was when she nursed her, which was less and less now, as Hel had long been nibbling on whatever Angrboda ate. And now Hel had taken to whining at her father for food at mealtimes.

"Stop feeding her that," Angrboda snapped at Loki as he made for the pot of honey she kept hidden in one of her chests. She knew exactly what he was up to, for Hel had refused her rabbit stew—as she often did when she knew she could get away with it, which was when Loki showed up with fresh apples and oatcakes he'd brought on his way from Asgard.

"But she loves it!" Loki protested as he sat back down at the table and set the clay honeypot down next to his own dinner. He extracted a linen-wrapped bundle of oatcakes from his haversack and plopped them into a shallow wooden bowl for Hel. Beside him, Hel licked her lips, her little dead feet swinging merrily from the bench as she watched him dribble the cakes with honey.

"She'll eat little else if you keep feeding her such things," Angrboda said. "And she gets so excited afterward that she doesn't sleep."

Hel leered at her mother and munched on a slice of apple Loki had cut up for her. Then she eagerly observed her father preparing her special dinner, and her eyes grew enormous with delight when Loki set the bowl down in front of her. By the time she had finished, her face, hands, and body were sticky with honey.

"Come now, don't you ever feed her?" Loki teased his wife.

Later on, Angrboda was the one who had to wash sticky layers of honey from an excitable toddler, who screeched for so long that she began to turn blue. It had happened several times before that Hel would overexert herself in this way when she became furious or agitated, but she bounced back fairly quickly and showed no other signs of illness, so Angrboda did not worry too much about it.

Late one winter night, when Loki had put Hel in her little nest of furs on the bed—as now, when he was around, he was the only one allowed to put her to sleep—he came over to where Angrboda was sitting on her chair in front of the fire. He sat on her lap as a child would, and when she rolled her eyes, he looked concerned that she wasn't playing along with whatever it was he had in mind.

"Are you angry with me?" he asked.

"Yes."

"Why?"

"You should put her to sleep when I *tell* you to put her to sleep."

"Oh, is that all?"

"Is that *all*? It's important!"

"She wasn't tired!"

"She wasn't tired because *you* keep pestering her and getting her excited. We have a routine. You're ruining it. You don't *listen* to me."

Loki's voice grew cold. "If I wanted to be nagged, I would go back to Asgard and spend five minutes with any given person."

"Then go back to Asgard, if it's so much like here. Though I fail to see how that's even remotely possible, Asgard being the center of the universe and Ironwood being a half-dead forest at the edge of nowhere."

He stood. "I don't need this from you."

"So everyone else is allowed to criticize you, but when I do it, it's unacceptable?"

"Yes," Loki said matter-of-factly, and with that he slunk back into bed and curled up around Hel, obviously having no intention of leaving.

Angrboda sat seething in her chair for a while longer before slipping into a restless sleep.

SHE awoke to Loki shaking her frantically, and the first words that came to her mind upon seeing his expression were "Is something wrong with Hel?"

Loki pointed. "Your dress is all soggy."

Angrboda stared down at her lap for a few moments before saying, in a small voice, "He's still so small . . ." But even as she said it, she could feel the contractions and wondered how they hadn't awoken her before Loki had.

She lowered herself onto the ground slowly—she could hear Loki doing something, but she couldn't hear his footsteps. She heard the door open and close and wondered if he'd left, but she found that she truly didn't care what he was up to unless he awoke Hel, which would only make things worse.

If Angrboda couldn't calm *herself* down, she had no hope of calming her toddler.

This isn't like before, she thought, recalling with trepidation the last time she had awoken to find herself in premature labor. *He's still alive in there.*

And he wants out.

Loki had gone outside to fetch a bucket of snow to melt over the fire, and he left again and returned to her side with a pile of fabrics and blankets from one of her storage chests. He must have taken that time to pull himself together, for she was now startled by his composure.

He put the blankets behind her so she could lie back on them, and the two of them looked at each other. Angrboda's breathing became labored and the contractions became more intense, and Loki's expression grew pained as he dabbed at her face with a cool cloth.

"He's probably not going to make it," Loki said very quietly, putting his hand on her stomach. "He probably could if he was bigger, but . . ."

"Don't say such things," Angrboda snapped. "Not right now. Hand me a scrap of cloth from that pile."

Loki obliged and sat down at her feet again, hiking her dress up to her waist. "I'm just being realistic. I've been where you are, re-member, although I suppose it might've been a bit different for me as a horse." He forced a smile, put his hands on her knees and squeezed, and peered down. "This may be over sooner than you think—are you pushing already?"

Angrboda had been in labor for nearly a day before Hel finally decided to make an appearance, but she didn't mention as much, as she had stuffed a rag into her mouth to muffle her screaming. Periodically Loki would glance past her to ensure that Hel was still asleep, before looking back to Angrboda and offering what small comforts touches and words could provide—she eventually placed her hands over his and scratched up his skin as her fingers clenched. He didn't say a word, didn't so much as flinch.

Within the hour, their second child was born.

She knew something was wrong just by the look on Loki's face as he picked up the creature she had just delivered: a grayish wolf with its eyes closed. It was nearly the size Hel had been when she was born—far bigger than the average wolf born in a litter.

"He's a wolf," Loki said unnecessarily as he cut the cord with a knife. He then held said wolf in a blanket like he wasn't sure what to do, and a dozen different emotions flashed across his face, one right after another.

Angrboda did not stop to identify them—she held her arms out, having eyes only for her son. Loki handed over the blankets with a slow, stiff motion. He now looked just tired and dazed and more than a little uncertain. For her part, Angrboda dried off the pup and put him to her chest, and he made a small squeaking sound and immediately started nursing.

"Well," Loki said as he looked on, scooting over to sit beside her. "Do you find this odd? I find this odd. Why is he a wolf?"

"We're odd. He's odd. Does this displease you?" Angrboda asked evenly, not looking up.

"Not in the least. I'm just . . . confused."

"I was arguably more confused when you showed up here as a mare and gave birth to a horse with eight legs."

Loki had nothing to say to that.

He was saved from having to say anything, because there was a small grunt from the corner of the cave as Hel hoisted herself down from the bed, then toddled over to where they sat by the fire.

"Hel, come see your new brother," Loki said, throwing a blanket over Angrboda's bottom half and hoisting Hel into his lap. "He's like the toy I made you, see?"

Hel seemed intrigued as she sucked on her wolf figurine. Loki smoothed the sleep-tousled ringlets of hair away from her face.

"What's his name?" Hel asked, after she decided that she'd spent a sufficient amount of time staring at her baby brother. The fact that he was a wolf did not seem to faze her in the least.

Then again, her legs were composed of dead flesh. Angrboda recalled that even before Hel could talk, it took quite a lot to surprise her.

"Fenrir," said Angrboda.

"'Fen-dweller'?" said Loki, making a face. "But why, though?"

"I just like the way it sounds. Don't you?"

"I mean, I suppose . . ."

"Fuzzy ears," said Hel, reaching over to touch her brother's face with her grubby little hand, with a gentleness the average toddler would not have used. "And wet nose. Why he decide to look like that?"

Her parents just looked at each other. Eventually Loki put Hel back to sleep, and by then it was dawn and Fenrir was asleep as well, nuzzled into Angrboda's chest. Loki tossed the soiled blankets outside and sat down right behind her with his legs on either side of her. He then leaned his head on her shoulder, ran his hands up and down her upper arms, and said nothing.

"Hel was right," Angrboda told him quietly. "Even if he didn't decide it—he's a wolf, aye, but moreover, he's a giant like we are, only in wolf form. I wonder if he had any control over it."

"Spontaneous shape-changing in the womb?" Loki said, putting his arms around her and smirking. "I suppose we've reached a new level of oddness. But did you not say once that you might have birthed wolves before, and you don't remember?"

"Indeed, I wonder." Angrboda turned as much as she could and looked at him. "*Are* you displeased?"

"No. Wolves are interesting and people are scared of them. It'll be exciting to have a son who's a wolf. Maybe we can train him to eat people we don't like."

"*Loki.*"

"*Boda.*"

"You are not training our son to eat anyone."

"I hear your nagging tone, but not the words you're saying."

"No eating people," Angrboda repeated tiredly, leaning back against him.

Loki kissed her shoulder. "I can make no promises on our son's behalf."

IT became apparent over the rest of the winter and spring that Fenrir was developing at a pace somewhere between that of an actual wolf pup and that of a typical child. He opened his eyes after only a few days, and they were the same color green as Loki's, leaving no doubt as to his parentage. And he was weaned after only a few months, which was good news to Angrboda, because unlike Hel, Fenrir often bit her while he was nursing.

Angrboda came to understand that her daughter had been a rare case as children went. Indeed, Fenrir seemed entirely without empathy—which often put him at odds with his sister, who seemed to feel everything, although her resting expression was one of indifference.

When he was barely a year old, Fenrir's head was only level with Loki's knee. This led Angrboda to conclude that their son was not done growing by any stretch of the imagination. He already had a mouthful of sharp teeth and enjoyed gnawing on bones. Yet Angrboda wondered if he would ever be able to talk, and *how* such a thing could be possible. She also pondered Loki's comment about "spontaneous shape-changing in the womb" on the night their son was born and wondered if he really *had* inherited his father's shapeshifting nature, but thus far Fenrir had not exhibited any such abilities. He had simply been born a wolf.

By the time Fenrir was two, his head was nearly level with Angrboda's hips, though he still had the appearance of an overgrown puppy. At this point he went off and came back with his own food, which he would not share with his mother and sister—which was fine with Angrboda, whose snares caught only so much game.

The one good thing that happened was that Fenrir began to talk, though not aloud as Hel had. Rather, his voice appeared in their heads; it was a small voice, a child's voice, and it spoke little and about simple things, like food and the weather and the goats.

But from the first moment Angrboda heard the word "Mama"— his infantile voice in her head speaking with confidence—and turned to see Fenrir looking at her and wagging his tail, she had hope, and she smiled then and embraced her son. She had *hope*, despite the fact he'd often snap at her and Hel for what appeared to be no reason at all.

Fenrir seemed to at least be trying to control his animalistic urges and was frustrated when he couldn't, which caused him to lash out further. Angrboda wished so badly that she could help him, but she didn't know how. She wished that she *had* been—or at least *remembered* being—the witch who had mothered the wolves who chased the sun and moon, or that she could find this old woman and ask her for advice.

Instead she asked her husband for advice. But as Loki was still going back and forth between Asgard and Ironwood, he found his son's ferocity entertaining rather than troublesome. He didn't have to deal with Fenrir every single day.

"Forget your silly spells—you'll be safe enough here with an *attack wolf.* This is going to be great," he said one time. "I still think we should train him to eat people."

"No," said Angrboda.

"But he wants to eat people! He would *love* to eat people. Isn't that right, Fenrir?"

Yes! Fenrir wagged his tail, his tongue lolling out of his mouth excitedly.

"See? Excellent," said Loki. "We'll just have to keep him away from the goats. Hel will be heartbroken if he eats one of them."

"It doesn't help that you named them all," Angrboda muttered. "She's so attached to them, now that they have names."

Loki just grinned at that. He had taken to calling Angrboda's goats by the names of the Aesir, which oftentimes did not correspond to the sexes of the goats. He did this for the sole purpose of narrating stories about them, only some of which were actually funny, in Angrboda's opinion.

Unsurprisingly, Hel was as enamored of her father as she'd been the first time she saw him; Angrboda got the feeling sometimes that Hel was the only reason he even returned to Ironwood, although he swore up and down that this was not the case. Then again, there weren't a whole lot of things Angrboda *wasn't* willing to put up with just to see her daughter smile and to keep her within eyesight:

Hel had taken to wandering past the clearing with the goats and Loki, and sometimes by herself, despite her mother's protests. It was then that Angrboda showed all of them the boundaries of the enchantment that hid their home and implored them not to go past the borders of her spell. Fenrir and Hel seemed to understand. Loki just gave her a crooked smile.

Hel was now three and a half and as active as any child should be, though she seemed to tire easily and would fall short of breath when she overexerted herself. Once Loki made her laugh so hard that she couldn't breathe and her fingertips began to turn blue, and only one of her mother's calming potions would help her recover.

"You need to stop getting her so excited," Angrboda snapped at him after that incident.

"You mean I need to stop being so funny?" Loki replied, unruffled. "Unlikely. But for our daughter's sake, I'll give it a try."

Angrboda stitched Hel a pair of long, thick stockings to wear under her dresses—not to hide her legs, but rather to make sure the salve underneath did not rub off. By now Angrboda had perfected her recipe and the flesh on Hel's legs was still growing *with* her, although it was bluish and dead. Angrboda did not know what to make of this at all and attributed it to her own clever witchery.

It gave her a certain sense of pride to do so, considering how long she'd been blaming herself for her daughter's condition.

After Fenrir's birth, Angrboda decided that it was high time to add a new potion to her repertoire: a contraceptive. She did not know what raising a wolf would be like, and with Hel and Fenrir so close in age, she had no desire to add a third child to the mix so soon. Loki seemed to agree with this, even though he made it perfectly clear that it didn't affect him in the least—either way, they still lay together nearly every night when he stayed in Ironwood. Angrboda tried not to let his attitude bother her too much, and mostly failed.

Skadi warned her that such a potion would probably not sell as well as the healing salve and the hunger reducers she usually bartered. She explained what Angrboda already knew: that most women in the Nine Worlds were keen on having as many children as possible. But nevertheless Skadi agreed to trade the contraceptive potions, a few here and there to those who desired them.

"Are you certain you're not the old witch from the stories?" Skadi had teased her the first time she laid eyes on Fenrir, when he was still just a smallish ball of fur. "Are you sure your wolf-children don't chase the sun and moon?"

"I'm not," Angrboda had replied. "Certain, that is. I'm not certain."

As it happened, Skadi had an affinity for wolves, which became only more apparent as Fenrir got older. He was always the first to hear her approach and would bound up to meet her, and Angrboda even allowed him to go hunting with Skadi so long as they stayed within the boundaries of the charm, which both Skadi and Gerd now knew of. When they returned, Angrboda's wolf-son would often start wrestling with the Huntress as he would with a fellow pup, and Skadi would laugh and oblige him; it turned out they were pretty evenly matched.

When such commotion would take place, Hel would look on with the same impassive expression she usually wore, and sometimes Angrboda would catch Skadi looking at Hel as if she were seeing someone familiar.

Every day Hel looks more like her father, Angrboda often thought, for she was sure that Skadi was seeing the same thing. She wondered how often Skadi saw Loki in Asgard, wondered when her friend would make the connection between Loki and her daughter, between Loki and herself. And naturally, not for the first time, she wondered how her husband's behavior in Asgard differed from his behavior in Ironwood.

"Have I not seen all these faces of yours?"

"I'm afraid you haven't."

In her mind's eye she saw that smirk, saw the darkness lurking behind his eyes on that night—just one summer night among the many they'd spent together, and yet she remembered it vividly as the night that planted the seed of doubt in her: that look he'd given her after he'd called their marriage an "arrangement" and wondered how long they could "keep it up." And he'd said these things to her with their infant daughter contentedly sleeping a few meters away.

Part of Angrboda had moved on from this conversation, had locked it in the back of her mind where she could access it at only the darkest of times. And yet another part still could not forgive him.

That was also the night she'd first told him of her dreams—the dreams that continued to plague her even now, though she still had not given in to the chanter, had not allowed herself to be drawn from her body. Each night she spent asleep brought the chanter on stronger, until she felt afraid to sleep at all, for fear that one day she would give in to his demands and allow herself to be taken.

And if she *were* to be taken, what would happen then? She did not want to find out. For the more the chanter tried to draw her out, the more familiar he felt, and the more heavily she suspected this person to be Odin in disguise.

And if that man wanted something from her, she was not going to give it up without a fight. Especially because she feared that no good would come of his having the dangerous knowledge he wanted her to access. Was she the only one who *could* access it, or the only one he didn't fear putting in harm's way to do so? Had he still been unable to get to it himself, in his travels with *seid*? Had Freyja and the Norns refused to help him, or was he simply not willing to put them at risk?

I refuse to do his dirty work. Her thrice-burned heart was set on this matter. *Not after what the gods did to me.*

It was on a sleepless night in early summer, around the time Hel was four and Fenrir was two and a half, that she forgot to take the contraceptive potion, and within a few days she had a sinking feeling that the damage had already been done. While she lay awake with Loki snoozing atop her one night, she recalled Skadi's words from years ago about letting him *use* her, and she almost wanted to weep.

Instead she cast a glance to the bed, where Hel was sleeping. Fenrir was curled up on the ground—Hel refused to sleep in the bed with her brother if her mother was not present. Angrboda felt the urge to push Loki off her and crawl into bed with her children so that one of them would not have to sleep on the floor, but she did not want to wake any of them, so she remained where she was.

She ran a hand through Loki's hair. He stirred but remained asleep, breathing on her neck with his forehead pressed against her cheek, drooling on her shoulder. Her hand traveled down to her stomach and rested there, on the loose skin and stretch marks that were the result of carrying her first two children, and wondered what sort of child she would bring into the worlds this time.

And to her distress, it was a question laced not with excitement, but with fear.

LOKI left soon after, and Angrboda did not see him again for many turns of the moon. It was the longest he'd been absent from Ironwood since Hel was born. Angrboda saw that with each passing day, Hel grew more depressed, and Fenrir grew more skittish and took to staying inside.

For this, Angrboda found herself growing angrier with Loki. She, by herself, was fighting with her son's fierceness, fighting with her daughter's despair. And she could not even sleep, for in her dreams, she fought with the chanter.

And she was fighting with her body as well; her lack of rest fatigued her, and it seemed that, as when she was carrying Fenrir, this new child inside her did not want to grow as a normal child should. Even four and five months into her pregnancy, she still vomited up most of the food she ate. Fenrir did not ask questions about this, but Hel was frightened by her mother's sickness, so Angrboda tried her best to hide it.

Once again, though, she could not hide her condition from Skadi—who was of course still coming by to trade, and gradually more just to talk. Skadi admitted she did not much care for children, but Angrboda's were quite the exception. In addition to allowing Fenrir to tag along on her hunts, Skadi had taken Hel out into the woods multiple times and shown her how to set up a snare.

"Ready to go, little one?" Skadi always asked before they left, and Hel would only nod with the faintest smile as she pulled on the child-sized haversack Skadi had brought her on their first outing. Skadi had become something like a second mother to her during Loki's long absences and was the only one who could get away with calling her such a thing as "little one"; a tiny child though she might be, Hel did not like to be reminded of this fact, and she seethed whenever Angrboda attempted to call her anything diminutive.

Going "trapping" with Skadi made Hel feel like a grown-up, even though Angrboda doubted the girl enjoyed it.

"Just like my father taught me," Skadi said to Angrboda one

night when they returned with two rabbits and a squirrel, which Hel refused to even touch. "She may balk at the idea of killing animals—"

"She's a child yet," said Angrboda. "Animals are her precious friends. She doesn't mind eating meat, but she doesn't wish to think about where it came from." Hel still turned away in disgust every time her mother had to skin a rabbit for dinner.

"That's true, but they're also food," Skadi replied.

"If she had the choice, Hel would subsist entirely on the oatcakes her father brings her," Angrboda muttered before she could stop herself; she knew better than to mention him in Skadi's presence. Fenrir and Hel might not know Loki as anything other than "Papa," but she was nervous about the day when one of them would blurt their father's name during one of Skadi's visits. Angrboda had a feeling that warning them against it would only bring that day sooner, as she wouldn't put it past either of Loki's children to purposely disobey her. Her insistence that they stay within the boundaries of her protection charm seemed to be the only warning of hers they took seriously—and that may have been only because Skadi was also very strict about it when she took them into the woods.

Angrboda shifted, wishing she hadn't mentioned Loki, albeit not by name. Luckily, Skadi only rolled her eyes and for once didn't press the matter of Angrboda's husband.

"Be that as it may," said the Huntress, "the reality is that trapping is a useful skill if one doesn't wish to hunt. Besides, you let no part of the animal go to waste. It's given you the gift of its life, and you cherish that. Hel is too small to understand this, but she will someday."

Angrboda conceded this point.

"Something else troubles you," Skadi observed several moments later.

"Is it that obvious?"

"How long has he been gone this time?"

"Since the beginning of summer," Angrboda said with a sigh. Apparently they were going to have this conversation today after all.

"What is he *doing*?"

Angrboda looked at her cup of goat's milk and wondered how long she would be able to keep it down. "Whatever he likes."

"I still mean to kill this man," Skadi said heatedly, her fist tightening around her cup. "One day I shall."

"You will do no such thing."

"I can't promise that," Skadi said, and gave her a stern look as she finished her ale; she left soon after without many other words passing between them.

THEN one rainy night in the middle of autumn, when the children were sleeping and Angrboda sat on her chair in front of the fire to unbraid and comb out her hair after a long day, she heard the door open and shut. She set her jaw, pulled her fur mantle closer about her, and leaned forward to put another log on the fire, determined not to give him a warm greeting.

He did not deserve as much.

"An entire season has passed since I saw you last," she said.

"Why's there green stuff on the table?" he asked her as he slung his cloak across the bench. Both of them spoke in hushed tones, as the children were asleep.

Angrboda's expression darkened as she stood and walked over to him. He looked the same as ever. "I must have forgotten to clean it up. I made it this morning. Fenrir was snapping at the goats and scaring them, and when Hel shouted at him, he bit her forearm and would not let go. It took me the rest of the afternoon to get her to stop crying."

"Oh," said Loki, turning to look toward the bed. "Is she all right?"

"No. She's not. The bite is deep and it will leave scars, ones far worse than yours. She was hysterical for an hour and then she passed out. Her face and fingertips had turned blue. I thought she might actually die. You know how easily she tires . . ."

Loki sat down on the bench and leaned against the table, setting his elbows upon it and resting his ankle on the opposite knee. "Pays to have a witch for a mother, I suppose. And for a wife as well."

Angrboda scowled and scooped up his cloak to let it dry near the fire, muttering, "Wife indeed."

"What is it now?" Loki pulled her into his lap when she returned, and she just gave him a withering look. "Are you angry with me *again*?"

"You were gone too long this time."

"Sigyn had another child. I couldn't get away so soon after. I brought you a present." From some invisible pocket, he pulled out a string of polished amber beads. "I thought you could wear them between your brooches, if you had any—I could bring you some next time, too, if you wanted to make yourself an apron dress to wear them with."

"I find brooches and apron dresses to be cumbersome when doing chores and chasing children," Angrboda said. *Such styles are more suited to women of higher status, like those in Asgard.*

"They will make a fine necklace for you, then."

Angrboda leaned over to place the beads on the table and said, "Thank you. But this still doesn't make up for the fact that you were gone *too long*."

"Look, I'm sorry," he mumbled. He leaned up to kiss her and she pulled away, and he frowned and stared at her for a few seconds. "Are you still mad about Sigyn? That was ages ago. If you were going to be angry about it, Boda, the time has long since passed."

"This isn't about Sigyn," Angrboda said through gritted teeth. *I have enough to worry about besides trying to plot an undoubtedly ill-fated revenge scheme against my husband's other wife, even though I'm sure Loki would delight in my undertaking such an endeavor over the likes of him.* "This is about your responsibilities as a father."

"And as a husband?" he prompted.

"Hel is miserable without you."

"And Fenrir?"

"Less so."

Loki lowered his voice even further. "He's savage, isn't he?"

"He's not," Angrboda said coldly. "You don't care for him, so you would accuse him of savagery? Shame on you."

"He's a *wolf*. And you said that he bit Hel. Sounds savage to me."

"Have you ever even spoken with him?"

"Of course I have. He's intelligent, but—"

"But he's *trying*." She stood, speaking in a harsh whisper. "Which is more than one can say for the likes of you. What's so great about Asgard, anyway, besides the opportunity to make mischief and spin lies to a wider audience?"

"When have I ever lied to you?" Loki stood as well, angrily, his scarred lips twisting in a sneer. "Name one time."

"You always say you'll come right back. And then an entire season passes."

"Time isn't an issue for us, you may recall."

"It is when you have two young children who need their father."

"I have two young children in Asgard as well, and a wife."

"And tell me—do you lie to Sigyn about where you go?"

"Never once," he ground out, "have I lied to Sigyn about where I go. I told you once that she thinks more highly of me than you do, and never has this seemed more true. And yet she has always seemed more bitter about my absences, where you have been indifferent until just now."

"It's not indifference, my love. I cannot have the children see me pine for you as they do, or all three of us would find ourselves in a constant state of misery. That wouldn't do at all."

Loki seemed amused. "And yet you *do* pine for me? What sort of woman are you, then, to sit back and watch me do as I please?"

Angrboda fought back a surge of rage. She needed to get away from him before she slapped him across his smarmy face. "Skadi has asked me the same question on more than one occasion. She thinks me spineless, though she doesn't say as much. She thinks it's a sign of weakness that I can't control you, in that secret, subtle way a wife has control over her husband."

"And what do you tell her?"

"That this is the way you are, and I accept it. It's not the same as being weak." Angrboda folded her arms, facing the fire. "Or at least I hope it's not, for my own sake."

"You're not weak," said Loki, coming up behind her and putting his arms about her waist, leaning his head on her shoulder.

Angrboda barely suppressed a sigh.

"You were burned three times and had your heart stabbed out," he murmured into her neck, "and you're still standing. And you've welcomed me into your home and bed for years with not a complaint until now."

"Until the children."

"Yes. Until them." Loki released her suddenly, sat again, and looked down at his lap, where his hands were trembling. He gripped his knees to still them. "I don't know why I do the things I do. I can't stop myself."

"It's in your nature to do such things." Angrboda, watching this gesture, sat and took his hands in hers. "I wonder if anyone else understands this as I do."

"The Aesir don't. Only Sigyn even tries. I think she would forgive me anything if I asked, but I don't want to. She *trusts* me not to lie to her." He grimaced. "I sometimes wonder if her trust is misplaced."

A beat passed, in which Angrboda felt something not unlike sympathy for the woman. "I know the feeling well."

He looked at her then, and his expression seemed softer in the firelight. "And yet you're both still by my side. Why is that?"

Angrboda thought for a moment. There were plenty of things she could say: that he was the father of her children, that she loved him despite herself, and that she knew he loved her, too. She could say that if he would just *stay*, she would be content to remain in his arms for as long as he would have her—which would be either until the next morning or for all of eternity. It was hard to know with him.

And yet after all this time, she wasn't sure if this was something that belonged on the list of reasons she loved him so dearly, or if it was a reason to hate him instead.

But last time they'd had that conversation it had ended with them both wanting to change the subject, so she replied instead, "This doesn't mean I'm not still angry with you right now, but you did, after all, return my heart to me."

"Hmm," he said. "At least I can do something right by you."

"Yes, well. I wonder about that sometimes."

"Wondering whether it wasn't right to give it back?"

Her silence was all the answer he needed.

"Come," said Loki at last. "Let's go to bed."

THE thunderstorm had started up again, but inside the cave, despite the night's events, there existed a sort of calmness. Hel and Fenrir hadn't been awoken by the conversation, and their parents were grateful for it.

Perhaps it was a result of their argument that Angrboda found that her role this night was not as a mattress; rather, she settled down on her side, and Loki did the same behind her and pulled a woolen blanket over them.

Before he fell asleep, he reached around her and placed a hand on the solid bump of her lower stomach. "It's small again. Think it'll be another wolf?"

"I don't know," Angrboda murmured, putting her hand over his. He kissed her temple and set his head back down beside hers, burying his face in her hair. And for the first time in recent memory, listening to the beating of her heart and his, Angrboda went right to sleep.

She did not remain asleep for long.

THE voice drew her out.

The words pushed her down, down, down, to the deepest, darkest place she had ever been: a place as empty as the very beginning of the worlds, the beginning of time.

She no longer had a form. She was spread out, her very soul dissipating like ripples in a stream, out over all the worlds, like the World Tree itself. For a moment, she knew everything. She was part of everything.

And she could see it all from there.

❖ ❖ ❖

ANGRBODA gasped and sat bolt upright, shaking violently, gasping for breath, covered in a cold sweat. The fire had not even fully died. Loki, who had still been asleep with his arms around her, awoke as well.

He asked her what was wrong, pushed her hair out of her face, tried to hold her. She pushed him away. Nothing calmed her down.

"What happened?" he asked her, again and again, until finally she just looked at him, fighting back tears, and his concerned expression turned to one of alarm.

"I know who it is," she said, her voice sounding dead to her own ears. "The man in my dreams. I know what he wants. I've seen it." She let out a deep, shuddering breath. "It's Odin. It has to be."

Loki scooted closer to her, his brow furrowing. "What did you see?"

Angrboda shook her head, took a shaky breath, pulled her knees up to her chest, and stared at them.

"But what did you *see?*" Loki pressed.

"I've seen how the end begins." Her voice was a hoarse whisper as the words tumbled out. "I saw everything in the Nine Worlds. I saw the Aesir, the giants, and shades and dwarfs and men. I saw Yggdrasil, and the dragon who gnaws its root. I saw a wolf so big that his jaws could swallow armies whole, and a great serpent rearing out of the water, and I saw the sun and moon go dark as the wolves who chase them finally swallow their prey, and I saw a ship crewed by dead souls. I saw so many faces that I can't recall every one of them, so many names that I don't know which matter, so many events that I can't even begin to put them together—"

She stopped abruptly and pressed her lips together. There was something else, too. But she found that she could not bring herself to describe it to him.

Loki reached out to touch her shoulder but recoiled as she put her hands up and pulled at her hair. So he scooted up behind her and drew her into his lap, and she leaned against him, trembling. He pushed her hair over one shoulder and kissed the other as he put his arms around her.

But he didn't sound quite certain when he said, "It was only a dream, Boda. Nothing more."

"I want so badly to believe that," she murmured. "I didn't tell him anything. He'll be back. He'll be back . . ."

Loki didn't respond except to kiss her shoulder again, and she could feel his breath and scarred lips on her skin, and they did not comfort her.

They sat that way for a while, until he got up and fed the fire and then coaxed her into lying down beside him as they had done before. But even with his arms tight around her, she feared she would never sleep again.

He drew me out and bade me travel to the most hidden place in the cosmos for that horrible vision of the future, but he didn't get what he came for.

I didn't tell him a thing.

And there were things she'd held back from Loki—things she couldn't bring herself to say. *Things he wouldn't want to know.* Three things in particular.

The first was that the wolf she'd seen—the enormous beast breathing fire from its knife-toothed maw—had been green-eyed and strikingly familiar and caused her to study her own son, an overgrown pup, who was sleeping peacefully at the end of her bed. *It can't be . . . can it?*

The second thing was death. So much death—that was the part where she'd jerked away, the very end, so she wouldn't have to see how it all played out. She didn't want to know. *So if it really is Odin who's bidding me to access this information*—and she was now certain it was—*then he* wants *to know how he's going to die.*

And the third . . .

Angrboda rolled over carefully and looked at Loki, who stirred but did not wake; she ran her hand over his scarred mouth, brushed her nose against his, closed her eyes.

I saw you lead a ship full of dead souls into battle against the gods, she wanted to tell him. *But how could this be? The dead obey no one, and you reckon yourself among the Aesir . . .*

The second time she'd seen his face in the dream it had been worse, and the memory of it made her stomach churn.

I saw you bound.

I cannot remember what you did, or if I even knew in the first place, but you were punished for it.

And you were in pain. You were in so much pain.

What will you do to deserve this, and how can I stop you from doing it?

But somehow Angrboda knew that it was not her place to become involved in these events, for in the dream he was not alone: There was a woman at his side when he was bound—a woman she somehow knew distinctly to be Sigyn. Even now that the woman's face had grown fainter in her memory, she remembered the emotions she had seen there: unhappiness, even grief. Arms outstretched, clasping a bowl near Loki to catch the venom of the snake fixed over him, tears running down her face every time she had to move the bowl to empty it.

Angrboda could still hear his screams in her mind as the venom burned his face. And yet it was Sigyn who was by his side, the picture of perfect loyalty.

But I will never see you suffer this way. What will stop me from coming to free you from this fate?

What will happen to me, to us, to prevent me from standing by your side as well?

Angrboda pulled the blanket over them again and pressed yet closer against him, felt the heat of his skin against hers. Thunder crashed outside, but still Loki did not wake. She envied how peaceful he seemed in sleep—the only time he *was* peaceful. And yet he was unaware of the woman who was holding him so tightly now, so unwilling to let go of him.

Indeed, Loki did not know how safe he was with Angrboda at his side.   •

Some part of her knew that things between them would not last forever, for *forever* was quite a long time, and her husband was easily bored. And yet, the question continued to eat away at her:

Where will I be when this terrible fate befalls you?

AFTER that night, Loki seemed hesitant to leave again for any length of time. Hel and Fenrir had been overjoyed to see him the morning after Angrboda's dream. They, too, seemed unwilling to let him out of their sight.

Angrboda felt uneasy in the days following for reasons she could not quite articulate. She suspected at first that it was because of the vision but knew part of her unease was due to her pregnancy; she couldn't help but wonder what form her next child would take, and this troubled her.

She was mixing potions one afternoon under Hel's watchful

gaze—which switched constantly between her mother and her father—when Skadi and Gerd dropped by. At the time, Loki was playing tug-of-war with Fenrir on the floor, using a large bone as a rope. This resulted in the massive wolf pup dragging him around the cave and, eventually, right up to the door. *Papa, Skadi's here— there's someone with her!*

Angrboda stiffened and she and Loki exchanged a look. Two seconds later there was a knock at the door, and Loki, still sitting on the floor, dropped the bone for Fenrir to scoop up. Then he scooted over to the cave's entrance and reached for the door handle.

"Loki, don't—," Angrboda began.

"What? I'm not scared of her," he said, and he opened the door to find Skadi glaring down at him. Hel screeched with delight and ran to her, Fenrir loping at her heels—both of them had pushed past their sitting father, who seemed offended.

But not more offended than Skadi, who scooped up the child in her arms and ruffled the wolf pup's head without tearing her gaze from Loki.

"What are *you* doing here?" she demanded.

Loki pointed over his shoulder with his thumb and said, "We're married." And then he hopped to his feet a fraction of a second before Skadi's boot came down to stomp his testicles into the ground.

"Hey!" Hel cried. "Leave my papa alone!"

"*This?*" Skadi said, ignoring her and gesturing wildly to Loki. She looked at Angrboda with fury. "You're married to *this*? This dreadful piece of work is your husband and the father of your children and the love of your life and so on?"

"'Life' is sort of a loose term when you've been thrice reborn from fire," Angrboda said, turning away from her potion making. "'Love of my existence' would probably be more accurate."

"Aww, and here I assumed you thought *so* little of me," Loki said. He sauntered over to her and made a show of putting an arm around her shoulders and planting a fat kiss on her temple.

Angrboda rolled her eyes and gave him a playful shove. She then turned to Skadi, who was positively twitching with rage. "You can come inside now, you two, and share a drink with us. And dinner, if you'd like. It's chilly out there."

"We're well aware," Gerd said, pulling her hood off and pushing past Skadi. "And we would be most grateful. Thank you."

To Angrboda's surprise, Fenrir trotted right up to the maiden and laid the bone at her feet, wagging his tail bashfully. *Hi.*

"Well, hello there." Gerd did not hesitate to lean down and give him a pat on the head. Fenrir licked her face, and she smiled and scratched him behind the ears.

"I could have castrated you nine times over in Asgard, Trickster, had I known *you* were the useless husband of my dear friend," Skadi sneered at Loki as he plopped down at the table. She sat on the bench across from him and set Hel down next to her. Gerd poured them each a cup of ale and went straight to Angrboda's side, intent on staying out of this particular conflict.

Loki sneered right back at the Huntress. "Well, obviously you weren't thus informed, as my balls are still where they're supposed to be. I'm surprised no one has tried to lop *yours* off."

"She deserves better than the likes of you," said Skadi with feeling. "Anyone does."

"Gerd, will you help me prepare dinner?" Angrboda asked tiredly.

Gerd nodded and leapt to the task, and they started skinning rabbits by the cave's entrance. For all that Angrboda could say about the girl, at least she was helpful.

"Your scars look more disgusting up close. Almost as disgusting as the things that come out of your mouth," Skadi was saying to Loki in the meantime.

"My scars are *dashing*. It's not my fault you have poor taste."

"*Pfft*. If I have poor taste, then *you* have no taste at all."

"Why do you insult my wife like that?"

"Saying you have no taste isn't an insult to—"

"Oh, but it is. You see, I taste her all the time. I'd bet you wish you could say the same."

Angrboda turned and raised her eyebrows at Loki, then looked at Skadi, whose face had turned a very bright red.

"Don't be lewd, Loki," said Angrboda, taking that as the reason for her friend's embarrassment.

Skadi kept her eyes on Loki and said, a little too loudly, "How about you taste my fist down your throat?"

"No, thank you," said Loki as casually as someone refusing more drink. "Threatening me in front of the children, Skadi? What sort of goddess *are* you?"

"Or, better yet, my hunting knife?" Skadi ignored him and took said knife—the length of her forearm and razor-sharp—out of its sheath at her belt and stuck it pointedly in the table. "How do you think *that* tastes, Trickster?"

"Poor," Loki said, eyeing the quivering knife cagily. "Not unlike your fist—or the rest of you, for that matter."

"Stop it, you two," Angrboda called to them, but they did not heed her.

"And that reminds me," Skadi said, as Angrboda gathered the chopped-up rabbits into a bowl, "I don't suppose you know of his double life in Asgard, do you?" She cast a look beside her at Hel, who was listening very intently to the entire exchange, her green eyes comically large.

"Aye, I do," Angrboda said, giving her friend a significant look. "I know all of it."

Skadi stared at her. "You . . . do?"

"Is that not what I just said?" Angrboda turned to see Gerd staring at her as well. But Gerd quickly averted her gaze and occupied herself by moving all the rabbit gristle to a pot to dump outside later. Fenrir stuck his face in the pot and started eating the contents without missing a beat.

"If you know, then how can you stand for it?" Skadi demanded, recovering from her surprise. Then, a few moments later, she stood slowly and asked, "Are you all right? You look pale."

"I'm fine," Angrboda said breathlessly, one hand clutching the small bump of her stomach. "Don't worry."

Across the table, Loki frowned and stood. "She hasn't been sleeping well."

"She never sleeps well, or sleeps much at all, from what she's told me. It's no small wonder you haven't noticed."

"For your information, I *have* noticed, and it troubles me."

"Oh, right. Because you're a quality husband."

"*Quiet*, both of you. Please." Angrboda suddenly felt a wave of dizziness and swayed. Seconds later her knees gave out, and Skadi sprang forward and caught her before she hit the ground. She couldn't be made to stand, despite Skadi trying to heave her upright.

Not again, Angrboda thought, squeezing her eyes shut as Skadi reached a hand under her knees and picked her up, cradled her like a child.

"How can it be time already, with the baby so small?" Skadi asked, panic in her voice.

Small, but alive. Angrboda kept her eyes closed as she felt the child twisting inside her. She was not panicked as she had been when she had thought Hel had died in her womb. Fenrir, like this child, had been very much alive when she'd gone into labor.

"We didn't think Fenrir would make it, either, and she only carried him for six months," Loki said. He grabbed all the furs and blankets off the bed and put them in a pile on the floor in front of the fire.

"It's been less for this child," Angrboda said weakly.

"Put her there, Skadi. I'll make her comfortable. Go fetch some water from the stream." Loki gestured to the pile he'd just made as he rummaged in the back of the cave and produced two buckets and an armful of rags.

"Don't tell me what to do," Skadi said, but she put Angrboda down anyway.

Loki shoved the buckets at her when she straightened, and the two of them glared at each other for a solid thirty seconds.

Angrboda tugged at Skadi's tunic. "Do as he says. Please. There isn't time."

Skadi looked down at her uncertainly but took the buckets and continued to glare at Loki. "I'm willing to allow that perhaps you're not as useless as I thought."

Loki stared at Skadi dead on, with an intensity that Angrboda had never before seen from the likes of him. Even Skadi recoiled just the slightest bit.

"And I'm willing," Loki said with utmost seriousness, "to take your concession and file it away with the rest of the things I don't care about, what with my wife about to give birth." When Skadi opened her mouth to reply, he said coldly, "You really don't want to get into it with me right now."

Skadi turned her back on him and stomped out without another word. When Loki turned to Gerd, the girl said quickly, "I'll take the children outside." Hel had started to cry and was clinging to Gerd's leg, and Fenrir was skulking behind Gerd and giving a high-pitched whine.

"Keep them occupied, and keep them *out* of here," Loki called after her as she ushered them out the door. A few minutes later, Hel came sprinting back in to throw her arms around her father, wailing. He hugged her for a moment before turning her back around and saying, "Why don't you go tell Gerd about your goats and the silly things they do? Mama will be fine."

"She will be," Skadi said as she came in after Hel, holding two buckets of water. She dumped them into the cauldron over the fire, set the buckets aside, and crouched down to Hel's level, smoothing the worry from her face to give the child a reassuring smile. "And I'd like to hear about those goats, too. Will you come outside with me and let your mama and papa have some time alone?"

THE labor was over before nightfall, but at that point, Angrboda didn't even have the strength to sit up. Instead she fell back against the blankets Loki had piled up behind her and asked heavily, chest heaving, "So? What is it?"

"I'm not sure," Loki said as he stared down at whatever it was Angrboda had just pushed from her body. There was minimal mess and no afterbirth, but that didn't seem to be what was troubling him.

"How . . . are you not sure?" Angrboda asked, struggling to sit up straighter and get a better view of her newest child.

"Well, it's sort of in a sac of some kind— What the—?" And then he yelped and scooted back, his eyes wide.

"What? What's wrong?"

Her question was answered when she felt something slither up her leg and, as she lacked the energy to jerk away, she found that a small snake was peering at her over her knee—peering with the same green eyes of his father, brother, and sister, bright against the dark green of his scales. When Angrboda laughed in surprise, the snake squeaked and toppled onto her lap.

The snake was nearly the length of Angrboda's arm, but the width of only two of her fingers. Like Fenrir, he was larger than the newborn animal whose shape he took, but smaller than Hel had been. Angrboda picked him out of her lap and cuddled him, and his forked tongue grazed her cheek. He had but one tooth, which he had used to rip his way out of the sac in which he'd been delivered.

"First a half-dead baby girl, then a wolf, now a snake," Loki said. "It seems as though our children are getting progressively less normal. The next one will just be a quivering blob with eyes at this rate."

"What do baby snakes eat?" Angrboda wondered aloud.

"I have no idea." Loki moved over to sit beside his wife, and they both looked down at their snake-baby, who was now looking at Loki and flicking his tongue curiously. Like Fenrir, he had intelligent eyes.

Eyes that were familiar not only because they were his father's, but also because Angrboda had *seen them before.*

In her vision of the end of the worlds. *The great serpent coming up out of the waves . . .* She looked down at the tiny creature in her lap, peering up at her with such innocence. *No. It can't be. It can't . . .*

"Boda?" Loki asked, rubbing the small of her back. "Are you all right?"

Angrboda snapped out of her reverie. *Ridiculous. What am I thinking?*

"Yes, of course," she said. She plastered a smile on her face.

"What shall we call this one? It's your turn to come up with a name."

Loki thought for a moment and held his arm out. The snake slithered up it as clumsily as a baby taking its first steps.

"Jormungand," Loki said.

"We are *not* calling our son 'awesomely powerful magical stick.'"

"Yes, we are. It's a great name. *That's* how you make names, Boda. Just stick a bunch of words together until it means something. Besides, his name doesn't need to be as depressing as your own. Isn't that right, Jormungand?" The snake nuzzled his chin and Loki grinned, triumphant. "See?"

"I take back what I said on the day we met. *You* bring *me* sorrow," Angrboda said. "And I also take back when I said you have a way with words."

"I have a way with giving my snake-babies really great names, if that's what you'd prefer to say about me now."

"I'd prefer to say a *lot* of things about you," Angrboda muttered.

"Maybe he likes meat." Loki reached into the nearby bowl and took out a chunk of rabbit, and Jormungand eyed it curiously before unhinging his jaw to swallow it right out of Loki's hand. The piece was too big for him, so Loki grabbed Skadi's hunting knife off the table and chopped it up into smaller bits, then held them out to his son again.

This time Jormungand was able to eat the meat, though it took him some time to swallow. Then he slithered back onto his mother's lap and curled up. Once Loki had shoved the soiled blankets aside and helped Angrboda onto the bed, he told Gerd and Skadi to bring the children back in.

The two women took their leave shortly after, despite Angrboda's attempts to make them stay the night.

"You have a new child," Gerd said, waving her hand. "We don't want to impose." Skadi looked hesitant, though, and gave Angrboda a meaningful look when Loki's back was turned. Angrboda looked back at her as if to say, *It's fine—you can go.* So Skadi went.

Hel seemed unperturbed that her second brother was an animal—she was perhaps too full and tired to care, as her dinner had consisted of dried meat from the stores, and Skadi had let her eat her fill of that and goat's milk. Fenrir had caught a few rabbits for himself for dinner, and for his part, he seemed disappointed that Jormungand was not another wolf for him to play with.

Later on, when she and the children had piled onto the bed, Hel snuggled close to Angrboda and ran her finger over the scar on her chest as she had done when she was a tiny baby, but she did not take her eyes off the snake curled up on her mother's stomach. Clutched in her other hand was the wolf figurine Loki had made her when she was a baby; it was worn and grooved with teeth marks from her gnawing on it, but she loved it all the same and took to hiding it around the cave for safekeeping. Angrboda would often find it stuffed under a pile of furs when she was cleaning out the bedding.

She whispered, "Mama, why did he choose to be a snake?"

"Maybe someday soon he'll be able to tell you," Angrboda whispered back, then kissed her forehead. A flash of the great serpent from her vision appeared in her mind like a bolt of lightning, and she pushed it aside just as quickly.

She knew there would soon come a time when she would have to process what she'd seen—both the serpent and the wolf, for wasn't it too great a coincidence that she now had not one but two sons who took the forms of the creatures in her vision?—and would have to come to terms with what it all meant for her and her little family.

But tonight, she just wanted to be happy.

Loki was the last to get into bed, as he had been tending the fire, making sure it would last. He lay pressed against Angrboda, facing her and the children, his elbow bent and his head propped up on his hand.

"He's endearing," Loki said, eyeing Jormungand. "In his way. I wonder if he'll talk, like Fenrir. I wonder if he'll grow massive fangs and eat people. That would be great, wouldn't it?"

Angrboda once again forced down thoughts of her vision and instead rolled her eyes. "What's your obsession with eating people?"

"I have a lot of enemies. Which is why I think it would be convenient to have sons who can swallow them whole. And that's the end of *that* problem."

"Sometimes," Angrboda said dryly, "I wish all our problems were solved as easily in reality as they are in your head."

"You and me both," Loki agreed, pulling the furs over them, and soon all were asleep.

LOKI did not leave much that winter, and Angrboda was grateful for that; the season was long and harsh. They spent most days huddled in bed with the children, not willing to waste too much energy on moving about—though the children didn't seem to understand this. Hel was still wary of Fenrir after he'd bitten her arm, but that did not stop them from running around the cave together, shrieking with delight, and of course Loki would only encourage them to tire themselves out. On the warmer days Jormungand would slither along with them.

Then they would all collapse in bed again and Loki would tell them stories as Angrboda dozed. She had slept more this winter than she had in recent memory and knew that this was due largely to the presence of her husband and children, who were never more than a few feet away at any given time. It helped steel her mind against the chanter, whom she could still feel on the periphery of her dreams—he seemed to be keeping his distance ever since he'd almost sent her over the edge.

As a result she'd only dipped her head into the vision before she'd pulled away. She hadn't completely submerged, gotten all the details, seen the bitter end. And she preferred to keep it that way.

Sometimes, when Loki and Angrboda were sure the children were sound asleep, they slipped away to lie by the fire. Most of the time they were too sluggish to do anything but curl up together and say nothing for a few hours, listening to the snow blowing and the wind howling outside, listening to the fire crackling and feeling its warmth on their hands and faces.

There was nothing special about such interactions, but she treasured them all the same. Time had meant little to Angrboda before the children and Loki; but the four of them had given her a new appreciation for those small secret moments that might have seemed ordinary to others but meant more to her every time she noticed them.

Jormungand spent most of the winter hanging about his mother's neck or curled up on her chest, leeching her warmth and not doing much else; when he was not with her or in front of the fire, he was lethargic. He didn't eat much, but when spring rolled around, he became active and started growing immensely. He also caught food on his own in the woods, which were greener than ever before that spring.

By the beginning of summer, he was as long as his father was tall—which is to say, rather long indeed—and nearly as thick as Angrboda's neck. She suspected he *could* swallow a person whole if he really tried, though to her relief, he didn't.

She kept an eye out, though—Hel would be his easiest target.

Now five, Hel was still very small. Her wavy black hair tumbled down to her waist, and her green eyes were enormous in her tiny pale face. She was helpful enough when working the garden with Angrboda but otherwise would take to pacing the clearing out of boredom, turning her wolf toy over and over in her hands.

Jormungand had not started to talk yet, but as he was only six months old, Angrboda was not exactly worried. He sometimes made sounds in her head, but just syllables—not even "Mama," which had been Fenrir's first word. And he and Fenrir—whose big puppy head was now level with Angrboda's elbow—often snapped and hissed and growled at each other, but in a playful way, as brothers do.

Loki, of course, only egged them on. He had not been absent for more than a month since winter's end. Angrboda was glad of this.

The chanter still kept his distance. She'd done her best to forget the horrors she'd seen in her vision that night, but she found she could not lock the knowledge away as cleanly as she wished to— both her sons' resemblance to the creatures she'd seen and the image of her husband's torture were always closest to the surface. But even that was pushed from her thoughts when he appeared, grinning, at the mouth of the cave with a new story to tell. The children always rushed to him, and seeing his face and seeing them happy made her feel content.

One day, when Loki and Hel were sprawled out on their stomachs in the grass of the clearing, she caught a snippet of their conversation as she was making dinner, with Jormungand curled around her waist with his head on her shoulder. He was getting too heavy to carry around, but she didn't mind.

"I don't know, Hel," she heard Loki say. "I think Frigg has the longest beard."

"*No*, Papa. She's a *girl* goat. She *can't* have the longest beard," Hel replied, with all the certainty of a five-year-old. "Odin has the longest beard, see? You said he was the wisest of *all* goats. *That* means he has the longest beard, too."

"I don't think so. Frigg's is longer. Girl goats have beards and horns, too, just like boy goats do."

"Well, in that case, I think Thor has the longest beard."

"I still think it's Frigg."

"Well, you're wrong. Why do girl goats have beards and horns?"

"I'm not sure, but that's the reason I mixed up their names when I named them. Remember?"

"Mama said it was because you do dumb things."

"Oh, she did, did she?"

"Yes. She said you did it on purpose because you're an idiot."

"Why are you poisoning my daughter's mind with your wicked lies?" Loki called back into the cave.

"Did you not tell her the other day that the scars on your mouth came from getting into a fight with the squirrel that climbs Yggdrasil?" Angrboda called back, and Jormungand butted her chin with the flat of his head. She generally took this to mean that he was amused.

"It was a verbal fight at first," Loki told Hel now, for she was giving him a suspicious look that Angrboda could see from where she stood. "And then he wanted me to stop talking, so he attacked my mouth with his squirrelly little claws." He curled his own fingers into claws and tickled her, and she giggled and yelled and rolled away from him.

Jormungand disentangled himself from his mother and slithered over to join in, which made Fenrir jump down from his perch atop the cave's mouth to pounce on his father—and soon the four of them dissolved into one writhing, shrieking mass. As charming as Angrboda found this, she called to them that dinner was ready, and they ignored her. She tried twice more with the same result. So she picked up a pail of water, strode out of the cave, and dumped it on them.

"Dinner is ready," she said calmly, and tossed the bucket aside. "Are you all right, Hel?"

Her daughter nodded breathlessly. For a moment Angrboda caught a hint of blue in Hel's lips and fingertips, but it went away as the girl calmed down. Hel herself hardly seemed worried about this condition, but Angrboda couldn't help but fret. It was her motherly instinct, she supposed.

"Fenrir, shake yourself out *before* you come inside. You, too, Loki," she said to them. But of course Loki waited until he was right in front of her to shake his wet hair in her face, and she whacked him with a spoon. "Sometimes I feel as though I'm raising four children instead of three."

"We could *make* it four." Loki grabbed her hips and held her against him.

At the table, Hel giggled and spooned stew into her mouth. Fenrir and Jormungand were present on either side of their sister, but as they had already eaten their fill of their own catches earlier on, neither was eating stew—nor did they have any desire to eat anything their mother had cooked, so Angrboda set out a plate piled high with chunks of raw meat for them as a snack.

Neither of her sons possessed anything even remotely resembling table manners. Often it was less sickening to eat without them, but she didn't want them to feel left out.

"Only if you're the one to birth it this time," Angrboda told Loki lightly. "Perhaps then it won't be a quivering blob with eyes."

"Or perhaps it will, and I shall have to carry it around in a sling."

"You *still* carry Hel around in a sling."

"That's because she likes me best. Only maybe this blob will become so big that it will eat all the Nine Worlds, and that will be the end of us."

"Are you really implying that the worlds will end with one of our children devouring everything?" A shiver went up her spine and she pushed the thought of her vision down once again. She knew better than to remind him of what she'd seen that night, and when she'd tried to tell him—well, she didn't think she could bear being written off again, so she kept her mouth shut.

"I still think we should get them to devour people. I think Hel would be especially good at it, even with her little mouth. Look how she's devouring her dinner."

Angrboda pushed him down onto the bench. "Why don't you make your *big* mouth useful for something other than talking and eat your dinner?"

"My mouth is useful for lots of things other than—"

"And how many times have I asked you not to say lewd things in front of the children?" she added, because he still had her by the hips and she could sense a crude remark coming on.

"I suppose you just know me too well," he said, releasing her, then turned around and proceeded to make faces at Hel, who giggled so madly that she almost choked on her food.

Annoyed though she was, Angrboda would hold good days like this in her heart forever and cherish them, for something told her they would be few and fleeting indeed.

SOON after that day, Gerd showed up at her door one morning with a basket of loose-spun, undyed wool and a look of determination Angrboda had never seen before.

"I've come to spend some time with Hel," Gerd said matter-of-factly. "You say she's grown bored of gardening, and she can't do much but wander around lest she overexert herself. So I've come to teach her a craft to keep her hands busy. I've seen her worry that wolf toy of hers—soon there will be nothing left of it."

Angrboda stood from her gardening and tipped her straw hat backward so she could see Gerd more clearly. Then she looked to Hel—who sat miserably drawing in the mud with a stick near the tree line while her brothers were out hunting—and back to Gerd. The witch certainly knew how to sew and weave, but she cared little for it.

"By all means," Angrboda said at last. "What do you wish to teach her?"

Gerd just grinned. "Can I drag a bench outside?"

Angrboda nodded and Gerd did so, then beckoned for Hel to come over and sit beside her. The girl trudged across the clearing and plopped down on the bench next to Gerd. Angrboda went back to weeding her garden but kept a keen ear on the conversation.

"It's called *nalbinding*," said Gerd, extracting something from her bag: a pair of socks. They seemed to be made from the same loose-spun woolen yarn Gerd had in her basket, and one sock was half-finished. The yarn attached to it was threaded through the largest needle Angrboda had ever seen, half the width of her finger and carved out of smooth wood.

"Weird," Hel said, eyeing the socks. "Why are they so big? Are they for an ogre?"

"I'll soak them in water and rub them together to make the fibers tighten up, so water can hardly get in, and then they'll be person-sized. See?" She reached into her bag and pulled out a mitten made in the same way, but the stitching seemed more condensed— solid, even. Angrboda was impressed.

Hel took the mitten from Gerd and ran her small fingers over it, curious. "It feels interesting. I like it."

"It's very easy," said Gerd with a smile. "See, you just take this piece of yarn here, and loop this around your finger, and . . ."

By the time Gerd left that afternoon, Hel had taken to the craft so fervently that her hands had not stilled since the moment Gerd handed over the needle and wool. Angrboda thanked Gerd profusely even though it seemed a little soon to be doing so—Hel had not stopped working even to eat and could not even be tempted by oatcakes and honey.

"That's quite a fine square you've created. What is it supposed to be?" Angrboda asked later on in the evening, when she was trying to usher them all to bed. "It's time to sleep."

"I'm just *practicing*, Mama," Hel said. Only reluctantly did she allow her needle and yarn to be set aside for the night. Although Angrboda was grateful that Gerd had given Hel something to do, she quite feared that her friend had just given her daughter a new obsession.

THERE came a day in late summer, when Loki had been gone for nearly a week, when Gerd came by to check on how Hel's crafting was going. Angrboda invited her to stay the night so she did not need to hike home in the dark. Gerd gladly agreed to this, as she was wary of walking Ironwood alone in the daylight, let alone after sunset.

Angrboda nodded in understanding, though Ironwood had been her home for many years and to her it was safer than anywhere else in the Nine Worlds. She was secretly glad that outsiders still found it frightening—it meant they would continue to leave her in peace. That was all she could ask for.

"I've not seen Skadi for two weeks now," Angrboda told her. It was early evening and the women sat at the table as Fenrir and Jormungand tussled out in the clearing, and Hel sat on the grass working on her *nalbinding* while it was still daylight. "I'm nearly out of ale."

"The word in Jotunheim is that something is going on in Asgard, or so my parents have overheard. Perhaps she was called to council—she *is* numbered among the gods now, after all," Gerd said. "You could ask your husband about it when he returns."

"Yes, but I want to know what's *really* happening. Which means I shall just wait to ask Skadi instead of him." *I'll probably see her sooner, anyway.*

"Why is that?" Gerd asked.

Because I never know when he's telling me the whole truth, Angrboda thought, but she said, "He tends to add a flourish to the stories he tells. Skadi is far more straightforward in her narrations."

"By 'straightforward' do you mean 'boring'?"

"No, I mean *straightforward.* Skadi's stories aren't boring. I listened to them for an entire winter and was never bored."

"Hers are all about shooting things and cutting people. They're men's stories."

"So what are women's stories, then?"

"Perhaps the kind your husband tells. Sweeping gestures and all." Gerd thought for a moment, and before Angrboda could argue that stories need not necessarily be gendered, Gerd went on. "Does it trouble you that he tells women's stories? He *is* quite handsome, if I may say so, but from the one time I met him and from what Skadi has told me . . . he seems a bit off."

Angrboda laughed. "That's an understatement."

"His handsomeness, or his peculiarity?"

"Both."

"Why do you say that?"

At that moment Angrboda heard Fenrir's excited barking and Hel's gleeful shriek, and a few seconds later Loki appeared at the door, carrying Hel in one arm as she clutched her ball of yarn, with Jormungand wrapped around his torso and Fenrir nipping excitedly at his heels.

Loki was clothed in a dress and a veil, and Angrboda guffawed into her bowl at the sight. When she looked at Gerd, she saw the girl's mouth hanging open and her stew dripping out of it and onto the table.

"*That* is why I say that," Angrboda said to her.

"Say what?" Loki asked innocently; he put Hel down and stepped out of Jormungand, who slithered away. Hel crawled onto the bed and began *nalbinding* again.

"We were discussing your manhood," Angrboda said, straight-faced, and Gerd spit out what little stew was left in her mouth.

Loki looked down at his dress and then back to Angrboda. "As in my masculinity, or my parts?"

"We were talking about the first, but we probably would have ended up on the topic of the other sooner or later," Angrboda replied, and Gerd flushed bright red and took to patting Fenrir and not looking at them.

"Why are you always so keen to talk about what's in my pants?" Loki asked. "Or under my dress, at the moment."

Angrboda shrugged. "It's relevant to my interests, you being the father of my children and all. Why are you dressed like that?"

"You know, that should have been the first thing out of your mouth: voicing your concern that your husband was in a dress. Why are you not surprised?"

"I'm neither surprised nor concerned. I suspect that this is just another day in your life, my love. Although as I said, I'm curious to know the story behind it."

"Do you two always talk to each other in such a manner?" Gerd wondered aloud.

"Absolutely," said Angrboda.

Loki gave Gerd the sweetest look he could. "Would you mind keeping an eye on these three while I tell my wife a story?"

"I don't mind at all," Gerd said quickly, for she seemed eager to no longer be part of this conversation.

"We won't be gone long," Angrboda said, kissing her children goodbye. Hel didn't react to her one bit, so focused was she on her *nalbinding*, but Jormungand flicked his tongue at her affectionately.

Gerd was busy petting Fenrir's belly. "I mean to help Hel with her crafting, so take your time," she said, and they left, fully intending to do just that.

LOKI led Angrboda off into the darkening woods, and they ended up by the small stream, which had been nearly flooded by the summer rains. They walked so far down that they were past the boundaries of Angrboda's protective charms, but as it was just the two of them without the children, she told herself it was all right. She cared only for the feel of her hand in his.

As she was about to ask him about the dress again, he pulled it off and cast it aside, kissed her like he hadn't seen her in an age, and took her there on the grassy bank soon after. When they were done, sweating and panting under the full summer moon, Angrboda sat up and asked, "So, as to the matter of you in a dress—"

"Oh!" Loki sat up as well and scooted over to sit on a large rock looming over the stream. Angrboda sat down beside him, and he began. "So, one morning, Thor woke up and couldn't find his hammer, Mjolnir."

"How could he possibly misplace such an item?"

"Thor isn't exactly the sharpest ax in the armory. Anyway, he couldn't find it, and he came to me first for some reason—probably thinking I'd taken it."

"Had you?"

"For once, I hadn't! So, anyway, he came to me and we decided the giants must have done it."

Angrboda's brows knitted. "That was your first logical conclusion? Our people?"

Loki waved his hand. "No, no, see, Thor's hammer is used almost exclusively for giant slaying. And he doesn't discriminate, either."

Angrboda remained silent, staring down at the water below, and decided to dangle her feet in it.

"So I said I should probably find out who took it," Loki went on, putting his feet in the water as well. "So we went to Freyja and asked for her falcon cloak—"

"Why in the worlds did you need Freyja's falcon cloak when you can turn yourself into a falcon at will?"

Loki opened his mouth to reply, then paused and shrugged.

"Because you wanted to make things difficult for her?" Angrboda ventured.

"Because I wanted to make things difficult for her," he confirmed with relish, "since I know how much Freyja hates loaning it out. But she gave me the cloak because Thor asked her. So, I flew to Jotunheim and found this giant named Thrym, who said that he'd stolen Thor's hammer—who even knows how?—and would give it back if he got Freyja for a wife. I went back and Thor told me not to change out of the cloak, because as soon as I sat down, I would forget everything—"

"Very true, my love."

"It is *not*."

"Oh, really? Do you remember what you had for breakfast this morning?"

"I had a very exciting day."

"Just as I thought."

Loki made a face at her and continued. "So, I told them Thrym had the hammer and would trade it for Freyja, and Freyja said no. Which was very inconvenient for the gods. So they held a council to decide what to do. And then Heimdall—the watchman, my archnemesis—"

Angrboda raised her eyebrows. "You have an archnemesis?"

"He sees *everything*, Boda. He's like what would happen if Odin decided to sit in his chair constantly and see all the Nine Worlds, all the time. That's Heimdall. He makes it really hard to sneak around Asgard. Which I do, often. So, anyway, he suggested that we dress *Thor* up as Freyja and send him to marry Thrym." Loki sighed wistfully. "Would that I had come up with such a brilliant idea myself."

"And Thor was content to go along with this?"

"Of course he wasn't. He said it would be a catastrophic failure of manliness, in not so many words. But I told him to shut up and do it, and that I would go with him as his handmaiden."

Angrboda snorted. "So you donned a dress. But you're a shape-shifter—you've taken on female forms before, so why not just change yourself into a woman?"

"Because that wouldn't have been *nearly* as fun," said Loki. "So, we dressed up Thor and went to Jotunheim, and he proceeded to act like his usual self, so I had to cover for him. Then, finally, they brought out the hammer as a wedding gift, and Thor picked it up and killed everyone there."

Angrboda said nothing.

"And that's how Odin's son got his hammer back," Loki concluded, "and why I was in a dress. That was earlier this evening—as soon as we got back to Asgard, I left for here. Wasn't that a great story?"

"It ended with a feast hall full of our dead kinsmen," Angrboda said dully.

Loki screwed up his face. "'Kinsmen'? I'll bet neither of us knew *any* of those people. They were the worst kinds of giants. Stupid, brutish, vicious. They're not our kin. They're not our family. What do you care for them, anyway?"

Angrboda gestured between them. "*We* two are giants. And for all I know, some of those people could have traded with Skadi or Gerd or have been saved by my potions, or—"

"Oh, Skadi? She was *so* angry when she found out Thor had killed everyone at the feast. She was about to stomp right out of Odin's hall, until he demanded to know whose side she was on."

Angrboda had no trouble picturing this. "And how did she respond?"

"She didn't. And trust me, the Aesir found this most worrying indeed. But Njord spoke out on her behalf, and so they bear her no ill will." Loki looked up at the moon. "He explained that Skadi is simply very attached to this land and to its people, as nasty as some may be. Njord understands this, as he is just as fond of the sea. Perhaps they're not such a bad match after all."

Angrboda was frowning, lost in thought. Loki took one look at her serious expression and stuck his tongue out at her. By way of a response, she shoved him into the water and curled her legs up to her chest so he couldn't drag her in.

Loki made no move to do so, though. In fact, he did not even surface for a few moments, and Angrboda was honestly starting to worry that he had drowned when he popped up and spit a stream of water at her. She put her hands up to block it, laughing.

"Come down here," he said. The water level was high—settling right below his pelvic bone, while usually it barely came up to his knee.

Angrboda slipped down into the water, not taking her eyes off him. "You're going to do something."

"No, I'm not," he said innocently, and she shook her head at him.

When she was in the water, he began to splash her, and when she shrieked and backed away, he laughed and sprang forward and dunked her. When she surfaced, he ducked when she tried to spit water in his face as he had done to her, and she settled for splashing him profusely instead.

Then he pulled her close, and she ran her hand down the thin trail of hair on his lower stomach. His lips were level with her forehead, as always, and he kissed her there.

"We've been alive a long time," he said suddenly. "I mean, a thousand years ago, we were around. Not as we are today, but we were here. And for at least some of the gods, some form of them was worshipped by humans in Midgard even back then. Don't you agree?"

Angrboda shrugged, then nodded. "Does this trouble you?"

"A little," Loki conceded, and pushed her long wet hair back from her face. "It's just . . . I've known you for so long, and yet it feels like no time at all. Will the rest of our time pass just as quickly? Will we change again and again as we have before, or are we stuck the way we are now forever, because more people will remember us this way?"

Angrboda said nothing. She tilted her head up to look at him, and his nose brushed hers, and in his eyes she could see that this was concerning him more than he would like to admit.

"What will they think of us a thousand years from now, if our stories are remembered?" he whispered. "Will I be counted the best among the gods, or the worst?"

She took his face in her hands, ran her thumb over his ruined lips. "Don't dwell on it. It's out of your control what people will think of you a thousand years in the future. What is a thousand years to us, anyway? The humans may pray to Odin and Thor and even Skadi, but those people will all eventually die, whether from battle or sickness or old age. And what of these stories of which you speak?"

"The people die. The stories continue, in poetry and song. Stories of their deeds. Of their gods." He tore away from her then, angrily. "Why am I not worshipped like the rest? What are gods if they're not worshipped? What does that make me? Reckoned among them, but not *one of them. Never* one of them."

"Is that really all that matters to you?" Angrboda demanded. "Worship and being well-known? Is that really why you make mischief, just for attention? Just so people will remember you in some far-distant future?"

"It beats hiding in a cave at the edge of the world, being scared of everything," Loki shouted in her face now, his scarred lips twisting in scorn. "You don't understand. You'll *never* understand, because all they will remember of you is the name you chose for yourself, Angrboda. Not that you were Gullveig, not anything else. They will know you only as my wife and the mother of monsters, because you choose to be *nothing more.*"

Angrboda felt as though he'd just kicked her in the chest. She wondered at just how much her face had crumpled, because Loki's cruel expression had dissolved into a look of alarm.

"I shouldn't have said that," he said unsteadily, reaching out to touch her arm. "Please—"

Her voice was deadly quiet as she twitched away. "Monsters?"

"Boda, I—"

"*Monsters?*" Angrboda slapped him hard across the face, and then she stomped out of the water and pulled her dress back on as he reeled. "You may say whatever you wish about me. But you leave our children *out* of—"

But then Angrboda heard Fenrir howl, and a few seconds later he bounded out of the trees, Jormungand slithering along beside him. She could hear Gerd and Hel tromping through the underbrush not far behind.

Mama, there's someone here. There's someone in our woods—I heard them, I can smell them, Fenrir said to Angrboda, and she hugged him tightly as Jormungand brushed her ankles.

Gerd and Hel appeared a second later, and Hel sprang at her mother and latched onto her waist tightly, whimpering.

"You all need to get back behind the boundary," Angrboda said with mounting apprehension. She tried very hard to keep her voice even. "Right *now.*"

"I'm sorry. I'm *sorry,*" Gerd said, panting. "They all just took off, one right after another. I tried to make them go back, but—"

"Loki?" came a shaky voice from the opposite bank, and all of them turned.

Out of the shadows on the other side of the stream stepped a woman in a cloak of feathers. Her clothing was fine, as if she'd just come from a feast, and her chestnut hair was done up and threaded with gold.

Her soft brown eyes were huge in the moonlight, and they were fixed directly across the river: on Angrboda's children.

"What are you doing here?" Loki asked her, thinly veiled panic on his face.

"I got lost," said the woman, turning her gaze ever so slowly from the children to him. "I followed you when you left Asgard—I borrowed Freyja's falcon cloak. I just wanted to *know*. I finally just wanted to see for myself. Now seemed as good a time as any, with everyone drunk on the victory of Thor's hammer returned. Everyone except you." She took a few tentative steps forward. "Who are . . . *they?*"

Angrboda could feel Gerd slink into the shadows behind her, and her arms tightened instinctively around her trembling children.

For she knew who this woman was. She had seen her before in a dream, and her face stirred up images of that part of her vision she'd tried the hardest to lock away: Loki's binding. His torment. The woman at his side.

The woman who was not Angrboda.

"Who *are* they?" this woman asked again.

Still in the river, Loki raised his hands, palms up in surrender, and took a step toward her. "You know of them. I've told you about them. This is not a surprise to anyone."

Silence passed, indicating otherwise.

"Sigyn," Loki said to her, "this is Angrboda. And these are our children."

"Does she not know I'm your wife as well?" Angrboda said loudly. "You refer to me as such but do not introduce me that way?"

Loki winced and looked over his shoulder at her. "She knows. I've not lied to either of you. That's the truth."

"You had not told me of the *nature* of your children," Sigyn said through gritted teeth. "I trusted you to be honest with me. I trusted you to—"

She sounded frightened, and Angrboda could not stop herself from asking, her voice loud and clear and cold, "And what *is* the nature of my children?"

Sigyn turned to her then as if seeing her for the first time. Her expression was perfectly blank, but Angrboda knew that she was passing judgment.

Angrboda had pictured this meeting so many times and always told herself that, if she ever found herself face-to-face with her husband's other wife—as she was sure she eventually would—she would handle the situation with as much dignity and grace as she could muster. But now, in that moment, Angrboda found her own face twisting with disdain as the other woman appraised her.

"Well?" Angrboda demanded.

At her tone, Sigyn's expression contorted to mirror Angrboda's, and the two women stared each other down with outright contempt. Angrboda's sons picked up on this immediately and sprang to their mother's defense: Fenrir leapt forward past Gerd and growled, baring his teeth, and Jormungand hissed and reared back as if to strike.

And this seemed to tip Sigyn's final verdict in favor of fear.

"They're feral," she said, backing away from the riverbank. "They're . . . they're *monsters*."

Angrboda's vision flashed red.

She was free from Hel's iron grip in an instant and launched herself through the water, meaning to wring the neck of the woman across the stream, wanting nothing more than to rip her limb from limb—but Loki grabbed her by the waist and forced her back toward the bank.

"Don't do this," he pleaded. "I swear, she's not usually like this—she's just scared. She doesn't know—"

"Let go of me!" Angrboda snarled, thrashing. "Let *go* of me, *let go*! Did you not hear what she just said?!"

Loki cringed, for he himself had said something similar mere minutes earlier. "You don't understand—"

"*Enough*," said Angrboda. *Mother of monsters.* His words were unforgivable. But hearing this sentiment echoed by a stranger—by a *goddess*—had caused something within her to come undone. Her fingers twitched at her sides as she stared the woman down and channeled every ounce of fury in her heart.

You called my children monsters . . .

And I'll make you swallow those words.

She closed her eyes and went still in Loki's arms, rooting around in the back of her mind for the place where she'd sealed all the things she'd learned from her vision of the end of the worlds. When she found it, she released it and let the knowledge course through her.

Head bowed, brow furrowed, eyes squeezed shut, she searched through it all until she found what she was looking for. And she smiled.

"Boda?" Loki said cautiously. His grip on her loosened a little, but not enough for her to break free if she wanted to lunge at Sigyn again. "Are you—?"

Angrboda's wet hair was dangling in her face, head still bowed and eyes still shut, as she addressed the woman across the river.

"You think you have the right to judge me, to judge my children, to judge my *people*," Angrboda hissed. "You and your gods think you always have the right of things. But I know better—so there's something I'd like to share with you."

Angrboda whipped her head up, and when she opened her eyes,

her pupils and irises had gone a dead white, causing Sigyn to gasp and step back before the witch even spoke.

And when Angrboda did speak, it was not just with her own voice; her words echoed with a deep, hoarse whisper, a cacophony of the dead speaking in unison with her.

"Despair, Sigyn," rasped the witch, *"for your gods will forsake you in the end."*

"Loki," Sigyn whispered, "what is she talking about?"

Loki had released his grip and stepped back from Angrboda, his expression knitted with confusion and concern. Then he seemed to realize in an instant what was happening—like his memory of what she'd told him of *seid* had all come rushing back—and he grabbed her by the arm and shook her. "Stop this, Boda."

She ignored him.

"Knowing the future would be too much of a burden." It was something Angrboda wouldn't wish on anyone—anyone *else*, that is.

But Sigyn had proven herself more than deserving of such a burden this night.

And although the witch knew what was to come, she would share only this scrap of prophecy, and this alone:

"Your sons will suffer greatly at their hands," Angrboda intoned, her attention still fixed on Sigyn. *"Do you want to know more?"*

"This isn't the way," Loki said, shaking her more fiercely. "Snap out of it!"

"What is she talking about, Loki?" Sigyn said. "What's wrong with her? And why are her eyes so—?"

Angrboda raised one hand and pointed a finger at her, and Sigyn suddenly shrieked and collapsed to her knees, digging her hands into her hair.

"Stop this *now*— What are you doing to her?" Loki said with increasing panic, taking Angrboda by the shoulders, stepping between her and his other wife. "Angrboda, please—"

Sigyn was still wailing, keeping her eyes shut and shaking her head as if willing the vision to go away. "No, no, no! I don't want to see it, I don't want to know!"

"*Brother will slay brother,*" Angrboda intoned, ignoring Loki completely.

"I'm begging you." Loki stopped shaking her but kept his hands there on her shoulders as he leaned down, whispering, pleading. "Stop this."

But Angrboda still did not acknowledge him.

Sigyn fell in a heap on the ground, sobbing. "Make it stop . . . make it stop . . ."

"Angrboda, *stop!*" said a new voice from behind Sigyn.

The sound caused Angrboda to snap out of her trance abruptly and stagger, and she regained her balance to see Skadi emerging from the trees on the opposite bank.

For a moment Skadi looked confused, as if the scene was not what she expected: Sigyn appeared unharmed save for that she was weeping quietly, and Angrboda and Loki were both far enough away that there was no way they could have harmed her.

Not physically, at least.

Skadi knelt beside Sigyn, whispered some words of comfort, and helped her to her feet. Sigyn wiped tears from her eyes and shook violently, her expression a conflicted mixture of terror and shame.

"Are you all right?" Skadi asked her. She cast her eyes across the river at Gerd and the children, and then finally at Angrboda, and comprehension dawned. "Is this— Sigyn, is this the first time you've met the—the children?" *And the other wife* went unsaid, for that much was obvious to all involved.

Sigyn looked up at her then, hurt in her eyes. *"You* knew? Even you? And you didn't think to tell me? I thought you were my *friend."*

Angrboda suddenly felt a deep hollowness in her chest, and her entire body went still.

And Skadi looked back across the river, her expression set in stone.

"Get over here, you cretin," she said icily to Loki as she held Sigyn steady in her firm grasp, "and take your wife home."

"Don't tell me what to do," Loki snarled, releasing Angrboda, who stumbled backward onto the grassy bank.

"You *really* don't want to get into it with me right now," Skadi said. Her voice was low and dangerous and did not so much hint at murder as guarantee it. "You'll end up in pieces."

Loki's glare was nothing short of hateful, so irked was he at his own words getting tossed back at him. But he turned and looked at Angrboda, who had regained her composure and stared him down unapologetically. He looked like he was about to say something, to reprimand her, but then his gaze moved past her to just over her shoulder, and his eyes widened.

Angrboda whirled around to see what he was looking at and gasped as she remembered—her children were present, and had been for the entire ordeal. For a horrible moment she thought they might fear her now, would look at her the way Gerd was looking at her—aghast, disgusted, terrified—but no, their eyes were locked on their father. Hel's face was dripping with snot and tears, and Fenrir and Jormungand were both glaring at him with something not unlike resentment.

They aren't bothered by what I've done. They know why I did it.
They heard what Sigyn said.
They see their father going with her.
He's broken their hearts.

Angrboda stepped in front of her children with her fists clenched at her sides, her dress damp in the front from her long hair and soaked at the bottom from when she had stormed into the stream. She faced Loki across the river with a baleful expression.

"Go," she said.

Loki reached out to her, helplessly. "Boda—"

"*Go.*"

So he exited the river on the other side and Skadi pulled off her outer tunic and shoved it at him. He put it on for the sake of covering himself and draped Sigyn's arm over his shoulder, and she sniveled and leaned against him.

"I saw her leave after you and then left the feast myself, fearing the worst, as she'd taken the cloak," Skadi told him in a steely voice, but so softly that Angrboda almost couldn't hear her.

"Your fears were justified, it seems," he responded in a matching tone.

"If they ask, I may be back tonight. And I may not." Skadi cast a glance across the river, then grabbed him by the collar. She was of a height with him, but much stronger. "If you care anything for Angrboda and your children, you will not tell the gods where I am. And you will not tell them of this night."

Loki set his jaw but nodded. He looked over his shoulder and locked eyes with Angrboda.

She was the first to look away, and then he and Sigyn disappeared into the trees.

Skadi waded across the river, and all were silent for a time. Angrboda knew her friends were both burning with questions, and she was grateful that neither woman voiced them at that particular moment.

Then Angrboda said, her voice cracking, "Skadi, Gerd, thank you for tonight. But I would like to be alone with my children right now. You are welcome to stay the night in our home—as I promised Gerd—but if you do, we four will be sleeping outside."

"Angrboda," Gerd began feebly. She seemed less scared now and more concerned. She was holding the dress Loki had arrived in, which he had cast aside, and held it out for Angrboda to dry herself. "We—"

But Skadi put a hand on the girl's shoulder and said, "We'll sleep out in the clearing. Take your bed. We'll just need some furs to sleep upon, that's all."

Angrboda knelt down to pick up her daughter. Hel's arms closed iron tight around her neck, and her legs did the same about Angrboda's waist. She cried into her mother's damp hair.

Then Angrboda placed one hand on Fenrir's head and one hand on Jormungand's and said, "Let's go home."

SKADI and Gerd settled in the clearing as they'd said, and inside the cave, Angrboda changed out of her wet clothes and curled up with her three children on the bed. Hel was pressed against her with her face buried in her mother's chest, and Fenrir was pressed close to Hel, and Jormungand nearly encircled them all, his head resting near Hel's and Fenrir's. He still could not talk, but his green eyes were woeful.

"She said my brothers were monsters," Hel whispered, clutching her wolf figurine, running her little fingers fretfully over its worn, chewed features. "Am I a monster, too, Mama?"

"Of course not. None of you are," Angrboda said, and kissed her forehead, smoothing back her black hair. "Don't you ever believe it."

Papa said it, too. He said himself that we were monsters, Fenrir said dismally.

"He did not," Hel snarled. "Papa would *never* say that."

I heard him—I heard him say it with my own ears! Fenrir whimpered. *Mama, are you really scared of everything? Is that why we live here all by ourselves?*

Angrboda silently cursed her son's heightened sense of hearing. *If he could hear Sigyn plodding through the trees, of course he heard part of our conversation.*

And the worst part, at that.

She chose her next words carefully, for all three of them were staring at her as if they were trusting her to hold their world together. "We live here because long ago, some people did some bad things to me."

Is it because of what you can do? Fenrir asked, for this night was the first time they had witnessed their mother doing that sort of magic. *Like what you did to that woman?*

"What *did* you do to her, Mama?" Hel asked quietly.

Angrboda took a deep breath. "I made her see something. Something terrible. Something no one should ever have to see. I could not allow her to come into our woods and speak of you three the way she did. So I chose to punish her in the worst way I could think of. It was . . . not right of me to do, but I did it because what she said made me so angry."

No. It wasn't bad of you to do. Whatever she saw that made her so upset, she deserved it, Fenrir whispered. *And Papa went with her because he thinks she's right about us, didn't he?*

"She's wrong," Angrboda said fiercely. "They're both wrong. Don't listen to them."

"Is she one of the bad people who hurt you before?" Hel's finger once again moved to the scar on her mother's chest. "Is that how you got this, Mama?"

"It is," Angrboda confirmed. "They stabbed out my heart and

left it on the pyre where they burned me. Your papa returned it to me after he found it there."

He did? asked Fenrir. *How?*

"He just handed it back to me. And I stuck it back in my chest, and now it beats, just like yours." She smiled and smoothed the fur away from his face. "But where it counts, he gave me the three of you."

Hel sniffled and cuddled closer to her. "I want Papa."

Papa hates us, said Fenrir.

"Shut up!" Hel cried, kicking her little dead legs in their stockings, her linen dress bunching up about her. "Shut up, shut *up!*"

It took at least an hour to calm them down after that, but Angrboda finally succeeded in doing so, very late in the night. Hel refused to listen to a word her mother said, opting instead to cover her ears and sob. But after her brothers were asleep she seemed to cry herself out, and she slept as well, clinging to her mother.

Angrboda gently disentangled herself from Hel and stood, went outside to where Gerd and Skadi lay awake, and sat between them. Skadi had grabbed a ceramic jug of ale from Angrboda's stores and was taking sips of it from the small wooden cup she carried at her belt.

When Skadi offered the jug to her, Angrboda took it gratefully and drank, then passed it to Gerd, who took a long swig.

"What happened tonight?" Skadi asked, and Angrboda told them the same thing she had told the children, except in more adult words. As with her children, she didn't describe the specifics of what she'd made Sigyn see.

Skadi and Gerd listened, rapt, and Angrboda braced herself to field questions about the vision and her abilities—but to her surprise, the conversation took a different turn.

"Sigyn said such things?" Skadi said, frowning. "That's hard for me to believe."

"Do you truly think so well of her?" Angrboda asked tightly, and felt that same hollowness in her chest she'd felt when she saw Skadi display such tenderness toward Sigyn at the river.

Skadi narrowed her eyes but didn't look up from her cup. "There's a reason I was upset when I found out Loki was married to you—it's bad enough Sigyn's married to him, but you, too? So, yes, you're both my friends and you both deserve better."

Angrboda said nothing but decided to let the matter rest. Skadi already had more than enough reason to hate Loki—he'd been more or less responsible for her father's death, after all.

"What did you make her see, anyway?" Skadi asked after draining the last of her ale. Gerd passed the jug back to her to refill her cup.

"It was the fate of her sons with Loki, and it was most unpleasant, as you could tell from the way she reacted to it," Angrboda said. Her friends didn't need to know that this vision was part of a larger, more terrible truth.

Skadi let out a low whistle, and she seemed thoughtful. "You never *did* give me a straight answer when we first met and I asked you if you knew *seid*."

"Prophecies are hardly marketable goods, my friend," said Angrboda.

"You truly don't get out much, do you?" Skadi asked. "Yours is a valuable skill. Make no mistake about that."

"Well, it's a skill I'm loath to use," Angrboda said shortly. *It's gotten me killed more than once, after all.*

Her friends only nodded, which surprised her. But she knew it must make sense to them that she'd be reluctant to use this particular form of witchery. She was glad they didn't question her further—after all, she'd never spoken about her past to either of them before, and tonight was not the night to begin.

"Well, I think you have bigger problems than that now," said Skadi. "Not only have you given Sigyn reason to hate you, but now she knows what you're capable of. She knows of your gift of foresight. And if she goes to the Aesir with what she knows, *that* will get Odin's attention most of all."

Angrboda's stomach twisted horribly at the mention of the god's name, which suddenly brought back images of the chanter and her visions and the end of all things.

But more important, she realized the severity of the mistake she had made tonight.

If her visions weren't a coincidence and her sons truly *were* the creatures of prophecy fighting against the gods during the final battle she'd foreseen, Odin would surely want them dead to ensure his own victory.

I've as good as killed them.

I shouldn't have done this. I shouldn't have done any of this. It was all a mistake. The memory of Sigyn's wails had satisfied her for only a moment—and now the very thought of her own actions earlier that night made Angrboda sick.

"How long do you think we have?" Angrboda whispered.

"Well," said Skadi, shifting, "that depends entirely on how long your husband and his other wife can keep their mouths shut."

Angrboda pressed her lips together. "So not long at all."

"I'm not sure," said Skadi. "For all that Loki is a slippery little weasel who will do whatever he can to save his own skin, I know he loves those children—if only because he's kept their nature a secret this long, even from Sigyn. If he suspected they could be in danger and cared about them enough not to breathe a word to anyone . . ."

"Perhaps *that* is his form of love. How annoying." Gerd sighed. "But that other wife of his. That Sigyn . . ."

Angrboda let out a strangled cry. "I shouldn't have lost my temper. I should've at least *tried* to be civil to her. This is all my fault, *all* my fault. And now my children are doomed."

"She was not being civil to *you*," Gerd said, suddenly fierce. "You lost your temper because she looked you dead in the eye and told you that your children were monsters. Had I your power, I would have done the same as you. I would have done *worse*."

"Believe me," said Angrboda darkly. "I wanted to."

Skadi shook her head in disbelief. "Sigyn is a good woman, and she was not herself tonight. I blame Loki for that—if he would've prepared her for this, I feel that things would've gone much differently. I think she would have been curious about your boys, and I think she would have been glad to know you and your children both if given the chance. I don't think she meant it, Angrboda. I truly don't."

"But she said it, and what's worse, my children heard it," Angrboda said bleakly, neglecting to mention the part when Loki himself had called them monsters as well. "Was I wrong to not tell them the world may not accept them the way they are?"

Neither responded.

"The way things were was normal for them," Angrboda said, tears pricking her eyes. "And that was how I had intended it to remain. Myself, Loki, you two, and these woods—that's all they've ever known. Should I have told them right from the beginning how different they truly were? Or was I right to let them think there was nothing wrong with them?"

Gerd put a hand on her shoulder and squeezed, at a loss for words. Skadi put an arm around her back, and Angrboda leaned into her and couldn't stop shaking until she was so exhausted that she simply fell into a dreamless sleep, with her last conscious thoughts being of Hel, Fenrir, and Jormungand and how much time they had left together.

I will stop this, she thought before she slipped under. *I will do whatever it takes.*

AT the end of autumn, Angrboda collected her pouches of enchanted stones and recast the spell that hid her home. She strengthened it, and she poured every part of herself into it, willing it to work with every fiber of her being.

After much deliberation, she tweaked the particulars slightly. When she had first created the spell, one could find her cave only if one had been there, and thus there were only three people who could visit her: Loki, Skadi, and Gerd. But now she changed it so that, besides herself and her children, only Skadi and Gerd would be able to return.

She did not tell the children about this, for they were still distressed about their father, and she felt no need to upset them further. And yet Loki's absence seemed only to reinforce what they thought to be his opinion of them: that they *were* monsters. Angrboda knew that she could not win by telling them she was keeping him away, or by allowing him to stay with them and keep up his act. It had gone on long enough.

For whether or not Loki had truly meant what he'd said, the fact was that he'd said it—and for Angrboda, it was enough to know that such a thought existed somewhere, if only in the back of his mind. This, to her, was intolerable.

Intolerable, and devastating.

The children became yet more distant from her with each passing week. Hel would spend days just sitting outside with the goats, working furiously at her *nalbinding* and hiding whatever she was making whenever Angrboda came near. Fenrir, now almost four, would slink off into the woods from sunrise to sunset, and Angrboda would reprimand him for being gone so long and scaring her, but he would only look at her blankly.

And Jormungand, who was by now a little over a year old, spent more and more of his time curled up in front of the fire as the days got colder. By now he was twice as long as his mother was tall, and as thick as her waist. He still did not speak, not even in the few jumbled syllables of before; he seemed to have given up. And no amount of coaxing from Angrboda would elicit any sort of response from him besides the occasional hiss.

Fenrir felt threatened by his brother's enormous size, and they often snapped at each other, but not as playfully as they once had. One time, Angrboda had to use her magic to pry them apart, on an occasion when Jormungand had wrapped himself around Fenrir and Fenrir had his fangs buried in his brother's tail. Hel looked on, ever impassive, and not without a flicker of grim amusement in her large green eyes at the spectacle, at the blood.

It was at that point Angrboda realized, with complete and utter dismay, that her children had taken their father's words to heart. And she felt as though the age-old wound of her heart had broken open, engulfing her in darkness, and she resisted the urge to rip her heart from her chest and cast it into the fire, for all the good it would do her.

But to do so would be to give up, and her children needed her now more than ever.

"I see you still cover your hair. Does this mean you still consider yourself married to *him*, then?" Skadi said to her one frosty morning when she came by with her reindeer. The animal was laden with winter stores, which she traded Angrboda for her hunger potions: always an invaluable commodity during the cold months.

"It's more out of habit than anything," said Angrboda, though she did not know how true that was. "Plus it keeps the hair from my face."

"Right," said Skadi. "Habit. Please tell me you will make a *habit* of allowing me to murder him in his sleep?"

"He *is* a rather heavy sleeper, surprisingly enough."

"So does that mean I can—?"

"No, you may not."

Skadi looked disgruntled by this answer. By way of a sort-of apology, Angrboda offered her lunch. Skadi accepted.

"They may soon be too much for you to control," Skadi said when they broached the subject of her children. "When they were smaller, surely it was easier, but your sons have grown bigger each time I've seen them."

"It's not their size," Angrboda responded as quietly as she could. "It's about what happened, that night by the river. They've not been the same since."

Skadi put her hands on Angrboda's shoulders and lowered her voice. "As far as I know, neither your slimy husband nor Sigyn herself has breathed a word to anyone about that night. But still, be wary. The gods do not play fair. I know this firsthand."

"I understand. Thank you, my friend. I have taken precautions," Angrboda said, and told her of the enhanced protective charm.

Skadi nodded, then shifted, all of a sudden looking a little uncomfortable—like there was more she wanted to say but it was not her place. But then she merely nodded again and said, "I'll pass the word on to Gerd, that she will still be able to find you as well. And if you need help—if your sons become too much—"

"We shall cross that bridge when we come to it," Angrboda replied. Skadi seemed dissatisfied with this answer but said no more on the subject.

One day, when Angrboda was sewing a new pair of stockings for Hel, her daughter rushed into the cave, weeping inconsolably. When Angrboda could finally get her to speak, she sobbed, "They're eating my goats, Mama! They're *eating my goats!*"

"*Who* is eating your goats, Hel?"

Hel looked at Angrboda like her head had just fallen off and rolled away. "My *brothers!*"

By the time Angrboda and Hel exited the cave, three of the goats had been eaten and the rest had scattered off into the foothills of the mountains and into the gnarled trees of Ironwood. Angrboda doubted they would be coming back.

She looked to Fenrir and Jormungand. The first was gnawing the meat off a leg bone, and the other was swallowing a last massive chunk of goat.

Hel sniffled and clutched at her mother's dress. Angrboda knelt down and put an arm around her, then looked again to her sons. "Why would you do this?"

Because it's nearly winter and there's not enough food, and we're hungry, Fenrir said, with the innocence of a child. But there was a derisive edge to his tone. *We'll chase the rest of them down later for food for you, Mama.*

"Those goats were not food," Angrboda said coldly. "They were your sister's beloved pets, and we used them for milk."

You've butchered them before, Fenrir observed. *Why can't we?*

Angrboda balled her fists and willed herself to calm down. She was used to such back talk from Hel, but it was becoming increasingly common from her middle child. "We butcher them in moderation. I understand you're growing quickly and have hunger to match, but can you not hunt in the woods as you always have?"

Fenrir spit the bone at her feet and stood. His eyes were level with her chin when she was standing, but as she was still kneeling beside Hel, he peered down his short snout at her dangerously. He still had the look of an overgrown pup.

There was barely any food in these woods to begin with, he said, and Jormungand hissed in agreement and rehinged his jaw. *There's nothing here except us and some rabbits, and the boundaries of your spell—*

"Have been extended, which you *know*. That's no excuse," she said, standing. Hel buried her face in her mother's dress and Angrboda stroked her hair, not taking her eyes off her sons. "And Skadi has offered more than once to bring larger game for you to supplement what's in the woods. There will *always* be more food for you. You need only ask."

Fenrir said nothing. He simply brushed past Angrboda and Hel and skulked back into the cave, Jormungand slinking behind him. Hel looked up at her with a blank, broken expression, and Angrboda held her close and led her inside.

It was then that she realized that her two sons had finally kindled some brotherly camaraderie, over the slaughter of the goats: Jormungand and Fenrir slept by the fire together that night. Even though the bed was getting too small for all of them, Angrboda still hated to see her sons sleeping on the floor. Hel seemed glad of her brothers' absence and clutched her mother and her wolf figurine as she slept.

And when Angrboda finally fell asleep, she had the worst dream of all.

THE gods' council was pure chaos, and for once, Loki wanted no part of it.

His wife was front and center, standing before the Aesir with an air of determination as she spoke of what had happened that night at the river.

And he stood to the side, leaning against the wall of the chamber, arms folded, his face cast in shadow.

Loki knew it was his fault that she'd finally gone to the gods. He'd begged her to keep her mouth shut. Following her encounter with Angrboda, Loki had played the part of Sigyn's dutiful husband the best that he could to mollify her. He'd stuck around Asgard. He'd lain with her, doted upon her, played with their sons. He thought it would be easy enough to keep her quiet. He'd always thought she loved him so much that she would forgive him anything.

He was wrong.

She had seen right through him in the end. He supposed it had been easy enough to pretend that he was hers alone, before she had met Angrboda face-to-face. Now there was no going back.

He had underestimated her. He had underestimated both of them.

The Aesir grew more and more enraged as Sigyn spoke, although she did not tell them what Angrboda had made her see. She didn't tell Loki, either—she kept it close to her chest, this terrible secret that had broken her heart. She wept as she told them about the pain the witch's unwelcome visions of the future had caused her, so no one asked her to go into detail, not wishing to distress her further.

Loki was grateful for this, at least. Because he still didn't want to know, either.

All the gods had assembled there in Gladsheim, the council hall—and even the goddesses came in solidarity with Sigyn, though they had a meeting place of their own. As the shouting around him grew louder, Loki half wished Skadi were not off on a hunting trip with the god Ull—although he was certain that her reaction to all of this would cause the gods to cast her out of Asgard for sure. Her love for Angrboda would not allow her to stay silent.

For his part, Loki did not speak a word—although this did not stop the

*rest of the Aesir from attacking him, for the unusual nature of his children
with Angrboda was, to them, the most frightening part of Sigyn's tale.*

"Shape-shifter. Mischief-maker. Wolf-father."

"His antics have gone too far this time. He bred a den of monsters."

"He probably birthed them himself."

"Unnatural. Unmanly."

"Nothing good can come of him."

*When Sigyn finished and the uproar died down, Odin finally spoke.
He and his wife, Frigg, had sat silently among the clamor of the other
gods, Frigg looking troubled and thoughtful, Odin with his expression as
blank as those of the two ravens perched on either side of his chair. He
hadn't even moved, except to occasionally stroke his long gray beard in
thought, and his eye had not moved from Sigyn once.*

*"You've done well to come forward with this information," Odin said
at last, in his deep, quiet voice: a voice that made even the last whispers
still floating around the hall stop abruptly. When the All-father deigned
to speak, everyone listened.*

*Sigyn nodded and bowed her head as the gods murmured their agree-
ment. She looked sideways just the slightest bit—sad but resolute—to
regard her husband in the shadows.*

*"You can't do this," he'd pleaded with her earlier. "The children are
harmless—"*

*"It's not the children. It's her. I must tell them what she did to me,"
she'd replied, stone-faced. "I can't keep it in any longer. I will always be
your loyal wife, but I have other loyalties, too." Her expression had softened. "You don't know what she made me see. Even though I don't believe
that what she showed me will come to pass, she made it seem so . . . real.
The gods have to know she has this power. Odin has to know—"*

*"Then tell him. Only him. And leave the rest of the Aesir out of it.
Odin can be reasoned with, but you know how the rest of them can be."*

She'd shaken her head. "That's not what Freyja advised. She insisted I seek an audience with all the gods and goddesses. She said they all must know, for the safety of Asgard and all the realms."

"And you trust Freyja's counsel more than mine?"

"Right now?" The hard look in her eyes had returned. "I'm afraid I do."

And in the end, he couldn't stop her.

"So, what are we going to do about Loki's witch-wife and these monster-children of theirs?" Thor demanded loudly. The gods around him filled the hall with their loud voices once more, and Loki's mind snapped back to the present.

"Surely we can't let them get away with causing poor Sigyn such anguish," agreed Tyr. "And the children could be dangerous—"

"And surely," Freyja said, mostly to Odin, her eyes gleaming with avarice in the lantern light of the hall, "we must investigate the witch herself. Whatever vision she made Sigyn see, maybe she knows more. Maybe she knows—"

But Odin needed only hold up a hand to silence them. He stood from the high seat, giving Loki a sideways glance.

Loki stepped out of the shadows, holding up his hands. "Brother—"

"With me," Odin said, and left the hall. Loki followed him in silence, without looking at any of them—not even Sigyn, whose eyes he could feel on him with every step he took. As soon as they crossed the threshold into the cold night air, Loki shut the door behind them, and shouts erupted from inside the hall.

Odin led him across Asgard to his hall Valaskjalf, its silver-thatched roof shining in the moonlight. Loki continued to follow wordlessly and stood beside Odin as the highest of the gods sat down in his chair, from which he could see all the worlds. His two wolves rested at the foot of the chair, and raised their heads to acknowledge their master's return before fixing their eyes on Loki, who ignored them.

"Brother," Loki said again, unable to stay silent any longer. "Listen. The children—"

"I could never see her before," Odin said. "After she escaped the burning, I arranged for the only woman in Vanaheim who'd truly mastered the craft of seid to join us. And while Freyja has been an asset indeed, there are things even she cannot see, nor the Norns who arrived in the witch Gullveig's wake."

Loki did not know what to say to this.

Odin sat back in his chair. "When Gullveig was reborn from fire not once but twice, I knew that she was more powerful than I'd realized. But the commotion in Asgard that ensued after the Vanir's proclamation of war prevented me from tracking her down when she rose from her pyre the third time." He looked at Loki sideways with his one eye, pale blue and as cold as ice. "But you found her. You knew. You knew what I sought, and you withheld it from me."

Loki held up his hands pleadingly. "I—I knew who she was, yes, but I didn't understand what she was capable of. I know nothing of seid, brother. She kept the extent of her power from me. Until that night—the visions come to her in sleep, she says. I thought they were just dreams." It wasn't the whole truth, but he hoped it would be enough to convince Odin to drop the matter.

He didn't.

And the silence that followed his words was ominous indeed.

"It's as I feared," Odin said as he stood, resigned. "I thought her flight as Gullveig would have weakened her resolve, but I was mistaken. If burning her thrice wasn't enough, how could I command her in sleep? No, it seems to me that drastic measures must be taken . . ."

"What?" Loki asked, and then a horrible realization hit him. The chanter in Angrboda's dreams, the one she thought was Odin—she had been right after all.

"Brother, you must listen to me," Loki said quickly. "Angrboda, she's not—"

"Is that what she calls herself now? 'Sorrow-bringer'? A fitting name," Odin said, staring straight ahead.

"She's of no harm to anyone."

"Sigyn seems to feel the opposite."

"She'd do anything to protect her children. Both my wives would." That's why Sigyn had gone to the Aesir in the first place, after all, despite what Angrboda had told her that night. "The gods will forsake you in the end . . . brother will slay brother . . . your sons will suffer greatly at their hands . . ."

"Your unnatural children with the witch are another matter entirely. Some are calling for their deaths," said Odin, gesturing toward Gladsheim—the distant shouts from the council hall were audible from across Asgard.

Loki repressed a shudder and puffed out his chest. "My children with Angrboda are your kin as well, by our blood oath. Killing them would make you a kinslayer, and everyone knows this to be true."

Odin sighed and made to leave. "Yes, brother, in some ways my hands are tied. For your sake, I wish Sigyn had brought this matter to me privately. Now I must seek counsel from Mimir and the Norns."

"Brother, please—"

But Odin was already gone, leaving Loki with nothing but cold, creeping dread in his wake.

ODIN went first to Urd's well, at one of the three roots of Yggdrasil, the World Tree. There he found the Norns—Urd, Verdandi, and Skuld, the three sisters of fate—and relayed to them Sigyn's tale; he asked them what they knew about Loki's three children with the witch Angrboda.

The Norns told him little, but enough.

"*The mother is of a bad nature, and the father is worse still,*" said Urd.

"*They'll be the cause of much mischief and disaster among the gods,*" said Verdandi.

"*Great evil is to be expected from these three,*" finished Skuld.

"*How?*" Odin asked them. "*How will this happen?*"

But the Norns would speak no more.

So Odin thanked them and went on to Mimir's well, which lay at Yggdrasil's second root. Mimir had been decapitated as a hostage in the war, but Odin had smeared his severed head with herbs and chanted a spell over it, which preserved Mimir's knowledge and wisdom within it, as well as preventing it from decaying. Mimir was Odin's most valuable adviser; his counsel had always been unparalleled, so much so that Odin had given up an eye to drink from Mimir's well of wisdom.

But that was a long, long time ago.

When Odin came to that very well and spoke to Mimir of all that had come to pass, Mimir's advice was just as Odin had expected.

"*You cannot slay your blood brother's kin,*" said Mimir, "*but you can take them and place them where they will do the least harm.*"

Odin's eye glinted beneath the broad brim of his hat. "*And the mother?*"

WORLDS away, the mother in question awoke in a cold sweat, horror creeping like ice into every corner of her thrice-burned heart.

They're coming.

THE next evening, Angrboda was sitting in the clearing with Hel, watching the stars, while Fenrir and Jormungand sat inside in front of the fire. Hel had not said one word to her when she'd suggested that they go outside, nor when Angrboda had grabbed a pile of blankets and left the cave. Hel trailed behind her, sat down, and bundled herself up. It was very cold that night.

Every waking moment, Angrboda fought down the panic rising like bile in her throat. *They're coming. They're coming. They're coming.*

But she'd done everything she could think to do. Everything she possibly could. Her protection spell was stronger than ever, and no one but the only two people she trusted in all the Nine Worlds knew where to find her.

All she could do now was wait, and hope that her efforts had not been in vain.

It took every ounce of her strength to act like nothing was wrong—and for her children's sake, she had to.

Angrboda and Hel sat there in silence for a time, and every now and then the witch rubbed her hands together to keep them warm, until suddenly Hel shifted and pulled out a small bundle of something she'd been hiding under the blankets.

"What do you have there?" Angrboda asked.

"I made these for you, Mama," Hel said. For the first time since her birth, she seemed suddenly shy, and she handed over what appeared to be two *nalbinded* tubes. "They're like mittens, only I made them different for you. I made them so your fingers are free so you can wear them while you work. There's a space for your thumb to be free, too. See?"

Angrboda slid them on without hesitation. They were long enough to cover her second knuckle and reached halfway up her forearm, and fit so perfectly that she had all range of movement. She rolled her wrists and looked down at her hands.

"I wanted to make them perfect," Hel said, seeming worried by her mother's lack of response.

"They're wonderful," Angrboda whispered, touched, and wrapped her daughter in a sudden, smothering embrace.

"You better wear them," Hel said loudly, squirming.

"I'll treasure them," Angrboda said. "Thank you."

Hel made an annoyed sound, but Angrboda could tell that she was secretly very pleased.

"Do you see those two stars?" Angrboda asked, pointing, when they'd settled back down onto the blanket. "The brightest ones, just there?"

"The stars are *all* bright, Mama. We're at the edge of the worlds. Papa says everything is brighter here." Hel sounded extremely uninterested but climbed into Angrboda's lap in an attempt to see what her mother was seeing. "What about them?"

"Those are Skadi's father's eyes," Angrboda explained, hugging her tightly. "When he died, Odin made his eyes into stars for Skadi."

"The gods killed him," Hel said, ever unsmiling. "They killed him and then gave Skadi an unfair payment for his death. Papa has told us all the stories about them. I hate them."

Then Angrboda saw Fenrir stick his head out of the cave, his ears perked up. Before she could ask what he heard, Hel turned and looked at her, and in that moment Angrboda could have sworn her daughter had the look of someone who was a million years old or more.

"They're horrible and terrible and they break oaths and kill people," Hel said. "I don't know why anyone would look up to them."

"I ask myself that all the time," said a voice from the trees, and Loki stepped into the clearing. Gerd was beside him.

Angrboda's heart jolted at the sight of him as she remembered her dream—remembered how Loki had felt, as though she had been inside his mind. He'd fought for her, appealed to Odin on her behalf—but had he won? *Has he come to warn us, or has he led the gods straight to our door?*

Hel screamed, "Papa!" and ran for him, but Fenrir and Jormungand stayed put in the mouth of the cave, glowering.

Loki scooped Hel up into his arms, laughing. Angrboda rounded on Gerd and said in a very quiet, very furious voice, "*Why* did you bring him here?"

"I'm sorry," said Gerd, who was holding a skein of yarn in her shaking hands. She seemed ashamed to be faced with Angrboda's wrath. "I've just brought more yarn for Hel—"

"I've been looking for you for *weeks*, Boda," said Loki. "What happened?"

"I cut you out of my protection spell," Angrboda said, raising her chin.

Loki looked crestfallen, and Hel turned in his arms and glared at her, appearing horrified. "*Mama!* Why would you do that?"

Because we don't want him here. He thinks we're monsters, Fenrir said from the doorway, and Angrboda was silently grateful that at least one of her children shared her opinion. When she turned to regard him, the look in his eyes told her he felt the same—he was grateful for her keeping their father away. Jormungand inclined his head, as if agreeing.

"That's not true," Loki said to his son heatedly.

"I knew it!" Hel said, and hugged him around the neck.

I heard you say it, Fenrir shot back, then retreated into the cave. Jormungand gave them all a spiteful look and followed his brother inside.

Gerd looked back and forth between Loki and Angrboda and said, "I'll go put the yarn inside, then, and let you two have a moment. Perhaps I could try to comfort your boys, too."

"I would appreciate it," Angrboda said, and then turned to Loki. "You, however, need to leave."

"*No*, Mama, he's *staying*," said Hel, clinging to Loki.

"Gerd, would you mind keeping an eye on Hel as well?" Loki asked. "I should like to have a private conversation with my wife."

"You're leaving," said Angrboda. *Even if he hasn't led the gods to us—the longer he stays, the less safe we are.* "There is nothing you can say that I want to hear."

Hel wailed and fussed, but eventually Loki ended up prying her limbs from around him and handing her to Gerd, who carried her inside.

Loki turned to Angrboda then and said, "Shall we go down to the stream?"

"Oh yes, because I have such *fond* memories of conversation by the stream," Angrboda said. She did not want to go far from the cave, from her children—not after what she'd seen in her dreams the night before. Not without knowing whether the gods were stalking these very woods, searching for her. "Can we not talk right here?"

"You really want your children to overhear every obscenity you wish to spew at me? Fenrir can hear the grass grow."

Angrboda was willing to concede this. With one last glance at the cave, she sighed. "Fine. Lead the way. But make it quick."

And so he led her off, the same way they usually went to the stream. After all the times they'd gone there to get water, there truly existed a path now, weaving between the twisted trees. Now, at the end of autumn, the trees arching over the path were sparse and orange in color, and the moon was huge and yellow in the sky.

They did not walk as far downstream as they had the one night, for Angrboda stopped him about halfway there, unwilling to further increase the distance between herself and her children.

"Don't you want to sit on the rocks?" he asked her.

Angrboda put her hands up. "What is it that you want to talk about? I don't exactly have time for your nonsense. I'm busy trying to repair the damage your words caused our children. It has not been an easy task."

"What words?" Loki asked, confused. "My absence of late has been *your* fault—"

"Fenrir spoke the truth earlier. He heard what you said that night, about me being the 'mother of monsters.' And who are the monsters, then, do you think?"

Loki's face fell. "Oh *no*."

"I hope you're happy with yourself," Angrboda said, folding her arms.

"I feel terrible," he said, and put his hands on her shoulders.

Angrboda was unconvinced. "Because you said it, because he heard you, or because you even thought it in the first place?"

Loki mulled this over. "All three, really."

Angrboda took a step back, and he released her. She narrowed her eyes at him. "So, what did you have to say to me that you couldn't say within earshot of the children?"

By way of a response, he stepped forward, and she looked at him in suspicion. Then, in one fluid motion, he put his hands on her waist, pulled her close, and kissed her. For the sake of reminiscing about a time when things weren't nearly as broken as they were now, she relented; she kissed him back and put her arms around his neck.

She expected that when the kiss ended, she would look into his eyes and see that he was amused, or pensive, or perhaps as full of regret as she wished he would be. She expected that he would offer to leave Asgard and stay with her, with the children. She expected that maybe things would change. Such was the nature of this kiss.

Angrboda pulled away a bit and murmured against his lips, her anger temporarily softened, "I heard what you said to Odin. That's the only reason I came with you tonight. I saw Sigyn go to the gods and I saw you defend us. And then I saw Odin visit the Norns . . . and heard what they told him . . ." She closed her eyes and leaned her forehead against his cheek. "I know you tried. In Asgard. For us. I want so badly to forgive you and to trust you, but you understand that I cannot let you back into the protection spell now that the gods know what—"

But Loki tensed against her, and he said, in an odd, strangled voice, "Is that all you saw? Nothing after that?"

"Yes, that's all. What's wrong?" When Angrboda pulled away, she saw in his eyes something she had never before seen there—he looked like the very ground beneath him was caving in. She made to pull away farther, but he kept her locked in their embrace.

"I'm sorry, Boda," he whispered, brushing her nose with his as he always did.

Angrboda twisted her face away. "Loki—"

"I'm so, so sorry," he said again.

And that was when she heard Hel scream.

She broke free in an instant, looking at him with such complete disgust and loathing that he visibly recoiled.

She very much wanted to strike him then. But instead, she ran—and without slowing down, she ripped the covering from her head and tossed it into the underbrush, letting her hair fly free, streaming long and loose behind her.

She cared little where the kerchief landed, a fine gift though it had been.

She was no longer married.

She wouldn't need it again.

Her feet carried her automatically back down the path, one step after another. She heard a loud hiss, the high-pitched whining of a wolf, her frightened little girl still screaming—her fists pumped; her feet moved faster—

"Mama, look out!" she heard Hel cry, but too late.

Just as she entered the clearing, a bolt of golden light hit her across the face, sending her reeling backward, dashing her head against a tree. She could feel the blood drip down her cheek and could not see, for the light had been so bright as to momentarily blind her, and the back of her head was throbbing and she could feel blood dripping down her scalp—

As she struggled to regain her footing, she suddenly felt a cord across her waist and arms, pinning her to the tree—but she wriggled her arms free, fearing the worst for her children, whom she could hear struggling still—

Then someone from behind her pulled the cord tighter and secured it, and then grabbed one of her wrists, and then the other, and tied them together behind the tree.

No. No. No. She struggled as hard as she could, summoning all the strength she could muster, to no avail. So she squeezed her eyes shut and whispered a few hasty, furtive chants, pouring all the energy she had into the words, but it was like talking to a stone— like someone had put up a wall, blocking her magic from having any effect on the world around her.

A fellow witch had cursed these bonds of hers—she could feel the magic, so familiar to her somehow, almost like she knew the person who had wrought the spells. Power pulsed through the ropes around her wrists and strengthened the cord securing her to the tree at the waist.

The person who'd crafted these ropes had bewitched them to restrain her specifically. To negate *her* magic. And there was naught she could do to fight it.

By this time the stars had left Angrboda's eyes, and she could see the scene before her by the light of the moon.

The scene she'd always feared.

A massive man with a red beard and steel blue eyes was holding the end of a huge, writhing, hissing sack, which Angrboda knew contained her youngest child, and she knew the man to be Thor by the hammer at his belt. There was a second man, who had dark hair and a dark beard and a sword at his hip; he had muzzled Fenrir and put a huge, thick collar around the wolf's neck and held on to it now. Fenrir had stopped whining and stared at his mother piteously. Angrboda realized in a second that these must be magical objects indeed to be able to restrain her sons.

The third man—brown-haired, golden-eyed, slightly smaller than the first two and with a thinner beard—looked very uncomfortable in his task: holding on to a twisting, sobbing five-year-old girl.

"What's wrong with that one, Frey?" Thor asked loudly, nodding at Hel. "She doesn't look like a monster."

Angrboda then knew the man who was holding her daughter, for Loki had mentioned him once in passing a very long time ago: Freyja's younger brother. Frey was looking more uneasy with each passing second.

"There is *nothing* wrong with her," Angrboda hissed. "There's nothing wrong with any of them. Release them now. Do what you will to me, but release them."

"I'm afraid not," said the man restraining Fenrir, giving her a stony look.

"I'm surprised the wolf didn't put up more of a fight, Tyr," said Thor.

Tyr's face remained impassive. Angrboda knew of him; some

said he was the son of a giant; others said he was the son of Odin. She was inclined to believe the latter this night.

"My children are innocent," Angrboda said vehemently, but her tone was desperate, and her voice cracked. "They haven't done you or anyone else any harm. And if you leave them here with me, they never will. I promise you."

Thor snorted, keeping a firm hold on the sack with his gloved hands. Though Jormungand was still flailing madly, the god didn't even flinch. "Leave them with *you*? All the way out here, where you could be teaching them who knows what? I think not, witch. The creatures come with us."

"If you cooperate, we may even do you the kindness of killing you before we go," said Tyr.

Hel started to sob more loudly upon hearing this, and Angrboda could not bring herself to tell her daughter that everything was going to be all right.

That would make me a liar, and lying is her father's job.

"Perhaps we should do as she says," said Frey. "At least with the girl. Thor is right—nothing seems to be wrong with her."

"It's her legs, under those stockings of hers. They're dead," said a woman's voice, and Freyja stepped out from behind the tree to which Angrboda was tied. "Or so your wife has told us, brother."

Angrboda raised her eyebrows in shock at the sight of the goddess—her pupil of old, recognizable even after all this time—but her surprise quickly gave way to scorn.

Of course that's why the energy in these ropes feels so familiar.

Of course she knew how to bind me.

She's familiar with my magic, so she had to make sure I couldn't fight back.

"Well played, *sister*," Angrboda said frostily. They'd used to call each other such, back in Vanaheim. Sister witches. But not for an age, and they would no longer. "This is magic skillfully woven. I hadn't expected it of you."

Freyja tossed her bloodred hair and smiled. "When the All-father told me it was you I'd be fighting, I came prepared, *Gullveig.*" Her necklace was the same golden color as her eyes, and both glinted ominously in the moonlight. "I am not the only one here tonight who was not unlike your sister once, I'm afraid."

"Can't you help me? Can't you calm her down? You *know* her," Frey was saying to someone in the shadows.

"Perhaps your new wife has worn out her usefulness," Thor said derisively, "eh, Frey?"

Angrboda turned. Frey had been pleading with a woman who had just come out of the cave, looking like she was actively trying to disappear. But Angrboda knew her as well, and this recognition came along with a suffocating wave of betrayal.

It was Gerd.

She has her hair covered now, Angrboda realized in horror as Gerd went to stand beside Frey. *I haven't seen her since I last saw Loki, and that's why. She married one of them since then. I should have known; I should have suspected.*

"I'm sorry, I'm sorry, I'm *sorry,*" Gerd said when she noticed Angrboda staring at her. She rushed forward but was held back by Freyja; the words spilled out of her nevertheless. "It was sudden—one day I was in Jotunheim and then I was married to Frey, and I didn't have a choice; it was all—"

"This isn't happening," Angrboda whispered to herself.

"And Sigyn finally went and told Odin about you and your children," Gerd went on, crying now, "and said she saw me that night as well, so he asked me what I knew, and I *couldn't* lie to him—"

"This witch here seems every bit as wild as Sigyn described," Tyr observed.

"I wonder which sort of giantess she is," said Thor, examining Angrboda through narrowed eyes. "She may not be as ugly as some, or as beautiful as others. It's hard to tell *what* to do with this one. Trust a mate of Loki's to confuse us."

Mate, Angrboda thought spitefully. *Like Loki cannot have a wife or a lover, because he's an animal and I'm an animal.*

"Agreed. Look at her, hissing and spitting just like her snake-child," said Tyr, but he didn't seem very confused as to which *sort* of giantess he thought Angrboda was.

"Do you think she's mad?"

"She'd have to be, to lie with Loki willingly."

"She's not Sigyn, that's for sure," said Thor.

"Let me go now and I'll show you just *how* unlike Sigyn I can be," Angrboda spat. "You have no right to—"

"Quiet, witch, or my hammer will silence you," Thor growled.

Angrboda could only glare at him in response, for she fully believed the threat. Though she didn't know if she was scared of it.

As long as she was still breathing, there was a chance she could talk them out of this. There was a chance she could *do* something. But the bonds were tight—and hot, burning the bare skin of her wrists.

"Speaking of Loki," Tyr said, "where *did* he slither off to?"

"I'm right here," Loki said tonelessly as he came up the path. He looked at her for a fraction of a second—just enough for her to see him notice her and her pain and her loose hair and to quickly mask his own grief with an empty expression—before he averted his eyes.

Angrboda saw then just how much of the odd man out he truly was when compared with the gods present: Thor, Tyr, and Frey were all three of them large and muscular and bearded. While tall—nearly of a height with Frey, the shortest of the three gods—

Loki was thin and lithe and clean-shaven and looked rather scrawny in comparison. His expression of unhappiness was also at odds with the satisfaction evident on the faces of the gods and Freyja—with Frey once again being the exception, as he still seemed quite uncomfortable with the situation.

"Papa!" Hel exclaimed when she saw Loki, wriggling more violently, trying to free herself from Frey. "Papa, help us! They're going to take us away!"

Shut up, stupid. He's not going to help us, Fenrir said. *He's one of them. He's just as bad as they are.*

All four of the gods looked at him, wide-eyed.

"It can talk," said Thor.

"In our heads," said Tyr.

"Most interesting," said Freyja, but Frey just looked even more troubled.

"Can we just go?" said Loki. "You have what you came for. Let's leave this place."

Hel gasped at those words and her huge eyes widened further, again filling with tears. Loki would not look at her.

"Why did we even need him for this, anyway?" Thor asked Tyr. "Couldn't Gerd have just led us here herself? If he's just going to stand here and whine—"

"We needed him to distract the mother, remember?" said Tyr. "And he failed."

"I could have just bashed in her skull in the first place," Thor muttered, seeming almost disappointed that he hadn't gotten the chance to.

"Is that so? You were the distraction?" Angrboda said to Loki. "Thor has the right of it—he could have taken care of me swiftly enough, but they made you play a part in this as well? To add insult to injury?" She shook her head. "You gods are cruel indeed."

"I didn't have a choice," Loki said under his breath. "If I wished to remain among the Aesir—"

"I see. So it *was* your choice." Angrboda spat at his feet. "I wish I could conjure words vile enough to describe you."

Loki pursed his scarred lips and looked away.

"You won't be conjuring anything anytime soon, witch," said Tyr. "Just because Loki is the All-father's brother—"

"You are *not* his brother," Angrboda said to Loki, who did not turn back to her again. "And I am not your wife. You do me a disservice by taking my children and leaving me alive to mourn them."

"You would do well to be silent," Loki said quietly. Pleadingly.

"She's asking for it," Thor said. "Go on, then, Loki. Take Tyr's seax and do it. She's *your* wife. Do her a favor. Put her out of her misery."

"*Enough,*" said Freyja, wrinkling her nose. "You remember what the All-father said. Leave her be, and let's go. It's bad business to kill a kinsman's wife, troll-woman or not."

"It's as you say. I tire of this anyway," Thor said, hoisting the bag over his shoulder. "Let us return to Asgard. I'm missing a most excellent feast for this monster-children nonsense. And, Frey, you had better keep that girl *quiet.*"

Hel let out a loud sob and shrieked, *"No!"*

Angrboda once again lurched forward against her bonds, incensed by her daughter's screaming. "Tell them, Loki. Tell them that your children aren't monsters. Tell them to stop this madness and give my babies back to me."

Loki looked to her again, but his expression was vacant. Tyr and Thor exchanged amused glances and Freyja folded her arms and rolled her eyes. Frey looked yet more anxious, because Gerd was still sobbing and Hel was screaming now, and he was responsible for them both.

"We don't hurt anyone," Angrboda said, still appealing to Loki. Tears were beginning to stream freely down her face now, and she was shaking so forcefully that the gods might have thought that she was still struggling to free herself. "We *never* hurt anyone, and you know it. We mind our own business. Tell them. *Please.*"

"I told you," Loki said simply, "that I was sorry."

"If you ever held any love for me at all, you would do this," Angrboda whispered. "You would tell them."

But Loki said nothing and turned from her once more.

Thor dragged the writhing sack away first; then Tyr followed, leading Fenrir, who gave his mother a last lingering look and whimpered loudly. Angrboda started struggling anew, screaming, *"No, no, no,"* and Gerd dashed away after Tyr and Thor, no longer able to bear looking at the scene she'd helped create.

Frey was struggling to pick Hel up—she squirmed aggressively, trying to get back to her mother.

"Mama, I'll be good, I'll be good!" she sobbed, reaching for Angrboda. "Don't let them do this, Mama! I promise, I won't be bad ever again! I'll be nice to my brothers and I'll eat all my dinner *all the time* and I'll talk more, I swear! I'll even go to bed when you tell me to! I'll be better! I promise!"

"I can't do this," Frey said, his expression bleak, but he did not release Hel.

"Come, brother," Freyja called back to him. "She's only a child. Throw her over your shoulder and be done with it."

Loki pushed him aside and said thickly, *"Give her to me,"* and gathered up his daughter into his arms, where she clung to him for dear life. Then he marched after the rest of the gods and did not look back.

The last Angrboda saw of her daughter were those tearful green eyes as she screamed over her father's shoulder.

Angrboda's chest started to heave as she gasped for breath, trying to keep herself from dissolving into sobs, part of her not believing what had just happened, another part trying to be strong for her daughter—but her daughter was gone and her sons as well, and her mind was racing, and this *couldn't be happening.*

But as she struggled, she felt Freyja's bonds begin to loosen. Hope welled up in her chest as she fought harder, summoning every bit of magic she had within her. The cords cut painful red lines into her wrists as she strained—her head began to pound so hard she felt her skull would burst—she could feel hot blood trickling from her nose, snaking down her upper lip and into her mouth, its sharp copper tang on her tongue—

Hel was still screaming. Angrboda was still screaming, too—*"No, no, no."*

And suddenly Thor reappeared in the clearing. He cast a brief look over his shoulder to make sure that the others had gone on, and then studied Angrboda with the same disconcerting lack of emotion that Tyr and Loki had before.

The bonds were starting to slip as she struggled. Thor saw this, and his expression hardened.

Angrboda didn't notice the way he was looking at her, as though she were a wounded animal who needed to be killed for mercy. She was close, *so close*, to escaping, almost there—but then Thor moved toward her.

"You *are* different," he said, more to himself than to her. "Different than the other giant-wives I've slain, so I'm not sure slaying you is the right thing to do. But my father says there's no other way. You're too dangerous to live."

She looked up at him, wide-eyed, pleading, shouting. "Please, you—"

But Thor raised his hammer high and brought it down, silencing her with a swift blow to the head.

The last thing she saw was the brief look of uncertainty that flashed across his face just before the stroke fell and Mjolnir made fatal contact with her temple.

Crack.

At Angrboda's voice being cut off so abruptly, Hel stopped crying and let out a horrified gasp—and even Loki hesitated, a look of shock frozen on his face. Fenrir ceased straining against Tyr's iron grip and emitted a high-pitched, pitiful whine. Jormungand began to writhe so fiercely in the sack that he almost escaped, but Thor stormed over at the last moment and took the sack from Frey, who had been struggling with it in his absence.

"M-Mama?" Hel whispered, breaking the long silence that followed the sudden absence of her mother's cries. Her breathing was shallow, her fingertips blue from exertion.

"Hush," Loki whispered back. "You must calm down, Hel, or you'll be ill. Your mama will be just f—"

But the child would not be stilled.

"What have they done to her? What have they done? Mama!" Hel wailed, over and over again. Her shrieks echoed through the empty, dead forest as they walked, and now not even Loki could silence her.

ANGRBODA slumped to her knees and fell forward onto her face.

It occurred to her that perhaps her bonds had been cut now that she was dead, but no—that was not so. She was cold. Very cold.

And she wasn't breathing, and she didn't know if she could even move, but she could feel the ground beneath her. The dirt of the clearing where she lay, facedown. She felt something wet on the side of her head but felt no pain.

What's going on? How am I—?

And then she knew. Sickened, she *knew.*

"Rise, Seeress," she was commanded, "and tell me what you know."

Her fingers clutched the dirt as she struggled to lift her head, her wild hair parting just enough for her to make out the man who towered over her.

The world around him was colorless, muted—as if she were seeing it through a fog—and completely and disturbingly silent save for the man's voice. She was still just outside her home, but she knew she could not really be there. The trees of Ironwood looked even grayer now, as if all traces of color had been washed away. The leaves blew too slowly. And when she glanced over her shoulder, her physical body was still there, tied to the tree, unmoving.

The man was the only thing she saw with any definition; he was clear as day. In another world, a raven was perched on each shoulder, and he was flanked by a pair of wolves. But the creatures were back in the same world as the trees and the grass and the cave, and the man himself was the only one there with her. He had many names, but not one came to mind.

The two of them were the only ones in this place.

Angrboda rose to her knees and looked at him blankly, somehow seeing with her dead-white eyes. The man wore a traveling cloak, which hid any features of his body; his height was imposing, if not extraordinary. His long beard was gray with hints of red still remaining, and one cold blue eye was fixed on her from under the broad brim of his tall pointed hat.

The name came to her then: Odin.

He spoke again. Angrboda didn't understand him—at least not on the surface. But something within her understood: He'd finally won. She was at the edge of the void now, staring down into the never-ending darkness.

His words pushed her over the edge and dragged her down, screaming, into the void. Her surroundings faded to black—even the man in front of her disappeared—and other images took their place. She was sinking. Falling.

"What do you see?" asked his voice from very far away, and against her will she began to speak—ancient words, sacred words.

And she told him everything.

THEN she was back in Ironwood, slack against her loosened bonds. Crusted blood under her nose and on the side of her head, matting her hair. A cut on the opposite temple from where she'd been knocked off guard the first time. Burns around her wrists from her fetters. But no pain. Only the cold.

Alive. Still alive. Or as alive as she had always been: in a sense.

And for nine days and nine nights she remained tied to the tree.

She lingered there in the darkness, somewhere between consciousness and oblivion: somewhere where the emptiness was comforting and naught could harm her, for she didn't have to think or feel a thing. Sometimes it seemed she could hear voices calling to her, but they were too far off and nearly indistinguishable and she didn't *care*, for they spoke only her name and her name was of no interest to her.

Visions flashed before her eyes when she surfaced enough, just before she sank back down: *Little Hel in Asgard, dressed in a fine green gown long enough to cover her legs and the thick stockings her mama had sewn for her. She was slouching near the outside of a hall. Her eyes darted this way and that, and she turned a pebble over in her hands without looking at it, picking at its surface with her short nails.*

No nalbinding and no wolf toy to keep her hands busy, and her mind would not calm down.

Suddenly a ball rolled around the corner of the building, and Hel gasped and jumped away into the shadows. A young beardless man came running over to fetch it. Hel could hear his friends shouting a little ways away. He had a stick in his hand, and he was blond and bright-eyed. When he bent to pick up the ball and saw her, he smiled. "Oh! Hello there."

Hel just swallowed, and her small shoulders shook.

He cocked his head at her, concerned. "Are you all right?"

Hel was silent.

"Are you new here?" he asked. "What's your name? I don't think we've met."

"Oi, come on!" one of the other young men called. "What's taking so long? Did you wander into the wolf's gaping jaws?" The others laughed.

Hel bristled at the mention of her brother—and in such mocking tones. No one talked about her family like that. Were she not so terrified of everything in this strange world of the gods, she would march over and punch those stupid boys in the face. But at least their words, however scornful, meant that Fenrir was still here.

That was more than she could say for her other baby brother. She had no idea what they'd done with Jormungand.

"Coming!" the young man called over his shoulder. He tossed the ball in the air once and caught it, then turned to leave.

"Hel," said Hel. When the boy turned to ask what she meant, she stammered, "M-my name. It's Hel."

"It's good to meet you, little Hel," he said with a dazzling smile.

"Come on, Baldur!" cried another one of his friends, and then a few

others yelled his name. "We want to finish this round before nightfall! You'll make us lose!"

Baldur took something out of his pocket—a golden apple—and tossed it to Hel. She dropped the stone and caught the apple in surprise, and he grinned at her and said, "Welcome to Asgard."

Just then her father came around the side of the hall and said, "Hel? There you are." His eyes flitted between her and Baldur before resting on the latter and narrowing. "Run along. She doesn't have time to play with you."

Baldur's eyes narrowed in return, but only slightly; he knew not to argue with his father's blood brother. He nodded once, gave Hel another fleeting smile, and dashed back around the corner to rejoin his friends.

Hel turned to Loki as he knelt before her, and her small, shrill voice was shaky as she gestured angrily with the apple. "Papa! We were having a conversation."

"Were you? It seemed a little one-sided to me," Loki said. He took the apple from her and threw it aside, and when she made an indignant sound, he said, "It won't do you any good anyway."

Hel stuck out her lower lip.

Loki smiled thinly. "I didn't expect to be having to talk about boys with you for another ten winters yet, at least. Then again, you did have a full vocabulary before your second . . ." But despite his playful tone, he seemed shaken. Almost as much as his daughter was.

The Aesir had been in talks for hours now and had finally dismissed him to make their final judgment in private. He was reckoned among the gods only when it suited them—and in this instance, it did not.

Hel sniveled, sensing his distress. She had never seen her father like this before: so on edge, so close to breaking. He was able to keep up his mask of nonchalance in front of the gods, of course. But in front of his only daughter, it was finally starting to crumble.

"Papa," said Hel, "what's going to happen to me? Why won't they let *me see my brothers? Where's Mama?" She swallowed and screwed up her reddening face, preparing to wail. "I want Mama! What did they do to her?"*

"Listen to me," he said, taking her by the shoulders, looking her in the eye. It was so much harder to lie that way, but lie he must. "Mama is fine. Your brothers are fine. Everything is going to be all right."

"Do you promise?"

"I promise. I just need you to be brave. Be brave and keep your chin up. So long as you do that, you'll always remember who you are. And so will everyone else."

Hel sniffled. "Who I am?"

"Yes. Who you are. Sometimes it's all you have, so you should never let anyone make you feel ashamed of it." Loki tapped two fingers under her chin, lifted it. "There, now. You look just like your mama." His voice faltered on the last two words.

In front of the gods, his straight face betrayed only what was expected of him, and only when appropriate: the exact amount of anger that a man was justified to have when others decided the fates of his kin. But it was different for him because he knew that he could not do a thing. His anger was a show, covering something he could never, would never, let them see.

She could not bear this vision anymore. In her physical body she felt something wet freeze on her face and despaired, for tears meant she truly was still alive. This, above even the theft of her children, seemed to her to be the greatest injustice: that they had not managed to destroy her and put her out of her misery.

She wished so badly that all her sorrows would be over, that all her tears would be spent. But the witch was not so lucky.

Hel was somewhere dark now, her green dress torn and stained, her little dead legs wobbly—she was afraid to peel off her stockings and look at the flesh beneath, for she felt a bit odd, even more so than usual.

The man on the eight-legged horse had left her there, and his form was vanishing into the fog. She did not miss him. Even if she were all alone down here, she would rather be alone than with him. She hated him. His people had taken her and her brothers away from her mama, and he himself had taken her away from her papa.

The ground shifted beneath her and she yelped and hopped away and looked around in panic. There was nothing in sight save for yet more fog in the distance—the bridges they'd crossed were so far away, but perhaps if she continued forward she could reach the far-off, jagged cliffs, perhaps find a cave in which to find shelter for the night—but was it night?

Wasn't it always night in Niflheim? That's where they said they were taking her, even though she wasn't dead. Even though she was only a small girl, and so very scared. Even though her papa had been yelling for her and holding on to her for as long as he could before the one-eyed man had ripped her from his grasp and shouted something, and her papa had shouted back, but she didn't know what they had said because she'd been screaming.

Something grabbed her foot and she shrieked. An entire skeleton was dragging itself out of the ground, and more of them beyond it. The fog started to form into shadowy shapes, getting closer, circling her.

There was no way out.

Hel batted the thing away from her foot and stood, screeched. The skeleton was made of dirt, animated by the shades, for there were no bodies in Niflheim: only souls. And the rest of the shadowy figures were closing in, their dark hands reaching for her—the ground roiled like the sea during a storm, dead things churning below the dirt. Rising.

Rising to get her. Monsters in the endless night.

And then suddenly two solid forms joined the fray: one prowling toward her on the ground, the other circling in the air. She saw the wolf Garm's slavering maw as he approached, felt the blast of air from Nidhogg's wings as the dragon landed.

They rounded on her, the monsters and the dead. The dragon's nostrils flared. The wolf growled. The shades reached for her, and she squeezed her eyes shut, held her hands out to bat at them, but her fingers slipped right through their smoky forms and they just kept coming. She could not fight them, but she could feel their ghostly touch and it made her skin crawl. Why could she feel them and not the other way around? It wasn't fair. Her knees started to buckle.

"Get away from me!" she cried, spinning frantically, her hands still outstretched. "Get away, get away, GET AWAY!"

A burst of air erupted from all around her in a circle, knocking the dead things back.

Hel stood there, trembling. When she finally opened her eyes, the dead were all back on their feet, though they had withdrawn into a small ring around her. Even Nidhogg and Garm had stopped their advance. They looked confused and perhaps even a little frightened.

Garm wiped his snout with a paw and lowered his head, and Nidhogg's nostrils flared again, his orange eyes burning. He was wary.

They were all wary of her now.

Maybe she had just done sorcery. Maybe her mama and that awful woman with the gold necklace weren't the only ones who could do it— maybe Hel could, too. She looked down at her palms, and then back at the hosts of Niflheim.

And she lifted her chin.

THE last thing Angrboda remembered was what she'd told Odin. The prophecy. The end.

She saw it again and again, and she could not look away.

Baldur, son of Odin, shining god of Asgard, is slain by a sprig of mistletoe sharpened to a deadly point, shot right through the heart by his own brother, and thus begins the end.

Loki, bound in torment—for what? She sees not.

Three years of winter with no summer in between. In Midgard, the bonds of kinship and social order begin to break. Wars erupt over dwindling resources. Many are slaughtered in this savage sword age of men.

A loud sound echoes through all the worlds and the bonds holding back the forces of chaos break. Loki is free, and so are his sons.

The wolves that chase the sun and moon finally catch their quarry, and the worlds go dark and all the stars go out.

Garm barks loudly at Hel's gate. Yggdrasil trembles.

The gods march to battle against the giants. Loki crews a ship of the dead. The gods and giants fight and kill each other. The Midgard Serpent makes for Thor, the Great Wolf for Odin. All four fall.

Surt approaches from the south with his fiery sword and sets all aflame.

A green new world rises from the ashes, and the dragon Nidhogg circles overhead.

The witch saw no more as she sank back down.

PART II

TIME PASSED AS SHE LINGERED BETWEEN LIFE and death. An eternity could have gone by and she would not have known; the end of the worlds could have come to pass and it would have meant little to her, for she knew what was going to happen now. All of it. She hadn't been able to look away this time.

I saw my sons die.

She'd told it all to Odin, and now it seemed to her that perhaps her time as Angrboda was over and done—that she would pass out of this role just as she had done with Gullveig. And what then? A true death, she hoped. She'd foreseen so much death already. Why should she remain alive to watch it all unfold?

I'll stay here forever.

Nothing mattered anymore. Not without her children.

It's not fair to them. They didn't do anything to deserve this. This isn't the way things are supposed to be.

Something tingled at the very edge of her consciousness: small but sharp, like a pinprick.

Oh, but maybe it is, said a voice, so soft that it seemed to be echoing from the deepest recesses of her mind. It was achingly familiar, like something out of a dream she'd forgotten long ago. *The question is, what are you going to do about it?*

Nothing. I can't do anything. I'm no one. I'm nothing. Just a sad old witch who's had everything taken from her. Betrayed by her husband. Deprived of her children. Forsaken by all.

Not all, the voice replied. *You know this. Even now, she calls you back. Do you hear her?*

"Angrboda," a different voice shouted, but it was muffled, as if she were hearing it from underwater. "Angrboda, are you here? Are you—no. *No!*"

The pinprick in the back of her mind turned into a pull—not a forcible one, not like Odin's pull when he'd dragged her out and forced her down, but a gentle touch that steered her in the general direction of consciousness.

"No, no, no . . . Please . . . wake up . . ."

Come now, the voice said, and Angrboda felt herself being hauled up through the darkness of an endless sea to a pinhole of light at the surface. The light got brighter as she rose, but she could not see who or what was pulling her.

She resisted. She was safe here. Up there was where everything went wrong. Down here, she could remain nothing and no one for as long as she pleased. She *never* had to go back.

"Wake up," a woman's voice pleaded. Angrboda could hear it more clearly now, could hear the anguish in the words. "Please, *please* wake up . . ."

It's time to rise, the voice said, still gently guiding her upward, and the light became brighter still. *She's waiting for you.*

Soon enough she felt the prickling sensation of her limbs awakening, felt that awful heartbeat again, felt the hair hanging in her face, felt the blood crusted around her nostrils and mouth. As she surfaced she let out a quiet, agonized sob but did not open her eyes.

"You're alive," said the woman's voice, rising an octave in relief. Angrboda felt a calloused hand gently lift her chin, and she felt almost comforted by the touch. She tried dimly to connect the voice with a person.

The other woman's fingers moved across her face to the side of her head, to softly brush aside the hair from the bloody crater at the witch's temple, where Thor's hammer had hit home. The woman let out a strangled gasp and a stream of curse words at the sight of it, and Angrboda's brain suddenly put a name to the voice: *Skadi.*

Angrboda's arms and legs wouldn't move. She screwed her eyes shut. Her head was pounding, *throbbing,* and it hurt so much that she wished she were still asleep so she didn't have to feel it. She tried to murmur something, but Skadi only said, "Shh. Don't talk. I need to cut you down. I heard Freyja made these bonds especially so *you* couldn't break out of them, but I wonder if that goes for anyone else who gives it a try."

"Leave me here to die," Angrboda finally managed. Her voice was barely a whisper and sounded alien to her own ears.

She heard Skadi scoff as she unsheathed her hunting knife. "Shut up."

There was the sound of snow cracking under leather shoes, the snapping of cords; Skadi's knife had indeed managed the task. Angrboda felt the bonds loosen and she fell forward, but Skadi broke her fall and gathered her up into her arms like a child. Angrboda's eyelids fluttered as Skadi carried her over the threshold into her cave, and she got a glimpse of her clearing and the barren trees beyond: all covered in a layer of snow, just like herself.

She felt herself being set down on her own bed, heard the sounds of Skadi starting a fire in the center hearth, then felt her clothing being cut away. Angrboda didn't even flinch, for her dress was frozen stiff and she knew that if it was still on her when it thawed the dampness would only make her colder. When Skadi was done and had cast the remains of the dress aside, she took to swaddling her friend in furs.

Angrboda's hands and feet continued to prickle painfully as more feeling returned to them. She heard water being poured into the cauldron over the hearth, and then a short time later felt a warm, wet cloth dab tenderly near her temple, but she did not open her eyes.

"I can see your skull. It should be broken. How are you still alive?" Skadi murmured. When she had cleaned away the blood to her satisfaction, she applied some sort of poultice to it, hands shaking—whether from rage or distress, Angrboda couldn't tell. The poultice was undoubtedly something from Angrboda's own stores; Skadi knew the witch's tinctures well from having traded them for so long.

Angrboda felt a hand lightly brush the ice out of her hair, then her eyelashes, and the rough fingertips lingered on her cheek. She opened her eyes to slits and saw Skadi, her face ruddy and windblown, leaning over her.

The Huntress pulled her hand back and a smile, full of relief, tugged at one corner of her mouth.

"Welcome back to the Nine Worlds," she said. She'd been sitting next to Angrboda on the bed but eased herself onto the stool at the witch's bedside. Angrboda immediately missed her warmth but said nothing; there was only one thing on her mind.

She closed her eyes again and asked, "What has become of my children?"

"You should rest before you hear the answer to that question," Skadi said. "Gain back some of your strength. They're alive—that should comfort you. Get some sleep and I'll go hunt some game for dinner. I know you have dried meat in your stores, but I think broth would do you better in this state."

The last thing Angrboda felt like doing was eating. "I've been sleeping for some time already. I'm not tired."

"You weren't sleeping, though, were you?" Skadi asked, studying her. "You were . . . somewhere else."

"I wasn't. I was asleep," Angrboda insisted. But her lie sounded weak to her own ears, and she knew Skadi didn't believe her.

"No one gets tired enough to just *sleep* for nine days and nine nights. Let alone someone who's—who's been through what you've just been through, my friend."

Nine days. How could she have let herself stay in the dark place for so long? If only she'd come to sooner. If only she'd been able to *do* something.

When Angrboda didn't reply, Skadi braced her hands on her knees and hauled herself to a standing position.

"I'm going to go catch dinner, then," she said at length, then gave Angrboda a stern look. "Don't go anywhere."

Angrboda only blinked at her. Between her head wound and her half-frozen body, she was hardly fit to move about, and she said as much. She could barely even lift her head, let alone walk out of the cave on her own.

"That's not what I meant, and you know it," Skadi said darkly as she donned her kaftan and lashed it closed with her belt. "I won't be long."

Angrboda moved her eyes to the ceiling as she heard Skadi

leave. Her mind went back to some of the visions she'd experienced while she'd been under: Hel in Asgard. Then Hel in Niflheim. Her daughter's confusion, her fear, her *power*.

She closed her eyes.

Was I seeing the truth of things, or was my grieving mind playing tricks on me?

Skadi would be able to confirm her worst fears soon enough.

THE next time Angrboda opened her eyes, Skadi was carefully lifting her head onto her lap and holding a bowl of broth to her lips, urging her to drink. Angrboda was still not hungry, but the broth was hot and she appreciated the warmth.

"What has become of my children?" she asked again when she was finished.

Skadi put the bowl down on the stool beside the bed without removing Angrboda's head from her lap. "I was out hunting with Ull at the time—he's a stepson of Thor's. We were out in Midgard until the day before yesterday. But as soon as I heard, I pressed Frey for details of what had transpired and came here straightaway when he told me."

Angrboda nodded. Frey was Skadi's stepson and had been the only one among the gods to display any sort of discomfort with their actions that night.

Skadi had paused. Angrboda gave her an expectant look, but the other woman only looked away and balled her fists and said, "I should've been there. I could've *saved* you, and the children, too."

"I doubt that very much," Angrboda said gently. "It seems to me that nothing could have stopped them. Don't trouble yourself with such thoughts."

"So you forgive me?" Skadi's head whipped down to face her. "For not being there?"

"My friend, there is nothing to forgive. I promise you that. Now, please, continue."

Skadi swiped at her eyes and seemed to regain her composure.

"The children were brought before Odin," she said. "Jormungand was cast into the sea first thing, and Frey swore he saw your son grow larger as they watched. So he is not dead."

Angrboda nodded again, expressionless. *I know. It's not his time . . . yet.*

Skadi inhaled sharply through her nose before continuing. "They're not quite sure what to do with Fenrir, for he, too, has grown in these past nine days. The gods have decided to keep him close in Asgard, where they can keep an eye on him until he becomes too much to handle. No one will go near him but brave Tyr, who feeds him, and your husband doesn't even dare go within his sight for fear that Fenrir will kill him. Your son holds no love for his father." She hung her head. "I tried to approach him myself, but it's clear he thinks I'm one of *them.* That I betrayed you, as Gerd did, though nothing could be further from the truth."

"And what will they do with him later, when they cannot stand to have him there any longer?" Angrboda asked, even though she already knew that, too; she'd seen Fenrir breaking free of *something* in her vision.

"Your husband or your son?"

"My son," said Angrboda. "I have no husband."

Skadi started, but then a look of approval flashed across her face before being quickly replaced by a sober expression more befitting their conversation. "What will happen then is anybody's guess."

"Jormungand cast into the sea and Fenrir trapped indefinitely,"

Angrboda whispered. Something was nagging at her. But then her stomach twisted itself into a knot, and she asked a question to which she already knew the answer: "What of Hel?"

Skadi took a deep breath. "Frey said she was quiet on the way to Asgard because it was Loki who carried her. She did not let go of him even for a second, and he did not speak to her except to try comforting her, and that seemed to work until they separated the children. Once they rid themselves of Jormungand and made sure Fenrir was safely muzzled, they had to decide what to do with Hel."

She seemed to be bracing herself for the next bit, and Angrboda waited.

"And then Odin himself tore her from Loki's arms." Skadi finally looked at her then. "They cast her down into Niflheim, body and all. I understand Odin has granted her jurisdiction over the dead, being half-dead herself."

"Of course," Angrboda said, eyes closed. The last pieces had fallen into place. This was her vision of the end times: the massive serpent rising from the waves and the huge wolf breaking its bonds as all the worlds descended into chaos. And the ship of the dead, who were her daughter's subjects, sailing into battle against the gods . . .

Only now she'd seen the rest. The entire thing, from start to finish.

She'd seen the deaths of Odin and Thor themselves. Seen Thor fight Jormungand and Fenrir swallow Odin whole, and seen both her sons die. She tried to force the images back down, put them out of her head, but she couldn't forget them. *Wouldn't* forget them.

It seems the more answers I receive, the more questions I have.

"Of course?" Skadi echoed, confused.

Angrboda only shook her head and didn't elaborate. "Thank you for telling me the truth of things, and . . . thank you. For caring for me. But if you don't mind, I'd like to be alone for a little while." She swallowed heavily. "I just . . . I need time."

"I understand. I won't go far, though. And you'd better not go where I can't wake you," Skadi warned her, and it was with much reluctance that she stood so Angrboda could rest her bandaged head upon a pillow.

"I won't," Angrboda replied.

Skadi hesitated for a moment before nodding once and exiting the cave. As soon as Angrboda heard the door shut behind her, she closed her eyes, took a deep breath, and thought about her vision.

She'd told Odin what he'd wanted to know that night. And before that, she'd begged, *pleaded* with, the Aesir to leave her children be; whatever the Norns had told Odin wouldn't come to pass as long as Hel, Fenrir, and Jormungand remained with her. She was certain of it. And then, once Odin had forcibly taken the information from her—when she was too vulnerable, too heartbroken, too *weak*, to fight him—he'd known it, too.

So why hadn't he simply returned her children to her the moment he'd learned what was to happen? Even if Odin thought her dead, why not release the children to Loki, or even into the wild to fend for themselves? If he was so concerned about his terrible fate, why make enemies of the very creatures who were to slay him and his son in the final battle?

Before she could think on this any further, she shifted in bed and felt something hard underneath the furs on the bed platform. She reached down between the layers to retrieve the object: Hel's much-loved wolf figurine, its features barely distinguishable, the bite marks weathered down by little hands turning it over and holding it close.

Clutching the toy in a tight fist, Angrboda pressed it against her chest, her entire body shaking with silent sobs as it all finally hit her.

Her children were gone.

Not gone, said that familiar voice in the back of her mind, the one that had guided her back to consciousness some hours before.

"They are lost to me," Angrboda whispered aloud. "If I free my sons, the end will begin. My visions have been very clear on that, and they haven't lied to me yet."

And what about your daughter?

"Hel . . ." She held the wolf figurine more tightly. *I should be dead. I wish I were dead so I could be with her. How unfair it is, that I've died so many times and yet . . .*

And then the thought struck her. *Maybe I don't need to die to reach her. Maybe I can reach her in my own way, and my sons as well.*

She squeezed her eyes shut and took a deep, calming breath. Cleared her mind, listened to the steady thump of her heartbeat. Waited to feel that separation, to sink down, to travel as she willed. As she'd always done.

But nothing happened.

She opened her eyes and furrowed her brow in confusion, and she willed herself to calm down and try again. But this time, instead of nothing, something worse happened: a flash of burning pain all over her body, flames like the ones that had burned her as Gullveig, which left her trembling and confused.

She tried a final time, and as soon as she began to leave her body, it brought everything back from that night, brought back Odin's iron grip on her very soul as he ripped her up out of her physical form and forced her down into the dark place like he was holding her below water, as he took what he wanted and did as he pleased with her.

Her stomach lurched and her vision swam and she landed back in herself. And then a sickening realization occurred to her.

She had—somehow, whether because of her own shortcomings

or from some kind of spell he'd put on her that night—lost the ability to perform *seid*.

Am I still a prophetess if I lack the skill of foresight?

Am I still a mother if my children are gone?

He has taken everything from me.

He and Loki both.

Her thoughts strayed back to Loki and she seethed. *Would that he had never given me back my heart in the first place. He deserves to suffer as I saw him suffer in my visions. He deserves every bit of it after what he's done to me.*

But as Angrboda fell asleep, she let go of that image, let it fade into the recesses of her mind: the binding, the snake, the bowl, the *pain*. She did not need it any longer. She did not need to keep herself up at night wondering about it, for she realized now why it did not concern her any longer, why it never concerned her to begin with.

There is a reason that I will not be by your side during your torment. And that reason is you.

SOMEWHERE between dreaming and waking, the voice spoke to her again.

Do you remember how Odin earned his knowledge of the runes? it asked. *He hung on Yggdrasil for nine days and nine nights. Sacrificed himself to himself.*

Angrboda did not understand.

You were a sacrifice, too. What did you learn while you were tied to your tree, Mother Witch? What did you bring back with you that you didn't have before?

What indeed, Angrboda thought sullenly. *Hopelessness? Despair?*

No, the voice said. *Me.*

But who are you? And why did it feel so familiar when you called me "Mother Witch"?

The voice offered no answer.

She woke up then, groggy and disoriented. She lay there for some time attempting to wrangle her thoughts. But the pieces were starting to come together in her foggy mind, and the picture became clearer with every breath she took.

Odin isn't trying to learn of the prophecy in order to prevent its coming true—that's what I thought originally, but I was wrong. He can't prevent it. He knows it's unavoidable. But then why would he want to know every little detail of his own death, of the deaths of his kin? Wouldn't everyone be happier not knowing? Is anyone truly so grim?

No. He's seeking information because he needs to know as much as possible if he intends to subvert it all somehow or find some kind of loophole to achieve his own ends.

And that means I can do the same.

But the question was *how.*

Angrboda didn't have an answer, but she knew someone who might; she just had to find them, this person who was speaking to her in dreams—once she learned who they were in the first place, of course.

Mother Witch. The name stuck with her. Made her think of when she'd first come here to Ironwood, as Angrboda, and found the stone foundations some ways away from her cave. *Perhaps that would be a good place to start.* Even if the place yielded nothing, perhaps there would be at least a clue there to point her in the right direction.

And if that amounted to nothing as well, then she had the whole Nine Worlds to search.

I suppose I'd best get started.

Still holding Hel's wolf figurine, Angrboda peeled herself out of the layers of blankets and furs in which Skadi had so carefully wrapped her—she winced as the colder air hit her bare skin, despite the warmth coming from the hearth fire—and sat up with much effort. She dragged her legs over the side of the sleeping pallet and stood, then braced herself on the table to make her way over to her chest of clothes.

Once she'd found her spare linen underdress, she donned it as gingerly as she could, then pulled a woolen dress atop it. The dress she'd been wearing, as well as the linen underdress beneath it, had been cut off by Skadi in an attempt not to jostle her head wound; she ambled back across the floor and picked them up, satisfied that she could repair them on her journey, so long as she remembered to pack a needle and thread.

It was as Angrboda was piling provisions into her pack basket that Skadi entered the cave carrying two dead rabbits by the legs, and the woman stopped short and stared after she closed the door behind her.

"What," said Skadi, "are you *doing?*"

"Leaving," said Angrboda.

"To go *where?*"

Angrboda shook her head, which had a fresh bandage tied around it. "You wouldn't believe me if I told you."

Skadi set the dead rabbits down on the table and folded her arms, drawing herself up to her full height—nearly a head taller than Angrboda, who was not a short woman herself—and effectively blocking the door.

"Try me," she said.

They stood there staring each other down until Angrboda sighed and sat down heavily in her chair. As she considered how to explain, she traced her finger along one of the swirls she'd carved into the arms an age ago and didn't meet Skadi's gaze. For her part, the Huntress settled herself down backward on one of the benches at the table, facing her, following the movement of the witch's finger with her eyes.

"Does it have something to do with . . . where you were? For those nine days?" Skadi ventured when Angrboda didn't say anything. She leaned forward to rest her elbows on her knees, laced her fingers. "Something to do with *seid*? You never did explain how you knew this sort of magic, and I didn't want to press the matter the other times it's come up."

"I don't know how I know it," Angrboda said, finally meeting her gaze. "I don't remember much before I first came here to Iron-wood. I remember next to nothing from Asgard save for what they did to me before I fled, and nothing at all before that."

Skadi straightened. "You were in Asgard? When?"

"A very long time ago." Angrboda shuddered as she thought back to it. "I went there from—somewhere—and passed through Vanaheim on my way. I taught them *seid*. Freyja was the only one of the Vanir to really catch on, and Odin was the only one of the Aesir. But I suppose that was enough to start a war—"

"*The* war?" Skadi stared at her. "You . . . *you're* Gullveig? I've heard her mentioned before, and it was so long ago that not much is known—most people think she's Freyja, or *was* Freyja. Because of the name, you know? A goddess who knows *seid* and has a thirst for gold fits the description rather well."

"Good—let them think it. I want nothing to do with the gods," Angrboda said firmly. "They stabbed out my heart and tried to kill me thrice more after the fact."

"How did you survive, then?"

Angrboda had always wondered this herself, and now that

someone had posed the question to her directly, she was forced to admit that she hadn't the slightest clue. "I don't—I don't know."

"And that doesn't trouble you? The fact that you came back to life not only after they'd stabbed your heart out, but also burned you three times?"

The witch shifted in her chair. "I—I guess not."

Skadi seemed hurt. "Why didn't you tell me all this before?"

"Because I hoped it would never become relevant again," Angrboda said. "My involvement with Odin and Freyja and my trials as Gullveig are all I remember. Nothing before that, nor why I was even traveling to the realms of the gods in the first place. And then there's the matter of the prophecy—"

Skadi scowled. "Which prophecy? The one you made Sigyn see at the riverside, or a different one?"

Angrboda sagged in her chair. "What I showed Sigyn that night was one piece of a much bigger puzzle. It started one night when I was pregnant with Hel, and she was dying—I called her soul back from beyond, and that's how he found me. He sensed it."

Skadi's eyebrows shot up in surprise, but all she said was, "He?"

"Odin. He started haunting my sleeping hours. I had a dream about how the worlds would end, but I didn't see it all. Loki just shrugged it off, but—"

"You should've told me," Skadi said hotly. "*I* wouldn't have shrugged it off."

"I'm sorry," Angrboda said, and she meant it. She went on to describe how Odin had pushed her to access that prophecy to end all others. She explained how she resisted at first—how she saw enough to know her sons were somehow involved but did not see how everything would end—until that night when Thor killed her and Odin *made* her see it. Made her *speak* it.

She kept the matter of Loki's torment to herself, though. He wasn't important to her anymore, and another mention of him wouldn't improve her friend's mood.

Skadi considered the gravity of her words. "So you know how they're going to die? Sigyn's sons, and Fenrir and Jormungand? And—and the gods?"

Angrboda nodded.

"What about me?" Skadi asked softly after a long moment. "Did you see how I . . . ?"

Angrboda opened her mouth to say that even if she *had* seen it, she'd never tell—but then she realized she *hadn't*. She searched her mind for any trace of her friend in her vision and found none.

"I—I don't know," she said at last.

Skadi clearly didn't believe her, but tried to be nonchalant about it. "Fine. I didn't really want to know, anyway."

"No, I really don't," Angrboda said, sitting up in her chair so quickly that she felt a distinct *pang* in her head. She sat back and winced, then took a moment to catch her breath. "I didn't see you die. And if I didn't see it, it's not certain it'll happen, right?"

"I mean, not necessarily," Skadi began, "but—"

"Maybe I didn't see *everything*," Angrboda said. "Maybe the only things I saw were the ones that are set in stone. That's why Odin wanted to know what he can't change—so he can figure out what he *can*. That's the key to finding a loophole, isn't it?"

Skadi opened her mouth. Shut it again. Shrugged.

"So what I need to focus on is what I don't know rather than what I do," Angrboda finished, speaking quickly and thinking even faster. *More questions than answers.* "I don't know how you die; I don't know how Hel—"

She paused. *Hel. I didn't see her at all. I saw Loki crewing a ship of dead souls, but I didn't see their new ruler on board. Which means she may not even be at the final battle. Which means . . .*

Which means there is hope for her yet. I can save her . . . somehow.

"Angrboda?" Skadi prompted, for the witch's eyes were wide with the realization. "Care to finish your thoughts aloud so I could be party to what in Ymir's name is going on?"

Angrboda leaned against the arm of her chair to steady herself as she made to stand. "I need answers. And to find them, I need to be able to perform *seid* again, to be able to contact Hel—and my sons—and from there, maybe we can figure all this out together."

"You can't do *seid* anymore?" Skadi asked, frowning.

"I . . ." Angrboda bit her tongue. "I tried last night, but I couldn't. Something is stopping me—or maybe I'm stopping myself, subconsciously, out of fear. I don't know. *Seid* is part of me, but it makes me feel vulnerable right now. It's like my mind is trying to block out what happened and in doing so is blocking out my ability to travel out of body."

Skadi looked thoughtful. "So where do we start? Reawakening your magic, contacting your sons, saving Hel by subverting this prophecy and whatnot?"

"*We* don't start anywhere," Angrboda said. She finally hauled herself to her feet but wavered, and when Skadi sprang forward and reached out to steady her, the witch held up a hand to stop her. "I must go alone."

Skadi dropped her arm. "Why?"

"This is something I have to do on my own," Angrboda said. She thought of the voice, the presence that had guided her out of her dark place and back to life: "*What did you come back with that you didn't have before? Me.*"

How did *I survive my burnings? And why am I still alive after Thor killed me, too?*

Who am I, really?

Skadi didn't say anything, but her face became red with anger and she looked like she wanted to argue but was too furious to even speak.

Angrboda braced herself. While Skadi may have taken everything in stride so far, something made Angrboda want to hold the presence of the stranger to her chest. This was more intimate than she could possibly explain to another person, and she knew she couldn't hope to succeed in moving forward if she happened to be held back by feeling that this whole quest was foolish. That she was chasing a ghost—or worse, a hallucination.

Whoever they are, maybe they know why I can't die, because they know who I was before I was Gullveig. And maybe that's the key to figuring out how I can regain my seid, *reach out to my sons, and save my daughter.*

"Besides," Angrboda said, "I've not been by myself for a while. And you have Asgard still, and duties as a goddess, don't you?"

Skadi's expression darkened. "The gods were dead to me from the moment I found you tied to that tree."

"But they don't know that, and you're reckoned among them. Worshipped by those in Midgard, even. I beg you, don't toss that aside for me."

"I shall never again return to Asgard," Skadi said fiercely, leaning forward and squeezing her shoulders. "The gods could die screaming in the flames of Muspell and I wouldn't bat an eye, so long as I could remain by your side. I know you won't forsake this mission of yours—and I won't ask you to. But you could come to the mountains with me first. You could spend some time healing and planning in my hall. I'll take care of you, and then we can set off and do whatever it is you mean to do. The worlds won't come to an end tomorrow, will they?"

"No—trust me, there will be plenty of signs," the witch said darkly, thinking back to her vision. *I saw Odin's son Baldur killed by his own brother, saw Loki bound, saw three uninterrupted winters, and then an endless night . . . to start.*

"Then what's there to lose?" Skadi demanded.

A moment passed in which Angrboda was uncertain. She saw that future laid out before her: Skadi forsaking her godhood, the two of them living together in the mountains or in her cave, offering each other comfort, keeping each other warm in the cold, dark winters.

It would not be a bad life. After all, Skadi was truly one of the only people who had ever brought her peace. It seemed a bright future, the two of them together as companions.

And maybe more, Angrboda thought, swallowing, for the thought sent a jolt of excitement through the pit of her stomach. She was tempted. She was so very tempted. After everything she had been through, did she not deserve the opportunity for such happiness— if only for a short time, before her quest began?

"I can't," Angrboda said softly.

"I'm sorry." Skadi took her hands off the witch's shoulders and stepped back, wounded. She looked down at her boots. "I've overstepped."

"You haven't. You misunderstand me," Angrboda said. "It's not that I don't want to. It's just—I fear if I go with you to your hall, I won't leave again."

And I have so much to do.

Skadi's head jerked upward, and she held the witch's gaze, questioning. Angrboda's own expression betrayed nothing; she did not know how long she would be gone, after all, and the last thing she wanted was for Skadi to hold out for her the way she herself had always waited for Loki.

Skadi straightened and looked away. "Then it seems I can't stop you. When will you depart?"

"As soon as possible," Angrboda said, gesturing at her half-packed basket.

"You intend to travel on foot?"

The witch nodded.

"How will you eat?"

"I'll forage. Perhaps if I come across a settlement, I'll barter my services for some food." She looked toward her worktable—which Skadi had built her so long ago—piled high with clay pots and vials of all sizes, plus baskets and jugs and linen-wrapped items, and then she glanced up at all the dried herbs hanging from the wooden rack on the cave's ceiling. "I'll take as much as I can in my basket and forage for the rest, I suppose."

"That won't do." Skadi shook her head and reached for one of the smaller pots, stopped with a cork. "People will recognize this pottery—we've reused it enough times. It'll lend credibility to your wares."

"It's too heavy for me to carry, though. It's just as well—"

"If you won't let me come along, then at least let me do this one thing for you," Skadi said hotly. Then she took a breath and added, in a more level tone, "Go back to bed and rest. Don't leave until tomorrow, and by that time I'll have figured out a way to make all this easier for you to carry. Please. Do this one thing for me."

Angrboda agreed.

ANGRBODA was readjusting her pack basket the next morning when she opened the door and found a freshly built wagon, sized for her to pull comfortably. It had been left next to her winter-bare garden and smelled of the linseed oil that had been used to seal the newly assembled wood.

"Skadi?" she called into the clearing, but she received no response.

She carefully lowered the pack to her side and stepped outside to look around. But all she saw were Skadi's light footprints and the wagon's wheel tracks.

There was no other sign of her. Angrboda knew in her heart that her friend was gone, and it made her feel both sad and relieved—she hadn't been looking forward to that particular goodbye, and part of her knew that the wagon was Skadi's version of a farewell.

Angrboda went back inside and packed two boxes, stuffing un-spun wool around the ceramics to keep them from breaking on the trip.

One of the clay pots rattled when she shook it. Inside she found the polished amber beads Loki had given her, and she frowned; she'd never thought to wonder what had happened to them, be-cause he'd gifted them to her on the same night her prophetic dreams started—perhaps he or Hel had hidden them there to sur-prise her later. The thought of Loki made her want to toss the beads into the fire, but she'd already put it out, and so instead she tied them around her neck and tucked them under her hood. They'd be a valuable item to trade if she needed to.

When the wagon was packed, Angrboda took a last look inside her cave. It wasn't as desolate a place as she'd first found it, but it wasn't home anymore. She wondered how much longer her pro-tection spell would last once she left, wondered how long things here would remain undisturbed, and then realized it didn't matter. She wasn't leaving anything of value behind.

Angrboda took a deep breath and closed the door.

And then she was off.

❖ ❖ ❖

FIRST she headed in the direction of the stone foundations. It seemed like so long ago that she'd stumbled upon them, but somehow she knew the way back, which made her feel even more certain that this spot held some significance in her previous life.

But she'd barely left her cave before her head began throbbing and she felt so dizzy that she could hardly walk straight, so she rooted around for a fallen branch to use as a walking stick to keep herself steady as she pulled the wagon behind her.

Ironwood seemed to grow quieter the closer she got to her destination, just as it had the last time she was there. When she reached the clearing, the air itself had stilled as though trying to preserve the site in time.

Angrboda dropped her wagon's handle and sagged against the nearest tree. *What now?* She thought back to when she'd first approached this place. How she'd thought she'd heard voices on the wind, felt a presence following her, heard it come up behind her and whisper the words "Mother Witch."

She closed her eyes and tried to remember, but her memories went only so far back—that was her entire problem. But maybe there was something useful in what she *could* recall.

"There was one witch here who bore the wolves that chase the sun and moon and raised many others still," she'd said to Loki on the day they'd met at the river. How had she known that, when she'd barely remembered anything else?

"Right," he'd replied, because he'd heard the stories, too, so she hadn't thought too much about what she did and did not remember. *"The Old One and her wolf-children."*

And then Skadi's words came to her, from the day the Huntress had shot her way into Angrboda's life with one stray arrow: *"They say the witch who birthed the race of wolves is still here somewhere. She's one of the ancient giantesses of the forest—supposedly they all lived here in Ironwood a long, long time ago."*

Angrboda slumped into a sitting position against the tree and looked down at her hands.

"Am I one of them?" she wondered aloud. "Or was I . . . their mother?"

The clearing yielded no response.

She dropped her hands down into her lap and sighed. She tilted her aching head back against the tree and looked up at the barren, ancient canopy of twisted gray branches above, then closed her eyes. "Oh, what did I expect—that the answer would just fall out of the sky?"

She opened an eye and peered upward as if expecting just that. Of course she knew better, but she was still disappointed when nothing happened.

With another sigh, she extracted a strip of dried meat from her pack basket to munch on, even though she wasn't particularly hungry. Night was beginning to fall. She made a small fire and wondered if she should just go back to her cave and shelter there tonight before taking off into the wider worlds.

But where would she go? She chewed dismally on her jerky. She'd been so certain there would be a clue here—something that would lead her in the right direction.

Just when she was beginning to believe she had truly imagined the entire thing—the voices, "Mother Witch," the presence itself—the wind picked up. The tree branches began to sway above her in the dying light. She finished her jerky and was seconds away from dousing her fire and going back to her cave when she saw the little girl.

At first she thought the girl was Hel, and her heart jolted in her chest. But no—the girl was a bit older, with copper red hair and gray eyes, and she didn't seem to notice Angrboda sitting there, watching her. She was circling the clearing, looking intently at the plants that bordered the tree line.

Angrboda perked up. "Hello?"

The girl ignored her. She was wearing rough-hewn wools and what looked like a fur cape about her shoulders, pinned with a rough circular brooch. Feathers and small animal bones were threaded into her hair, and her gaze was determined. The witch could not remember ever seeing anyone dressed like her.

Angrboda tried to stand abruptly and faltered, her head pounding, and so instead she approached the girl on all fours, her palms and knees crunching loudly in the snowy underbrush. The child didn't look up.

"You'll have to go farther than that to find willow, dear," a woman's voice called, sounding amused. Angrboda looked around wildly as she tried to determine where the woman was—her voice seemed to be coming from nowhere.

"Who are you?" Angrboda whispered, but as she crawled forward, she noticed something disturbing: In the firelight, the little girl no longer appeared solid, and the witch suddenly sat back and stared as she realized she was seeing a ghost. That's why the girl wasn't paying her any mind. Angrboda was witnessing something that had already happened, long ago.

"It'll be closer to the river," the woman's disembodied voice continued. "And be quick about it—Mother Witch is going to show you how to make her healing salve. Don't keep her waiting."

"Yes, yes." The little girl sighed and started to walk away from Angrboda. Her small leather shoes didn't leave footprints in the snow.

"Wait," Angrboda called after her weakly, certain she'd receive no response.

But to her utter and eternal surprise, the child stopped and looked over her shoulder, her stone gray eyes boring into Angrboda's blue-green.

"Do you understand yet?" the girl asked her.

"I'm starting to," Angrboda replied, though it was at least half a lie. "But where do I go from here?"

The girl gave her an impish smile. "You'll always know where to find me, Mother Witch."

Angrboda understood then that what she was seeing was a manifestation of that presence in her mind, and her heart leapt again. "But that's just it. I *don't* know—"

But she blinked, and the girl was gone.

ANGRBODA slept little and awoke with the sun. She ate more jerky and pondered what she'd seen the night before. She tried once again to perform *seid*, to no avail. She paced back and forth across the clearing, leaning heavily on her walking stick and muttering to herself. Willing herself to remember more. Willing the presence in her mind to bring back the little ghost girl from last night so she could talk to her in person again. Willing something, *anything*, to present a clue for what to do next.

"*What did you bring back with you that you didn't have before?*"

"*You'll always know where to find me . . .*"

"Whoever this person is, they sure seem confident that I already have all the answers I need," Angrboda murmured to herself. She paused in the center of the clearing, next to the ruins of the fire pit, and closed her eyes. *Perhaps I should be more confident, too.*

"I know where to find you," she declared to the empty clearing, feeling foolish. But then her voice grew stronger. "I know where to find you. I know where—"

She felt a nudge. Not a strong one, but a push that felt similar to the one she'd received when she'd been under, had felt the gentle presence guiding her back up to the surface. Only now, when she opened her eyes, it was guiding her west. A clue. A tug in the right direction.

Come find me, it said.

She took up her wagon and began to walk.

IT took her nearly a day before she made it out of Ironwood and found herself at the river beside which she'd first rested after fleeing Asgard.

She could almost see herself sitting on the other side in the shade of a tree. The heartless witch, skin still healing from the burning, heavy wool obscuring her from the sun. Unaware that her life was about to change, that a man would slither up to her out of nowhere and give her back her half-burned heart.

And then break it so completely.

Angrboda shoved the thought of him from her mind. She walked upstream for a ways until she found a shallow point where she and the wagon could cross; then she continued on to Jotunheim, following the presence's weak tug.

The days went on. The presence, it seemed, tended to come and go as she journeyed. Some days she would have a clear idea of where she was headed and felt she was closer than ever to finding out just what she was looking for; other days her wandering was aimless and hopeless, and she wondered over and over again if she should just go back to her cave and wait out the end of the worlds.

But she kept on. Eventually she was led from Jotunheim and into Midgard and back again—for those two worlds were very close—and in both realms she was welcomed into homes here and there, and with her potions and charms she cured the sick, healed wounds, attended births, eased the pain of the dying. It all felt natural to her, this aiding of those in need. As if it was something she had done before, in an earlier time.

She mostly slept alone under her cloak in the forests or the mountains. She bartered her potions and produced more as she went, pulling her little wagon behind her. She no longer needed the bandage wrapped around her head; nonetheless she kept her head down and her hood up to hide the scar.

Everywhere she went, the people whispered, and the whispers in Midgard were not always kind. She learned by eavesdropping that they called her "Heid," a name meaning "bright one," though she was not sure her presence in Midgard was a positive one. When she passed back into Jotunheim it was to visit the markets, to make sure her potions were getting to the people with whom Skadi usually traded, who had been relying on her wares for many winters.

At least Skadi had been correct about her clay pots. In both worlds, humans and giants alike recognized them. Some even went so far as to give her back their old empty pots so she could reuse them when she brought them something new. If she happened to pass through a market or settlement twice, people were kinder to her the second time.

They also tried to trade her fine things in exchange for her services—but she would accept nothing save a roof over her head on a night of ill weather, or a bite to eat before she was on her way. The only finery she possessed were the amber beads Loki had given her, her tablet-woven belt from Gerd, and her antler-handled knife from Skadi, which still hung from the sturdy leather belt she wore beneath Gerd's woven one. Upon this belt she also wore a pouch, in which she kept her most cherished possession: Hel's wolf figurine.

Some days her head hurt so badly that she could not walk at all, and she huddled up in the woods to rest. Other days, she could barely stagger to the next village before collapsing. And still other days she was fine, and the worlds were beautiful, and nothing hurt.

On those days she'd sit in the woods and clear her mind and try to contact the presence again, or have another go at *seid*. The latter never resulted in her favor, as she continued to be pushed back into her body again and again, which frustrated her to no end.

There came a day when she was traveling and she got the distinct impression she was being followed. At the same time, the presence's tug had been stronger that day, and it was guiding her somewhere more insistently than usual. Soon enough she found herself in the middle of a sparse forest with rocks piled in moss-covered heaps all around her.

The tug ceased all of a sudden when she reached a small, burbling creek. Angrboda scowled and looked around. It was nearly dusk, and this didn't seem to be a suitable spot for camping.

"Where were you leading me?" she wondered aloud.

Then a wolf jumped down from the pile of rocks behind her, and she whirled to face it in surprise. The creature was nearly as big as a horse. Angrboda could tell by looking at it that it was old, battle-scarred as if from swords and spears, with a nicked ear and a grizzled maw.

It bared its teeth at her and snarled, and said in a rough, feminine voice that echoed through Angrboda's head, *You're scaring away every other animal in the forest with that rickety cart of yours. I suppose if I can't kill a deer for dinner, you'll do just as fine instead.*

Perhaps it was that she had a son who was a wolf, or perhaps it was because her tolerance for being mistreated had gotten lower and lower the longer she existed, but Angrboda only pulled off her hood and gave the animal a withering look.

"It's a wagon. And it's not *rickety*. It's brand-new," said the witch with a sidelong glance at the object in question, which looked a little worse for wear. It often made her wonder just how much time had passed since she'd left Ironwood.

You can hear me? The she-wolf had stopped snarling when it caught sight of her face. Now the creature sat back and stared at her and said in wonder, *It's you.*

"Of course I can hear you." Angrboda's heart leapt. "You know me?"

Of course I know you, said the she-wolf with a sideways tilt of her head. *Don't you know me?*

"You—are you—are you the one that led me here? The"—she made a vague hand motion at her temple—"person? In my head?"

No . . . The she-wolf blinked once, slowly, and seemed disappointed. *I've no idea what you're talking about. Maybe you're not her after all.*

Angrboda swallowed her disappointment and pressed on. "Not who?"

Mother Witch, the creature replied. *My companion of old, and my dear friend.*

"But—but I think I *am*," Angrboda said, taking a step closer, blinking back sudden tears. "I just—I don't know. I'm sorry I'm not what you expected, but I need answers."

You don't remember me at all? The she-wolf's ears wilted.

Angrboda shook her head sadly.

Well, said the she-wolf, *what's the last thing you do remember? What happened to you?*

"I think perhaps I should make camp before I tell you this tale,"

Angrboda said. She felt fatigued from standing and longed to pull her bedroll out of her pack basket and sit down.

The she-wolf regarded her, then bobbed her head in assent. *Now that you've stopped moving with that cart of yours, I have a chance of catching dinner. I'll be back.*

Once the creature loped away, Angrboda found an outcropping of rocks with an overhanging ledge she could camp beneath to stay out of the elements. She pulled her wagon over as quietly as she could, started a fire, and unpacked her blankets to sit on. Then she took out the last of her jerky and ate it as she waited.

The she-wolf came back a few hours later, when it was dark. Angrboda had started to lose hope that her new companion would return and was relieved beyond words when the she-wolf bounded up and sat opposite the fire from her, seemingly in a better mood than before.

So, what do you remember?

"I went to Asgard and Vanaheim," Angrboda said. "I taught them my magic—"

The she-wolf's eyes narrowed and she asked sharply, *You taught them to travel?*

"Yes, and I don't know why." She then explained her trials as Gullveig and eventual escape from the Aesir, and everything that came after. She had to pause every now and then to fetch a drink of water from the creek to wet her throat, for she did not remember the last time she had talked so much, if ever.

They were well into the night by the time Angrboda's tale was complete. The she-wolf was silent for a long time after the witch had finished speaking.

So you did go home after Asgard, said the she-wolf at length. *Home to Ironwood, that is. You just didn't know what led you there. And then things went sour for you.*

"I suppose," said Angrboda. "So Ironwood . . . *is* home?"

Of course it is. We two are of the Jarnvidjur.

"Jarnvidjur," Angrboda breathed. The ancient giantesses of the forest. She thought back to the stone foundations, which of course triggered the memory of the ghost girl. "What happened to everyone else?"

When you never came back, they left. Or died. It was so long ago. The she-wolf shook her head, then set it down on her front paws. *I don't even remember why you left in the first place, but I stayed behind to protect the other Jarnvidjur. And then they dispersed or passed on, and so I left, too.*

Angrboda felt a sudden ache in her chest, for reasons she couldn't quite describe.

It's all so foggy—I'm so very old, the she-wolf went on. *I wish only to die now.*

"I understand," said Angrboda, with feeling. "Can I ask what your name is?"

I don't think I ever had one, and I'm too old to care, said the she-wolf. *And what should I call you, then?*

"They've called me Heid in my wanderings."

But that's not your name. What do you call yourself?

The witch thought for a time before saying, "Angrboda."

"Herald of sorrows," said the she-wolf, amused. *Are you sure you weren't practicing* seid *when you picked that name? Seems rather prophetic to me.*

"I suppose not," Angrboda said with a smile. Then she sobered. "Would that I could practice *seid* now. It would help me get to the bottom of things."

Well, I can be of help. Several things became clear to me over the course of your tale, said the she-wolf. She lifted her head and held Angrboda's gaze. *The first is that presence of yours—the one who brought you back when you sank too far down—is you.*

"Me," Angrboda repeated, unbelieving.

You, as you were. As you were meant to be. As Mother Witch. It seems to me that she's the part of you that you brought back into the light. The part of you that you lost as Gullveig, the part of you that you can't remember. She—you—led you to me, to reunite us. It was your own instinct that brought you here.

"But—that can't be. It can't . . . *she* can't . . . be me. Can she?"

Indeed, said the she-wolf. *Tell me, what did you feel while you were down there?*

"Comfortable," whispered Angrboda. "Safe. And powerful. I never wanted to leave." She shivered. "I could feel the void just below me, though. I wonder what would happen if I went there willingly and not under Odin's control—if I embraced it. But the truth is, I fear going down there again. I fear I would be lost to it this time."

Why? To tap into that power is to reach your true potential. To become yourself again. I wouldn't doubt that's the next place Mother Witch will call you to, to that place deep inside yourself where the power lies. You'd be a fool not to access it, after what you've just told me.

"Well, unfortunately for her—I mean, for *me*—I won't be doing any traveling of that sort anytime soon, since I'm still unable to perform *seid*."

That is troubling, the she-wolf said pensively. *You need that to tap into your true power, and you need your true power to save your daughter.*

"But why do I *need* that power to save her? I don't even know *what* I'm going to do, let alone how I'm going to go about doing it."

The she-wolf set her head down on her paws again and let out a small huff. *Tell me again how the worlds are to end?*

"Three years of winter," Angrboda said, recalling her vision, "in which there are wars and slaughter all over the worlds. Then the wolves who chase the sun and moon will catch their prey, plunging everything into darkness. Yggdrasil will tremble and all the bonds in the universe will break." *Including those holding my sons,* she thought, though she hadn't heard yet of Fenrir being bound, and Jormungand was trapped nowhere other than beneath the sea. "Then the gods and giants will go to battle, and the fire giant Surt will burn all the worlds down, from which a new world will be born."

Ah, said the she-wolf. *Does anyone survive?*

Angrboda fought the urge to roll her eyes. "Some of the young gods, yes. But I don't know how they—" She paused. "I don't know how *they* survive."

And your daughter doesn't go to the battle, does she?

"Not that I saw," said Angrboda carefully, "but—listen. There's something else. I saw Odin's son Baldur die—that's what sets all this off. He was slain by a dart of mistletoe, loosed by his brother's own hand. And if I saw it, then Odin knows it. And if he's not trying to prevent it, then he's going to let his own son die—but while the rest of the gods are all slain, Baldur comes back when the new world is born. Odin still wins, doesn't he? Because his son survives. But *how*? How does *anyone* survive Surt's fire? It's to burn *every* realm, even that of the dead."

It's a good thing, then, that your daughter has a mother who's survived a burning not once but thrice, isn't it?

Angrboda stared across the fire at the she-wolf. The she-wolf stared back at her.

"That's it," Angrboda breathed. "That's the answer. I just need—some kind of protection against fire. Like some kind of shield, or . . ." But then her hope faded. "How did I survive the flames as Gullveig, though? Did I truly die three times, or did I just protect myself somehow?"

That would be a good question for yourself, the she-wolf said dryly, looking up at her, eyes huge and pale in the firelight. *Perhaps your next step is to figure out how to get your* seid, *and you can go from there.*

"You're not wrong, my friend," Angrboda said. She was feeling very tired all of a sudden from all the talking and thinking she'd done today, but her mind was abuzz with the possibilities before her. "It seems to me that going back to my cave will do me no good in that regard, and something is telling me to keep on this path."

That's your instinct again, Mother Witch. Trust it.

Angrboda nodded. "Maybe it means there's someone out there who can help me reawaken my abilities—I just have to find them." She paused. "Will you come with me?"

I suppose it's better than dying, the she-wolf said wearily, closing her eyes, *although not by much.*

ANGRBODA'S journey continued, but after she met the she-wolf, the presence of Mother Witch was no longer in the forefront of her mind; perhaps it sensed that its purpose had been served in its leading her to her old friend—who, despite not having the answers Angrboda sought, had at least pointed her in the right direction. *Or maybe,* she thought more than once, *I can't feel her anymore because I am her, and now I'm fully me again.* But if that were true, wouldn't she have all her memories back? She had to wonder.

So she and the wolf traveled on through the worlds, continuing as she had before, but now with a better sense of what she was looking for—even without the presence to guide her.

That was all well and good with her. If she truly was Mother Witch, then it was as the she-wolf had said: She needed only her instinct as her guide. And besides, the she-wolf was a far more substantial traveling companion than the nebulous ghost of her own past life.

So on they went. Whenever she passed by populated areas, the she-wolf would linger far enough away not to upset the inhabitants, and Angrboda would now ask questions in addition to bartering her potions. She asked if anyone else had passed through recently, anyone who said they could perform magic or who displayed any unusual skills. Most just shook their heads and said that she herself was the only one they were aware of—aside from the occasional fraud who *said* they knew charms or could use runes to cure sickness but usually ended up making things worse. Angrboda needed more than one hand to count the times she'd reached beneath a sick person's pillow and pulled out an antler carved with the wrong runes, making them sicker.

Sometimes Angrboda would cast a charm to disguise herself as an old woman in areas where she didn't feel particularly safe, in which case she'd also magic the she-wolf's form into that of an elkhound so the creature could stay at her side. The more harmless they looked, the less likely people were to feel threatened by them. But those times when she herself felt threatened were few and far between. Angrboda now moved through the worlds with purpose.

And she found that if she acted like nothing could touch her, it seemed nothing would.

It's good to see that you're still making your concoctions, the she-wolf observed one day as they walked. *Mother Witch was a healer first. It pleases me to see that you remember how to work this magic.*

"That and *seid* were the only things I could never forget," Angrboda admitted. "Both seemed to be a part of the very fabric of my soul—until now, that is."

Don't lose heart. There must be others in the Nine Worlds who can help you.

Angrboda stopped for a moment and clutched the side of her head, wincing. These days the headaches would come on with no warning, and she'd be unable to move for hours, dizzy and nauseated. She had yet to devise a potion that would take the pain away.

You could always ride on my back, the she-wolf suggested. *And I could pull that dratted cart of yours.*

"It's a wagon," Angrboda muttered. "And it's fine. I'm fine."

You used to ride me, you know. In the old days.

"I did?"

Put your walking stick in my mouth.

Her head hurt too much to question this, so she obliged her companion and the she-wolf clamped her teeth down on the stick. Angrboda had expected it to snap in the creature's mighty jaws, but the witch gasped with surprise when it instead transformed into a pair of thick reins stemming from either side of the wolf's mouth.

Reins patterned to look like snakes: green and yellow scales, and amber eyes.

Angrboda's eyes bulged. "What—?"

The she-wolf's black lips parted so that Angrboda could see it: a tiny symbol carved into one of her canine teeth. *It's an old spell between us. You weren't the only one among the Jarnvidjur with some magic in them, after all. You wove these reins yourself. Do you remember?*

Despite the pain in her head, a smile tugged at the corners of Angrboda's mouth.

"It seems that wolves and snakes appear wherever I go," she mused.

So would you like a ride?

"I think I'll be all right. I just need to rest." Angrboda reached out to take the reins from the she-wolf's mouth, and they turned back into a walking stick as soon as the wolf opened her jaws.

By the time night fell, her headache had subsided. Angrboda made camp and sat by the fireside in a contemplative silence. The she-wolf was asleep at her back.

"Perhaps *I* did protect myself with a spell," Angrboda whispered. If this was the case, it had been instinctual—unavoidable, even. And she'd hardly escaped the flames unscathed in the end.

A shield, perhaps. With a deep breath, she squeezed her eyes shut. She forced down her fear of that ancient pyre upon which the gods had burned her and focused every ounce of her energy into a barrier around her hand.

Then, slowly, eyes still closed, she extended her hand into the fire.

For one joyous moment, her spell held up. She felt the heat, but it was distant; the flames licked her hand but didn't burn. Her eyes snapped open and—for the first time in possibly her entire existence—she grinned with triumph.

"*And to think,*" came Loki's words suddenly to her mind, "*you were once a powerful witch who did interesting things.*"

The thought of him broke her concentration, and Angrboda yelped with pain and immediately pulled her hand out of the fire, clutching it to her chest. When she finally drew it away to examine the damage, a low hiss escaped her clenched teeth as she scowled at her blistered fingertips.

That's a good start, said the she-wolf, who was staring at the witch's hand.

Angrboda started at her companion's voice. "I didn't know you were awake."

Do you have a healing salve for that?

"Of course."

Good, the she-wolf said with satisfaction. *Then you can try again.*

❖　❖　❖

NIGHT after night, Angrboda practiced her spell. And the more she practiced, the more it became clear to her that she'd need more power than she currently possessed to be able to protect herself— let alone someone else—for any extended period of time.

It was now more important than ever that she find a way to perform *seid*, to reach that well of power, to reach her daughter. But was it a matter of getting past her own subconscious fear, or something more? Was there something else holding her back?

Angrboda had reason to think so. Soon they passed through a seaside market town in Midgard, where they came across a crowd assembled on the shore, greeting a crew of returning raiders, and she saw the opportunity to barter some of her wares; Viking men rarely arrived home without a scrape. But then she spotted a flash of copper hair making its way to the front of the crowd of towns- folk and felt a stab of recognition. *Don't I know her?*

The copper-haired woman threw her arms around one of the burliest sailors, and when he picked her up and spun her around, Angrboda could see her face, and her stomach sank in disappointment. For a moment, she thought she'd seen one of the Jarnvidjur: a grown-up version of the little girl's ghost she'd spoken to in Ironwood. But that was nonsense—that had been just her imagination.

What's wrong? asked the she-wolf at the look on her face.

"Nothing," Angrboda said, but now she took in the entire crowd, the townsfolk and their returning raiders—talking, laugh- ing, shouting, crying, hugging, clapping one another on the back—and for a moment she felt horribly, starkly alone. "I just—I thought I saw someone I knew, that's all."

They do *look alike,* said the she-wolf, eyeing the copper-haired woman. *Her, and one of our Jarnvidjur. A descendant, perhaps. Who knows where they all ended up after Ironwood?*

Angrboda took a shaking breath, voicing aloud that feeling she'd had since the she-wolf's revelation about the Jarnvidjur on the night they met, that feeling she'd since put a name to: shame. "I failed them. I failed you all. It's my own fault I had no one to come home to. It's my fault I forgot them. My fault I left . . ."

If I'd stayed, maybe I'd belong somewhere.

The she-wolf studied her with viciously intelligent eyes. *Guilt is a heavy thing, Mother Witch,* she said. *It's best left behind if you want to move forward.*

"But if I'd stayed . . ."

It would've made little difference in the end. The she-wolf butted her shaggy head against Angrboda's shoulder. *So the Jarnvidjur fell apart without you—that's the way of things. Even if it happened a hundred years ago or a thousand, it would have happened sometime. They left home, found new friends, founded new families. And so have you.*

"I did. And now that's lost, too," Angrboda said bitterly.

Lost, but not gone, the she-wolf reminded her. *Just because that time is over with doesn't mean it didn't matter. Your time with the Jarnvidjur, with Loki and your children, with Skadi . . .*

"And now with you," Angrboda said, stroking the she-wolf's muzzle. Her eyes strayed to the copper-haired woman once more, and something bittersweet blossomed in her chest as she thought of the Jarnvidjur, all over the worlds, all with their own lives—and she, still an old witch with her wolf, the same as she'd been back then, but so much more yet.

"Thank you," she said at last. "That does make me feel better."

The she-wolf pulled away and said gruffly, *Good, because that's all the validation you're going to get out of me today. Now, come. Let's move on.*

"Yes," Angrboda whispered, with one last look at the people assembled on the beach, and she felt lighter somehow. "Let's."

SHE and the she-wolf were passing through the craggy wastes of northern Jotunheim when they passed a settlement and decided to stop. Angrboda had not visited this hall before, so to be safe, she magicked herself into the form of an old woman and glamoured the she-wolf into a hound, and they approached with the wagon.

Angrboda went first to the kitchen area at the back of the massive longhouse, for she always had more luck speaking with the women than going through the front door and announcing herself to the men, as was proper. The owner of the hall was named Hymir, and he happened to be hosting a feast that day. Angrboda could hear the raucous laughter coming through the walls.

Hymir's wife, Hrod, was organizing the servants, who were coming in and out of the hall to refill their serving plates and pitchers of ale. They all seemed rather haggard, and Hrod answered the witch's questions curtly, for she was very busy, so after Angrboda confirmed with her that there were no sick or injured in the settlement who might require her aid, she decided not to ask if anyone had come through lately who knew magic.

"But we may need a healer before the night is over, considering how much these men are drinking," Hrod added tiredly. "So if you wish to stay and help me serve, I'd be happy to provide you with supper and a roof over your head tonight."

Angrboda agreed. "I may look old and withered, but I can certainly pour ale without spilling it."

"Excellent," said Hrod. "What do they call you?"

"Heid" was becoming too noticeable a name. For a split second

Angrboda floundered, then decided to make something up. "Hyndla."

"Well, Hyndla, your help is greatly appreciated," said Hrod, handing her a clay pitcher and sending her on her way.

The feast hall was even more raucous on the inside and was full of a larger variety of giants than Angrboda had seen for quite some time: hill trolls, dark elves, frost giants, rock giants, and the odd dwarf or two, along with a few other giants who were roughly the same size and shape as she was, indistinguishable from a human or god. Their host, Hymir—an enormous man—sat in the high seat and was recounting in a booming voice how he and Thor had gone fishing for the Midgard Serpent.

Jormungand. She barely kept her face straight as she milled about the hall, filling cups as she went, and listened to the tale. Thor had arrived under a false name and was offered hospitality but had quickly taken advantage by eating two whole oxen, so Hymir suggested they go fishing for their next meal. Thor then killed another of Hymir's oxen and used its head to draw the Midgard Serpent from the sea, and then had broken Hymir's boat as he struggled to keep the Serpent on his line. Hymir had ended up cutting the line, but that hadn't stopped Thor from getting a blow in to the Serpent's skull with his hammer, at which point Hymir realized just whom he'd gone fishing with.

Angrboda was livid.

To add insult to injury, Thor had then stolen Hymir's mile-wide cauldron to brew enough ale for the gods. By the end of the story, the entire hall was as furious as Angrboda.

"The Aesir are thieves and deceivers all," an ogre bellowed, and the rest of the hall shouted in agreement.

"Something should be done about them," screeched a vicious-looking giantess in the corner, a woman twice Angrboda's height and covered in boils.

And then, near the front of the hall, a very familiar voice called out: "I've a tale to tell, if you need more proof of the gods' treachery."

Angrboda's heart skipped a beat as she turned to see Skadi stand up on a bench to address the congregation. The woman's face was ruddy with drink, and she brandished her large cup of ale like a weapon.

Stay calm, Angrboda told herself, though her heart was positively palpitating now. *It's just a coincidence that she's here. Don't make yourself known.*

"Sit down, Skadi Thjazadottir," Hymir said dismissively. "We all know the story of how they killed your father." He leaned forward in his chair and leered at her. "And yet you're still one of them. Why is that?"

When the crowd started to shout, "Boo!" Skadi waved them off and said, "*Pfft.* I was going to tell the one about the binding of the Great Wolf. It's a tale near and dear to me, though I only heard it told from another."

"We know that one, too. It happened quite some time ago," grunted a hill troll. A couple of others in the hall voiced their agreement, but there were others still who urged Skadi to continue.

"They stole him and his brother and Hel away from their mother, you know," Skadi went on, raising her voice so it would reach everyone in the hall, although her words were rather slurred. "Tied her up and stole them in the night. But the joke was on them, for Fenrir grew so big that they knew they couldn't keep him in Asgard for long. The only way they could restrain him was trickery. Fenrir allowed the gods to try binding him because he knew he could easily break any fetter they had. So they went to the dwarfs to craft a special one, made from the beard of a woman and the footfall of a cat and other such magical nonsense. The trick was that it didn't *look* strong, so they thought they could fool him into putting it on, saying there was no harm in it because he'd broken bonds that were made of iron.

"But Fenrir was smarter than all that. Before he agreed to put on the fetter, he said, 'If it's truly so easy to break, then let someone put their hand in my mouth as a token of good faith that you're not deceiving me.' And that's how Tyr lost his hand, and how the Great Wolf became trapped." Skadi raised her cup. "My point is, friends and kinsmen, that we giants have outsmarted the Aesir before. We can surely do it again."

The assembled giants broke out into more cheering and jeering, but Angrboda stood rooted to the spot. She had not heard the tale of Fenrir's binding before. *So, that's how he came to be bound—in those same fetters he broke free from in my vision.*

She watched Skadi step down from the table and sit back down on the bench, watched a servingwoman refill her friend's cup. Angrboda could barely breathe as she processed what she'd just heard.

Truly, her sons were exactly where they needed to be for her prophecy to come true.

"Bold of you to tell a tale of how my son Tyr was maimed, in my very own hall," said Hymir once the assembly had quieted. "But the truth of it is that he's as bad as the rest of the Aesir and helped Thor steal my cauldron to boot."

Hymir is Tyr's father? Angrboda had heard conflicting stories of Tyr's parentage in the past, but to hear him confirmed as a giant angered her. *Our bloodlines are truly not so divided, and yet the Aesir think they're so much better than us.*

Skadi became drunker as the night wore on, but as Angrboda was still in the guise of an old woman, Skadi barely even acknowledged her. Soon enough the longhouse began to quiet, and the various giants moved their benches to line the perimeter of the hall to sleep upon. Skadi passed out face-first on the table, and so her bench remained in place.

So that's your Skadi, the woman you told me of. It seems she's masking her pain with drink, the she-wolf-as-elkhound observed as she followed at Angrboda's heels. *Does that trouble you?*

"More than you know." Angrboda was tempted to reveal herself to the Huntress, but she could only think of what would happen. She knew the first words out of Skadi's mouth would be another invitation, and even after years of a hard life on the road, Angrboda knew in her heart that she would not be able to refuse a second time.

Besides that, it was a matter of respect. Skadi had not wanted to say goodbye, and Angrboda's mission was not yet complete. She had more to do before they could meet again. And she couldn't help but wonder if she was running out of time.

She slept in the kitchen with the servingwomen that night, curled up by the cooking fire with the she-wolf in her elkhound form, and they departed before first light.

THE next day Angrboda's head felt worse than ever—probably a result of enduring the noise from the feast the night before—and she accepted the she-wolf's offer to ride on her back, after the witch fashioned a harness out of spare rope so the she-wolf could pull the wagon behind her. Since Angrboda hadn't gotten a chance to trade anything at Hymir's, they stopped at a small settlement so she could barter her wares in exchange for some dried fish.

The villagers' eyes were wide at her approach. Angrboda felt too weak to cast a glamour to disguise herself and her companion, but it turned out the giants there were willing to trade with her anyway and thanked her as she left. She got the distinct impression that they were glad to see the back of her.

When she and the she-wolf were fully provisioned and had traveled far west of Hymir's hall, they took shelter in a shallow cave along a river. Angrboda practiced her protection spell a few more times with varying levels of success, and once she'd treated and bandaged her hand, she sat back against the she-wolf's shaggy fur and fell asleep.

It was the dead of night when a voice sounded from the mouth of the shallow cave: "Wake up, sister. I have need of your wisdom."

Angrboda flipped over at once and sat up, scowling. Behind her, the she-wolf stirred but did not wake, exhausted from the day's trek. Their sleeping area was now lit by a single torch, grasped in a hand belonging to a person she had hoped never to see again in her exceedingly long life.

It was Freyja. And when she caught sight of Angrboda's face, she drew back, startled.

"*You*," she hissed. "You're alive?"

"What are you doing here?" Angrboda was on her feet in an instant, all thoughts of rest forgotten. Her head spun, as it sometimes did when she rose too quickly, and the scar on her temple pounded for a moment as if the wound were new. "How did you find me?"

Freyja seemed at a loss for words but recovered quickly enough.

"I asked around," she said, shrugging, twirling a bloodred strand of hair. "I'm seeking a witch who rides a wolf with snakes for reins, but I didn't know you were she. You have many names now, it seems."

"Yes." News certainly did travel fast in Jotunheim. "Why are you here?"

"I've told you, I have need of a sorceress's knowledge. And I suppose that very sorceress is you, Angrboda Iron-witch."

Angrboda's eyes narrowed at the name.

Freyja gave her a venomous smile. "The nickname Loki gave you has gotten around in your absence. They say you died of grief and are buried in your daughter's realm. You've passed into legend since your departure, sister."

Angrboda ignored this. She didn't know what knowledge Freyja could possibly want from her, but she had a feeling she knew what the woman wanted her to do to get it. *Could she not have done this herself?*

But then she realized Freyja had no idea that she couldn't perform *seid*. She decided she might as well bluff, in order to divine the true nature of this visit.

"Come with me to Asgard," said Freyja after thinking for a moment. "Perhaps we could work something out. Strike a deal."

"I will do no such thing," said Angrboda. Her gaze strayed to Freyja's companion: a small boar standing at attention beside the goddess. There was something odd about it, she decided. Like the animal form was not its original one. It did not take her long to put two and two together. "Is that where you're taking this one, your lover in disguise?"

"You're confused," said Freyja, but anger flashed across her face for a second before she wiped it primly away. She shifted, and her famous golden necklace gleamed in the torchlight. "This is but a boar, Battle-swine, whom the dwarfs made for me. I would learn the lineage of my protégé Ottar, so that he can claim his kingship in Midgard. Will you tell me what I wish to know, or what?"

"Why not ask Frigg? It's said that Odin's wife knows the fates of all men." Angrboda suppressed a smirk, but she was suspicious. *Lineage? That's all she wants to know?* When Freyja didn't answer, Angrboda sighed and said, "Well, I'm sorry to disappoint you, but you've come all this way for nothing. I've not been able to perform *seid* since the night Thor slew me and Odin forced himself upon me to gain knowledge of the end times, and that's a fact. So I suppose you'll have to go elsewhere to find out what you want to know."

Angrboda did not know how much Freyja knew about that night—the woman had gone ahead with the rest of the gods and had not seen what happened to her—and therefore tried to gauge her reaction.

"It's a terrible business," Freyja said, feigning sympathy, "that you were so resistant, and the All-father had to resort to having you killed again to finally get the information he needed."

So she does know. Angrboda sat up straighter. *Maybe she also knows, then, why I cannot perform* seid. Here it was, what she'd been searching for all this time: finally, a fellow practitioner of magic, standing right in front of her.

Maybe she'd be willing to help me, if I paid her price. The thought of asking Freyja for help made her want to vomit, but as she saw it, it was the only choice she had.

"Did you know Loki tried to bargain for your life?" Freyja continued when Angrboda was silent, clearly mistaking the other witch's pensiveness for despair, and deigning to add fuel to the fire.

"Speak not of Loki to me," Angrboda ground out.

Freyja ignored her. "It was so sad. He agreed to distract you so I could bind you while we gathered up your little monsters, and he was *so* very upset when Thor put his hammer to your skull instead, on Odin's orders. I daresay the Trickster hasn't been the same since."

"Then add that to the oaths the gods have broken," Angrboda snapped. "Do you know why I can't perform *seid*, then? Did Odin do something to me that night? Did he—trap me somehow, in my body, and make it so I'm unable to travel?"

Freyja looked at her now with something not unlike pity.

"Such things we women are made to endure," Freyja said quietly, and with such feeling that Angrboda almost felt a twinge of feminine kinship with her. "No, he did nothing to you besides the obvious. It seems to me that it's fear that's holding you back. Fear of being forced down and held under. I've tried going as deep as you have, but I cannot. None can. If you tell me what it is I need to know, I will guide you down as far as I can go. Do we have a bargain?"

"I accept," said Angrboda.

"Excellent." Freyja's mouth quirked smarmily to one side. "Although I'm sure you regret teaching your *seid* to the Aesir and Vanir near the beginning of time, it seems it's paid off for you in the long run, hasn't it, now that one of your apprentices of old is the only person who can help you . . . ?"

"Just get on with it," Angrboda muttered.

Freyja put her torch down on the remains of Angrboda's fire to light it again and then knelt across from her, her gold eyes gleaming. The mysterious boar settled down beside her. From her belt she took a small drum and began to beat it in a slow rhythm—the rhythm of a heartbeat—and chanted the ancient words Angrboda had taught her long ago.

Angrboda needed no drum or spoken words to perform *seid* herself, but when she closed her eyes, she could feel the power of the chant. Part of her bristled with fear as she felt herself sinking down and out of her body. She started to shut down, to resist.

Freyja's chanting grew more forceful, and Angrboda felt the

woman's hold tighten on her. Her physical body began to panic as Freyja dragged her down. And while the other witch's body in the material world was still chanting, Angrboda could feel her presence there with her, in the place below.

But then Angrboda sank further. She could feel Freyja watching her from above, hovering near that pinprick of light at the surface.

See? Freyja said, above her own chanting voice. *You just needed a little push to leave your body. Like ripping a bandage from a wound.*

I know. Angrboda realized then that they had succeeded. She was back, back here in the place where she'd been for nine days and nine nights, from which she'd never wanted to leave. She had needed only Freyja's little push to break her own mental block, and now here she was. She could reconnect with Mother Witch. She could contact Hel. She could access that deep well of power at the very bottom, tip once more over the precipice Odin had forced her over—but this time she could control it. All of it.

But first, she had to send Freyja on her way.

I've forced you down, but no farther, said Freyja, her voice fading. She had stopped chanting. *The rest is up to you. Remember our bargain.*

Angrboda did. She reached out for what it was the other witch wanted to know, and the dark place told her. Her eyes opened, white and dead, and she began to speak the truth of Ottar's ancestry—and then something changed. The words changed; the images changed. The dark place was telling her, once again, of the ending of the worlds.

She had gone further than she'd intended and now she was being called deeper, back to the void.

She surfaced before the dark place could pull her in, and her eyes returned to normal. Freyja was staring at her. Angrboda glared and said, begrudgingly, "Thank you."

Freyja nodded once as she stood and took a horn from her belt, muttered some words over it, and fed it to the boar. "So that he remembers the names you've spoken, and his lineage," she said. "But not the rest. That was only for my ears."

"You must go, too," said Angrboda. It did not surprise her to learn Freyja's boar was not just a boar, but truly Ottar in disguise. She suddenly felt tired, drained. "Get away from here. You have what you want to know."

"And more," said Freyja. "You told me of Ragnarok. Not as much as you told Odin that night, but some."

Ragnarok. The doom of the gods, the word meant.

"By your expression," said Freyja, "I take it this is the first you've heard of such a thing? How can that be, if you're the one who spoke the words and made them so?"

Angrboda shivered. "It's only the first time I've heard my vision called by such a name." She folded her arms in an attempt to still her shaking hands. "Thank you. Again. For helping me recover my *seid.*"

"You're welcome. I hope I don't come to regret it, although I'm sure I will. I could just as easily have forced you, as Odin did—"

Angrboda rolled her eyes. "Oh, go away. Back to all your lovers, for they are great in number indeed."

"I'll burn this cave to ashes," Freyja snapped, "should you continue to insult me."

"All the worlds will burn. Curse you and curse the gods. And curse your Ottar as well."

"At least Ottar will thrive while mortal men still do," Freyja spat, and she turned and walked from the cave, the boar in question at her heels.

When she was gone, Angrboda sat up straighter and let the effects of what had just happened sink in.

I can do seid *again. I'm still myself.*

And now that she had this ability once more, she had much to do. And the first thing was to pay her daughter a visit.

She slipped from her body—this time with such ease that she felt almost giddy with relief—and reached out in that form until she could touch Yggdrasil, and the tree took her down, down, down.

THERE was darkness and ice and blowing snow, and she was walking down a pathway of icy, crumbling stone. As she continued to walk, she realized the pathway was a bridge, and if she looked over the side, she could see rushing rivers and empty valleys below.

Her hair flowed around her as if she were underwater. Though her surroundings were black and gray and desolate as far as the eye could see, she had a feeling that it was not missing any color.

She knew, without seeing herself, that her eyes had gone white, as they always did when she was in a trance. When she was somewhere only the dead should be.

Finally she reached the last bridge, which was thatched with gold, and beyond it milled the souls of the dead: the wicked, the unlucky, the old and the young and the sick. The ones who had not died in a glorious battle, the ones who had not been chosen and escorted to the halls of the slain in Asgard by the valkyries.

But a pale maiden, clothed in black, rose from the shadows and stopped her at the end of the bridge, and she could go no farther.

"I am Modgud, the guardian of the bridge. Only the dead can enter here," she said, studying the witch. "But you—you are neither dead nor alive. What business do you have in Hel's realm?"

"I've business with my daughter," said Angrboda. "Let me pass."

Modgud stared at her for a long moment before stepping aside.

So Angrboda continued along the path until she came to huge walls and a great gate, and she slipped inside.

She soon found herself in her daughter's hall, dark and fearsome and carved into the side of a cliff, lit by a phantom glow that came from nowhere. Hel, it seemed, had inherited her father's dramatic flair.

The inside of the hall, though, was surprisingly inviting. The dead milled about as they had outside—laying great golden decorations on a long table, goblets and plates and all manner of finery, with the honey-sweet scent of mead in the air. Angrboda frowned at the sight of this activity. *Surely this isn't for me . . . is it?*

Angrboda made for the rear of the hall, where a young woman in a long black dress sat in the high seat. Her skin was white and her hair was long, trailing down almost to the floor as she sat, and it was as black as pitch and wavy. Under the dress, her legs were crossed, and Angrboda could not see what her feet looked like.

She knew this woman to be Hel, though. Her eyes were the most obvious giveaway: green and bright, just like her father's, though they were sunken. And she possessed the same circles under them as her mother did, though they were black where Angrboda's were gray.

But for all Hel had looked like Loki as a child, she now was the spitting image of her mother—gravitas and all.

And she was staring Angrboda down with a look of solid contempt. In the shadows behind her, dark figures moved: misshapen things, some not even remotely human. Hel's servants. A child's creations.

Her only friends in this deep, dark place.

Angrboda swallowed heavily, at a loss for words under Hel's vicious gaze. All she could manage was a nod at the bustling skeletons and a shaky "Are you expecting company?"

"That's none of your business," said Hel, and Angrboda was startled at her daughter's hoarse, shrill voice. Then again, the last time she had heard Hel speak, the girl had been five years old. "So you've finally died, then?"

She realized then that there were to be no cries of joy, no tearful embrace. Mother and daughter simply looked at each other across the hall.

Hel considered her for another moment before her pale face broke into a disdainful grin. "No, of course not. All this time I thought that the gods had really killed you . . ."

"Until this very night, I had no way to reach you," Angrboda said. "Not even dying brought me here."

"For so long I thought you *were* dead. I mourned you," Hel went on, as if she hadn't heard her. "I even built a monument to you at the eastern gates. But I could never find you in my realm, so I wondered . . ." She leaned forward, her white hands clutching the sides of her chair in a death grip as she leered. "You have some explaining to do, Mother."

Angrboda took a deep breath to cover her internal wince. The last time Hel had spoken to her, she was "Mama."

Now she was "Mother," and when Hel spoke the word, it was as cold as ice.

"I couldn't leave my body, as I had before," said Angrboda. "I had no way of seeing you, nor of contacting your brothers—"

"A likely story," said Hel. Her expression was distant, like she was remembering something from ages past. "I waited to see you here. I've waited forever. You were dead. I thought you were just lost, but you never came. I knew my father would never come for me, but I thought you were different." She lowered her voice to a whisper. "He called us *monsters*. But I'm not a monster. My brothers were monsters, but I wasn't. I was just a little girl."

"Hel—"

"You should have come for me, Mother," said Hel loudly, and she stood and glared down at Angrboda from the dais.

"Hel, please—"

"I'd hoped you would come. But you didn't."

"If you knew what's been done to me, you wouldn't speak to me this way," Angrboda said, her voice breaking. This was not going at all how she'd planned.

"Do *you* know what's been done to *me?*" Hel shot back. "I should've never been born, but you—you had to meddle. Yes, I know what you did now; I've seen it myself. The dead know all. I was dying, and you summoned me back with your *magic*. Now here I am, with power over life and death but only a sad half-life to call my own, cast away from all the worlds, alone forever. Where have you been all this time, Mother? Where have you been while I *rotted?*"

Hel whipped aside the bottom of her dress to show her legs: merely bone now, with blue-gray flesh still clinging in some places, held together by only a few tendons and a *lot* of magic.

Angrboda stared. That was all she could do.

"I can still feel them, you know. And your salves worked well," said Hel snidely, covering her legs again with a flourish. "Unfortunately, I no longer had access to them."

"Hel, I'm . . . I'm so sorry. But you must listen to me. I've finally managed to travel again, and this—you're the first person I wanted to see." Angrboda attempted to steady herself under her daughter's cruel gaze and continued. "They killed me that night. The night—the night you and your brothers were taken from me—but I didn't die. But I also couldn't fight back, and Odin made me see how it's all going to end. The gods, the giants, and all the worlds. Ragnarok—"

"Aye, I know of Ragnarok. I see more than you'd think down

here. I know of fate, as do Frigg and Freyja and the Norns. You're not special to the gods because you can access this dangerous knowledge—you're only the most disposable to Odin. How many more times are you going to let the Aesir kill you, Mother, before you realize that?"

Angrboda clenched her teeth. "Why do you mock me so?"

"Because I see right through you," Hel sneered, stepping down from the dais. "You, the wise old witch in the woods, doing no harm so that no harm will come to you. You forget that your enemies strike first, and they strike harder, and they do not give you the same respect that you give them."

"Hel—"

Hel circled her like a predator, her bone feet making an unnatural *click-clack* sound on the stone floor. "Soon it will begin. And what will you do? Head back to your cave to wait out the end, when all the worlds go up in Surt's flame? You're nothing but a coward."

"You're not *listening* to me," Angrboda said. "I've not been idle this entire time. I've been trying to come up with a way to save you. I *can* save you."

"There you go, meddling again, Mother. Have you forgotten what happened the last time you tried to 'save' me?" Hel gestured at her covered legs. "I want none of it. I—"

Suddenly she let out a shallow breath and stumbled, clutching her chest.

"Hel?" Angrboda said worriedly, stepping toward her.

"Leave me be," Hel snarled. She stalked back to her chair and sat down heavily, hunched over, pain and anger in her eyes. Her hand was still at her chest as she ground out, "Don't you understand? *I don't want your help.* I don't want *you.*"

Angrboda took out the wolf figurine—somehow tangible, somehow every bit as real as Hel herself—and held it out to her. Hel stared at it, and her expression faltered, began to crumple just the slightest bit.

"Come to me when the end begins," Angrboda whispered. "When your father comes to you, come to *me*. I'll protect you, I swear it. You may have rejected me as your mother, but you are still my daughter."

Hel's mask of hatred was back up in an instant. "You have no daughter, witch, and I have no father. Begone. And take that worthless piece of wood with you."

No longer able to bear looking upon her daughter's twisted face, Angrboda closed her eyes and let herself float away, grasping for that deepest part of Yggdrasil—narrowly avoiding the dragon Nidhogg as it chewed the Tree's root, snapping at her as she went past—and following it up and up—

And then down again. Something—or *someone*—had sensed her presence through the Tree and was dragging her back. Angrboda's heart leapt for a moment at the thought that her daughter had perhaps experienced a sudden change of mind, but then she realized she was on the opposite side of Hel's realm now.

Why am I here? She turned to look over her shoulder at the runes carved into the doorframe: THIS IS THE EASTERN GATE AND IS DEDICATED TO MY MOTHER.

Oh, Hel . . . Angrboda's incorporeal stomach twisted as she looked around, hopeful.

But Hel herself was nowhere to be found.

Who would summon me to my own grave?

Suddenly she noticed movement in the distance. Barreling through the fields of shuffling dead, a solid figure was coming straight toward her, astride the oddest of horses.

Angrboda stood her ground and waited for the horse and rider to approach. When they were mere feet away from her, they stopped, and Angrboda recognized Sleipnir, the eight-legged horse her husband had birthed an age ago.

She took a step forward and raised a hand as if to approach the creature, but Sleipnir had grown large and fierce and did not know her. The man upon his back raised his head, and one icy blue eye stared down at her from beneath his broad-brimmed hat.

Here we go again, Angrboda thought with an inward sigh.

The feeling seemed to be mutual. "They said a wisewoman was buried here." He looked at the inscription on the doorframe and said, "Most think you died that night. Your daughter included. Perhaps I should have known."

My daughter knows the truth of things now, Angrboda thought, but she said nothing and put on her blankest face. It also occurred to her that Freyja couldn't have told him already that Angrboda was alive—the woman had just left her in the cave, after all. *So how did he find me?*

The answer was simple, she realized: She'd used Yggdrasil to travel, and Yggdrasil was his. No wonder he'd noticed her immediately once she started using *seid* again.

She looked at him, feigning confusion, and said, "What man is that who's summoned me here?" *Again,* she wanted to add. "A difficult road I have traveled to come to this place, and I've been dead a long, long time."

"Dead you are, many times over, and yet I've raised you again, for I have need of what you know. I am Vegtam, the wanderer."

Angrboda very nearly rolled her eyes at this false name, but she kept her expression the same.

"Vegtam" pulled back on Sleipnir's reins and commanded, "Tell me—for whom is Hel's hall so decorated? Whom is she to welcome?"

Hel hadn't answered Angrboda's same question, but suddenly Angrboda remembered what her daughter had said: *"I see more than you'd think down here. I know of fate."*

Suddenly she knew whom Hel was expecting.

"Despair, Vegtam," she said, her head whipping toward him, her face blank once again, "for Hel has brewed her mead for Baldur, son of Odin, who shall be slain by a sprig of mistletoe. And now I've told you too much, and I shall be silent."

"Do not be silent. Who will be his killer? Who will slay Odin's son, truly?"

Why is he asking me again, when I've already told him? Does he think the answer will change, or does he think there's more to know, more to Baldur's death than simply being pierced by a mistletoe dart?

"Baldur's blind brother, Hod," she said, recalling her vision, "who will in turn be slain by Baldur's avenger. I've told you this before, and more besides."

"You will tell me the details of his death. You will tell me all, so I can do him justice."

"Justice," she said, her chapped lips forming a cruel smile, "will be served when your son enters my daughter's hall, Odin Allfather."

"You are no wisewoman and no prophetess, Angrboda Ironwitch, mother of monsters," said Odin frostily, pulling the reins to turn Sleipnir around.

"A false man visiting a false grave you may be," Angrboda shot back, "but the only truth here is in my words."

She felt his hold on her loosen and she began to drag herself up and away. Before he could say anything in response, she grinned cruelly and said, "And beware—your own doom is fast approaching."

She awoke in her body then, with the wolf figurine still clutched in her hand, her mind reeling with emotions: grim satisfaction that she'd finally gotten the last word in a confrontation with Odin, and horrible guilt as she recalled every single sentence Hel had uttered to her.

She sagged against the she-wolf and held the figurine to her chest.

I will make this up to you. I swear it.

And I'll do it by making sure you survive Ragnarok.

IT took Angrboda some time to recover her bearings after that. The next thing she wanted to try was to reach out to her sons, but the thought of things going the same way as they had with her daughter was more than she could bear.

Nevertheless, she attempted it anyway. She sank down and reached for Yggdrasil, used the Great Tree to observe the hidden places of the worlds one by one, jumping back to her body every time she felt the slightest hint of Odin's presence—but thankfully he didn't seek her out again. In her mind she called out to her boys, but she heard nothing, saw nothing. Wherever they were— Jormungand at the deepest part of the vast ocean, Fenrir bound somewhere unknown—they were out of her reach.

She desperately hoped she would see them once more before they perished. Did they know what was to come? Had they accepted their fates, or should she be doing more for them? She didn't have an answer for these questions—and even if they survived the battle, even if their fates *could* be changed, she doubted her shield would be large or strong enough to protect both a wolf as tall as the sky and a serpent big enough to encircle a world.

As the days passed, she worked even harder on perfecting her shield—now she could protect her entire arm for several minutes—but found she was running into trouble. It had seemed so easy to sink down, go back to that void where she could feel the power flowing and tap into it. Use it for her shield.

But in reality, whenever she got close to the edge as she had before, she found herself hesitating. The power pulsed and hummed and beckoned her, and she found herself wondering if, this time, she wouldn't come back from it.

She'd almost been lost during those nine days and nine nights tied to the tree, hovering in the safety of that space between life and death. And Freyja had pushed her only far enough to skim the surface; Angrboda had been able to come back on her own. The farthest down she'd gone was when Odin had pushed her, his own knowledge of *seid* like a fishing line, ready to pull her back once she'd found out what he needed to know.

The power she sought lay deeper in that void than she'd ever been. What if she couldn't pull herself back up? That thought frightened her beyond all else. So she decided that she would venture there only as a last resort.

I am Angrboda Iron-witch, she thought. *The Old One, Mother Witch, who birthed the wolves who chased the sun and moon. Former wife to Loki and mother of both the ruler of the dead and the two creatures of chaos destined to bring about the doom of the very beings who ruined our lives.*

I can do this on my own.

MERE days later, the gods caught up with her again—this time in the form of two enormous black ravens. The birds fluttered to a dramatic stop on a branch just ahead of Angrboda and the she-wolf, blocking their passage.

"You," said one. "Witch."

"The Aesir require your assistance," said the other.

The she-wolf growled at them, but Angrboda sighed the long-suffering sigh of someone who had been burned, stabbed, killed, betrayed, hassled for information, woken up, and otherwise continuously bothered by the very same group of people who had stolen her children away from her in the night. *Will they never leave me alone?*

If the gods are so great, what do they need me for?

"I didn't know that Odin sent his ravens out to disperse information," Angrboda said to the birds, who were named Hugin and Munin, Thought and Memory. They flew around the Nine Worlds each day before returning to tell their master all they'd seen. "I was under the impression that your job was quite the opposite."

"A favor," said Hugin, "for one whose death you yourself foretold."

Angrboda hesitated. "Is it Baldur?"

Munin bobbed its head, confirming her suspicion.

Hugin said, "And it was by your husband's own hand that Baldur was slain."

"I have no husband," said Angrboda, as she had said to Skadi before, but she paused. "Wait—*Loki* killed Baldur?" *That's not what I foresaw—his brother Hod killed him. Not Loki.*

Her brow furrowed. *I saw . . . I saw Hod shoot the mistletoe into Baldur's heart.*

But Hod is blind.

Which means that someone must've guided his hand.

"How did this happen?" Angrboda asked.

"Odin's son had been dreaming of his own demise, and his mother, Frigg, made everything in all the worlds swear not to harm him," said Munin.

"All but a young sprig of mistletoe, which Loki the Deceiver sharpened into a dart for Hod to use to slay his brother," said Hugin.

Odin knew about the mistletoe, Angrboda thought. *If he truly wished to prevent Baldur's death, he would've warned Frigg to take extra care.*

But something still wasn't adding up. She herself hadn't known that Loki would be the one to slay Baldur, so how could Odin have known? Was Loki being framed? Punished for a crime he did not commit?

Angrboda's eyes narrowed. "You lie. Loki is many things, aye—but a murderer?"

"You must do a favor for an innocent," Hugin added, like it hadn't heard her.

Angrboda sighed again. *That's what I get for arguing with birds, I suppose.* "What exactly do they need my assistance with?"

"Pushing his pyre into the water," said Hugin. "The ship will not budge. Not even Thor can move it. The Aesir fear it's bewitched."

"Your safety is guaranteed," Munin finished.

"With us, Hyrrokkin," said the ravens together, and they fluttered ahead to the next branch and turned around to look at her as if bidding her to follow.

Angrboda arched her eyebrows and turned to the she-wolf. "Hyrrokkin. You hear that? 'Fire-smoked.' That's a new one, that is."

In response, her companion made a sound disturbingly close to a snort of derision. *We're not really going to do this, are we?*

"Well, I've no desire to set foot in Asgard ever again, or do the gods any favors. But I can't deny I'm tempted to heed this summons."

The she-wolf looked skeptical. *Why? I have a distinct feeling that you were their last resort . . .*

"For my own selfish reasons," Angrboda said, stowing the wagon behind a cluster of trees. When it was sufficiently hidden, she stuck her walking stick in the she-wolf's mouth, where it promptly transformed into reins. "To see how Odin feels to have his most cherished son taken from him. To watch him grieve with my own two eyes, after all he's done to me."

But he knew it was coming, and he didn't prevent it, the she-wolf pointed out.

"That doesn't mean he's not grieving." Angrboda pulled herself onto the she-wolf's back. "Besides, how often do you get to attend the funeral of a god?"

THEY followed the ravens out of the forest and to a rocky, crowded beach, where there was assembled the most diverse group Angrboda had yet seen in the Nine Worlds: the Aesir, the Vanir, light elves and dark elves, dwarfs, trolls, Odin's valkyries and *einherjar*—his slain warriors—and even some giants she'd seen before. Angrboda pulled her hood lower over her face so none would recognize her. If it was truly a spell keeping Baldur's funeral pyre from moving, she'd need all the strength she could muster to break it, and she didn't feel the need to waste her energy glamouring herself into an old woman when a hood would do just as well.

The assembly parted for the witch and the she-wolf as though they were lepers. The two of them rode right up to the beach, where a massive ship sat, half in the sand and half in the water. A few of the Aesir and one of the trolls were hanging back from it, doubled over and breathless. Thor was among them, seeming furious.

The witch dismounted the wolf and took the reins from the animal's mouth; they instantly turned back into a walking stick, which Angrboda used to brace her steps on the dark sand as it shifted beneath her feet.

She was just moving toward the ship when she heard her companion snarl from behind her—and she whirled around to see that two of Odin's berserkers had crossed spears between her and the she-wolf, and two more berserkers had spears pointed directly at the creature's throat.

"That is unnecessary," Angrboda said coldly to them, her hood still hiding her face.

The berserkers did not move an inch.

I'm fine, the she-wolf said. *Just hurry up and do what they wish, so that we might leave.*

So Angrboda walked up to the ship, and Thor stepped back, scowling. He looked to his father, and then Angrboda looked past him and saw Odin: dressed not in the heavy traveling cloak and hat in which she usually saw him, but rather now in the finery befitting the highest of the gods. He was staring her down with his one eye, and she could see the sorrow there, though she could not bring herself to feel sorry for him.

Next to him stood a woman Angrboda barely recognized from her time in Asgard—his wife, Frigg, dressed in the finest clothes she'd ever seen, with her dark hair elaborately plaited, her face tearstained, her raw grief laid bare.

She saw Frey, Freyja, and Tyr as well, all looking mournful. Angrboda did not feel sorry for them, either.

With one of her hands hovering a few inches away from the ship, Angrboda lifted her head such that her features were distinguishable only from Odin's angle. She arched her eyebrows, questioning. He nodded.

She reached toward the ship and immediately felt the spell

beneath her fingertips, saw the runes carved upon the prow, and knew that it was he who had cast it.

Her head whipped around to face Odin. "What trickery is this?" she hissed.

"It's no trick," the All-father said. "Merely a means to an end. As is everything I've done in my long life. Perhaps you know the feeling."

Angrboda opened her mouth to argue, but then she heard a yelp and whirled to see that every head had turned to where the berserkers were trying to restrain the she-wolf, who yelped again as two of them knocked her down and kept their spears at her throat. The wolf bared her teeth but did not move.

Hurry, the she-wolf said.

Angrboda turned back to Odin, who was giving her an unfathomable look.

"Why?" she asked. "Why did you really summon me here?"

"Because you wouldn't come otherwise, and I wished for you to see. It's all coming to pass, just as you said it would. We stand here as equals: me the father of the gods, and you the mother of the giants. Are you prepared for what comes next?"

"Yes," Angrboda lied, lifting her chin. She discreetly took out her antler-handled knife and scratched off the runes on the prow, movements hidden from Odin by her cloak. "Are you?"

He was silent, but his one eye followed her as she gave the ship a gentle push and it slid off its rollers and into the sea. Behind them, she heard Thor cry out in rage and disbelief.

Iron-witch and All-father waded into the shallows after the boat. Angrboda said, "I suppose you've done nothing *but* prepare."

"I only did what I had to do. I wanted you to know that," he replied, looking down into the boat at his dead son. "Plants die;

animals die. Men die and their kinsmen die. And so, too, must gods meet their demise, for not even we can prevent it."

"But you didn't even try," said Angrboda. She didn't ask him why; she already knew.

Odin did not respond to that. As Angrboda turned and walked back up onto the beach, he placed his famous gold arm ring inside the boat and leaned over to whisper something in Baldur's ear.

"We should kill her," Thor said loudly as Angrboda passed. She paid him no mind, but that old healed wound on her head began to throb painfully.

"She's done us a favor," said Frey, who stood leaning on his golden boar, Gullinbursti, as Baldur's pyre was lit and pushed farther out to sea by Odin's *einherjar*. The god himself watched, still knee-deep in the water, silent.

Angrboda's heart skipped a beat when another voice joined the fray.

"Leave her be," said Skadi, standing beside an older-looking man who Angrboda assumed was Njord.

After the briefest of pauses, Angrboda resumed walking, turning just enough to meet the woman's gaze as she passed.

Skadi's eyes widened.

The witch inclined her head just slightly, as if to say, *Now. Now I'm done.*

But before she could determine whether she'd been understood, Angrboda turned away quickly, hoping the Huntress had gotten the message. For next to her were two women whom Angrboda could not trust: first was Gerd, looking miserable, and next to *her* was Sigyn, whose expression was a mix of anguish and trepidation. As if she feared that the gods would turn on her for what her husband had done.

She's right to be afraid, Angrboda thought, noting that Sigyn's sons were nowhere to be seen.

Angrboda kept her head down and continued walking. When she reached the she-wolf, the berserkers lifted their spears and parted, allowing both woman and wolf to pass.

After that, Baldur's wife, Nanna, died of heartbreak and was placed upon the boat to burn with him, along with his horse, and Thor angrily kicked a passing dwarf onto the pyre. But by that point Angrboda had mounted the she-wolf and disappeared back into the woods.

The she-wolf found her way back to the wagon easily enough. Angrboda slid off her back and took her walking stick. "You've been through enough today, my friend. I'll pull the wagon."

Where are we going?

"Home," said Angrboda. She'd been thinking about it for the past few days, ever since her encounter with Freyja. There was no need for her to travel any farther—she'd found out all she'd needed to know. It would do her some good, she thought, to continue practicing her spell in the safety and comfort of her cave.

Part of her wanted to wait to see if Skadi would follow immediately, but another part wanted to get as far away from Asgard as possible. Besides, Skadi could be delayed by business with the Aesir—Loki was still on the loose, after all, and Angrboda did not doubt that Skadi would want to have a hand in capturing him.

And Angrboda suddenly understood that whether or not he was guilty, she knew he was going to suffer—she'd seen it herself—and now she knew why.

It made her stomach churn—the thought itself, along with the fear that she knew the first place he would hide: the only place he'd ever felt safe, in that cave on the edge of the worlds.

But that wouldn't scare her away from her own home. And if he'd indeed had the nerve to seek refuge there, then he had some explaining to do.

FINALLY they crossed the river into Ironwood, and Angrboda and the she-wolf both visibly relaxed as they were swallowed up by the dense trees. The woods—*her* woods—were no longer green as they had been during the years she dwelled there in her cave, raising her children, but the place still felt familiar, felt like *home*.

Looks the same as I left it, the she-wolf said. *Gray and dead.* She stopped and sniffed the air, then veered to the right. Angrboda frowned and followed her before she realized they were heading south toward the stone foundations. The she-wolf loped ahead of her through the thickets until she came to the clearing, where she sat down heavily and bowed her large, shaggy head, almost as if in reverence.

Angrboda came up behind the wolf and pulled off her hood. She stood beside her friend and leaned heavily on her walking stick.

"This is where they lived," she said quietly. "All that time ago."

It was, said the she-wolf, tilting her head to look Angrboda in the eye. *Do you remember?*

"More than before, but I wish I could remember it all." The witch squeezed her eyes shut. She had moved beyond guilt over the Jarnvidjur, but that didn't mean she'd let go of all her regrets. Now that she was standing here, taking in the ruins and *knowing* in her heart whom they'd come from and who she'd been before, she couldn't help but think again of how different it could've been if she'd never left, or if the Jarnvidjur had still been there when she'd returned . . .

"I wonder what it feels like," she whispered, "to have someone to come home to."

You still do, the she-wolf reminded her.

"You mean Loki?" Angrboda spat, whirling. "My home is no longer his. If he's there when we return—"

Calm yourself. I'm not talking about him, the she-wolf said, rolling her eyes. *I'm talking about your Huntress. Don't act like you have no one to come home to, when it's just as likely she heeded your call and forsook the gods the moment Baldur's funeral ended to make her way back here. And if Loki did in fact seek refuge in your cave and happened to cross paths with her, she could be bashing his face into the side of a mountain at this very moment. Isn't that a lovely thought?*

Angrboda felt the heat rise to her face and was about to reply, but then she felt a rush of air from behind her. They both turned to see a person shifting from the form of a falcon as they pulled off a feathered cloak.

Her first thought was that it was Freyja, and she opened her mouth to tell her to go away, but when the person's form solidified, it was Frigg.

Frigg, in her fine clothes with her dark hair styled intricately, a golden band around her head. Her face was lined and beautiful, and she was shorter and slighter than Angrboda. But there was something severe about her—though perhaps it was merely the look of a woman who had just lost her son.

Angrboda knew the feeling well.

I suppose my protection spell has run its course, if she could find us here.

"Your daughter, Hel, has decreed that if everything in all the worlds will weep for Baldur, he can return from her realms," said Frigg to Angrboda, her stern face set in determination. "We gods and goddesses have dispatched ourselves throughout the Nine

Worlds to see that this would be so. Will you shed a tear for him, so that my son can return to me?"

Angrboda and the she-wolf were both silent.

"There was a hag in a cave who would not weep," Frigg went on, her red-rimmed gray eyes narrowed to slits as she took a few steps closer to them. "She said, 'Let Hel hold what she has.' Freyja suspected it was you, Angrboda Iron-witch, so I came to speak with you myself. Mother to mother."

"It was not I," said Angrboda, "but I have cried enough over the loss of my own children. I have no tears left for yours. So now you have two who will not weep for Baldur."

Three, said the she-wolf, though Frigg couldn't hear her.

Frigg closed her eyes as if she'd suffered a blow, then opened them again. "Would you not wish someone to do the same, if it were your children?"

"If enough tears could have saved my children from their fates, I would have made all the worlds weep," said Angrboda after a moment. One tear dripped down her cheek, and she wiped it hastily away; the she-wolf imitated her. "There. It is done. But that was not just for Baldur."

"It will suffice," said Frigg. "Thank you." Her gaze lingered on the witch and her companion for a moment before she donned the falcon cloak again and flew away.

Loki stands by his deed, it seems, the she-wolf pointed out, *if he's so committed to Baldur staying dead.*

"*Let Hel hold what she has,*" Angrboda murmured, and suddenly the thought of Loki getting his face bashed into the side of a mountain didn't seem so sweet. She shook herself, unwilling to dwell on the implications of this, and said, "Come. My home's not far."

I know, said the she-wolf. *Lead the way.*

❖ ❖ ❖

THEY traversed the woods in silence until they came to the cave. Her heart ached at the sight of the emptiness of the clearing, the barrenness of her garden—and then skipped a beat when she saw that the door to her cave was ajar. No smoke rose from the chimney hole and no light could be seen within, but she knew it was not empty.

"Stay here," said Angrboda to the she-wolf as she started forward.

She found Loki slumped in her chair when she went inside.

He was staring at the empty hearth like a man already dead: green eyes glazed, scarred mouth set in a thin line, elbows on the arms of the chair, and long, thin fingers laced as if he were thinking. His deep green Asgard-style tunic was muddied and torn, and his unlined face was haggard.

How long had he been sitting here, without a fire, without food? Angrboda did not care.

When he saw her, he looked up, and his eyes widened as he sprang from the chair.

"They said you were dead," Loki said, his voice barely a whisper. He reached for her. "Boda, I'd been looking but—they said you were—they said—and like a fool I believed them."

"You did," Angrboda confirmed without emotion—although to be fair, she imagined that Skadi would probably rather light herself on fire than tell Loki that his ex-wife yet lived, and Freyja and Odin had only just found out.

For his part, Odin probably had his own underhanded reasons for not running straight to his blood brother with this information. *If Loki had known I was alive, what would have been different?*

It had no bearing on Angrboda's feelings toward him, however, and she only glared daggers at him until he wilted under her gaze.

"I killed Baldur," Loki said weakly. He collapsed back into the chair, hands shaking. "I killed Baldur and then I wouldn't weep for him, so he's staying with Hel. And the Aesir are out for my blood."

"And rightly so. It's not wise to be here," she told him callously as she took off her traveling cloak and hood and threw them on the table along with her pack. "Frigg herself appeared in my woods—my protection spell is spent. Make no mistake, the gods are coming for you. Just as they came for me all that time ago. Just as they came for our children. Thanks to *you*."

Loki stood and reached out to her again. "Boda—"

But Angrboda took a step back and put her hands up. She felt as though her heart had jumped up into her throat, for when she spoke, her voice was thick with rage.

"You," she said, "had the nerve to come *here*?"

"I had nowhere else to go," Loki said desperately. "This was my home."

"But no longer. Get out."

"If it's as you say, they'll be here soon. You have to help me."

"I will do no such thing. And how can I help you, anyway? You destroyed your own family—betrayed your own children. And now you've slain a son of Odin. You've slain your blood brother's kin—your *own* kin. I cannot help you. I cannot do a thing."

"Will you even let me apologize? I *wanted* to, but it was too late because you were—I thought you were gone. I never thought I would get the chance."

"It's not me you should apologize to," Angrboda snapped. "The boys are beyond my reach, but I visited Hel. She was not happy to see me."

Loki winced as if she'd hit him. "Is that so? How is she?"

"Cruel, powerful, and lonely. And she blames me for all of it—when she should be blaming *you*."

"I did what I could for them. For all of them. For *you*."

"And it all amounted to nothing." Angrboda recalled what Freyja had told her—that Loki had attempted to bargain for her life—and found it didn't dampen her rage.

"I know. But I *did* try." Loki clenched his fists. "The gods do what they want and have no concern for others."

"And that doesn't sound familiar to you?"

"What's that supposed to mean?"

Angrboda raised her chin. "It means that you don't have to be a god to do that. And you were never a god to me, Loki."

He ignored the jibe, too focused on himself to heed her. "That doesn't change the fact that I *am* a god. And the worst among them, at that. I'm the one who's done the most evil among the Aesir, and if nothing else, at least they'll remember my name. That's more than one can say for you." When she didn't respond, he switched to a different tactic. "If you turn your back on me now, you condemn me to death."

Angrboda shook her head and stepped closer to him. "Not death. Although I'd gladly condemn you to that, if it meant you'd be on your knees in our daughter's hall, begging her forgiveness."

Loki ignored this, too. "You have the power, don't you? To protect me?"

"Perhaps I could, but I won't." She held his gaze. "You were right. I married you and mothered your children. That's all there is for me. That's all anyone will ever know. The worlds go on, and you have a part to play in what's to come."

"A part to play," Loki echoed, looking at her as if seeing her for the first time. "Boda, I told you the very first time we met that I want nothing to do with your depressing prophecies. I make my own way—I choose my own fate. You can't take that away from me." His tone turned pleading. "You *mustn't*."

"Why did you do it, then?" Angrboda whispered. "Why did you kill your brother's son?"

"The gods took everything from us, Boda," he whispered back. "I thought it was high time I took something from them."

Tears pricked Angrboda's eyes at this. *Even not knowing what would happen, not knowing that he was fated to do so . . . Loki did it anyway.*

He thinks this is all within his control, within our control, and I envy him this ignorance.

And then another thought struck her.

Let Hel hold what she has.

"Took something—some*one*—from them," she said slowly, "and gave it to our daughter."

Loki gave her a wan smile. "See? Everybody wins."

Something about that was nagging her, something Angrboda couldn't put her finger on. Hel had always been Loki's favorite. Had he truly slain Odin's favorite son as a gift for his daughter? Had he had only Hel in mind when he'd guided that dart into Baldur's heart? She searched his face for any clue that he was deceiving her, but she couldn't decide.

And before she could ask, he saw his opening, saw that she had softened. He stepped closer to her and said quietly, "If you ever held any love for me, you would help me now."

Those words, her words from the night her children were taken, stabbed her like a knife to the gut. But she was ready for such a threat, for she had one of her own.

"And if *you* ever held any love for *me*," she said coldly, "you would understand why I cannot and will not help you. And you would leave."

You are destined to face the consequences of your actions, Loki Laufey-jarson. And there is nothing anyone can do about it.

Loki held her gaze for a solid moment, and she found herself astounded that he was actually taking her words to heart instead of discarding them as he had that night. He put his hand on her cheek for a moment before lowering it, brushing his fingertip over the top of her scar, which was barely visible above the neckline of her dress.

"Do you still wonder sometimes whether it might have been wrong for me to return your heart to you?" he asked her.

Angrboda grabbed his wrist and pushed it away. "You don't have permission to touch me. Not anymore."

"I suppose that's my answer." Loki dropped his hand and stepped back, smoothing all emotion from his face. Then he moved past her to the door.

"Where will you go?" she asked.

He shrugged, then squared his shoulders, not turning around. "The gods are having a feast at Aegir's, by the sea. I believe I'll drop in and give them a little piece of my mind. Or a big one, perhaps."

"Will you *ever* learn to keep your mouth shut, Sly One?" Angrboda asked him, a sad smile tugging at the corners of her mouth despite herself as she finally turned to face him.

Loki looked over his shoulder at her, the fading light framing him in the doorway, and his scarred lips twisted into a wicked grin.

"Not likely," he said.

And then he was gone.

ANGRBODA sat in her chair for hours afterward, absently turning Hel's wolf figurine in her hands, wondering whether she'd done the right thing. The she-wolf was rather too small to fit inside the cave comfortably—Angrboda had far less furniture inside the last time the she-wolf had lived in Ironwood with her—and so stood watch in the clearing, sheltering indoors only at night.

Eventually Angrboda got up and started a fire in her center hearth and started practicing her spell again. Then she remade her bed and unpacked her wagon and pack basket. She went outside and set up a few rabbit snares, and the she-wolf herded the creatures to their deaths before going off to hunt larger game to feed herself, as Fenrir had done so long ago.

And so Angrboda lingered there in that awkward state, where everything was so familiar—her home, her bed, and her rabbit stew, now made with foraged root vegetables instead of the ones from her now-empty garden—and yet so different.

Skadi arrived at her door a few days later.

Angrboda was sitting on her stool next to the fire, summoning up the energy to strengthen her shield enough to put both arms into the flames this time, when the Huntress entered. The two women stared at each other as Angrboda stood slowly, at a loss for words.

She had never been more relieved to see anyone in all her long life, and now that Skadi was here, she had no idea what to say.

"Your wolf almost didn't let me pass," said Skadi, standing awkwardly just inside the door. She had a jug of ale in one hand and was holding two skinned, headless rabbits by the legs with the other; she shifted from foot to foot. "You . . . did want me to come here, right? Or did I misunderstand that look you gave me at Baldur's funeral?"

"Yes," Angrboda said quickly. Then she cleared her throat. "I mean, no, you didn't misunderstand. I want you here."

"I see." Skadi stepped inside and set the jug down on the table. "So you've done what you set out to do?"

"I did as much as I could, and it was time to return." She went to her chest and pulled out two empty cups, uncorked the jug and filled them with ale, and passed one to Skadi, who sat backward on one of the benches at the table, facing the fire. Angrboda put the rabbits into her cauldron, added some water from a bucket so their dinner could stew, and put another log on the fire. Skadi was silent all the while, but Angrboda could feel the weight of her gaze.

"He came here, didn't he?" Skadi asked as soon as Angrboda sat back down.

"He did," said Angrboda.

"And you turned him away?"

"Aye."

"Because you knew what he'd done?"

By way of a response, Angrboda turned back to the fire and asked, very quietly, a question to which she already knew the answer—for she knew he'd be bound in torment, but she hadn't seen the events connecting Baldur's death to Loki's punishment. "What has become of him?"

Skadi leaned back against the table. "He went to a feast the Aesir were holding at Aegir's—probably right after he left here. I myself was present. He forced Odin to seat him, citing their kinship, and then proceeded to insult everyone present." Skadi pursed her lips, evidently recalling some of said verbal abuse. "The insults returned only served to roll off him like water from a leaf. Then Thor arrived and made him leave by threat of violence."

"Of course. How very like Thor." Angrboda tried very hard to force down a dark smile and failed. *Yet he knew enough to realize that, should he engage Loki in verbal combat, he would lose. A smart move on Thor's part to stick to his strong suit: brute force.*

"Indeed," said Skadi. "Anyway, he left and was hunted down. Then he was captured and bound, not two days ago. I don't know if I should tell you the rest."

"I should like to know."

Skadi sighed. "He was taken somewhere distant, somewhere in Midgard. One of his sons with Sigyn was turned into a wolf, who then disemboweled the other son. Loki was bound with that second son's guts, which turned to iron. The wolf then ran off." She shifted. "No wonder Sigyn reacted the way she did, that night at the river, if that's what you made her see . . ."

Angrboda nodded grimly. "What then?"

"Then a snake was hung above Loki's head, dripping venom on his face," said Skadi. "He writhed so powerfully, it felt as though all of Midgard shook. But the Aesir allowed Sigyn to stay with him, with a bowl to catch the poison— reluctantly, for they think he doesn't deserve as much. And so do I. But at least this way, he will be too distracted to try thinking his way out of this. It was necessary."

Angrboda let this sink in. *So this was it. This was how my vision came to pass.*

Skadi reached forward and put a hand on her arm. "Are you all right?"

"I am." Angrboda nodded. "Thank you."

"For what?"

"For telling me all of this. And for coming back."

"Of course," said Skadi. She looked like she was about to say more, but instead she said, "So, I'm assuming that your quest was successful?"

Angrboda smiled. "We have a lot to catch up on, my friend."

Skadi sat silently through Angrboda's tale, which took well into the night to finish telling; the only part Angrboda left out was how she'd seen Skadi at Hymir's feast. By then the rabbits had stewed so long that the meat fell right off the bone, and the jug of ale had run dry.

"So that's where the wolf came from," Skadi said when she was done. "You're she, then. The witch who lived here so long ago, whom I mentioned on the day we met."

"I am."

"Well," said Skadi, "then it seems to me, if you're she, you're more than capable of—well, whatever it is you're going to do about all this."

"I appreciate your confidence, my friend."

"Anytime. I'll be right back—I have to use the latrine." Skadi stood, went to the door, and opened it—causing a gust of unseasonably cold air to rush into the cave. Confused, Angrboda moved to join her at the door, where the Huntress had stopped short.

Angrboda soon saw why.

There was snow. Three feet at least, which had not been there when Skadi had arrived a few hours earlier.

Which was not terribly unusual, except that midsummer had been a month ago.

"Fimbulwinter," Angrboda whispered. When Skadi gave her a questioning look, she explained, "Baldur's death and Loki's binding are the start of Ragnarok—that's what they're calling my prophecy. And next comes three years of winter."

The she-wolf, who seemed to have been fast asleep in the clearing, stood up suddenly and shook herself, sending wet clumps of snow everywhere. Then she looked at the giantesses and said grumpily, *I don't suppose you have room inside?*

Angrboda and Skadi moved to either side to let the creature pass, and Skadi said, "She can talk?"

"You can hear her?" Angrboda's eyebrows shot up. "I thought it was only me. And so did she, for that matter."

Skadi shrugged. "I've always felt a certain kinship with wolves . . ."

Oh, I like this one, said the she-wolf as she settled down by the hearth. *Can we keep her?*

❖   ❖   ❖

THE winter escalated quickly, and Skadi left the cave before the mountain passes were snowed in. Angrboda did not expect to see her again for some time, and she wondered what she was going to do for three long years, sitting here with the she-wolf. *Work on my spell, I suppose.*

Skadi had not asked her to go to the mountains with her again, and Angrboda tried not to be disheartened by that.

But Skadi did something unexpected: She packed every single provision and possession she could from her hall, loaded everything onto three sledges, donned her skis, and led all her reindeer down from the mountains.

Angrboda could not have been more shocked if Freyja herself had suddenly appeared to apologize for restraining her bodily while the gods stole her children away.

"I know you didn't invite me to winter here, but your wolf did," said Skadi, amused, as Angrboda gaped at her from the doorway. "As I understand it, this is her home, too."

"This must be everything you own," Angrboda sputtered.

"Everything of value, at any rate. Would you care to lend a hand, or does your head pain you today?"

"You're . . . giving up Thrymheim?" Angrboda whispered. "Why? You wouldn't even do such a thing for your husband."

"A three-year-long winter anywhere would be rough, but I fear it'll be worse in the mountains." Skadi shrugged, but the look of amusement did not leave her face. "It's the end times, my friend. And while I'm hardly worried about us surviving, I cannot say the same for the rest of this realm. I suppose it won't surprise you to hear that the giants have been growing restless and angry."

Angrboda thought back to her visit to Hymir's hall—which

Skadi was still unaware of—and then realized Skadi was referencing the witch's own prophecy.

"It's our nature to be that way, but it's been worse ever since Baldur was killed and Loki bound—I heard enough on the way here to make me think they'd march tomorrow if most of us weren't from the mountains. It's been one thing after another with the Aesir for many years now, but Loki's binding was the last straw. Many believe his killing Baldur proves that the Trickster is on our side once and for all. Besides that, his insults to the gods at Aegir's feast have been chronicled in a poem by someone who was there—a servant perhaps—and are making their rounds. Can you imagine how Jotunheim feels, hearing someone talk to the gods that way? Loki didn't hold anything back."

"They're rallying around him," Angrboda murmured. "It's a flimsy excuse, but we've always been a combative sort of people, haven't we?"

"Yes," said Skadi. "The giants will take any excuse for a chance to take down the gods once and for all. But if we're to fight, Jotunheim must survive this winter."

"I've been thinking about that as well," Angrboda said quietly, choosing to ignore Skadi's use of the word "we" when talking about the giants marching toward Ragnarok—and their deaths. "You've always been my strongest connection to the worlds outside these woods—I believe we can find a way to help. As in the old days. I wondered if you could go to—?"

"Gymir's hall, to see what remains of Gerd's old garden, so you can resume making your hunger potions for me to dispense all over Jotunheim and Midgard?"

Angrboda blinked. "Well, yes. Exactly."

"Why do you think I'm in such a hurry to unload these and get going?" Skadi untied one of the ropes holding the supplies to the first sledge and handed Angrboda a thick bedroll with furs sticking out. "Put this next to your bed—it's where I'll sleep."

"That's nonsense," Angrboda said without thinking. "You'll share my bed."

Skadi opened her mouth and shut it again.

"That is—it's large enough for both of us to sleep comfortably. I'll not see you sleeping on the floor when we can both fit our separate beddings on my sleeping pallet." Angrboda was grateful that her face was already so red from the biting wind—it helped disguise the flush creeping up her cheeks.

"All right," Skadi said when she finally found her voice. "Put this next to yours, then."

AND so, as in the time before, Skadi traveled out into the worlds and back again with her reindeer and sledge, and Angrboda stayed behind in Ironwood and worked with the materials Skadi brought back for her.

Skadi's first supply trip was indeed to Gymir's hall. Gerd's parents' servants had continued to grow her garden in her absence, and all the plants had been harvested, dried, and stored as soon as the unexpected winter began.

Gymir parted with all of it: Every last leaf and stem was loaded onto Skadi's sledge. When Angrboda expressed her surprise, Skadi remarked offhandedly, "They need little."

The months passed. Angrboda counted them by phases of the moon, and soon there was one year gone. As the winter continued, Skadi's suppliers ran lower and lower, so she was forced to cover more ground in her search. The she-wolf often went with her, leaving Angrboda alone. Skadi was sometimes gone for weeks at a time.

Angrboda fretted over her absence, but in her heart she knew that if there was one woman in the cosmos who could take care of herself, it was Skadi Thjazadottir.

I suppose it's always been my lot to wait here for someone, Angrboda thought. Those times when Skadi did stay and spend the night, Angrboda could barely sleep, and it seemed to her that they were separated by more than just the several layers of fur of their individual bedrolls. Part of her was screaming to roll over and have the conversation she'd been meaning to have with Skadi for a very long time—a conversation that would explain the stab of jealousy Angrboda had felt when she'd heard Skadi was married, and much more yet.

She stopped herself every time, and before she knew it, Skadi was off again.

I'm overthinking, she told herself, but she still felt frozen with fear. *But what if I'm misreading things? What if I've misread her from the very beginning? What if it's all in my head?*

For her part, the she-wolf remained mostly silent and observant these days but would sometimes give Angrboda knowing looks when Skadi was turned the other way.

"Do you ever think about your cousin Gerd?" Angrboda asked Skadi one night as they sat across from each other at the witch's table. Skadi had just returned from one of her long trips, her cheeks still red from the cold, a steaming bowl of stew cupped in her hands. The she-wolf sat in the corner, gnawing on the leg of a small hoofed animal she'd killed earlier that day.

"I don't think about her often enough," Skadi admitted. "When I visited Gymir's for those supplies, her old mother was shuffling about the hall with her head down. She speaks of Gerd in the past tense, as though she'd died rather than wed. She has it bad in Asgard, though," she added, and her dark expression encouraged Angrboda not to inquire further.

Angrboda felt the tiniest stab of pity for her old friend, but she shook it off and sat up straighter over her bowl. "Well, she made her decision."

"She didn't have much of a choice in marrying Frey," Skadi said gently. "And from there, it was only a short step further to betray you to the gods, as she was compelled to do. I cannot excuse what she did to you and her family, but I do recognize why she did it. There is a difference between understanding and forgiveness. It's possible to have one without the other."

"Hmm," said Angrboda, raising her bowl of stew to her mouth to take a sip of broth. Angrboda often thought of Gerd when she looked at her own tablet-woven belt, which had weathered quite a lot with her over the course of her travels and had become dirty with age no matter how much she washed it. It was truly well crafted to have held up this long.

"I do understand," Angrboda said after a time. "But it's as you said—I cannot forgive it, and I hope never to see her again for as long as I live."

Skadi considered this. "You cannot forgive Loki and not forgive Gerd."

Angrboda froze with the bowl halfway to her mouth. "Who says I've forgiven Loki?"

"I didn't say you have; I'm only *saying*." Skadi shifted on her bench. "I spoke with Gymir for a long time when I went to him. He told me that the giants were beginning to amass in the citadel at Utgard to weather out the long winter together."

"And?" Angrboda sipped her stew. "Did Gymir go to Utgard, then?"

Skadi nodded.

"So that's why he let you take so many provisions from his stores."

The Huntress nodded again. "He and his wife needed only what they could take with them to Utgard. And Gymir spoke truthfully—many of my trading partners have abandoned their villages and homesteads and headed north to the citadel. More and more each time I venture out. Lately I've been going to Utgard to dispense your potions and gather new provisions."

"That's why you're gone so long these days," Angrboda said with a frown. But she had a feeling there was something Skadi wasn't telling her. "Do . . . do they know of Ragnarok? Or are the giants amassing of their own accord?"

"They're blissfully ignorant, for now. And I'm not about to tell them. They wouldn't believe me, anyway—they'd want proof." Skadi finished her stew and crossed her arms on the table, regarding Angrboda levelly. "When the long winter is over and the end begins, they're going to march against the gods. And I'm going with them."

Angrboda had sensed this coming, but her insides turned to ice nonetheless.

"Why would you do such a thing?" she asked, fighting to keep her voice even. Her head began to pound horribly. She felt dizzy with anger.

"Because what else can I do?" Skadi shrugged, and Angrboda's blood pressure rose further. "It seems a fitting end for me, does it not? I'm going to die fighting—fighting for my land, fighting for my *people*. Fighting to avenge my father."

"Is your father not already avenged?" Angrboda said through gritted teeth.

Skadi scowled; the witch's words had prodded a sore spot.

"The gods slew him and gave me a fool's recompense for his death," she said, her voice rising. "I shall have a proper vengeance and take down as many of his killers as I can."

Angrboda pushed her stew bowl away and laced her fingers on

the table. "Please, my friend, listen to me. I've seen much, but I haven't seen *your* fate. Or my own. I saw the deaths of the gods and my sons and many more—but not ours."

Skadi shook her head. "We're safe, sure, until Surt's flames consume us."

Angrboda took a deep breath. The flaming sword of the fire giant Surt, who was fated to kill Frey in that final battle, would engulf all the worlds in flame.

And just like that, it would end: the final act of Ragnarok.

"You know I've been working on that," Angrboda said. She hadn't gotten much further with her shield spell, but she still had two more years to work on it, by her reckoning. Two years before Fimbulwinter ended.

Two years to talk Skadi out of this madness.

Skadi shook her head again. "There's nothing that can stop it, Angrboda. There's no power in the cosmos that can escape what's coming. You've said so yourself." She rose from the bench. "I don't wish to fight about this. My mind is made up."

Angrboda rose with her and ground out, "You'll be killed along with everyone else. You *know* I've been working on a plan, a *spell*, to keep Hel safe. And it can keep you safe, too. You don't have to fight—"

"I *want* to fight."

"Then you will die," Angrboda said coldly.

"Then at least I can say I fought," Skadi said, suddenly shouting, "and at least in death, I'll be free from the pain of my father's loss and all my failures."

"You don't believe I can protect you from this?" The witch balled her fists, angry tears springing to her eyes. "You don't believe in *me*?"

Skadi stared her down: first incredulous, then with a swelling fury.

"You're an absolute fool," she said in a low voice, "to assume that this has anything to do with you. You cannot be angry with me for wishing to be selfish in this *one thing*. This is not about you or your feelings, however intent you are on twisting it. Because the truth is that I've done all for you, for the gods, for my family. I must do this for myself."

And with that, Skadi stormed out of the cave and into the snow, letting the door slam shut behind her, leaving Angrboda standing dumbfounded in her wake.

The she-wolf looked up from her goat leg and commented, *You are a fool, you know.*

Angrboda couldn't argue with that.

WITH Skadi gone, there was nothing for Angrboda to do but work on her spell. Some days she could lean over the fire and it wouldn't even singe her hair; other days, when she couldn't concentrate hard enough to protect so much as her fingertips, she felt herself inching ever closer to the void.

She couldn't help it. Looking inward, *grasping* inward, ultimately led her to that place—that expanse of power that dwelled before her as if she were looking down into a deep, dark well, with eons of primordial energy humming beneath the surface.

Waiting.

For her.

It was the same dangerous power she'd tapped into in order to gain knowledge of Ragnarok, but it had never been something she chose, never been within her control. To access this power willingly—to accept it, to *embrace* it—scared her beyond belief. But she had a sinking feeling that, in the end, she wouldn't have a choice.

Once she took that plunge, she knew she would not resurface.

But she kept practicing anyway. It wasn't good enough to assume that tapping into the power of the void was the answer—if she got only one shot at it and it didn't work, then all was lost. She would rather rely mostly on herself and use the void as a last recourse.

Her spell was improving every day, to the point where she was certain she'd be able to protect her entire body from being burned.

And that's how, some weeks after Skadi stormed out on her, she found herself standing on her chair, barefoot and clad in her thinnest linen gown, looking at her center hearth. She'd taken down the cauldron to give her more space, but now she was having second thoughts as she stared into the fire.

It must be done. One way or another, I'll have to do this sometime.

She took a deep breath, summoned every ounce of strength she had into her spell, and stepped into the hearth.

The flames lapped at the hem of her dress, as harmless as calm waves on the shore. Her skin remained unscathed, though the embers were uncomfortable under her feet. And all the while the dark place called to her—it would be so easy to reach out and tap into it. But she ignored the urge and kept her concentration locked on maintaining the barrier around herself.

She didn't know how long she stood there before she opened her eyes and saw Skadi standing in the doorway, staring at her in utmost awe.

Angrboda gasped in surprise and toppled sideways out of the hearth—and found herself free-falling one second and in Skadi's arms the next. They stared at each other for a long moment before Skadi set her upright and stepped away, looking embarrassed.

A beat of silence passed.

"I didn't hear the door open," Angrboda said, awkwardly shaking the ashes off the hem of her dress.

"I knocked. Sorry. I needed to clear my head," Skadi said, sitting down on a bench and staring into the fire. "I was afraid if I came back here too soon, it would be the end of our friendship for good."

"I understand." Angrboda sat down on the bed and regarded her.

"That was incredible, what you were doing just now. Is this— what you've been working on all this time? Your spell to save Hel?"

"Yes." Angrboda shifted. "I—I'm glad you came back. So I could tell you that I was wrong. What I said to you before. I'm sorry."

Skadi's head whipped around to face her, brows raised high over pale blue eyes. She seemed at a loss for words for a moment before sighing and coming over to sit next to Angrboda on the bed. "At least you admit it. Although, you know, sometimes I wish I had never met you. You exasperate me so."

Angrboda had nothing to say to that. A silence passed between them once more, but this one was less tense.

"I have something I've been meaning to tell you," said Skadi at last, and when Angrboda turned to look at her questioningly, she saw that Skadi's expression was resolute. "It was I who placed the snake above your husband's head after they bound him."

Angrboda didn't even bother to correct the "husband" part before the visions of Loki's torture surfaced once again in her mind, and her eyes widened. She hadn't seen who'd hung the snake, just that it was there. "Why would you do this?"

Skadi turned to the fire. "I wanted to see him suffer. Not just because he's always making trouble. Not just because he killed Baldur. Not just as a painful distraction so he wouldn't have the wit to escape his punishment. I wanted to see him suffer because I saw you suffer so much because of him."

Angrboda had nothing to say to this, and found herself staring into the fire as well.

"I told him, 'This is for Angrboda, and for your children,'" Skadi continued. "Then he spoke, for the first time since he was caught. He whispered to me, so no one else could hear, that it can't be for you because you would never add to his suffering this way. And I told him, 'That's why I must.'"

A long silence followed, during which Angrboda realized that while she was certainly overthinking her relationship with Skadi, she was definitely not misreading the signs. Skadi's confession had just proven that.

"Thank you," Angrboda said quietly, and turned to her.

"Huh?" Skadi blinked at her, arching an eyebrow. "For subjecting your former husband to bodily torture on your behalf without your approval?"

Angrboda took Skadi's hands. "For everything. For nearly shooting me with an arrow all those ages ago, and then sharing your dinner, and then making me furniture. You made me useful by trading my potions. I was desolate indeed when we first met, but you cared for me then."

Skadi's voice was very soft. "I care for you still."

"I know," said Angrboda.

"Do you?" Skadi asked, struggling to read the witch's expression. She must've seen something there that emboldened her, for she moved closer and said, "Loki may have loved you, if he could, but all he ever brought you was pain. You know it. We both know it. I wished to be more for you, Angrboda. So much more. I loved you then. I love you now. I will love you until I die. And even after, whatever comes then, I will love you still, even though you're a fool and you've used me the same way that Loki has used you. But I suppose that makes me a fool as well."

"We're both fools." Angrboda's heart swelled in her chest. "Things could have been so different . . ."

"Things can *still* be different," Skadi said fiercely, leaning in close, squeezing her hands.

"But the ending remains the same," Angrboda whispered back.

"The ending doesn't matter. What matters is how we get there. To face what's ahead with as much dignity as we can muster and make the most of the time we have left." And with that, Skadi reached up and took Angrboda's face in her hands and kissed her with ages' worth of longing. And Angrboda put her hands on the other woman's shoulders and returned the kiss.

"Grant a dead woman's last wish," Skadi whispered when they finally pulled apart, placing a trembling hand on either side of the witch's face, "and let me share your bed, *truly* share it, this night and every night until the end."

And Angrboda did.

THE months that passed afterward seemed almost like a daydream, but they both knew it to be the calm before the storm, the bowstring pulled taut before the release. Soon another year was gone, and then another, and this time passed more quickly than any other in Angrboda's life, for she did not know that she was capable of experiencing such happiness. Skadi came and went to barter her potions, but she left less and less as the winter wore on. Angrboda was glad of this; she did not want to waste a single moment, for moments were truly finite now. The she-wolf had grown so tired of seeing their affection that she mostly stayed outside unless the weather was worse than usual.

And in the dead of winter, pressed together under the wool and furs, limbs intertwined, the giantesses spoke of all the things that came before and tried to forget what was to come.

"I miss them," Angrboda whispered one night, turning Hel's figurine over in her hands as the child had once done. She'd tried several times to reach out to her sons, but to no avail. And every time she'd tried to visit Hel again, Modgud had stopped her. Hel had even chained up her guard dog, Garm, right at the gate to keep her mother away.

It was clear to Angrboda that Hel wasn't going to listen to her, wasn't going to come to her when Ragnarok began. And if she couldn't find Hel, the spell she'd been working on for so many years would all be for nothing.

Skadi sensed her distress and pushed a lock of Angrboda's hair behind her ear, fingers lightly grazing the scar at the witch's temple; she always sobered at the sight of it, but less now that she could press her lips against it as she pleased, as if just one more kiss could make it disappear.

Oh, how Angrboda wished.

"I do, too, and I didn't think I liked children until I met yours. Sometimes I wish I'd had some of my own. Sometimes it scares me to think that I'm leaving nothing behind in these worlds. That I will be forgotten, like I had never existed at all."

Angrboda had heard similar words from Loki before, but for some reason hearing such a thing from Skadi ignited something within her.

"Forgotten?" Angrboda sat up in bed—ignoring the burst of cold air against her bare chest—and stared down at her, aghast. "You? The woman who showed up to Asgard clad in chain mail, armed with all manner of weapons, demanding justice for her father? *Forgotten?*"

Skadi didn't seem convinced, so Angrboda leaned down and cupped her chin. She looked so beautiful, Angrboda thought, with her white-blond hair out of its usual braids, flowing over the pillows like the silk she'd once brought Angrboda. Skadi's hair was thick, but much softer than it looked.

"The people die," Loki had observed one night long ago. *"The stories continue, in poetry and song. Stories of their deeds. Of their gods."*

"You will be remembered for all you are and all you've done," Angrboda whispered, touching her nose against Skadi's, brushing a lock of silvery hair away from her face. "Your bravery. Your pride. Your conviction. I don't see how anyone could ever forget you."

"If stories are all I'll leave behind when I'm gone," Skadi whispered back, "what happens when there's no one left to remember them? It seems to me we'll all be forgotten in the end."

Angrboda pulled away, looming over her. "Baldur is to survive Ragnarok somehow. Do you think he'll ever forget how you wanted to marry him? I would've paid my weight in silver to see *that* exchange."

"You've ruined the moment," Skadi complained. "He was too young for me, anyway. He was just the prettiest and, I suspected, the least awful of the Aesir. That's why he was my first choice when they offered me a husband." She grabbed the nearest pillow and whacked Angrboda with it, her voice rising. "And don't forget, that entire incident was the same one in which *your* former husband tied his testicles to a goat to make me laugh and seal the gods' deal with me."

"You're deflecting," Angrboda shot back, snatching the pillow from her. "And you *did* laugh at him, need I remind you?"

Skadi smirked. "Well, you know that since he was acting out something that already happened, that means—?"

"That he's tied his testicles to a goat more than once, yes. I knew what I was getting into when I agreed to be his wife—don't worry."

"That was back when he'd do anything for a laugh. Back before . . ." Skadi suddenly looked guilty. "Before you died."

The thought sobered Angrboda, and she sank back onto her pillow, still clutching the wolf figurine. Skadi settled in beside her again and put a hand over hers to still it.

"You're worried," she said. It wasn't a question.

"Hel hates me. I asked her to come find me when Ragnarok begins, but I doubt she'll listen. I *can* protect her; I know it. My shield is stronger than ever. But . . ."

"Is there someone she *will* listen to?"

"No one who can reach her, anyway. You'd have to die, or . . ." Angrboda sat up again as a thought struck her. "Loki."

Skadi arched an eyebrow and propped her elbow on the pillow and her cheek on her palm, looking up at her lover with displeasure. "Must you speak his name in our bed?"

"Loki goes to Hel," Angrboda said excitedly. "In my vision, he goes there to muster the dead and then leads them to battle on the ship of nails. She won't listen to me, but maybe he can convince her. He does have a way with words, after all."

"Hmm, except that he betrayed you and got you killed and got her and her brothers taken away from you and all of that . . ."

"But he's still her father. He was always her favorite, and she his," Angrboda said begrudgingly. "I'd be willing to bet she'd hear him out."

"You'd be betting the start of the apocalypse. You'd have to free him to get him there, and you know what happens when he's free."

"It's worth a try, though, isn't it?"

Skadi looked at her in skeptical silence.

"I don't know how he's freed, but it happens somehow, and the three winters are just about over. He'll be loose one way or another, after all. It might as well be by me, for my own purposes. For our child."

"So you've decided, then? You're going to do it?"

"It seems to me that it's the only way."

"I just . . ." Skadi squeezed her eyes shut and dragged her arm out from underneath her, laid her head on the pillow. After a moment she let out a low sob, and tears began to stream down her face as her expression crumpled into despair.

Angrboda had not seen her cry since the day she learned of her father's death, and she lurched forward to drag Skadi's head into her lap, petting her hair.

"I want more time," Skadi whispered. "I just want more time . . ."

"Me, too." Angrboda slid back down under the blankets and held her, felt the woman's tears against the scar on her chest as she sobbed. Soon Angrboda was crying, too.

"But at least we had this time," she murmured against the top of Skadi's head. "It's been the happiest of my life, and I'm sorry to see it end. There's no one else I would rather have weathered this winter with than you."

Skadi breathed deeply a few times to calm herself, then tightened her arms around the witch. When she was composed enough to speak, she said, "You should do it soon. Tonight, if you can. Get it over with. The three years are almost up and you don't want someone else to get to him first."

Angrboda knew this was Skadi's way of accepting her decision. "Where did they take him?"

THAT night, after Skadi was fast asleep, Angrboda slipped away without leaving the safety of her lover's embrace.

If she hadn't known exactly where to go, she would've missed the cave's entrance entirely; it was barely visible in the cliff face save for the small ledge jutting out at its mouth and the treacherously narrow pathway leading up to it.

But she followed that path through the rocks and up the cliff and entered, as silent as the grave, her loose hair and the nightdress she'd donned fluttering soundlessly around her. Down, down she walked into that darkness, not feeling the cold or the damp in this form despite her bare feet, but she knew the cave's occupants must feel both, and she pitied them.

Angrboda had a plan, though. First she would bargain with Loki, and if he accepted and agreed to go to Hel for her, she would free him. If he declined, she'd find some other way to reach Hel, and she would leave him to rot until . . . well, he was fated to be freed eventually in any case, and Skadi was right: it might as well be by Angrboda's hand in exchange for what she wanted.

But when she reached the heart of the cave, the scene that awaited her was even worse than she had seen in her visions—in a way she wasn't prepared for.

By the dim light of a handful of nearly empty oil braziers strewn about the interior, she could see Loki: kneeling in the center, painfully thin, knees bloody from scraping against the rocky ground, arms secured by iron bonds that stretched out to embed themselves in the cave walls. Similar fetters wrapped around his shoulders and chest, binding him to the cave floor. He was unconscious, dressed in only a dirty pair of pants ripped off midthigh, his chest barely rising and falling, ribs standing out with every breath.

But that was not the worst part.

His *face*. It was all Angrboda could do not to recoil in horror at the fresh blood and the blisters, layers upon layers of old scars, starting at the bridge of his nose and stretching across both cheeks, all the way to his ears. She could see almost every spot where the snake's venom fell and dripped down his face like tears, gouging rivers of red in their wake. Some drops had even trickled onto his chest. She had never before seen him with a beard because he'd always shape-shifted it away; now that he lacked the energy to do so, the venom had sloughed entire chunks of hair from his face, and skin with it.

She finally raised her white eyes to the snake above his head. It stared her down, amber-eyed and hateful, and opened its mouth wide, two huge drops of venom ready to drip from its exposed fangs.

The witch glared back at it with all the force of her rage; she willed its head to twist sharply sideways, and it fell to the ground, dead.

The resulting *thunk* did not rouse Loki from his unconscious state—but it did cause someone to stir in the shadows just to Angrboda's right, and she turned to see Sigyn crawling into the glow of one of the braziers. The woman's face was a mask of exhaustion and grief as she grappled about in the darkness before finding her bowl—the one she'd been holding above Loki's head to catch the venom from the snake, to give him some respite from his pain.

For the entire length of Fimbulwinter, she's been doing this, Angrboda thought. *Almost three long years.*

"I was only asleep for a second," she croaked, her voice seeming long unused, and she clutched the bowl and began to stand—but froze when she noticed just who their visitor was.

Angrboda moved closer to Loki and regarded her warily. Having had only one other interaction with Sigyn, Angrboda expected screams, sobs, accusations.

But what she got was calm resignation.

Sigyn struggled to her feet, not taking her eyes off the witch.

When she was fully upright, she straightened her spine and cleared her throat, and Angrboda realized with a start that she was at least three inches taller than Sigyn; the other woman was smaller than she had seemed from across the river an age and a half ago.

"You were right," Sigyn said at last. "What you showed me that night. My sons . . . I tried to hide them once Loki disappeared, but the gods found them anyway, and they . . . they . . ."

"I know," Angrboda said with a sideways glance at Loki's bonds. Though they were made of iron, she knew them to have been magicked from something far more sinister.

"I shouldn't have told you what I did," said Angrboda, looking back to Sigyn. "It was wrong of me to put this knowledge on your shoulders, and for that I am truly sorry."

"I provoked you," Sigyn said, staring down at the clay bowl in her hands. "I was just so angry."

"But I should have known better. I lost my temper. I thought of the worst possible way to get back at you for what you—for what you said about my children, and I went through with it when I should have taken a step back and thought things through—"

"It was bad for the two of us to meet the way we did." Sigyn closed her eyes. "We both lost our children in the end. But the difference is that I was the cause for you losing yours. I thought I was doing the right thing. I'm sorry."

"No," said Angrboda. "You were not the cause. Ultimately, it was the Aesir alone who were responsible for their crimes against our families."

She realized the truth of these words as soon as she spoke them. She'd accused Loki of being the one who'd wronged her and their children, and he'd made some inarguably terrible decisions—but at the end of the day, he was no more responsible for Angrboda's fate than Sigyn or Gerd had been.

One way or another, she would have lost her children.

One way or another, Odin was going to get what he wanted.

And Loki had suffered enough for it. Angrboda's entire family had.

A sound somewhere between a laugh and a sob escaped Sigyn's throat before she whispered, "*'Despair, Sigyn, for your gods will forsake you in the end . . .'* I should have believed you. I should have taken your warning more seriously."

"It wasn't a warning," said Angrboda sadly. "It was my revenge. You had no reason to trust what I made you see."

"But still, if I could have prevented—"

"There was no preventing this. Any of it. Do not blame yourself."

Sigyn looked down at her bowl again. Then at the dead snake on the ground. And suddenly, viciously, she hurled the bowl at the cave wall, where it shattered into a million pieces.

Loki still did not wake.

"He wouldn't even talk to me," said Sigyn with a strangled cry. "He has not uttered a word since they left us here. Do you know what that's like? I loved him so. I love him still. I am loyal. I have stood by him until this very moment."

"And you've received nothing but grief in return," Angrboda said. "I can sympathize. I cannot imagine what it must've been like for you. But there is nothing more for you in this cave."

"There is so long as he's trapped here," Sigyn said firmly.

"Which won't be very much longer."

Sigyn stared at her. "You mean to free him?"

"I do," said Angrboda. She knew in her heart that he was in no state to strike a deal with her; she would have to free him first and worry about that later. It was a risk she was willing to take.

"I've tried before and gotten nowhere. But if you succeed, I don't know what that means for me." Sigyn gestured at the broken shards of her bowl on the ground. "Was this my only purpose? What shall I do now?"

"I don't know," Angrboda replied. "But maybe you two can decide that together."

It took Sigyn a moment to understand what she was getting at—that this was it, a true end to the strife between them—but when she realized it, she nodded once and held out her hand to Angrboda. After a brief hesitation, the witch reached out and the women clasped forearms tightly.

"I must do this final thing," said Angrboda. "I don't think we'll meet again."

"Then do it," said Sigyn, "and let us part as friends."

They released each other, and Sigyn stepped back while Angrboda stepped forward and knelt beside Loki, brought a ghostly hand up to the side of his face. Her cool touch was what finally caused him to stir. His eyelids fluttered for a moment before opening, and Angrboda's heart dropped into her stomach when she realized that the venom had blinded him in one eye.

He stared at her, bewildered.

"Do you still wonder sometimes," she whispered, "whether it might have been wrong for you to return my heart to me?"

Comprehension dawned, and he rasped, "Never."

Angrboda snapped her fingers and his bonds shattered, the sound so loud that—even in the quiet of the cave—it seemed to echo throughout all the worlds.

Because it had.

Chaos would begin to rage outside the confines of the cave, she knew. But in this moment, she caught Loki in her arms as he fell, and she held him on her lap like a child as he panted and writhed, his body unsure of what to do with itself now that it wasn't fixed in one awkward, painful position.

"What—what are you doing here?" he asked between deep breaths.

"Well, I came to ask you to deliver a message to Hel on my behalf in exchange for your freedom, and then I saw the state you were in . . ." Her face twisted with sorrow. "This is a terrible thing they've done to you. Worse than I had imagined."

Once Loki's breathing had steadied, he found the strength to quip, "How kind of you. And here I thought for sure I'd be left to writhe in pain for all eternity."

Angrboda peered at him. "Do you still not know what is to come?"

Loki shook his head and closed his eyes. "Not the slightest clue. And I'd prefer to keep it that way."

"Where will you go now, then? What will you do?"

Loki opened his good eye to peer at her. "Why ask me what I'm going to do, if you already know?"

Angrboda gave him a small smile. "Because you make your own way, and you choose your own path. I cannot take that from you. I mustn't."

His face twisted with emotion at these words, but naturally he disguised it by clearing his throat. "Hmm. Well, then. Don't tell me. I don't want to know."

"As you wish," she said, and helped him to his feet, his arm around her shoulders. Loki seemed confused about this. "Hang on. You're not even really here. Why can you touch me in this form?"

"Because I've willed it so," said Angrboda. "The Seeress may be a manifestation of my very soul, but right now, I need to be able to touch you. So I can."

"Huh," said Loki after a moment, giving her a small pained smile. "I wonder if you'll ever cease to surprise me, Angrboda Iron-witch."

As they stumbled toward the mouth of the cave, Loki leaning heavily on her, Sigyn stepped forward out of the shadows without a word and threw his other arm around her shoulders, taking some of the weight off Angrboda.

Loki staggered to a stop and stared at her. Once he'd regained himself, he managed to choke out, "Sigyn? You're—you're still here?"

"Until the bitter end," she replied.

"And bitter it's been, indeed," Loki murmured, shaking his head, but his ruined lips still had the same upward quirk as they soldiered forward.

They reached the mouth of the cave and stopped on the ledge, for it would take some time to navigate the perilously narrow path that would take them down to the shore. But the ocean was roiling as fiercely as it did in the worst of storms, though there were no clouds in the sky—and though the sun had just risen, the full moon was still visible as well.

But they were both slowly disappearing, bit by bit. *Eclipsing.* The sun and moon had a slow, steady, identical shadow moving across each of them, their light disappearing second by second. It would take hours—maybe even a day—for them to be swallowed completely, but once they disappeared, the worlds would be completely dark.

"A *double* eclipse?" Loki asked with a scowl. "That's impossible . . ."

"It's not an eclipse," Sigyn whispered.

Angrboda slipped his arm from around her shoulders and stepped forward, white eyes wide. "It's started."

It started the moment I freed you.

The breaking of your bonds was the breaking of all bonds.

Including our sons'.

"That dream you had," Loki said quietly behind her, leaning fully on Sigyn to keep himself upright. "This is it, isn't it? What Odin wanted to know all along. It's finally happening."

Angrboda nodded. *I saw the sun and moon go dark as the wolves who chase them finally swallow their prey.*

I saw . . .

The cold wind that had been blowing for three years had finally stopped, but the ocean's churning reached a fever pitch.

Then stopped, very suddenly.

"What's happening?" Sigyn asked in a shaking voice, but Angrboda and Loki looked at each other and knew.

"Run," Loki told Sigyn. "Go down the path *now*. I'll catch up with you. I swear it."

"But—"

"*Go*. Trust me. Please."

She gave him one last look and then dashed off. She had barely made it to the bottom and into the trees before a creature burst forth from the waves, so massive that—even standing on a ledge several hundred feet above sea level—Loki and Angrboda were already looking up at it before its entire head was even out of the water. Its scales were blue-green, pointed webbed fins running from the top of its head and down its back. It—*he*—peered down at them with familiar luminous green eyes and bared a mouthful of sharp teeth.

He had been a tiny green snake when Angrboda had birthed him; now his head looked more like that of a dragon.

"I'll be damned," Loki breathed. "Jormungand?"

At the name, the creature reared back so that even more of his gargantuan body was out of the water, and he angled his head down toward them, nostrils flaring.

Angrboda was so overcome with emotion that she could not speak. But one emotion was fear, after her earlier confrontation with Hel—for if her youngest bore the same ill will toward her as her eldest, then she would surely be swallowed whole.

And she had too much left to do.

Jormungand regarded them for a moment longer before rearing back and letting out a guttural cry, so loud that it shook the very foundations of the rock beneath their feet, and Angrboda and Loki clung to each other to stay upright as chunks of rock detached themselves from the cliff face around them and toppled into the sea.

The Midgard Serpent's roar ceased abruptly.

As they cowered on the ledge, Loki said to Angrboda out of the corner of his mouth, "So, this is either going to be a heartwarming family reunion, or he's going to tear us limb from limb. Please tell me you foresaw this and have a plan?"

"I did have a plan, but it didn't involve this," Angrboda replied.

The Serpent seemed to have lost interest in them; he craned his head to the left as if waiting for a response to his roar. When he did, Angrboda was startled to see that the side of Jormungand's skull bore a craterlike scar similar to her own. She remembered Hymir's tale of Thor "going fishing" for the Serpent using an ox's head and dealing the creature a blow from Mjolnir that should have been deadly: much like the one Thor had dealt her the night her children were taken.

Pride and fury swelled in Angrboda's chest, momentarily pushing the fear aside.

It will take a lot more than that to keep us down for good, won't it, my son?

None of them spoke. Jormungand didn't move. And then his

call was answered—from all the way down the shoreline, an enormous, shaggy shape rounded the corner and made its way toward them, each step shaking the earth.

Angrboda stepped away from Loki, gaping as her middle child approached them. Fenrir was a hundred times bigger than he'd been the last time she'd seen him, his fur darker, his snout longer, and his *teeth* . . .

As she neared the cliff's edge, Jormungand's head moved toward her until he was mere feet away and their eyes were nearly level, and an infantile voice said in Angrboda's head, *Brother.*

Tears sprang to Angrboda's eyes. She reached out a shaking hand to touch the smooth, wet scales on her son's snout; his massive eyes slid closed, as if he was savoring the touch of another being after so long at the bottom of the ocean.

All alone.

"You can speak," Angrboda whispered.

He does his best, said Fenrir, in a voice much deeper than the child's voice Angrboda had heard in her head an age ago. Though he was still some ways away from them, she could hear him loud and clear. *It's a good thing we're strange enough to be able to communicate in our heads, or both of us may have gone mad in confinement.*

Mad, Jormungand repeated. *Both of us.*

"I called out to you both. Did you ever hear me?" Angrboda said weakly. "You never answered. I tried so many times . . ."

We were placed beyond your reach. Beyond anyone's reach, Fenrir said. *It could've been some spell or another the gods put in place, or maybe we were just too far.*

Fenrir was upon them now, and was large enough to sit upon the rocky shore and still have his head hovering near where his parents were so precariously perched.

It's been a long time, Mama, he said, blinking his large green eyes once.

Mama, Jormungand echoed.

"I'm sorry," Angrboda said, tears springing to her eyes. *This is it—this is going to be Hel all over again.* "I'm sorry I couldn't stop them."

A massive pink shape suddenly moved toward her, and before Angrboda knew it, her entire body had been *licked* by her colossal wolf-son: covered in drool from just one swipe of his tongue. A moment later Jormungand leaned forward and gently butted his enormous head against her, just as he had when he could fit around her neck, only this time it caused her to stumble a bit.

There was nothing you could have done, Fenrir said.

Angrboda very nearly sobbed with relief, but she was too busy wiping drool and seawater from her face and gown.

Fenrir's gaze drifted toward Loki. *And as for you, Father . . .*

Angrboda moved in front of Loki, blocking him from their view. "Believe me, my sons. Your father has suffered much as of late. I won't ask you to forgive him, but at least spare him your wrath." *Although I suppose letting you kill him would be one way for him to reach Hel . . .*

We'll make his a quick death, Fenrir sneered, his upper lip curling over wickedly sharp teeth. *He's not worth our time.*

"Fenrir, listen to me," Angrboda said in her most commanding motherly tone. "Your father isn't blameless, not by any stretch of the imagination—"

"Don't help me," Loki muttered out of the side of his scarred mouth.

"—but he wasn't the cause of all this," she finished. "The Aesir are the ones truly deserving of your ire. Not him."

Angrboda heard Loki let out a long, relieved breath behind her.

Fenrir and Jormungand both considered her. Then they looked at each other and Fenrir said, *You're right, Mother.*

"I don't know about you two, but I've just been tortured for three years by the Aesir. I've half a mind to go north to join up with Jotunheim's army in Utgard when I leave here," Loki added helpfully from over her shoulder. He gestured to his disfigured face. "Revenge and all that. What do you say? I'm sure they'd be happy to see you at the citadel."

"How . . . did you know there's an army in Utgard?" Angrboda asked, remembering what Skadi told her and arching an eyebrow at him.

"I may have been stuck in a cave, but I know where giants go when they get hungry. And by now, they're probably angry, too. Angry enough to march against the Aesir, who've surely weathered this long winter in safety and comfort, as they do."

Angrboda eyed him. "Are you *sure* you haven't heard my prophecy?"

Utgard? Fenrir looked to his mother, curious. *Does he speak the truth?*

"He does," Angrboda said.

Then we head north to join them, said Fenrir. *And if we have to fight side by side with the likes of him in order to have our vengeance upon the Aesir, then so be it.*

"That's the spirit," Loki said bracingly. But his forced cheerful veneer was starting to chip. She could tell from looking at him that he was still in terrible pain.

Fenrir turned to Angrboda once more and said, *I'm sorry we didn't have more time, Mama. But I've dreamt of revenge for too long to waste another moment.*

Revenge, Jormungand hissed, eyes narrowing.

Angrboda pressed her face against each of their snouts for a moment in turn to say goodbye, and when she pulled away to look at them both, she whispered, "Go, my boys. And show them what you're made of."

And with that, Fenrir let out a final howl and bounded away down the beach, and Jormungand disappeared beneath the waves. The water churned as he descended before going still once more, the vanishing moon having no effect on the tides.

Indeed, the ocean seemed eerily still in the Serpent's absence.

"That was a close one." Loki let out a long breath and sagged back against the rock.

Angrboda stood there, stricken. Her cursed heart ached, and as much as she swiped at the silent tears coursing down her face, they just kept on coming.

"Did you mean what you said?" Loki asked her. "About . . . about not blaming me? For *everything*?"

"Yes," she said, still staring off in the direction her sons had gone.

Loki opened his mouth, closed it again, and said, "Well, since you just freed me from my three years of torment—you said something about needing me to go to Hel for you. I thought you said you saw her already."

Angrboda had very nearly forgotten about that in the wake of her unexpected reunion with Fenrir and Jormungand, and she whirled around to face him.

"Yes, I did, and she won't let me see her again. I've tried," she said with a renewed sense of urgency. "But you—I think she'd let you in, if you could get there. I need you to tell her something."

"If I can get there," Loki echoed, bemused. "Okay, sure. What do you need me to tell her?"

Angrboda put her hands on his thin shoulders and looked him dead in the eye. "Tell Hel to come to me. Tell her I can save her.

Make her believe you. Her life depends on it. Swear to me you'll find your way to her and you'll tell her."

"I swear it."

"Swear it on your life, and hers, too."

"I do. I do," Loki said. He tilted his head sideways in a catlike motion. "Angrboda—you're disappearing."

Angrboda looked down at her hands—they were fading, though she did not will it so. "I must go," she said, gritting her teeth. "Or I may not be able to get back. My means of travel is in turmoil." Her hands started to pass through his shoulders and she pulled them away. "Yggdrasil trembles. The alignment of the worlds has been thrown off. The lines separating one realm from the next are beginning to blur, and I fear that soon, nothing will separate even the living from the dead. But at least that will make it easier for you to get to Hel."

Loki nodded but still looked worried. "Boda—"

Angrboda felt the ground lurch beneath her. The last thing she saw was Loki's hands reaching for her as she fell, and she closed her eyes and braced herself for impact.

And when she opened her eyes again, in her bed, tears were flowing down either side of her face. She was exhausted, panicked, trembling, cold—and alone. Relief settled over her when she saw Skadi standing in the doorway, looking out, her face skyward. Beyond her, the she-wolf sat in the clearing, her massive shaggy head tilted upward as well.

Angrboda stepped up next to Skadi, who started at her approach, then put an arm around her shoulders. Neither woman tore her gaze away from the dying sun and moon.

Skadi's voice shook as she whispered, "You did it. It's time."

"I know," Angrboda whispered back, leaning in close. "I know."

❖ ❖ ❖

SKADI spent the next few hours packing up what few supplies she'd take with her to Utgard. Meanwhile Angrboda struggled to make as much of her hunger potion as she possibly could with what few resources she had left. She packed all her tiny clay pots into a large wooden box and padded it with wool, and Skadi packed as much as she could onto her sledge.

"And with that," said Angrboda, shoulders sagging, "I've done all I can do for Jotunheim."

"You've done more than enough," Skadi told her as she secured the last strap. "And our people will be grateful for it." She took something out of her pocket: Angrboda's sheathed antler-handled knife, the one she usually wore at her belt. "You left this on the table when you were dressing, so I sharpened it for you after I sharpened my sword."

"Thank you," Angrboda said, and untied her belt to thread it through the sheath's loop. Then she cast her eyes to the sword at Skadi's hip and asked, "Your father's?"

Skadi nodded solemnly. "None other."

The snow and wind that had battered them for the past three years had stopped, and the air was warming; it was still bitterly cold, but they could now be outside for longer than a few breaths before experiencing extreme discomfort. But just as on that seaside cliff, the worlds seemed to be unnervingly still, silent, waiting.

Like a bowstring drawn taut . . .

And any moment now, the arrow would be released.

"Where's your wolf gone off to?" Skadi asked, looking around, at the exact moment the creature in question materialized out of the forest—and she was not alone.

There was a figure walking with the massive wolf, whose form seemed to be flickering back and forth the same way Angrboda had when she'd left Loki on the cliff. She recognized this man as Baldur, his white hair luminous even in the low light of the disappearing sun.

Angrboda bristled at the sight of him, but then her gaze moved to the woman slung across the she-wolf's back, whose face was hidden by cascading waves of thick black hair.

I heard them wandering through the woods, the she-wolf said.

Baldur looked first at Skadi, whose jaw had dropped, and then his eyes fell on Angrboda. He took a step toward her, arms spread imploringly, and said, "Thank goodness we found you."

The woman on the she-wolf's back made a noise of discomfort. Baldur's brow knitted with worry, his eyes darting to her and then back to Angrboda. Then he raised his hands palms up in surrender and said, "Please. You have to help her."

"What?" Angrboda said at the same moment the woman lifted her head and groaned, "Mother?"

Angrboda froze. "Hel?"

Skadi was already rushing toward the wolf and had Hel down and upright within seconds. She could not stand up on her own and leaned on Skadi for support.

Angrboda could've wept with relief. *Loki convinced her.*

"It's good to see you, little one," Skadi said, tears welling up in her eyes.

"I wish I could say the same," Hel said in a weak voice.

Skadi turned to Baldur and demanded, "What have you done to her?"

"Nothing but try to help. I'm here and then—then I'm not," said Baldur, holding out his flickering hands. "Sometimes I could support her and help her along. Other times, she'd fall, and . . ." He balled his fists. "And there was nothing I could do about it. We'd still be out there in the snow if your wolf hadn't found us."

Angrboda turned to her daughter. "You can no longer walk?"

"My legs have finally failed me," Hel muttered, avoiding her gaze.

"But before," said Angrboda, "when I saw you, you looked fine—"

"That was before," Hel said flatly. "That was when I was ruler of a realm. In that place, a little girl's dead legs functioned without her mother's healing salves. But now that they've rotted to bone . . ."

"You're . . . no longer ruler of a realm?" Skadi asked, but Angrboda knew the answer.

Hel's green eyes finally turned to her mother. "My realm is empty; I relinquished the dead to my father. They're all sailing to join my brothers and the giants in their fight against the gods. I have no power over anyone anymore."

"Which explains this," said Baldur, holding out his hands again. "I'm . . . becoming more and more solid. More *alive*. And the rest of the dead, too . . ." He swallowed. "My brother Hod went with them, to fight. And I—I don't even know which side he'll fight for. But how can the dead come back to life? None of this makes any sense . . ."

"Of course it makes sense," Angrboda said. She relayed to them what she'd told Loki: "With Yggdrasil thrown off its axis, there is nothing separating the world of the dead from that of the living. That's how the dead could sail out of Hel's realm in the first place."

Skadi understood. "So the Nine Worlds are bleeding into one another because the natural order of the universe is in complete chaos, and everyone who has ever died a nonglorious death is now fighting on the side of the giants? Lovely."

Hel reached up and brushed her hair out of her face, and Angrboda was startled by how sickly her daughter looked: her features gaunt, her eyes sunken and dark-rimmed, her breath coming in short gasps.

"She needs rest," Baldur said nervously, and Angrboda noticed for the first time that his wife, Nanna—who had been so upset by his death that she'd died of grief and been put on the pyre with him—was conspicuously absent from Hel's undead Asgardian escort.

"She'll get it," Angrboda said. "I'll take care of her."

Hel muttered something unintelligible but allowed herself to be carried into the cave by Skadi, who set her down on the sleeping pallet. Baldur followed, and once inside, he planted himself at Hel's bedside.

"Angrboda," Skadi said, pulling the witch outside, "it's time for me to go."

Angrboda knew she was right. She reached up and cupped Skadi's cheek, but paused when she looked over Skadi's shoulder and saw the she-wolf sitting beside the Huntress's sledge.

Your reindeer seem to have run off, the she-wolf said. *I hope you don't mind a grizzled old dog in their place.*

"You mean to go with Skadi?" Angrboda said, but she found she wasn't surprised. Even if her shield was strong enough to protect the she-wolf, too, the creature was old and tired.

It seems the thing to do, the wolf replied. *It's as good a way as any to die. Better than being burned alive, at least.*

Angrboda didn't disagree.

"I guess this is goodbye, old friend," she whispered, and the she-wolf licked her face, then allowed Skadi to secure her to the sledge using the old harness Angrboda had crafted for her wagon, which had been buried in snow for some time.

And then Skadi turned to Angrboda.

Tears had started forming in Angrboda's eyes before Skadi's arms were around her, and they clung to each other for dear life.

"Please don't go." Angrboda's voice was almost a whimper as her tears soaked into Skadi's shoulder. "I can protect you. I *will* protect you. Just stay."

"I cannot," Skadi said, her voice thick with emotion. "The dead are joining forces with the giants. Don't you know what that means? I'm to see my father on the battlefield, and I will make him proud."

"You've already made him proud," Angrboda argued. "Who wouldn't be proud of you?"

Skadi put a hand on either side of the witch's face. "Even if you could protect me, it would be at your expense, wouldn't it?"

Angrboda had at some point, without realizing it, come to terms with the fact that she was going to burn again. It never occurred to her to save herself; her shield was meant only for Hel.

"If that's the case," Skadi said, "if I were to stay here, with Hel, under your protection—do you think I would stand to see you die for my sake, too?" She shook her head. "No. Never."

"That's a good point," Angrboda admitted.

Skadi leaned in and murmured, "Exactly. So if there's a life after this one, then that's where I'll see you again."

"And if not?" Angrboda managed to choke out. *If I'm unable to die . . .*

"Then this is it," Skadi whispered, and kissed her a final time. Angrboda clung to her until Skadi turned to leave, her hand slipping out of Angrboda's even as the witch reached for it. She did not look back.

When Skadi and her sledge disappeared from the clearing and into the woods, Angrboda collapsed to her knees and cried.

I just . . . want more time . . .

When she finally turned her face to the sky, she saw that the sun and moon were nearly spent. The sight caused her to compose herself, slow her breathing, stumble to her feet. She dried her eyes with the hem of her sleeve and looked toward her cave.

The witch still had work to do.

WHEN Angrboda stepped back inside the cave, she saw that Baldur had pulled her carved chair over to Hel's bedside and was sitting there, looking more solid by the second, not taking his eyes from Hel's face.

Angrboda said, "If you could please give me a few moments alone with my daughter, I should like to make her comfortable and get her out of her muddy gown. Would you go fetch some more water from the stream? We've put a hole in the ice—it'll be easy to spot."

Baldur stood, nodded, and said, "I'll gather firewood as well." When he leaned down to grab a wooden bucket and his hand passed right through it, he added sheepishly, "To the best of my abilities, that is." The second time he reached for the bucket he was solid enough to grab it, and he left the cave.

The door shut behind him, and silence ensued.

Angrboda sighed as she peeled off the fingerless mittens Hel had *nalbinded* for her so long ago and set them on the table. She had a little water sitting in a cauldron over the hearth, which she'd been using to mix her potions. She lowered it farther into the fire to heat it, and when she was satisfied, she took out some clean rags, stripped off Hel's filthy dress, and bathed her—the top half of her, at least.

Hel's face remained carefully blank the entire time, and she didn't utter a word.

"You were like this when you were little, you know," Angrboda said as she pulled a clean dress over Hel's head, fed her arms through the sleeves, and pulled it down to cover her body.

"Like what?" Hel said at last.

"Angry when you couldn't do things for yourself," the witch replied, arranging the blankets and furs around Hel. "Furious at being helpless."

Hel's eyes moved past her mother to the *nalbinded* mittens on the table, and she made a face. "You still use those horrid old things?"

"I've barely taken them off since the night you gave them to me. They've held up just as well as this belt Gerd made," Angrboda told her, but Hel only turned away so the witch couldn't see her expression.

Eventually, when Angrboda had gone back to her stores and started digging around for any food she had left, Hel called weakly from the bed, "I was so angry at you both. Especially Papa. I'd planned to throw him into an eternal river of ice or a very deep crevice when he finally came to my realm. But when he showed up, he looked such a fright that tossing him into a bottomless pit actually might've been an improvement, and that rather took all the fun out of the idea."

Angrboda paused and gave a wan smile, having found the large pouch of jerky she'd been rummaging for. She brought it to the table and said, "He would've talked his way out of it somehow. It's what he does."

"He talked me into coming here. Told me to give you another chance. I'm glad it was in private, so Baldur wouldn't see me cry. It was so embarrassing," Hel said, staring up at the ceiling of the cave. "Papa said I looked like his mother, Laufey. She's where I got this dark hair from, while you and he are so fair."

Angrboda sat down on the chair beside her. "He told me long ago that he didn't remember his mother."

"He said that seeing me reminded him," Hel whispered. She finally turned her head and met Angrboda's eyes. "I assume you two made up, or he wouldn't have come?"

"In a manner of speaking," Angrboda said, putting a hand on her forehead. Cold, cold—her daughter's skin was ice. "I harbored a lot of hatred toward him for a long time after what he did. But in the end, I realized that we're all victims of fate."

Hel looked away but didn't move her head. "I came to the same conclusion after Papa came to me. Thank you for not telling him all the terrible things I said to you. Why would you even want to save me, after the way I treated you?"

Angrboda smoothed back her hair. "Because I'm your mother."

When Hel squeezed her eyes shut, several tears leaked out, and Angrboda wiped them with her sleeve. Hel was too weak to bat her away and said, anguished, "It's not fair. My entire life was wasted down there, and when we finally could've seen each other I kept you away . . . and now we're all doomed . . ."

"I have a plan," Angrboda whispered. "I'm going to protect you, Hel."

"That's what Papa said. Baldur doesn't know, though. But he came with me anyway. To see me safely to you, if you could help me . . ." Hel closed her eyes again, and this time her voice began to fade. "I'm sorry to disappoint you, Mother, but I doubt I'll live long enough to see Ragnarok . . . let alone . . . live through it . . ."

Angrboda bit back a sob at the words. Hel had passed out, her chest barely rising and falling underneath the mountain of blankets. When Baldur returned with a bucket of water and some kindling, he found Angrboda sitting there, eyes not moving from

Hel's unconscious form as she tried to assess just what was wrong with her daughter.

Is it sickness, or something worse?

"How is she?" Baldur approached her and crouched at Hel's bedside. He glanced down at Hel, set his mouth in a thin line, and then looked up at the witch. There was something in his expression, something in his eyes—the warm blue of the summer sky, the exact opposite of Odin's—that gave Angrboda pause. Then something began to nag at her.

And that *something* was the problem of Baldur being here in the first place, when Angrboda had expected only Hel. Could *save* only Hel.

"She's asleep." Angrboda did not take her eyes from her daughter. "Why are you here?"

"Well, as you said, Yggdrasil is thrown off its axis and the dead can come back—"

"No," she said, turning to face him, "why are you *here*?"

"She wouldn't have made it on her own."

"And why do you care?" Angrboda narrowed her eyes. "And where is your wife? Didn't she die with you?"

"She did," Baldur admitted.

"And where is she now?"

Baldur took a deep breath and seemed to steady himself. "If you're trying to dig up some underhanded motive for my escorting your daughter into your care, I'm afraid you won't have much luck."

Angrboda could've said any number of things to refute that, but she only sighed. "Well, if you know Hel so well, what do you think is wrong with her?"

"Her heart. It beats irregularly, and with much effort," he said with such certainty that Angrboda made a sound of surprise, which made him look up from Hel and shrug. "Hel is a witch like you, like my mother, like Freyja. Did she ever show her power as a child?"

"Never," Angrboda said, scowling. *That's not true*—she'd had that vision, when she'd been tied to the tree after her children were taken: the vision of Odin depositing Hel down in Niflheim. Hel had demonstrated her power to the creatures and dead things who'd come for her in the night.

She'd raised her chin and stared them down.

Then she'd gathered them all up and made them her subjects.

"Her power is tied to her realm," Angrboda whispered. "And her realm is empty and gone. And now . . ."

Her memory of that vision, though, suddenly slipped to the one that had come just before: of the youngest son of Odin tossing her daughter a golden apple and flashing a brilliant smile.

"It's good to meet you, little Hel. Welcome to Asgard."

"She's been deteriorating for the whole of Fimbulwinter, ever since I arrived in her realm," Baldur said, his voice strained. "And I've had to watch. I suspect she's had this condition since birth, but her power has masked it. Until now."

Angrboda's breath caught in her throat. *Little Hel, running around in the clearing, short of breath. Fingertips blue.*

"Before. It's been since before her birth." Angrboda stood suddenly, lurching forward on unsteady legs. "I need some air. Please, watch over her."

"Always," Baldur said. He let her pass and then took her chair.

Angrboda caught a glimpse of them as she left—Baldur reaching out to caress Hel's face, Hel stirring at his touch. The witch paused and listened.

"You're a ridiculous man," Hel rasped, "to have dragged me all the way out here when you didn't have to."

"Who says I didn't have to?" he chided.

"Me. *I* say you didn't have to."

"Well, you're wrong."

"Don't contradict me. You're still somewhat dead, which means I'm still your ruler."

"You're still *somewhat* my ruler. Now, stop talking and save your strength."

"You cannot tell me what to do."

"We're not in your realm anymore, so technically I can do as I please."

Angrboda could bear no more. And as soon as the cave door slammed shut behind her, she dropped to her knees in the thawing snow of the clearing.

Many realizations hit her at once.

The first was that there was a reason Hel had almost died in her womb, and that her legs were just fate's cruel manifestation of Angrboda's folly. There was a *real* reason that Angrboda had to call her daughter's soul back from the dead before she was even born, a reason that Hel had been dying in the first place. Maybe Baldur was right; her heart hadn't formed as it should have—and now that Hel was grown and had no magic to compensate for it, this condition would kill her.

The second realization was that Baldur had gotten close enough to Hel to hear her heartbeat. To know that something was not quite right.

And Angrboda knew then, in the way that a mother just *knows*, that it would be useless to save Hel if she wasn't going to save Baldur, too. A much younger Baldur had won little Hel's heart ages ago with that dazzling smile. Angrboda had seen it herself in her vision.

And so had Loki, who had actually been there.

"Why did you do it, then? Why did you kill your brother's son?"

"The gods took everything from us, Boda. I thought it was high time I took something from them."

So he had. Loki had taken Baldur from the Aesir—and delivered him to a lonely woman sitting on a dark throne. A spot of warmth for the frigid being ruling the coldest realm of the worlds.

Angrboda couldn't breathe.

Loki really had known exactly what he was doing all along— but did he *know*? Had he been in on Odin's scheme the entire time? He claimed not to know what she'd seen, what she'd told Odin, but—*but*—had he *known*? *Loki and his many faces*—had he and Odin been playing her for a fool?

That was it. That's why Odin wasn't trying to prevent Baldur's death.

Angrboda thought as she knelt there in the mud, as the last slivers of the dying sun and moon were slowly swallowed up by ravenous wolves.

Because the safest place for Baldur is with Hel.

So this was how he was to survive Ragnarok.

Let Hel hold what she has.

"Your father has given you a great gift, my daughter," Angrboda murmured, looking down at her pale, calloused hands in the fading light. "But it's nothing if you don't live to enjoy it. If you *both* don't live to enjoy it. And so . . ."

Angrboda put her chin to her chest and looked down at the scar between her breasts. The pale blue dress she wore had been modified for when she'd been nursing Hel and Fenrir: The keyhole neckline extended downward across her sternum. She had not taken it on her wanderings, so it was one of the last of her garments that had not gone completely threadbare; she required two delicate penannular brooches to secure it shut.

This suited her purpose today of all days. Without hesitation, she unsheathed the freshly sharpened knife at her belt.

And so I shall do what I must.

As the last of the light went out in the Nine Worlds, Angrboda Iron-witch held her breath.

The knife cut down.

And the bowstring released.

YGGDRASIL writhed, and she saw it all from there.

Armies marching onto the plain of Vigrid where it all was to end. First come the gods, with shining Asgard at their back: the Aesir, the Vanir, the elves, some dwarfs. The valkyries. Odin's berserkers and his einherjar, the slain legions of Valhalla; and Freyja's men, who make up the other half of the slain.

The army of the gods is uniform. They seem to radiate light, from their gleaming chain mail to their polished shield bosses.

Their opponents look like a torch-bearing hodgepodge in comparison as they march in from the opposite direction: creatures of all shapes and sizes. Frost giants, hill trolls, ogres . . . some human-sized, some not. Beings from other worlds have joined; dark elves and other dwarfs also march among them.

She cannot see Skadi or the she-wolf among their ranks. She doesn't want to look. Maybe they were too late getting to Utgard; they only just left Ironwood, after all. Maybe their tardiness will spare them. The witch can only hope.

Surt appears with his flaming sword, the bridge Bifrost breaking underneath his army of fire giants as they pass, joining Jotunheim and their allies.

Then there's Loki, pulling up in a ship of nails filled to the brim with dead souls, who spill out as soon as they reach the shore—and from the water behind him erupts the Midgard Serpent with a roar to shake all the worlds, his brother, Fenrir, appearing at his side from beyond the mountains, the ground shaking with his every loping stride.

With his sons at his back, Loki struts to the head of the army, defiant—he's shape-shifted the beard off his face, but not the scars or blisters; those he wears with pride. He grasps arms with the ruler of the citadel of Utgard, Skrymir, and the two of them look west at the enemy across the field.

"It's a good day to die," Skrymir booms.

"It is indeed," Loki says with a wicked grin.

From across the field, Heimdall blows Gjallarhorn, and the battle begins.

With fire in his eyes, Fenrir makes straight for Odin and swallows him whole—along with his horse, Sleipnir, the Wolf's own half brother—only to be kicked in the lower jaw by Odin's son Vidar with his legendary shoe.

Vidar grabs Fenrir's upper jaw and tears; the Great Wolf goes down with a cry that rips through the witch's very soul, and then he dies.

Jormungand goes for Thor, spitting venom, and after a struggle he incurs a death blow from the great red-bearded god—in the same spot as the previous blow, caving his skull in completely. Thor takes nine steps before the venom kills him, and the Midgard Serpent drops to the ground beside him, crushing members of both armies beneath his massive body.

She has seen this all before.

She finally spies Skadi on the she-wolf's back just as the Huntress runs out of arrows. Somehow they'd found their way to the battle after all.

Skadi casts aside her bow and unsheathes her father Thjazi's sword. Thjazi is there with her on the battlefield; he locks eyes with her as he's impaled upon a spear and dies—again. Incensed, Skadi begins to fight the valkyries surrounding her, and takes several down with her before she suffers one strike too many and slides from her mount just as the she-wolf takes a spear to the heart.

Skadi collapses, bleeding out on the battlefield for several minutes before she finally dies, right beside her father. Her pale blue eyes go glassy as she stares up into the dark, starless sky.

Finally the witch sees Loki facing off with Heimdall, the guardian of the now-shattered bridge Bifrost. Loki is quick and evasive—he's not fast enough to avoid every blow, but most. He is tired; he is pained; he has not had time to recover from his punishment.

But he's angry enough that it doesn't matter. He lands a blow on Heimdall that renders the god's right arm useless, blood gushing from a deep, fatal cut between his neck and shoulder.

Heimdall drops to his knees, his sword falling from his hand. Loki pauses and grins with triumph—but that one moment is all it takes for Heimdall to grab the short sword at his belt with his good hand and lurch up to slash Loki across the throat.

He falls and is lost amid the chaos raging around him.

Then, at last, at the other end of the plain, Surt overcomes Frey—who had lost his golden sword an age ago and fought with only a deer antler. His opponent dead at his feet, Surt raises his flaming sword to the heavens with a mighty cry. The sword flares brighter and fire spreads from it, engulfing those left alive on the battlefield.

They scream as they burn.

Flames begin to spread out from the plain of Vigrid in all directions, consuming everything in their path.

And as Yggdrasil burned, the witch slipped back into her body and staggered to her feet, cradling her still-beating heart against her chest.

WHEN Angrboda went back inside, Baldur recoiled at her bloody hands and the red spot growing slowly outward from between her breasts, staining her pale blue dress a violent crimson.

He was on his feet in an instant. There was only worry in his eyes—no fear—as his gaze moved to the pulsing bundle she clutched to her chest, wrapped in a strip of cloth she'd torn off the bottom of her gown.

"Has it happened?" he asked in a low voice.

"It is done, but not finished," the witch said vaguely. "Your fathers are slain, and now Surt's fire comes for us. We have little time. We shall be the last to burn, out here at the edge of the worlds."

"So we're to die after all?" Baldur asked, his shoulders sagging.

Angrboda stared at him in surprise. *He came here not knowing there was a chance he could be saved?* Then she remembered Hel telling her: *"Baldur doesn't know . . . he came with me anyway . . . to see me to you safely . . ."*

Baldur's worried expression didn't change. Either he was exceedingly good at bluffing, or he really *had* guided Hel here with absolutely no pretense of surviving Ragnarok.

He really does love her.

"Not if I can help it," Angrboda said at last. "Please step aside so I might say my goodbyes. This shall only take a moment."

Baldur acquiesced and didn't ask questions.

Angrboda sat down next to her sleeping daughter. The witch undid both her tablet-woven belt and her leather belt, upon which her bloodied antler-handled knife was secured, and set all of these items on the table next to where she'd left her fingerless *nalbinded* mittens when she'd taken them off to tend to Hel. After a moment's pause, she also took off the amber necklace Loki had brought her all that time ago, and put it down next to the rest of the cherished possessions she'd been gifted over the years.

She no longer had need of such things.

Hel had shifted onto her side, shivering under layers of bedding, her lips and fingertips a worrying blue. She didn't move, but Angrboda could feel shallow breath against her palm as she pushed the hair away from her daughter's face.

"My child," said the witch in a voice so low that only Hel could hear her, "I'm sorry for what's befallen you. But when you awaken, it will be in a better world than this one. I have seen it."

The witch lifted the covers and slid the pulsing bundle down the front of Hel's gown. Hel's breath came in small, short gasps, her chest barely moving.

After regarding her sleeping face for just a moment longer, Angrboda slipped Hel's ancient wolf figurine under her daughter's pillow. It was worn down by teething and by worrying little hands, but now there were new marks upon it: runes stained copper from the blood that had soaked the knife when Angrboda had carved them out in the clearing just minutes before.

She would not be there to see her final spell come to fruition, so she'd instilled the figurine with all the power she could muster. She could have carved the runes upon anything—an antler or a stick—but this figurine was also imbued with all the loving intent Loki had when he'd first carved it for Hel all those ages ago, and that made it more powerful that any other object Angrboda could think of to use for her purposes.

She did not have to hope that its magic would hold up after she was gone. She knew it would. It *had* to.

With that, Angrboda kissed Hel on the temple and covered her again, tucking the blankets and furs securely around her frail body.

Then the witch turned to Baldur and reached out to grasp his shoulders, giving him a hard look.

"Do not touch her," Angrboda said. "Do not move her. She will not awaken until the magic has run its course, and not a moment before. If you wake her before it's completed, the spell will fail and she will die." She dug her stained fingers into his biceps, dried blood flaking off onto his sleeves. "Do you understand me?"

"I understand. I won't touch her." Baldur hesitated. "But what have you done?"

Angrboda gave him a tight-lipped smile. "Perhaps one day you will see."

He blinked, confused. "But—"

"I will not be back," she said, releasing him from her grip. "Under no circumstances will you venture outside this cave. Not until the heat subsides and you can see light through the cracks in the door from the new sun rising."

Baldur seemed to realize what she meant to do and looked stricken as she turned to go.

"Thank you," he managed, his voice thick with emotion.

Angrboda said nothing and did not look back.

ONCE she was outside and the door shut behind her, Angrboda looked to the west, where Surt's inferno had reached Ironwood's border. A wall of fire had crossed the river and was burning up the gnarled gray trees of her ancient forest. From the thick clouds of smoke pouring into the sky and the orange flames in the distance, Angrboda judged that she had mere minutes left.

Suddenly she was Gullveig upon the pyre again: throat clogged with smoke, heat upon her face, a stabbing pain in her chest where her heart used to be.

For a moment she felt short of breath, and the memories threatened to overtake her. Her knees started to give, the old wound in her temple pounding in agony.

But she took a deep breath and steeled herself, not tearing her eyes from the fire.

It's different this time.

My heart is so much more than it once was, even if it now beats outside my chest.

And I will burn not for the gods' will, but for my own.

The wall of fire moved ever closer. Within the clouds of smoke billowing up into the endless darkness, she caught traces of *something* rising: tiny, glittering specks floating higher and higher until they separated from the smoke altogether and disintegrated into the black sky.

That was when she saw the shades marching toward her from within the flames, ghostly figures that began to dissolve as they advanced. Gods and giants and all beings of the Nine Worlds. Even from this distance, she could see the relief on their faces. They were finally free.

Only three souls made it all the way to where Angrboda stood. The first was the she-wolf, who made as if to nuzzle her, but her muzzle passed right through Angrboda's body. *I tried, Mother Witch. I tried to keep her safe.*

"You were glorious, my friend," Angrboda replied, tears pricking her eyes. "Be at peace."

You know, I think I will. She could've sworn the she-wolf was smiling as she disappeared.

The next to approach was Skadi, whose hand went right through Angrboda's cheek when she reached out. Angrboda leaned in as close as she possibly could without passing through Skadi's ghostly form.

"I told you I would remain by your side no matter what," Skadi whispered to her, their faces barely an inch apart. "So here I am."

"I must do this on my own," Angrboda whispered back. "Don't wait for me."

"But I always have."

A sob bubbled up in Angrboda's throat, and she clamped a hand over her mouth, forcing it back down. She needed all her concentration for what was ahead and could not cast her mind back. She could not afford to feel guilty. Not now.

"You have indeed," Angrboda managed. "But not this time."

Skadi began to dissipate from the feet up, but she was smiling just as all the others had been. "I'll see you again soon."

"Soon," Angrboda echoed, and she reached out as the last whispers of Skadi's soul dissolved into starlight. "Goodbye."

And then she was gone, and Angrboda dried her tears—but too soon, for the last ghost, of course, was Loki.

The wall of fire was mere yards away from engulfing the clearing when he stepped into her view. He looked just as he had that day by the river when he'd given her back her heart, that day at the beginning of time when everything had changed.

"Angrboda Iron-witch," he said, an impish slant to his grin. "You intend to stand against *this*?" He jabbed a thumb over his shoulder at the encroaching inferno.

"I do," Angrboda replied with more calm than she felt.

"Aren't you scared?" Loki asked, for now he was upon her, a hand hovering just inches from her cheek as if he wished he could touch her.

Angrboda gave him a tight smile. "I've been through worse. Shouldn't you be going?"

"You don't want me to stay with you?" Loki asked, head tilted sideways in curiosity.

"You've never stayed with me," Angrboda said gently. "I'll endure this as I've endured everything else in this life. Perhaps I will see you in the next."

"But what if there's nothing after this?" Loki's voice was barely audible above the roar of the fire behind him.

Angrboda thought of the ghosts smiling as they left this burning world; she thought of Odin and Thor and Freyja and the giants, disintegrating and becoming part of everything around them.

She'd seen a new world rise from the ashes of the Nine, and even though the old gods were gone, they would be a part of every tree, every rock, every drop of water, every snowflake. And so would the giants and the valkyries and everyone else who'd ever lived.

Including her.

"What comes next for beings like us?" Loki wondered.

Angrboda tore her gaze away from the fire and looked him in the eye. A sudden peace had settled over her unlike anything she'd ever felt before.

"Eternity," she said, and just as he leaned in as if to kiss her, he was gone, as though a gentle gust of wind had carried him off into the sky.

Then she was alone.

The fire was coming faster, roaring its fury. Every bone in her body screamed to put up the shield *now, do it*—*save yourself while you still can*—but if her practicing had shown her anything, it was that her sudden bursts of strength were only temporary. Unless she waited until the very last second—until the flames were directly upon her—she would not be able to hold her shield up long enough for the cave to withstand the fire.

Her face began to redden, to blister. Her dress whipped about and the hem caught fire, and as the tip of her braid caught as well, it unraveled, her hair fanning out behind her.

And then, suddenly, it was time. She could wait no longer.

Just as the wall of flames hit her dead on, she threw out her shield, willing it to surround her home and its occupants—but within moments she realized that she was no match for what she was up against. She'd only ever practiced with her hearth fire, and that was the equivalent of holding her hand over a tiny candle compared with this inferno.

No, she thought, panicking as flames began to lick the wooden door at her back. Her dress and skin and hair were burning, *blackening,* her body screaming with agony just as it had on the pyre. *No, no, no, no—I cannot fail—I cannot—*

She was down to her last resort.

Pushing down her pain, she frantically reached out to that deep well of power, the one that had always called to her, the one she had always resisted; now she would have to use it. Against everything she had fought for, in the end she had failed on her own.

It was the only thing that would save her daughter, this power she'd feared to tap into for so long.

I can't do it alone, she thought as she reached out and grasped for that darkness just beyond her consciousness. *I'm not strong enough.*

But you are, the presence's familiar voice replied. It echoed from the deepest part of the primordial well, from the beginning of time itself, and Angrboda finally—*finally*—recognized the voice as her own. *This power is yours, Mother Witch. It has always been yours. You need only reach out and take it.*

Angrboda did.

And the shield burned bright as the flames consumed her.

PART III

WHEN HEL AWOKE, IT WAS FROM A SLEEP like death.

She sat up stiffly, groaning, sunlight hitting her in the face through a crack in the door. Her body felt heavy, wooden; her muscles screamed with disuse. She swung her legs over the side of the bed and—

Her legs. Her *legs*.

She nearly screamed at the sight of them as she planted her feet on the cave's floor—feet with *muscles* and *skin* attached, not just bone. It was the same with her legs, *both* of her legs, all the way up to where they joined her hip. She pulled her dress up and pinched the flesh of her thigh, stunned. *Is this real? Is this—?*

A hysterical laugh escaped her throat. Then another, and another, until she couldn't stop.

Hel couldn't remember the last time she had laughed.

She twirled about the cave on her brand-new legs, laughter dissolving into giggles until she collapsed back onto the bed. When her head hit the pillow, she felt something lumpy underneath that she hadn't noticed in her deep sleep. She reached underneath it and her fingertips brushed smooth wood: a familiar shape.

Her mood was immediately dampened when she extracted the little wooden wolf. She turned it over and over in her hands like she had as a child, but it wasn't the same—the *texture* wasn't the same, for someone had carved runes into her beloved figurine, and it felt unfamiliar beneath her fingers. She slammed it on the table with a *thud* that echoed through the empty cave.

Empty cave.

She froze and looked around. "Mother?"

Nothing. Every single item in the cave—including her blankets, face, and hair—was covered in a layer of ash and dust, which Hel brushed off herself. There was a set of footprints leading out the door, but they seemed quite old.

Hel walked to the door and threw it open, immediately raising an arm to shield her eyes against the blinding sunlight and the dazzling green.

Green. Hel had never seen Ironwood such a color—the *whole* of Ironwood, at any rate. When she was a child, her clearing and the surrounding trees had become greener each spring, but now it seemed as if all the trees in the forest had bloomed.

Haven't all the worlds burned? Or is this the aftermath?

How long have I been asleep?

"Mother?" she called again, stepping out into the clearing. The feeling of grass beneath her feet was nearly enough to make her weep with joy. "Mother, where are you? Baldur?"

No one answered.

Just as when she'd been left in Niflheim as a child of five, Hel was completely alone.

So Hel made her home there in Ironwood, as her mother had done an age before.

She had nothing to wear but what Angrboda had left behind, so she was forced to don the witch's clothes: sad blues, undyed gray wools, plain linen. She wore her mother's old belts, and the old antler-handled knife, which was sheathed and caked with dried blood, but still sharp and useful after a good cleaning. She donned the amber beads she found—for she did so love shiny things, and she'd never seen her mother wear them—but moved the worn mittens to a worktable in the corner so she could ignore them. For some reason these items were her keenest reminders of Angrboda, and they made her mother's absence even more glaring, such that it hurt to even look at them.

She scoured the dust and ash from the cave and began to collect firewood, berries, and mushrooms from the woods. Hel had always had more sympathy for animals than for gods or giants or lost souls, but if she wished to eat, she had to set up snares as Skadi had once taught her. At least until the old garden revived—she had found Angrboda's store of seeds and rusted tools and made an attempt at planting them.

By what she estimated to be midsummer, the garden had blossomed beyond Hel's wildest dreams, and she emerged one morning from the cave to gaze upon it in satisfaction.

"And to believe I once ruled the realm of the dead," she mused aloud, examining a particularly fine turnip.

Then she caught sight of something circling high overhead, a familiar shape that she knew to be Nidhogg: the dragon who'd been one of the very first creatures she'd faced in Niflheim, who had become one of her subjects. Now he was only a reminder of what had been.

Of what *she* had been.

To think, I was once a powerful witch who did interesting things. Her mood soured considerably at the sight of the dragon. *And now here I am, smiling at a turnip. Preposterous.*

The seasons passed and there was no sign of Baldur. The footprints she'd discovered leading out of the cave when she'd first awoken were a testament to his having survived—but where was he? Her worry gave way to anger and then to apathy just as a chilly autumn gave way to a mild winter, then a balmy spring.

Wherever he is, she thought grimly as time went on, *I suppose he doesn't care for me as I cared for him.* She was unwilling to entertain the idea that the footprints belonged to her mother. *She would have never left me.*

Hel was bathing in the stream one day with her hair braided and tossed over her shoulder when she thought she caught sight of Angrboda, and her heart leapt—until she realized that it was only her reflection in the water. She sighed, disappointed, and began her walk home. *Where did she go?*

She didn't have much time to ponder this, because when she returned to the cave, there was someone waiting for her in the clearing.

Her breath hitched. She would recognize him anywhere, even before he turned to look at her: his blond hair shining in the sun, his eyes the same beautiful blue as the sky, crinkling at the corners when he smiled.

He was smiling now. At her.

She swallowed but didn't speak and kept her face carefully blank. So she wasn't alone after all—she was not the only one to survive Ragnarok. A thousand questions were bouncing back and forth in her brain: *Where have you been? How long did I sleep? Where is my mother?*

"They say a witch used to live in these woods," Baldur said conversationally, breaking the lengthy silence. "A long, long time ago."

"You're looking at her," Hel said. She moved past him, sat down on the stool she'd set at the cave mouth, and picked up the pair of mittens she had been *nalbinding*, just as Gerd had taught her to do so long ago. She began her work again, pointedly not looking at Baldur, and added, "Although it seems to me that there's no more magic left in the worlds at all. Where have you been?"

"You're angry with me," he observed. "I don't blame you. But as it turns out, there's just one world now, and we weren't the only ones to have survived."

"Is that so?" Hel said, disguising the hurt in her voice with disdain. "I suppose you have more interesting company to keep than me now. I might've known."

"It's not like that at all." Baldur brushed his cloak over his shoulder. Unlike the finery he'd died in, simple traveling clothes were what he was wearing now. "We've rebuilt Asgard—or, we've built Idavoll, right where Asgard was." He made a sweeping gesture that fell purposely flat. "A glorious place with a gold-thatched roof. We've been pulling all sorts of trinkets out of the ashes. Thor's sons found his hammer, even. And two of my other brothers survived by jumping into the sea—even Hod made it. More of us survived Ragnarok than I thought. And there's a waterfall . . ."

"Wonderful," Hel said dully, looking down once more at the mittens she was making. "So, what brings you here, then, after so long? What could possibly tear you away from your golden hall?"

"Listen," said Baldur. He crouched down until he was at eye level with her. "I had to leave you."

"Why?" Hel asked petulantly.

"Because your mother ordered me to."

"A likely story."

Hel made to go back to her *nalbinding*, but he reached forward and pulled the mittens out of her hands, needle and all. When she gave him a furious look, he shook his head. "Your mother saved both our lives, and she ordered me not to move you. She made sure I understood that if I touched you, I'd break the spell she cast to heal your heart. Otherwise I would've carried you with me. You know I would have," he added, with feeling.

"My . . . heart?" she asked, putting a hand to her chest. She had noticed the tender pink spot of skin between her breasts when she'd first awoken from her long sleep, but it had faded away shortly after, and she'd thought little of it. She'd thought that maybe the pain had gone away with fresh air or that good long nap she'd taken, just as it used to when she was a child . . . She never imagined . . .

"Hel?" Baldur said worriedly, for her expression had crumpled.

"My legs, too," Hel whispered as she stood. "She healed my legs. She carved runes into my wolf . . . She died, didn't she?"

"Yes," Baldur said, standing as well. "She died protecting you. Protecting *both* of us."

Hel let out a low moan and her chest began heaving with dry sobs. She shoved him away when he tried to embrace her. "But how could she have forgiven me for the horrible things I said to her, just like that? I don't understand . . ."

"She's forgiven you, just as you forgave her," Baldur said gently. "She saved us both. Isn't that enough to prove it? What were her last words to you? She whispered them in your ear before she left the cave."

"How should I know? I was hardly conscious at the time."

"*Think*," Baldur said, and it seemed to Hel that he needed to know more than she wanted to remember. She wondered vaguely if he had heard the words himself and only needed her to confirm them.

She closed her eyes, cast her mind back, and told him. "She said, 'My child, I'm sorry for what's befallen you. But when you awaken, it will be in a better world than this one. I have seen it.'"

Baldur held her gaze steadily and whispered, "Those words are the very same ones my father spoke to me before they lit my pyre."

"That's impossible," said Hel.

"Ah, but here we are." Baldur was smiling again as he moved in closer.

A jolt of hope ran through Hel's newly healed heart, but she twisted away from him. Hope had never served her well in the past. *Hope is for fools.*

"Go back to Asgard, or whatever you're calling it now," she said thickly. "Leave me in peace. I have no need for you gods and your nonsense."

"There are no gods anymore, Hel. We're all only men. And I was hoping," he said, reaching out to take her hands in his, "that you'd come back with me."

Hel started and glowered at him but didn't pull away. "That's quite bold of you, Baldur Odinsson. Don't forget, I was your queen once."

"And you can be my queen again, Hel Lokadottir, if you come with me to Idavoll."

"Angrbodudottir," Hel amended, looking down at their clasped hands. When he gave her a questioning look, she said, "My father went by Loki Laufeyjarson—he used his mother's name instead of his father's, so I shall do the same."

After a moment, she added, "Everyone knows I'm my father's daughter. It's my mother they always seem to forget."

Baldur gave her a sad smile. "I think she would be proud to hear that."

"I will not go to Idavoll with you," said Hel, finally tearing her gaze away from their hands and looking up at him. "Trouble me no more with your furtive glances. They're only because I'm the last woman on earth and because my corpse legs are healed."

Yet she still did not pull her hands from his.

"On the contrary, I've troubled you with furtive glances for some years now, and I plan to trouble you with them for many years to come," Baldur said, straight-faced. "And I should like to see these legs of yours to prove you're telling the truth of them."

"Oh, I'm sure you should, but you won't. Begone with you."

"Also," he went on, ignoring her, "you're not the last woman on earth. Just the only one whose company I desire. I fear life is quite dull without our ceaseless banter. It passed the time quite well when I was dead, didn't it?"

"Is that a roundabout Asgardian way of saying that you missed me?" Hel asked, arching an eyebrow.

"Possibly, in so many words."

Hel shook her head, forcing down the pleasant feeling bubbling up in her chest. Her hands seemed to move of their own volition as they disengaged from his and moved up to either side of his face, smoothing his short beard. "Your place is with your people."

"My place," he said, leaning in close and moving his hands to her waist, "is with you. And if your place is here, then so is mine. You won't be rid of me so easily."

"Ridiculous man," she breathed, and then Baldur's lips were upon hers, and she found herself completely lost in a moment she'd been dreaming of since she was very small.

If hope is for fools, then so be it.

I am my mother's daughter, after all.

❖   ❖   ❖

So Hel and Baldur raised their children in peace in the forest at the edge of the world, where she was born. Baldur's family would often come out from Idavoll to join them for some time, and they would laugh and talk of all the beauty and wonders of this new world and reminisce about the gods of the old, their kin. Their children—and the children of Idavoll—eventually spread out into the world at large, mingling with human beings for generations until their earliest ancestors were nothing more than a distant cultural memory.

And life went on.

Every night until the day they died, Hel and Baldur gathered their children and grandchildren and great-grandchildren around the hearth fire and told them stories of how things had been before, in the days when gods and giants walked the earth.

They spoke of one-eyed Odin and his quest for knowledge; of mighty Thor and his hammer; of beautiful, fierce Freyja and her treasured necklace. They told tales of how Tyr lost his hand, of the theft of Idun's golden apples, of the Norns and Mimir's head, of the mead of poetry and the intricate crafts of the dwarfs, of mortal heroes who had already faded into legend long before Ragnarok had come to pass. They told of Frey's marriage to Gerd and the loss of his sword, and Freyja's almost-marriage to a giant or two, and the building of Asgard's wall.

They spoke of a wolf so huge that his gaping jaws touched both ground and sky, and of a serpent so large that he encircled the earth. They spoke of the ancient giantesses of these very woods.

They told of brash, brave Skadi taking up all manner of armor and weapons and marching right to the gods' doorstep to avenge her father.

They told of handsome, cunning Loki, of his antics and wit and charm.

And every now and then a child or two would come home after catching glimpses of figures moving through the forest: a woman in a man's tunic guiding animals to their traps or aiding their hunt; a nimble man with grass-green eyes grinning at them as he dashed through the trees, as if walking on air, daring them to give chase; a man in a broad-brimmed hat inclining his head in pride as they passed; or a woman in a tattered traveling cloak giving them a serene smile from beneath her hood before vanishing into the morning mist.

In one case Hel's own great-granddaughter stumbled into the clearing and clutched Hel's knobby knees as she stood from her gardening work. Baldur had passed on some years before, leaving Hel alone once more in the cave, but their sons and daughters were never far—they'd founded a small village in the clearing where the Jarnvidjur used to live. And they visited her daily with fresh oat-cakes in their linen-wrapped bundle, which the little one held to her chest in fright.

"You needn't fear them, child," Hel said, bending down to the girl's level with much effort. "They mean you no harm. They're only watching over you."

"But you said the gods and giants were dead," the child protested.

"Dead, aye, but not gone," Hel replied. "Nothing ever dies. Not truly."

"Who was the woman? The woman in the hood?" The girl was young; she had not yet committed every tale to memory.

Hel smiled.

"They say a witch used to live in these woods a long, long time ago," she began.

And this is what the little girl would tell her children, and what they would tell their children long after the ones who came before were gone:

They say an old witch lived in the east, in Ironwood, and there she bore the wolves who chase the sun and moon.

They say she went to Asgard and was burned three times upon a pyre, and three times was she reborn before she fled.

They say she loved a man with scarred lips and a sharp tongue, a man who gave her back her heart and more.

They say she loved a woman, too, a sword-wielding bride of the gods as bold as any man and fiercer still.

They say she wandered, giving aid to those who needed it most, healing them with potions and spells.

They say she stood her ground against the fires of Ragnarok until the very end, until she was burned a final time, all but her heart reduced to ashes once more.

But others say she lives yet.

ACKNOWLEDGMENTS

Writing a novel may be a solitary endeavor, but what comes after is anything but. I would like to extend my heartfelt gratitude to the following people:

To my agent, Rhea Lyons: Thank you for championing this book, for being my biggest cheerleader, and for being so patient with me and so generous with your advice. I never in a million years dreamed I would have an agent who was so passionate about my work, and I would be utterly lost without you.

To my editor, Jessica Wade, for continuously challenging me to make this book better. Thank you for your brilliant insights, your meticulous edits, and your firm belief that I could work out a better ending for Angrboda without compromising my vision of what I wanted this story to be. The old witch and I are eternally grateful for your guidance; we couldn't have navigated Ragnarok without you.

To the team at Penguin Random House, with special thanks to Miranda Hill, Alexis Nixon, Brittanie Black, Jessica Mangicaro, Elisha Katz, and everyone else who helped bring *The Witch's Heart* to life. And to Adam Auerbach, for this absolutely stunning cover.

To Kristin Ell, Angela Rodriguez, Emily DeTar Birt, and Kirsten Linsenmeyer: You were the very first people to ever set their eyes on this book. Thank you for your encouragement, critiques, and feedback; it meant so much to me that you fell in love with Angrboda's story, and it helped push me forward when things were rough.

To Shannon Mullally, Mirria Martin-Tesone, Emma Tanskanen, Marisa Schamerhorn, Mel Campbell, Sarah Gunnoe, Jessica Lundi, Allen Chamberlin, Candyce Beal, Ryann Burke, and Terryl Bandy: Thank you all for cheering me on, and for looking out for me when I needed it most.

To my local authors squad: Andi Lawrencovna, Marj Ivancic, and Darlene Kuncytes, for hours of laughter, solid advice, and writerly commiseration, even.

To my Viking family, for keeping my spirits up when all else seemed bleak: "Stay the same. Be better."

To my Book Twitter family, for their support right out of the gate. Thank you especially to Kati Felix, Joshua Gillingham, Villimey Sigurbjörnsdóttir, Katie Masters, Siobhán Clark, S. Qiouyi Lu, Lizy, Miranda, Allie, and so many more.

To M. J. Kuhn, Hannah M. Long, and the rest of the #2021debuts: I wouldn't have had anyone else by my side as we went on our respective journeys together. We made it.

To Merrill Kaplan, for fostering my love of Norse myths and sagas, and for fielding my very specific novel-related Old Norse questions, both then and now. I wrote the first draft of this book over the course of three weeks when I should have been working on my term paper for your Norse mythology course, and suffice it to say, I was a different person before I stepped into your classroom. *Takk fyrir.*

To Daina Faulhaber: I may be a writer, but it's hard for me to find words to describe what your friendship means to me. Thank you not only for your steadfast support of this reclusive cave witch (and Angrboda), but also for being willing to yell about Norse mythology with me, for always telling me what I need to hear even when it sucks, and for climbing down into that cave to take my author photo. Everyone deserves a friend like you.

To my sister, Bridget; my mother, Lisa; my dad, Ron; my uncle Rory; and to Grama Jo and the rest of my (very large) family for blessing me with a lifetime of unwavering support.

To my grandfather, to whom this book is dedicated, and who I wish could be here to read it. A Swede by birth and an American by choice, he told me once, in conspiratorial tones, that he knew the old gods were still around. While I'll never know what he thinks of my interpretations, I can only hope he would be proud.

And finally, to you, dear reader: Thank you for giving Angrboda a chance.

APPENDIX

I chose to Anglicize the Old Norse place-names and personal names in this novel, so they may appear differently in other retellings and translations of Norse mythology (ex. Freyr instead of Frey, Oðinn for Odin, Àsgarðr for Asgard). The Old Norse names in their nominative case are listed in parentheses where relevant, indicated by "ON."

Please note that the *Prose Edda* and the *Poetic Edda*, the two main sources of what we know about Norse mythology, were my sources for this novel. Every translation of the Eddas is slightly different; the translations I used are listed below. All of the poems mentioned are compiled in the *Poetic Edda*.

People

Angrboda—a giantess, mentioned once by name in each of the Eddas, and both times in relation to Loki and their children. Some connect her to "the Old One," who lives in Ironwood and birthed the wolves who chase the sun and moon: "Fenrir's kin" (sometimes translated as "brood" or "offspring"), as attested in the *Prose Edda*. There is also cause to connect her to the seeress whom Odin, traveling in disguise as Vegtam, raises from the grave in the poem "Baldr's Dreams," and whom he calls "the mother of three [giants/trolls/ogres]."

Hyndla—a giantess whom Freyja visits in the poem "The Song of Hyndla" to ask for information about her lover's family line. The giantess reluctantly gives her this information, and then suddenly starts reciting a mini-prophecy of Ragnarok. Freyja tells Hyndla to get one of her wolves out of the stables and ride alongside Freyja to Valhalla for some reason.

Hyrrokkin—a giantess who appears riding a wolf with snakes for reins, summoned by the gods to push Baldur's funeral pyre into the water when no one else could, as attested in the *Prose Edda*

Gullveig/Heid—a mysterious witch mentioned in stanzas of the poem "The Seeress's Prophecy" (ON: *Völuspá*), in which Gullveig shows up in Asgard in its early days, is burned three times by the gods, and is reborn three times, before traveling as Heid to dispense spells and practice sorcery (ON: *seiðr*). Very little is known about her, but most believe her to be Freyja.

The Seeress—the mysterious woman who narrates the poem "The Seeress's Prophecy," sometimes in first person and sometimes in third person. She claims to have been present at the beginning of the worlds, and describes in great detail the event Ragnarok, the doom of the gods.

Loki—shape-shifting god of Norse mythology, whose father is thought to be a giant and whose mother, Laufey, is possibly a goddess. Blood brother to Odin, Loki is canonically handsome, cunning, and unpredictable, according to the *Prose Edda*. He is known mostly for getting the gods into and out of trouble with his trickery. He eventually orchestrates the death of Odin's son Baldur, is bound in torment soon after, and fights against the gods at Ragnarok. He is also said to have eaten the half-burnt heart of a woman and spawned the race of trolls, according to the poem "The Song of Hyndla."

Skadi—a giantess who is most famous for taking up sword and shield and marching to Asgard to demand compensation after her father is killed by the gods. Instead, she receives a husband from among the gods and "a bellyful of laughter" as her payment. She is also cited as being the one to hang a venomous snake over Loki's head when he is bound. Enumerated among the goddesses after her marriage, Skadi is represented primarily as the goddess of bowhunting.

Gerd—a giantess who is coerced into marrying the god Frey, as attested in the poem "Skirnir's Journey"

Hel—ruler of the Norse underworld, daughter of Loki and Angrboda; described as being half-dead, she is most commonly depicted with one side of her body rotting and the other side alive. Hel famously decreed that Baldur could come back from her realms if all the worlds would weep for him, proving how much he was missed.

Fenrir—the giant wolf, son of Loki and Angrboda. The gods attempted to bind him multiple times and failed, and it was only through trickery that they were able to tie him up—and at great cost (he bit off Tyr's hand in the process). Fenrir is fated to devour Odin at Ragnarok.

Jormungand—the Midgard Serpent, son of Loki and Angrboda, who is so large that he encircles the realm of Midgard and bites his own tail. He is fated to be free at Ragnarok, along with his father and brother, and to slay Thor.

Odin—the highest of the Norse gods. He likes to travel in disguise, in a broad-brimmed hat and cloak, and uses many different names, among them Grimnir and Vegtam. His valkyries choose who is to die in battle and escort them to Valhalla, Odin's hall of the slain, where they are said to feast and fight every day until Ragnarok. Odin has two ravens, Hugin and Munin, who fly around the worlds and report back to him what they've seen.

Thor—Odin's son by the giantess Jord/Fjorgyn. He is arguably the most well-known of the Norse gods, for his thunderous temper and his hammer, Mjolnir.

Freyja (or Freya)—a priestess of the Vanir and seid (ON: *seiðr*). Freyja is most commonly associated with sex and war, and receives half the slain in her hall while the other half go to Odin in Valhalla. Freyja's most famous attributes are her golden necklace, Brisingamen, and her feathered cloak, which turns the wearer into a falcon.

Tyr—Possibly a son of Odin, Tyr is a god associated with war and justice, and had his hand bitten off by Fenrir.

Frey—Vanir and brother of Freyja, who sits on Odin's chair Hlidskjalf when forbidden to do so and gazes out over all the worlds. He catches a glimpse of the giantess Gerd and falls in love with her, and gives his famous sword to his servant, Skirnir, in exchange for the latter convincing Gerd to marry him. As a result, Frey is fated to be slain by the fire giant Surt at Ragnarok. He is also associated with fertility.

Sigyn—Wife of Loki, Sigyn famously holds up a bowl to collect the venom dripping down from the snake above Loki's head when he is bound.

Frigg—Odin's wife and Baldur's mother, who is said to know the fates of all men

Baldur (or Baldr, Balder)—Odin's son, slain by his blind brother, Hod (whose hand was guided by Loki). Youngest, most beautiful, and most beloved of the gods.

Njord—Vanir, sea god, father of Frey and Freyja, husband to Skadi.

The Norns—While a norn is a female spirit associated with shaping fate, *the* Norns are three female deities somewhat like the Fates in Greek mythology, who dwell in a hall at the Well of Urd, at one of the three roots of the World Tree, Yggdrasil.

Mimir—a god traded as a hostage to the Vanir, who cut off his head and sent it back to Odin, who magically preserved it and its wisdom. Mimir's head resides at Mimir's well at one of the three roots of Yggdrasil, where Odin left his eye in exchange for wisdom.

Heimdall—guardian of Bifrost, the rainbow bridge

Skrymir—ruler of Utgard, the citadel of the giants, in Jotunheim. Famous for tricking Thor and Loki with impossible tasks while they are off on an adventure.

Surt—leader of the fire giants of Muspelheim, the realm of fire

Idun—goddess who is keeper of the gods' golden apples of immortality

Thjazi—Skadi's father, who orchestrates the kidnapping of Idun for her golden apples and is slain by the gods

Races

Aesir (ON: *Æsir*; feminine: *Ásynjur*)—the Norse pantheon of gods, the highest of whom is Odin. They inhabit Asgard.

Vanir—another race of gods, associated with fertility and wisdom, whose notable members (Njord, Frey, and Freyja) are essentially subsumed into the Aesir following the Aesir-Vanir War. The Vanir inhabit Vanaheim.

Giants—the sworn enemies of the gods. "Giants" was originally a mistranslation of *jötun* (plural: *jötnar*). The giants inhabit the world Jotunheim. Giants can be either large or small, attractive or grotesque, depending on the story. Interestingly, the first giant was the primeval being Ymir, from whom even the gods are descended.

Frost giants, fire giants, and many different kinds of **trolls, ogres**, and various other creatures are often grouped in with the giants.

Jarnvidjur—giantesses who reside in Jarnvid

Places

While the cosmology of Norse mythology is sometimes hard to pin down, it is agreed that there are Nine Worlds.

Asgard—the home of the Norse gods (the Aesir)

Valhalla—Odin's hall of the slain

Yggdrasil—the World Tree, which connects all the worlds

Gladsheim—Odin's hall, where the gods counsel

Valaskjalf—Odin's hall where his chair Hlidskjalf is located, where he can sit and see everything in the worlds

Bifrost—the rainbow bridge connecting Asgard and Midgard

Jotunheim—the land of the giants (ON: *jötnar*)

Jarnvid—"Iron-wood," a forest in eastern Jotunheim

Utgard—citadel of the giants

Thrymheim—Skadi's home in the mountains

Midgard—the "middle earth," the mortal realm. On some maps, Jotunheim is in Midgard.

Niflheim—the realm of ice, in which Hel's domain is located, although some sources cite Hel/Helheim as its own realm

Vanaheim—home of the Vanir

Alfheim—realm of the elves, ruled by Frey

Muspelheim—the realm of fire, ruled by Surt

Nidavellir—home of the dwarves

Svartalfheim—home of the darkelves. Sometimes grouped in with Nidavellir.

FURTHER READING

The Poetic Edda:

The Poetic Edda. Translated by Carolyne Larrington. Oxford, 1996.

The Poetic Edda. Translated by Lee M. Hollander. University of Texas Press, 1962.

The Poetic Edda: Mythological Poems, Volume II. Translated and with commentary by Ursula Dronke. Oxford, 1997.

The Prose Edda, by Snorri Sturluson:

The Prose Edda. Translated by Anthony Faulkes. Everyman, 1987.

The Prose Edda. Translated by Jesse Byock. Penguin, 2006.

Retellings:

The Norse Myths by Kevin Crossley-Holland

Gods of Asgard by Erik Evensen

Norse Mythology by Neil Gaiman

Norse Mythology: A Guide to the Gods, Heroes, Rituals, and Beliefs, by John Lindow (not a retelling, but an extensive glossary-style resource)